DAUGHTER OF MINE

DAUGHTER OF MINE

A Novel

MEGAN MIRANDA

MARYSUE
RUCCI
BOOKS

New York   London   Toronto   Sydney   New Delhi

MARYSUE
RUCCI
BOOKS

Marysue Rucci Books
An Imprint of Simon & Schuster, LLC
1230 Avenue of the Americas
New York, NY 10020

First Marysue Rucci Books hardcover edition April 2024

MARYSUE RUCCI BOOKS and colophon are trademarks of Simon & Schuster, LLC

Simon & Schuster: Celebrating 100 Years of Publishing in 2024

For information about special discounts for bulk purchases, please contact Simon & Schuster Special Sales at 1-866-506-1949 or business@simonandschuster.com.

The Simon & Schuster Speakers Bureau can bring authors to your live event. For more information or to book an event, contact the Simon & Schuster Speakers Bureau at 1-866-248-3049 or visit our website at www.simonspeakers.com.

Interior design by Erika R. Genova

Manufactured in the United States of America

1 3 5 7 9 10 8 6 4 2

Library of Congress Cataloging-in-Publication Data has been applied for.

ISBN 978-1-6680-1044-0
ISBN 978-1-6680-1046-4 (ebook)

For my family

DAUGHTER
OF
MINE

PROLOGUE

The drought started in the West. We watched on the news as the waters dropped in the reservoirs and lakes, and their secrets and ghosts slowly emerged. The Great Salt Lake was suddenly in danger of disappearing, threatening to release the toxic dust hidden at the bottom. Skeletons surfaced from the edges of a shrinking Lake Mead—in barrels, in boats, bare bones scattered on a dried-out shoreline. Missing persons, finally found. Unknown crimes, suddenly uncovered.

We watched from the safety of our enclave on the East Coast, where freshwater rivers cut down the mountain, sustaining our lake, our community. We watched from our living room couches, with lush forests of trees right outside the windows, the promise of the green North Carolina landscape. We thought ourselves protected, immune.

It came here on a delay, like everything else—the latest fashions, high-speed internet.

And then slowly, the rotted wood beneath the docks became visible, soft and black. Boats were raised up into dock houses, or anchored farther out, where they drifted back and forth like ghost ships in the night.

We were told not to water the grass, not to launch a boat onto the lake from Gemma's Creek, not to worry. Even as more things slowly started appearing: branches and trunks, reaching out from the surface; sunken beer bottles wedged into the newly exposed mud.

In the West, there were the bodies. But here, we were less

flashy, less prone to drama and sensation. We preferred our crimes quiet, our cases closed—that was my father's motto. He was the last of a dying breed, I thought. A detective who got no shot of adrenaline from either the chase or the justice. So very different from the craving of my youth: *Give me a wrong, so that I may punish.*

So when the drought finally arrived, I supposed it was fitting that the first thing to attract attention was not a body or a barrel or a bone. It was something quieter—something we didn't understand at first.

Quieter, but no less dangerous.

PART 1

FATHER

CHAPTER 1

62 Days without Rain
Wednesday, May 15
5:30 p.m.
Precipitation: Zero

They raised the car from the lake on the same day as my father's memorial, two unrelated but equally newsworthy events: Something lost. Something found.

My father had been gone for over three weeks, and in the days since, I'd found myself measuring time differently. A recalibration. A new reality.

I listened to the weather reports each morning on the radio in Charlotte—*sixty-two days without rain*—and thought, instead, *Twenty-three days without him.*

It seemed like half the town had come out for the celebration of life—crowding the deck of his favorite restaurant, raising a glass (or two, or three) to the portrait of Detective Perry Holt— while the other half was gathered around an inlet on the opposite side of Mirror Lake, watching as the salvage company hooked a crane to the car that had been spotted below the surface a few days earlier.

All I could think was: *Of course this is happening now.*

I'd always suspected that my father alone had held things together by sheer force of will—not only in our family but in the entire town. And without his careful gaze, his steady oversight, everything had shifted off-kilter.

Even for this, he had left us his guidance. A cremation instead of a burial. A party instead of a funeral. Food covered by the department. Drinks on him.

But the discovery of the car was big news in a small town, and no one had seemed sure what to do, with the outside world watching. It had made headlines all the way in Charlotte, even: the water level of Mirror Lake had dropped to the lowest it had been in decades, and a fisherman had practically run up on top of the sunken vehicle.

There was no evidence of a crash—no bent metal or crushed vegetation at the curve of road above the inlet—so the rumor spreading through the crowd was that the old rusted sedan must've been there for years, before the addition of the new guardrail. Apparently, a dive crew had been out to inspect the car the day it was found, but saw nothing inside.

And yet, it had the air of something I couldn't quite put my finger on: a sign of things emerging, changing.

A warning, that things were beginning here too.

There was something in the air, keeping everyone on edge: a buzzing of insects in the muddy puddles beneath the deck; the setting sun glaring sharply off the surface of the water, so we had to squint just to look at one another; leaves, dry and brittle and churned up in the wind, falling to earth at the wrong time of year.

This wasn't how things were supposed to go.

There were supposed to be stories on the mic set up beside the bar, for anyone who felt moved to speak. We were supposed to find solace in the liquor, and the laughter—a release, an acceptance. Perry Holt was gone too soon, and it wasn't fair, but my god, what a life he had lived.

So many people here attributed their lives to him. Whether he'd pulled them out of danger, or pushed them toward the help he knew they needed—today, we were supposed to remember it all. But now news of the car was splitting everyone's attention and sense of responsibility and propriety.

For every comment of *He was such a good man, a good leader, a good role model* booming from the sound system, there was a quieter whisper carried in the crowd around me.

It's coming up.

No license plate. No VIN.

Stolen and dumped, probably.

While the youngest Murphy girl—now a few years out of high school—told the story of how my father found her drifting in the middle of the lake as a kid, her tube cut loose from the dock, I heard the group to my side taking bets on what they'd find inside the trunk.

A body. Stolen goods. A gun.

I turned to stare, hoping to shame them into silence, but they were looking toward the entrance instead, where a group of uniformed officers had gathered in the doorway.

It didn't help that a lot of the people here were presently or formerly connected to law enforcement, either by profession or family ties. Or that men and women in uniform kept rotating in, alternating between paying their respects and relaying updates to my brothers.

Both of whom had suddenly disappeared again.

I didn't blame them.

I was pretty sure I'd find them on the long sliver of deck at the side of the building—the only reprieve from the crowd.

I saw Caden first, pacing back and forth, all frenetic energy. He paused periodically to hold his phone out over the water, trying to catch a signal. Any other day, he'd be out there himself. He'd been the very first on scene; the call about the car came in while he was working his normal shift on lake patrol.

Gage, meanwhile, remained perfectly still, arms resting on the wooden railing as he stared out at the water. From a distance, he looked so much like our father it stopped my heart: sharp nose, prominent jaw, dark cropped hair. Heavy slanted eyebrows that gave everything he said an air of gravity.

I slid up beside him, mirroring his posture. How many years had I mimicked him, idolized him, revered him as the hero of my youth? He let me follow him around far longer than most older brothers might, and I relished his praise: *Hazel can climb that tree*; and *Hazel will jump from that bridge*; and *Hazel can beat you in a race*.

All I'd had to do was show up, and prove him right. Now I tried to mirror not only his position but his emotions. *Find the balance. Rise to the moment.* Like our father, Gage was always the responsible one—and now he found himself in a new role not only in the department but in our family. Maybe that was the curse of being the oldest.

"Are we hiding out?" I asked, as Caden's footsteps retreated down the deck.

Gage tilted his head to the side, squinting. "We're hiding out."

Then I could feel Caden's footsteps getting closer again—a metronome, keeping time.

He stopped pacing behind us. "Mel's trying to send pictures. They're not coming through." I could see the pent-up energy in his stance, though his expression remained calm, controlled. The things he could hide under his cherub-shaped face, even at twenty-seven, with the dimpled cheek, and his brown hair swooped to the side, like he was still on the cusp of adulthood.

"What's going on out there?" I asked.

If anyone would be able to distinguish the facts from the rumors, it was my brothers—both of them had proudly followed our father onto the force. Though Gage would probably be the only one to tell me. Caden and I got along best when I remembered to bite my tongue, and he remembered to ignore me. Today, we were both mostly doing our part.

Gage was tall and lean-muscled, where Caden was more broad-shouldered and stocky. The only discernible features they shared were the color of their deep blue eyes and the low tenor of their voices. *The Holt voice*, my dad had called it, though his had turned more gravelly as he aged.

"Probably some insurance scam," Gage said, dark eyebrows knitted together. "The guardrail was installed fifteen years ago. The car must've been there for a while."

I knew that stretch of road, right before the narrow, single-lane bridge. "It's easy to lose control there," I said. I remembered the warning myself, from when I was learning to drive. My father's echo: *Careful. Slow it down, Hazel.*

It had always been a dangerous bend, especially in the night.

The township of Mirror Lake didn't believe in streetlights or painted center lines or regular pothole maintenance, it seemed. It *did* believe in respecting the natural geography that had existed before, which was why the roads forked sharply, banked unevenly, rose steeply. The side roads were generally only wide enough for one vehicle at a time. Growing up here, we had learned to be both cautious and aggressive, to maneuver through tight spaces, to step on the gas before someone else did first.

So driving was a dangerous activity, especially for someone from out of town.

I imagined someone speeding around the bend, unfamiliar with the dark mountain curves, the dark mountain roads, tires losing traction—how quickly something could sink below the surface, unnoticed.

"There was no one inside the car, Hazel," Gage answered. "They checked."

"Could've escaped," I said. I closed my eyes and saw it: someone clawing their way out of the vehicle as it sank. Their head finally emerging above water—that first, primal gasp.

"Yeah, well, no one called it in, if so. And the plates were removed. Seems more likely it was dumped there on purpose. It's a convenient spot." Gage was logical, pragmatic, levelheaded. All things that made him a good detective now. It was always so easy to believe him.

It made sense: here was a place no one would go looking.

Caden glanced up briefly from his phone. "I can't believe it's been there that long. I used to jump from that spot in high school."

Gage rubbed the side of his chin. "Me too," he said.

I shuddered. We had all jumped off the rocks at the edge of that curve, when the summer sun got too hot, and we were desperate for something to happen, despite the warnings from the adults. I could still feel the cold shock of that pocket of water, always in the shade no matter the time of day, the feetfirst plunge, and how the bottom seemed so endlessly far away.

How close had we come? How many of us had brushed up against a strip of metal and thought *boulder* or *branch*. How many of us had imagined something else instead?

"Jesus," Caden said, holding his cell closer to his face. He stopped breathing for a moment, his only tell. And then his eyes narrowed. "Someone really needs to help with the crowd control over there."

I tried to peer over his shoulder at the screen, but he was already on his way. He quickly rounded the corner back toward the guests.

Apparently by *someone*, he meant himself. I couldn't believe he was leaving like this.

"Seriously?" I began. "Dad would—"

"Dad would be out there himself," Gage cut in, squinting at the water, the surrounding mountains reflecting off the hazy surface. "And you know it."

I did. Over the years, I'd watched our father leave the dinner table for a break-in; a birthday party for an overdose; a soccer game for a high-speed chase. He made no excuses or apologies. We all understood that his responsibilities stretched beyond the boundaries of our family.

"You should head home too, Hazel," Gage said, turning back to face me. "This is only going to get worse. Everyone knows you've got a long trip back."

Two hours, really. But Charlotte might as well have been a different world from Mirror Lake. I was a different person out there, without the anchor of history.

"You sure?" I asked. "I feel like I should stay to help clean up. . . ."

But Gage shook his head, releasing me. "Drive safe," he said, like my father would do. "And, Hazel?" He looked at me with wide-open eyes, a wide-open expression. "Don't be a stranger, okay? He wouldn't want that."

I forced a small smile, even as a wave of panic gripped me from nowhere. I felt, then, the finality of this moment; I wasn't ready.

"You should be so lucky," I said before turning away, eyes burning.

Even as I joked, I wondered what would next bring me back. Thanksgiving? My niece's birthday in the summer, maybe, if Caden invited me? I felt untethered, ungrounded. All the emotions I'd fought to contain today suddenly fighting for the surface.

I kept my head down, weaving through the crowd, a study in evasion. Eyes forward, stride confident, hoping no one stopped me. It didn't help matters that I was the only one in black amid a sea of khakis and floral. Or that I looked like I was dressed for a business meeting—tailored A-line dress, blazer, stacked heels—while the rest of the guests had arrived in what I could only call Lake Casual.

I grabbed the bag I'd stowed behind the counter and slipped into the restroom. I wanted to change before the drive home—I had plans to swing by our latest renovation project on the way, which was still an active construction site. I needed to focus on something else, to let my work consume me again.

The bathroom was down a dimly lit, wood-paneled hall, and my vision was still adjusting to the change as I pushed through the door and nearly collided with the person on the way out.

"Oh." A hand on my shoulder, to brace herself. A whiff of coconut. A curtain of hair.

Even in the dark, I would know: Jamie.

She slowly removed her hand from the front of my shoulder,

then ran it through the ends of her long, honey-colored hair, an old nervous habit. "Hazel," she said, locking eyes with mine. Her voice was like something sharp and piercing, straight to the heart. Maybe it was because my guard was already down, or my nerves too exposed, or because I was already hovering so close to the edge. Her attention shifted to the bag in my hands. "Are you leaving?"

"Yeah. Just changing first." I gestured to my outfit. "No one told me the dress code." Jamie wore a spring floral dress and beige sandals.

A twitch of her lip—an almost smile. A portal to another time, before her gaze slid away again. She stepped to the side, closer to the exit.

And then, because I didn't know where to go from here: "Is Skyler around?" My six-year-old niece was always a welcome distraction.

"She's outside with some of the department kids." She cleared her throat. "Are you coming back this weekend?"

"For what?" I asked.

She frowned, peering at the door. "Caden said they're cleaning out the house. I thought you knew."

This was what happened when you were the only one who left home. I had to hear about things secondhand, default to my brothers' preferences, concede to their decisions.

I shook my head, grief giving way to anger—a familiar and welcome slide. "When?" I asked, louder than necessary.

"Sunday."

I did my best not to look surprised. Maybe Gage forgot to tell me in the chaos of the day.

Sometimes Jamie mentioned things in a way that sounded offhand but seemed almost intentional instead. As if she was still trying to bridge the gap between me and Caden.

Or maybe I was being too generous, blinded by nostalgia and the years of friendship that had once sustained us.

Back when we were in high school, Jamie used to say I had an A-plus asshole radar—warning her of the boys who would let us down; the teacher who would not give second chances; the classmates who would take particular pleasure in our missteps. But I felt my instincts went to something deeper than that, like I could see what was underneath—less action, more intention.

Unfortunately, it never rubbed off on Jamie, considering she married my brother Caden.

"Thanks," I called as she opened the door. "I'll be there."

After changing, I thought about going out to find Gage, tell him I'd be back Sunday—but there was currently a straight shot to the exit, the sun was setting, and this celebration was quickly becoming something else.

I had started to get that subtle, creeping feeling—like the walls were closing in, and I needed to escape. A reminder of why I'd left in the first place.

Stay too long, and you became exactly what Mirror Lake decided you would be.

Out front, the department kids were playing a game of hide-and-seek in the trees. One of their mothers leaned against the wooden railing, keeping tabs on them, like mine had once done. I caught a flash of Skyler's blond hair rushing past, and saw, instead, a group of us racing through these woods, a generation before.

I kept moving.

How quickly the past could grasp on to you here, and pull.

The dirt parking lot was overflowing, and several vehicles were combing the area, looking for free space. I raised a hand to the nearest car as I walked to my SUV, gestured I was heading out. I had gotten the last viable spot at the edge of the lot, half my car fully in the woods, tucked under the branches of a large oak.

The driver's side window lowered as the bright blue car slowly pulled up behind mine.

"Hi," he said. A familiar voice, a familiar face.

I froze, shoulders tensing.

Last I saw Nico Pritchard, he was driving away in a different car, and doing his best not to make eye contact.

I paused, one hand on my car door. "Hi," I repeated.

"Sorry I'm late, I got held up," he said. And then, when I didn't respond: "Been a while, Hazel."

Two years and two months, but who was counting?

"Yeah, guess it has," I said, like I hadn't just done the math. "Lucky timing on the parking spot, though."

He drummed his long fingers on the steering wheel, as if debating his next words. "Seems like I keep just missing you," he said.

I nodded. We'd been just missing each other for over two years, at holidays and family visits and birthday parties; I just wasn't sure which of us was the more active player.

It was a feat, considering he was Gage's oldest friend, and he still owned the house on the same inlet as my dad, bordering our property.

The pattern of evasion was broken only with the message he'd sent me the night my father had died: *Hazel, I'm so sorry.*

He'd been away on vacation when it happened. Even then we'd missed each other.

There was a time that Nico was anywhere Gage went, and was nearly as much a part of my childhood. Our fathers had been partners on the force—a different type of family, I supposed.

"Well," I said, "good to finally run into you."

It was, and it wasn't.

For years growing up, I had been singularly focused on Nico Pritchard. Attuned to the careful way he did everything, from baiting a fishing line to saying my name. The way he pronounced each syllable carefully, not letting the second half get swallowed up, like everyone else. The innocent look of his wide brown eyes, like he was always trying to take everything in, quietly and carefully, to file away for later. The shape of his down-turned mouth, so that his sudden smile was both a surprise and a game changer.

My infatuation was obvious in a way that bordered on embarrassing. As we grew older, the fact that it had been reciprocated by him was not nearly as evident.

"Sorry it has to be under these circumstances," he said. Even his words were carefully chosen. He'd managed to apologize twice in as many minutes.

"Me too," I said. I opened my car door, before it was too late.

"Hazel, hold on," he said.

I held on, hand tightening on the top of the door.

To my horror, Nico stepped out of his idling car: long, tailored pants; white button-down, tucked in; a silver watch that I knew had once belonged to his father; a flush along the top of his high cheekbones.

It didn't matter how much time had passed, or how badly we'd left things the last time—whenever I saw him, I pictured him at fifteen on our swim platform; at seventeen, leaning against my bedroom door; at twenty-one, home from college, eyes slowly scanning the room, before landing on me.

"I wanted to call," he continued, taking a step closer. "I've been meaning to. I just didn't know—"

"Nico," I said, cutting him off. "I'm sorry, but I really do need to go."

I needed to leave before he did something terrible—like resting a hand on my shoulder; placing a thumb under my chin.

I slid into the driver's seat, did my best at smiling. "If you can't find Gage, he's hiding out around the corner of the deck."

I started the car and didn't look back. I had learned long ago that this was the only way to truly leave.

———————

Since Mirror Highway was a loop, there were technically two ways out of town. Going to the right would be faster, but turning left would take me by the scene of the salvaged car.

Sorry, Dad. It was human instinct. I wanted to see it too.

There was a slowdown before the curve, a line of cars steadily crawling forward, inch by inch. Most of the traffic seemed to be due to the line of emergency vehicles along the side of the road, and the fact that only one lane could move at a time. I could just make out a man in the distance, directing traffic past the site.

When I finally approached, I realized that it was Caden in the road, guiding us on. He was still in his khaki pants and light-blue polo. There was mud on the side of his pant leg, like he'd been pressed up against the car, checking inside. Curiosity, before crowd control.

I paused for a beat, like all the rest before me, taking in the scene beside the lake.

The guardrail had been removed and now lay curved and crooked against the trees.

The old vehicle rested at a slight angle on the side of the road, tires flattened, rubber disintegrating. I felt myself holding my breath, like I did whenever driving past a graveyard.

The car was coated in a layer of mud, like something alive, sliding off the surface, dripping onto the asphalt. I couldn't tell the color underneath anymore, but the body was boxy and long, like something a grandparent would drive. The windows were either down or broken, and the inside was piled high with mud and grime. The trunk had been pried open, and it remained that way, like the mouth of an animal.

Goose bumps rose across my arms, the back of my neck. The car seemed like it had become something else under the surface. Something more visceral. A part of the landscape, swallowed up by it, pulsating with the place it had just been.

Caden's face didn't change as he waved me past.

But when I glanced in the rearview mirror, he had turned in my direction, watching me drive away.

———

My phone chimed once I had exited the town, on the weaving road toward the main highway that would bring me back to Charlotte. I thought it was probably Keira or Luke—my business partners and closest friends—checking in, updating me on the day's progress. Making sure I was doing okay.

I peered down at the phone, and saw a message from my uncle: *Did you leave?*

I ignored it, but then my phone rang, the name ROY HOLT on the display. Since I'd left Mirror Lake, he'd rarely reached out. But in the years before, he'd sometimes step in for my father when work called him away.

I answered on speaker. "Hello?" I said. A question, more than a greeting.

At first his voice was choppy, as if he was still in a dead zone himself. "Hazel?" he said, like he'd just repeated himself. "Are you still here?"

"No, I'm on the road already. I have a project I have to check in on."

If he was calling with a lecture, I wasn't interested. Though he'd often seemed proud that I'd set off on my own—building a business, charting my own course—he'd always had a closer relationship with my brothers. *Caden left already too*, was what I wanted to say.

"I was hoping to catch you before you left." A beat of silence, as he searched for what to say next. "I'm the executor of the estate, Hazel," he said, voice low, as if he was trying to find someplace quiet to have this conversation.

It made sense, since he was the only lawyer in the family. He'd begun his career as a prosecutor—he and my dad used to tell stories of the old days, when the cases would pass directly from one Holt to the next. He'd since settled into family law, so of course my father would entrust this part to him. I braced myself for whatever he was about to say.

"Look," he began, voice even lower. "There's something in the will you should know about."

CHAPTER 2

65 Days without Rain
Saturday, May 18
8:00 p.m.
Precipitation: Zero

*T*he house is yours. With every day that passed, the tension in my shoulders only grew.

My uncle's words had echoed in my head for the rest of the week—at work, at the gym pool, at Friday-night drinks.

The house is yours. Just yours.

Of all the things I could've imagined—this was the last on the list.

Do they know? I'd asked, once I'd gotten my bearings again. As if that was the place to begin. Instead of: *Are you sure? Why?*

I haven't talked to them yet, he'd said. *But they might. Perry's will was discovered in his office at work last week. I wanted to tell you first—in person.*

But three days had passed, and he *must've* told my brothers we had talked by now. And yet neither had said a word. Not a call, not a text. I hadn't expected to hear from Caden, but Gage . . . I thought he might reach out, to put me at ease. To say, *Of course he wanted you to have it, Hazel—he always wanted you to come back.* To still be on my side.

But no one had been in contact. Jamie had said they were

meeting tomorrow to clean out the house. No one had even told me the time.

I didn't know what I'd be stepping into.

Which was why, as soon as I had finished walking through our latest open construction site at close of day Saturday, I packed an overnight bag and decided to go.

I wanted the time alone in the old house first, before my brothers arrived in the morning with their questions and their judgment.

I wanted the opportunity to take it all in, to savor the memories one last time, before we stripped them from the walls, pulled them from the shelves, boxed them into the attic. I thought a night alone would help brace me.

To understand why he'd done it.

And if I was being honest with myself, I wondered if I might find something in the house that was meant just for me.

A letter, maybe, tucked under my childhood pillow—like my mother had done, before she left.

Or if, like her, he'd given no reasonable explanation for his decision.

As I veered off the highway, I was reminded why I didn't often make this trip at night. It was the way the trees closed up the view behind you with every mountain curve. And the way the streetlights turned sporadic, and then nonexistent, after the welcome sign for Mirror Lake.

The lake was nestled at the heart of a mountain valley, like the center of a bowl, and every street, every house, the entire town, was crafted with that firmly in mind. The main highway split as you approached the lake, winding up and around the border in either direction, tracing every finger, every outlet, rising and falling along with the terrain. Narrow mountain roads branched outward from the perimeter, sloping up the curves of the bowl. Houses were built into the landscape, their lower levels half buried in the earth, colors blending into the woods.

Sometimes, the wind rushing through the trees sounded like a river.

During high school, after hours of lectures from my father on the dangers of driving in the dark here, I'd made it my mission to know every bend of Mirror Highway by heart, the same way I could map the lake by memory. But it was still too easy to become disoriented in the night.

The moon reflected off the surface of the lake, and without streetlights to ground me as I rounded a curve by the water, for a moment I couldn't tell whether I was heading down or up. I felt a flash of panic, of vertigo, before the trees blocked the view of the lake again.

I pictured that car, pulled out from the depths. How long had it been there, with no one noticing?

Something glowed faintly orange in the distance, and I wondered if this was a new safety feature, after all. But the dim bulbs of a construction sign slowly came into focus, a hazy warning: *NO GUARDRAIL AHEAD.*

I tapped my brakes on instinct—out of curiosity, as much as caution. As if I might see something new in the glow of my high beams. But there was just a series of orange cones in the place the guardrail should have been, and remnants of mud that hadn't yet been washed away by a rainfall in the place the car had once rested.

The mountain wind shuddered against the side of my car, the tires threatening to drift, and I held the steering wheel a little tighter.

Careful.

One more curve, and the road slanted down over the narrower, single-lane bridge. I felt myself list sideways, from muscle memory.

No matter where you were driving in Mirror Lake, you were always circling the basin, bending toward it, like a galaxy spiraling closer to a black hole.

For years, that sensation had felt like home. Like coming back to something—to someone. Only now I was circling an absence. An abyss. Like I was traversing time instead of space, and it would be impossible to ever go back. Like crossing an event horizon.

———————

My wheels churned on the loose rock and gravel as I descended the uneven slope of our driveway. We lived at the bottom of the bowl, along the far edge of the lake, on a quiet, private inlet, sheltered from view. I rode the brakes down, gravity pulling me closer.

The high beams of my SUV illuminated the flat circle of drive, the two-car garage on one side, and the structure of the main house beside it. From the front, it was a quaint ranch home, but there was another level visible only from the back, built into the slope above the lake. Everything appeared dark.

The glare from my headlights reflected in the single garage window, sharp and garish. The last time I'd been here was a blur, rushing over as soon as I got the call from Gage, voice cracking—*It's Dad*. It had taken me a long moment to register what he was trying to say: *He didn't show up to work, wasn't answering his phone. Caden went by the house and found him. Heart attack.* I was already in the car by the time he finished speaking.

I hadn't stayed over then; had driven straight back to Charlotte, terrified of the silence. Our place had always been a hub of activity, a home base for our friends, with an open-door policy that extended to half the community. It wasn't meant to be this quiet.

I turned off the engine and let my eyes adjust to the night before I stepped outside. The glow of the moon, its reflection rippling along the surface of the lake. Stars gaining clarity in the clear sky.

And something else.

I was wrong about the house being completely dark. There was a light somewhere on the main level. Stepping out of the car, I could see the faint yellow glow through the gauzy curtains of the den.

My steps echoed in the night, rocks skittering in my wake. I approached the entrance, squinting into the window.

The house is yours.

Time snapped tightly, so that suddenly I could remember both the moment I first walked through that front door at the age of seven and the moment that I exited after my last visit home, twenty years later.

A cool breeze kicked up from the lake, the familiar scent carrying, evergreen and moss. And something faintly chemical. The exhaust from a boat; the remnants of gasoline in an emptied container. No one had been keeping an eye on things, and I was suddenly nervous about what I'd find inside.

I used the flashlight on my phone to see the keypad beside the garage. I didn't have a key to get inside the front door. The irony: that this house should be left to me, and I had no official way to claim it.

But my father never locked the door inside the garage: Who would ever attempt to sneak into the home of respected Detective Perry Holt? He had been a permanent fixture of town, from community events to school functions. I was convinced he knew the names of every resident in town.

The numbers of the keypad lit up as I pressed the code, gears churning to lift the double doors. The dim overhead light barely illuminated the tools on the walls and crates of canned food and bottled water stacked on the floor in the corner.

I'd teased him over Christmas, asked if he was becoming a prepper, but he'd laughed and said he was just preparing for the pleasure of our company. In his defense, when we were growing up, you never knew how many people would end up here for dinner.

I returned to my car and pulled into the empty spot beside my father's truck. Safe, now, from the threat of wind through the night, snapped branches and twigs already littering the surrounding area—an unpredictable landscape.

The drought had also brought fire warnings to the region, due to a deadly combination of low humidity and gusty winds. How quickly a spark could catch, and spread, if you weren't careful. I stared out the garage window into the dark, watching as the branches arced against the sky.

I had a moment of panic that the inner door to the house would be locked. That Gage had been through, securing the premises. Or Caden had dropped by and turned that dead bolt, knowing I had no way inside otherwise.

But when I tried the handle, the door creaked open, like always.

Every house has a story, and every renovation, a mystery—something the prior owners are trying to fix, or cover up. Something they hoped you wouldn't notice. An old leak, drywall patched over and painted in a slightly off-color shade. A shitty electrical job, wiring not up to code. An unpermitted addition. A secret.

I'd learned as much from my job, but I'd discovered it for myself, long ago.

In the week after Nico's father died, when we were helping him organize, we found a hidden room. *I* found a hidden room, I should say, tagging along with Gage, like always.

A closet tucked inside another, crudely hollowed out in the interior of the house. Hidden behind the closet in the guest room, where, I'd learned, Nico's father had been staying before the divorce. Hanging uniform pants covered the hidden alcove—a rectangular hole in the drywall, just wide enough for one person. We filed into the darkness. I could still see it in flashes. A red flashlight on an empty file box. Crime scene photos taped up on the wooden beams, seared into memory: pale twisted limbs, hair splayed in the dirt, blood on a broken charm bracelet, dangling from a lifeless wrist—cases the elder Nicholas Pritchard had presumably never solved, before he'd moved his family here from Raleigh, for a safer, quieter life.

A *murder* room, Nico had called it.

We'd been kids then—me, fifteen; Gage and Nico, seventeen—and drawn to it, standing there speechless, our hitched breathing echoing against the silence. Back then I wasn't afraid. I felt how consumed this man had become by the need for justice, but I was at the age where I wanted to consume, to be consumed. To fall deeper into everything, as if there were something honorable, beautiful even, in the commitment.

Nico was the first to act. He pulled a photo off the wall, tore it in half as he did, pieces scattering onto the unfinished floor. I pulled down the next, and the next. Until we were in a frenzy, desperately scratching at the walls, before someone else saw them.

We didn't speak. Gage stuffed the pieces into a trash bag before Nico's mother got home, and we dumped it outside. A gift. A promise. It had cemented something between us all right then.

We'd walked home in silence. Until Gage finally broke it.

Hazel, he said—was all he said. We had always communicated like this, with an easy understanding. A look, behind a word.

I know, I said. I understood.

It was our first secret.

———————

I stood in the dark hall of my father's home now, feeling along the wall for the light switch. It buzzed for a moment before catching, a delayed flicker before the series of three overhead lights guided the way, one dimmer than the rest.

I started a list in my head, an instinct that was hard to shake: paint; light fixtures; add a window maybe—

I could sense the potential in a building just like I could see it in a person. Better yet, I could convince others to see it as well.

A wood floorboard popped beneath my steps, as if it had settled with the changing season. As if the house had started to shift on me. I tapped at the hardwood, checking for signs of hollowness underneath—from water damage or time. I was nervous what I'd find if I pulled up the flooring. If the issues with the house were more than just cosmetic.

Everything felt off. The ticking of the grandfather clock in the foyer, like it was moving too slowly. A staleness to the air, like the space was reverting back to its essence, wood and brick, drywall and plaster. Cold and impersonal.

At the end of the hall, I could finally see the source of the inside light.

It was my father's reading lamp, set up narrow and snakelike over his recliner, a worn brown leather with a bookshelf behind it, stacked with equally worn mass-market mystery books. The light was glowing over his empty seat. Like a taunt, after years of him calling after me, *Hazel, the lights!* whenever I left a room. He always said if I ever went missing, all he'd need to do was follow the trail of lights I left behind. Standing in this empty room now, it was almost enough to make me believe in ghosts.

I flicked another switch as I passed—*Old habits, Dad*—and moved deeper into the house. The living room on one side, versions of us frozen in time in the pictures on the mantel: My dad in uniform, with his class from the police academy; I could still name most of them, had grown up thinking of them as my uncles and aunts and cousins. My college graduation photo. Gage's swearing-in ceremony, my father beside him, both of them with that same dark military-style haircut—so alike, both in mannerisms and appearance. And then Caden's, a handful of years later. He'd taken a wilder path, but he had gotten there, all the same.

The only baby pictures now were of my niece, who had the same rounded cherub face as Caden's, the same coy smile that let him get away with everything growing up.

When I got to the kitchen, it was obvious that someone had started without me. There was a pile of loose pictures on the rounded kitchen table, already split into sections. Organized, deliberate, and at first I thought, *Gage*.

The box with my father's medal was open in front of his customary seat, bronze catching the gleam of the chandelier. He'd received it many years earlier, when he saw the smoke from the Woolworth house fire and arrived before the fire trucks, barging straight in. He'd come out with a young boy in each arm and damaged lungs, a perpetually lingering cough that had become background noise, a familiarity of home. He didn't need to display any medal for people to know who he was, what he'd done—he'd worn his heroism across his body.

Now his badge was positioned beside the medal on the table, like a centerpiece.

And there was a small wooden box I didn't recognize, with a silver key wedged into the lock. I opened the top, and a compact handgun rested on a bed of maroon velvet inside.

"Jesus," I muttered, letting the lid fall shut again. This wasn't my father's familiar service weapon. No, this was something else.

I had no idea he'd owned another gun.

This shouldn't be left out, unsecured. This shouldn't be left out at all.

My brothers both would've known how to deal with this. The fact that this was left out felt like someone making a point, instead.

Here, it's yours. You handle it.

Caden, then.

I secured the lock, and looked for a safe place to store it. I settled on the china cabinet, which held no china, and never had. Instead, there was a collection of liquors and various specialty cups and shot glasses brought back from vacations, or gifted by others. I slid the box out of sight on the lower level, then dropped the key into a pewter beer stein with a shamrock on the upper shelf.

The wind blew outside, whistling through the weatherworn window seals. The deck seemed to shudder against the house, and a sharp clang came from somewhere out back—like something had come loose in the yard. A piece of the grill maybe, or one of the staked solar lights that lined the curving path down to the old dock but no longer worked.

I turned on the deck lights that hung over the glass doors and stared out into the night. The deck glowed almost white in the halo, but the ground disappeared below, into the shadows. I opened the sliding glass door and stepped out onto the deck, peering over the edge, where the stairs descended to the lower level.

There was no furniture visible, nothing that looked like it had come loose or fallen over.

The yard slanted downward toward the lake, and it seemed somehow bigger, deeper—the dark of the water even farther away.

The wind whipped through the trees, and then my hair— another clang, a little farther than I'd first thought. Someone out in the water, maybe. I leaned an arm onto the splintered wood of the deck railing, straining to see.

Shadows, slowly coming into focus in the moonlight. Things reaching out from the surface of the lake—branches, roots. And the rectangle of the swim platform, which now appeared closer than I remembered.

We used to race out there as kids, launching from the backyard, high-stepping through the muddy, silted water, before diving in. A mad-dash, gasping race that left me out of breath by the time my hand slapped onto the algae-coated edge, in triumph.

The swim platform drifted to the left in the next breeze, and the sound of metal on metal resounded once more. That's what it was, then. The chains underneath that anchored the platform were no longer pulled taut, given the lower level of water. They twisted against one another and pulled at the connections as the platform drifted back and forth in the current.

I rubbed my upper arms, chilled by the night wind, then re-treated inside and locked the slider behind me.

My father used to say you have to keep an eye on things, or they'd change on you. When I was younger, I had thought he was talking about other people, a quick bait and switch, like a magic trick. I'd thought it was a warning to stay alert, to be exacting, to not let anyone fool you. I'd thought he was talking about my mother.

But now I understood.

The way the edges of the lake kept shrinking, the yard expand-ing in response, roots and mud and rock emerging. A landscape reflected in a funhouse mirror, proportions off. Like it was someplace different from the one I'd once known.

I understood now that it wasn't just the watching but the caring. How quickly everything had gone and changed on me.

I hadn't been watching him—had missed the signs of his weakening heart, obvious only in retrospect, like so much else. And now he, too, was gone.

I brought my luggage inside—a single backpack, a small weekender bag—and wondered what else my brothers had already tackled.

My dad's room was the first door off the hall, and I flipped the light switch. His closet had already been cleaned out, everything pulled off hangers, dumped into piles. Boxes from the high-up shelves were now tossed onto the floor, contents emptied.

The other two bedrooms on the main level had once belonged to Gage and Caden, though Gage's had long been turned into a home office. Nothing appeared disturbed in either.

The flooring creaked below me as I moved—eerie in the emptiness.

Back in the living room, I opened the china cabinet once more, picked up a metallic shot glass I'd brought back from a trip to New York. There was a skyline etched into the surface.

I heard the echo of my father, opening a bottle for a crowd in the living room. *What's the best way to knock out a criminal?*

A shot. Two to be safe.

I opened the whiskey beside the box with the gun, balanced it carefully as I poured. I followed my father's advice: I took one shot, and then two to be safe.

I flicked the switch for the deck lights, darkness falling, and then hit every other light as I passed.

See? I wanted to say. *I listen. I was paying attention.* I stopped at his chair in the den, reaching for the reading lamp, last of all.

The only light left on was the one leading to the basement. The air was cooler in the stairwell, and I knew it would drop another few degrees at the bottom step.

My bedroom was on the lower level, with doors that opened directly to the outside. It was my mother's idea—*Hazel can take that room, she's not afraid of anything.* Which was not at all true when I was seven. For years, I'd stare at those sliding doors until I fell asleep each night, imagining all the things that might happen. But that claim of fearlessness became a state I tried to inhabit, an identity I eventually made my own.

My mother was always very persuasive.

I'd grown accustomed to the vulnerability down here, and when I got older, those doors worked in my favor instead.

My room was the smallest one—I wasn't even sure it counted as a bedroom, since there wasn't a closet. Over time, my things had steadily encroached throughout the lower level: a dresser in the hall with a mirror over the top, my desk in the rec space. Until I'd claimed it all, painting it, even, without asking.

It was still that same leafy green shade, which gave the impression that the space was larger than it was, even though it was dark, moody. There was a second set of sliding doors in the rec space, and the walls blended with the green outside, like there was no separation between outside and in. Even then I had a vision. Saw the way to optimize a place, turn a space into a home.

It sounded like a fan was running, and it took me a moment to realize it was the old desktop computer, on the desk pressed against the far wall of the rec space. I moved the mouse, and the monitor came to life. *System Crash*, the message read. I held the power button until the computer shut down, and the room fell fully to silence.

It was like a time warp, with the walls and the desktop and a cordless landline phone beside the television.

The sheer, gauzy curtains hanging at the sides of the glass doors swayed gently as I passed. The dimensions of the room felt off, somehow, like the ceiling was pushing lower. There was a growing collection of mismatched mirrors clustered together on the back wall, across from the glass doors, adding to the disorientation. There had been only two at Christmas—Dad said they lightened up the room in the daylight—but now there were five, eating up the majority of the wall space. They reflected different slices of me as I passed, distorting the whole.

The whiskey was catching up with me, or maybe it was the house. I brought my bag into the bedroom, slipped into my old daybed, and turned to my side, watching the sliding glass doors, like always.

I'd spent so many years like this, feeling prepared, instead of wary. Just waiting for something to happen. Craving the mystery, the danger, the adventure.

Back then I had naively believed they were all the same thing.

I knew much better now.

CHAPTER 3

There was someone inside the house.

After a childhood spent within these walls, this awareness came from a feeling as much as evidence.

But there was that too.

A fluttering of something overhead when I exited the shower, like an animal had found its way inside a vent. Or as if something was sliding across the floor.

I stared up at the ceiling, remained perfectly still, held my breath. I was used to listening to houses, deciphering their nuances.

Nothing. And then: A deeper creak, like the pop of a floorboard. A footstep.

A person.

"Hello?" I called, though my voice came out hoarse. I finished pulling on my clothes, then went to the base of the steps, expecting Gage to poke his head into the stairwell at any minute.

There was no response, but if he had gone into one of the bedrooms, he probably wouldn't have heard me. He might not have noticed my car in the garage either.

I crept up the stairs, not wanting to startle him. At the top of the steps, there was no sign of anyone else inside. Just the slanting sunlight coming in through the back windows that lined the kitchen and living room.

Through the foyer, I could see the dead bolt was still engaged on the front door. I frowned, then peered out the gauzy curtains of the den: no car.

A chill worked its way down my spine. I listened carefully: the old grandfather clock in the foyer; the drone of a boat engine somewhere out back.

Maybe it was just the settling house, left unattended for too long.

But then I heard it: the creak of a door, coming from somewhere inside—and then silence again.

My heartbeat picked up and the room hollowed out. I took three quick steps backward, toward the front door, my hand already reaching for it. How many empty houses ended up with people squatting inside, believing them abandoned?

I flipped the lock, opened the door, heard the rustling of leaves blowing across the drive.

"Who's in here?" I called, bolder than I felt. I already had one foot outside, ready to run.

The door creaked loudly this time, rapid footsteps rounded the corner, and I had about half a second to prepare myself for the surprised smile of my niece, before she launched herself into my arms.

"Skyler," I said, practically laughing in relief. I held her tight, smoothing the blond hair on the back of her head, my hand still faintly shaking from the surprise.

"I didn't know it was you," she said, burying her face into my neck. I felt the tremble in her arms, the rapid-fire heartbeat in her ribs.

"Hello, favorite girl. I didn't mean to scare you," I said, laughing again, trying to shake the nerves loose.

"You didn't scare me," she said, wide blue eyes peering out from under her overlong bangs. She slid down from my hip, brushed the hair back from her shoulders, crossed her arms. I couldn't help grinning. Skyler might've inherited her father's features, but she had definitely gotten the defiance and attitude from her mother.

"Well, you scared me," I said. "Where's your dad?" They didn't live too far—on the other side of Mirror Highway, partway up the slope of the bowl—though I couldn't imagine he'd let a six-year-old hike down here alone, crossing the road just before a blind curve.

"On the way. They're carrying the boxes," she said.

"How did you get inside?" I asked. The garage door was still closed. The front door had been locked.

Her eyes drifted toward the front of the house. "Grandpa showed me a trick," she said, smile coy.

"Did he, now?"

She leaned closer, as if preparing to tell me a secret. "The garage window," she whispered.

I pictured a lock that didn't latch. Another project to add to the list.

A shadow appeared in the doorway, and then Caden stepped inside, wearing brown work boots and jeans, a gray shirt with the logo of our local brewery.

"Look who's here," Skyler said, as if presenting a magnificent discovery.

"I can see that," he said with a tight smile. "Lucky us." Caden's face gave nothing away. The tops of his cheeks were red, and he brushed his brown hair off his forehead, like he'd been playing a game of pickup basketball, instead of trudging a stack of boxes down the hill.

"I thought she was a monster," Skyler said, which made her father let out a real belly laugh, easing the tension. "She surprised me."

"This one is always full of surprises," he said, dropping the pile of flattened boxes just inside the foyer, letting them slide to the floor, as if searching for the most inconvenient spot. "Speaking of, what are the rules now, Hazel? Do I have to knock first?"

I ignored him, even as he reached into the front pocket of his jeans and pulled out a single key. He held it between us, like an offering, or a dare.

Jamie appeared suddenly from behind. "Hi, Hazel," she said absently. And then, to her daughter, "I told you to wait."

She swept into the room, all business this time. Jamie's long hair brushed against my neck as she air-kissed my cheek, a pretense of affection. I didn't know whether I'd misinterpreted her intentions at the memorial, to have me here. I couldn't read her the way I used to.

Jamie used to have choppy bleached-blond hair, cut razor-sharp to her shoulders. She used to have a stronger edge, a slicker style. In school, she'd sold fortunes, before moving on to cigarettes, and occasionally whatever else she could dig up in her mother's medicine cabinet. She'd worn bold patterns, mismatched styles, Goodwill vintage layered with boutique-sale finds, a combination that somehow worked on her. She used to say exactly what was on her mind, no matter the audience or situation. She used to be my best friend. We'd been drawn together since middle school—a spark to a firecracker, my dad used to say. I never knew which of us was which.

But motherhood had softened her, curving her edges, tempering her voice, as if she was accustomed, always, to a baby sleeping in the next room. Her hair fell in gentle waves now. Even her expression was cautious.

Today she wore casual jeans and a soft T-shirt, pink lip gloss that matched her small cross-body bag, and sneakers that I'd seen on half the population this week alone. She hadn't told me anything real about herself in nearly a decade.

I could see her taking me in as well, and I wondered if she was thinking the same about me.

I was dressed the same as I'd be for a home renovation: loose worn jeans, torn at the knees, fraying at the hems. A black T-shirt, athletic sneakers. Dark hair pulled up high into a tight ponytail.

"Sky, help me bring the boxes in," she said, leaving me and Caden awkwardly in the hall together.

"Well," he said, placing the house key on the foyer table with dramatic ceremony. "He always was trying to get you to come home."

"I'm home all the time," I said, because I could never let a comment go. It was the rhythm of our youth. Even now I couldn't be the bigger person.

But he was right—I hadn't been here to see our dad since Christmas, and he'd died in April. Four months I could never get back.

"The gun's in the bottom of the china cabinet, by the way," I said, changing the topic, shifting the accusations.

Caden stared back, mouth caught half-open, like that was the dumbest thing he could imagine, before suddenly looking over his shoulder.

The sound of tires on the gravel out front was a relief. Things with Caden could go one of two ways: either he was in a good mood and generally ignored my existence; or he was in a combative mood and took every dig he could manage.

Growing up, my mom said our tension was because Caden and I were too close in age—too directly competitive. But she always was more willing to give him the benefit of the doubt.

"Gage is here!" Skyler shouted, weaving past her father. Skyler was at the age where anything could be exciting, every arrival an event. Gage still lived in Mirror Lake; she probably saw him often, and regularly.

I followed her outside to greet him. The morning was warmer than I'd been expecting, like the wind had blown in a new front overnight.

Gage parked his Jeep directly in front of the entrance, sunlight reflecting off the windshield, making me squint. I raised a hand in greeting, while Skyler ran to the driver's side door. I couldn't get a read on his expression. Couldn't tell if my presence was a surprise for him. And if so, whether it was a welcome one.

"Hey," I said, as Gage scooped up Skyler for a bear hug that made her laugh in delight.

"Hi," he said blinking twice, like he was making sure I wasn't a figment of his imagination. My heart contracted, waiting. "I didn't know you were coming. I didn't want to put this on you. I know you're busy. And you were just here." A series of excuses. Three of them.

God, how I wanted to believe him.

If every house has its flaws, Perry Holt tried to keep his small and obvious. The house showed its signs of age visibly, on the surface. There was a list, in fact, on the side of the fridge, of projects he needed to tackle: *Check basement. Check garage. Check crawl space.*

But wasn't that just like my father. He'd even itemized his valuables and left a detailed document of where to find his finances.

"He left this with the will," Gage said, holding the list, while the rest of us stood scattered around the living room. "He said everything's in the house. There's not too much of value left, after . . ." He trailed off, eyes flicking around the room briefly. He didn't need to say any more. We all knew.

After my mom left. After she took everything with her.

"But," he continued, "there's a safe, and we have the code, and of course we should go through the office carefully, make sure there's nothing from work. . . ." He drifted off again. Then he cleared his throat. "I think we should start there."

I could picture Gage then in front of a room of his colleagues, or standing over a scene—taking charge. Bringing a sense of order to the chaos.

I knew he would have a plan, that the rest of us would fall in line, wanting to follow him. This was how he'd gotten promoted so quickly—making detective before he'd turned thirty.

Caden trailed after him, but I was suddenly too hot, too worried about what they would say when we were crammed in that room together, alone. I opened the fridge, took a can of orange soda—Dad's favorite—and held it to the back of my neck, before cracking the top open.

Skyler was sitting at the kitchen table beside her mother, moving photos around.

I was glad I'd relocated the gun.

Skyler held a photo out to me. "Is this you?"

"It is," I said, grinning. I had been twelve or thirteen, standing beside my father, both of us with gold medals around our necks, the lake in the background. "We won the swim relay in the Lake Games that year," I told her. He'd called me his secret weapon. My dark hair was wet, hanging tangled down my back. His arm rested around my shoulders. His smile beamed. I still thought of that day when swimming laps at the gym pool.

"Who's this?" she asked, moving on to the next.

Jamie leaned closer, the only tell a twitch at the side of her mouth. "Me."

Skyler looked to her mother, then back to the picture, and I couldn't help but smile too. It was from BC—*Before Caden*—and she'd been doing a cartwheel in our backyard, white-blond hair in front of her face, so that all you could see was her wild, unrestrained smile.

"I took that picture, you know," I said. "Your mother was quite the gymnast."

Now Skyler looked particularly incredulous. She sorted through the stack, one by one. "There's a lot of pictures of you, Mom," she said. "You and Hazel."

"She was here all the time," I said. Like I was still trying to lay claim to something, years later. *Mine first.*

Jamie leaned over Skyler, frowning. "Okay, come on, help me pack up the clothes, Sky." She stacked the photos again, tapped the edge against the table, and turned them facedown. As if she was saying, in response: *You ruined it.*

I did not handle the news of Jamie and Caden well. I'd left for college, and by the time I came home first semester, she had *something to tell me.*

I was shocked, blindsided. The fact that Caden and I didn't get along should've told her everything she needed to know.

I tried to warn her. Asshole meter? I was sure he was one hundred percent sociopath, and the very worst kind to prove. Nothing so obvious, no actions to call forth as evidence. Just a centering of himself in every interaction, and every decision. Generally harmless to all but those who loved him.

And so I impulsively told Jamie that Caden's interest in her was just *part of his ongoing attempt to piss me off.*

I'll be the first to admit that I was wrong. But it turns out it's hard to recover from calling someone's boyfriend a sociopath, once they go and marry them.

Jamie and Skyler disappeared into my father's bedroom to tackle the mess of clothes and boxes from the closet. I headed for the room at the end of the hall—Gage's old bedroom, which Dad had converted into his home office.

Caden was sitting in Dad's chair behind the wide oak desk, feet up, head back, eyes closed, like he was lost in thought. Like he was putting himself in his father's shoes. I was momentarily taken aback by this display of vulnerability.

A memory rolled through me then: my father at his desk, his booming voice calling my name as I passed the room. So that suddenly I could feel him here, a shadow in the corner of my eye, something I could almost grab on to—

"This is how I found him, Hazel," Caden said, without opening his eyes. As if he could sense me, like a disturbance in the room. "Just. Like. This." His eyes shot open and he dropped his feet abruptly to the floor, making me jump. "Legitimately thought he was asleep." He ran a hand across his chin. "Good thing one of us checked in on him."

The memory was gone, and in its place, the horror Caden must've seen. I stood at the threshold of the room, unable to move forward or back. Unable to breathe, to shake the image from my brain.

He stared back at me, as if daring me to say something.

I finally had my answer about what I'd be walking into here: hostility. Definitely, one hundred percent, hostility.

"I think I've got it," Gage said, louder than necessary from his position inside the closet. He was crouched down in front of the safe, eyes on the spinning dial. I heard the click of the lock just before he pulled the door open. "Here we go. The essential stuff."

He removed the stack of documents, balancing it on two hands, before depositing it all onto the surface of the desk.

"Are you going to help?" he asked me. An invitation. A welcome. Always the mediator between me and Caden.

I joined them behind the desk. We combed through the documents, checking them off of his itemized list. Birth certificate, passport, deeds to the house and the truck in the garage. A checkbook.

Once we started, it was easier to continue. Caden and I started emptying the drawers, sorting the contents into piles of trash or keep.

"Jesus," Caden said, pulling out a bound package of envelopes, the ghost of a smile forming. "I think these are our report cards."

Gage returned from the closet with a large white envelope, edges crushed.

"What's that?" I asked.

"I think it's a copy of the will," he said. "It was at the bottom of the safe."

Even Caden paused, the momentary smile sliding off his face. I watched as Gage's eyes trailed down the document, as if he were checking it for accuracy. As if he were confirming it was as we'd all been told.

A line formed between his eyes, and he abruptly flipped the pages back to the start. His expression told me everything I needed to know: yes, it was; no, he didn't like what he was seeing.

"It matches the one they found at the station," Gage said as a loose sheet of paper fell from the bottom.

Caden scooped it off the pilled area rug. "Passwords," he said. "Banks, credit cards . . ."

"God," Gage said, peering over his shoulder. "It's a miracle he wasn't hacked."

I had to agree. It seemed every password was a variation of *Mirror Lake* and his birthday, in different orders. But then, he still preferred using the old family desktop computer instead of his work laptop—he had never been the most tech savvy.

The pitter-patter of Skyler's feet racing down the hall breached the silence, jarring us back to the task at hand.

The only thing our father had kept on the surface of this desk was half of the fancy pen set I'd gotten him for Father's Day one year—wood base with his name positioned at the edge of the blotter, gold pen engraved with the letter *H* currently missing. I couldn't bear to move it now.

The narrow top drawer contained just one thing: a gold wedding band. I hadn't seen him wear it in years.

I held it in my open palm, the light from the window glinting off the metal.

Gage frowned. His throat moved, and he raised his eyes to mine. "Can I have it?" he asked quietly.

I nodded. I didn't know why he was asking me, when it was currently extended in my outstretched hand. This was probably the only personal item of value remaining, and I didn't want to be responsible for it.

He took it from my palm, turned it side to side, as if looking for some clue. "I didn't know he kept this. It wasn't on the list."

"Probably not worth much," Caden said.

When my mother left, she took everything she could—jewelry, cash—in a whirlwind of chaos. She probably only missed this because he'd been wearing it.

I stepped out of the room, needing air.

At the kitchen table, Jamie was poring over the photos again.

"Hey," I said, startling her. She dropped whatever she was

holding, then turned around, hand to heart. "Find any good ones?"

She smiled tightly. "This house," she said, "feels like it's full of ghosts."

"Mom," Skyler said, bounding into the room. "Can I go swimming?"

Jamie looked out the window, frowning. As if it wasn't the lake she knew anymore either. "Not right now."

"Dad said—"

"Not *now*," Jamie snapped.

"What's going on?" Caden asked, joining us in the kitchen.

"Dad, you said I could go swimming today. You promised. You said Mom wouldn't want to be here anyway."

Jamie's shoulders stiffened, and I felt the tension in the silence that followed.

"I'll take her," I said. "It's fine." Like Skyler, I needed to get out.

Jamie pushed a small purple backpack into my hands without making eye contact. "She has to wear swimmies," she said.

"Well," Caden said, one side of his mouth rising, "it is your house. Guess you're in charge now."

CHAPTER 4

66 Days without Rain
Sunday, May 19
11:15 a.m.
Precipitation: Zero

don't need these. Grandpa let me, but I'm not supposed to say," Skyler said, as I started inflating her bright pink swimmies.

I smiled tightly. "I follow your mother's orders," I said.

Skyler looked toward the edge of the lake. "Grandpa said you can't be scared of your own backyard," she said.

"That sounds like him," I said. "I'm still listening to your mother."

When we were younger and charged into the lake to race out to the platform, Caden would always start swimming long before me. To anyone else, it probably seemed like he wanted to win, to get a head start. Only I knew he hated the feel of his feet on the bottom of the lake. That he was afraid of what might be down there. It was actually faster to keep running until the water got too deep. Fear only slowed you down.

Now the earth was parched and thirsty, and I could feel the chunks of grass, brittle under my soles.

"My dad says you're not really my aunt," she said, watching me intently.

"Really," I said. A pause. "What does your mom say?"

Skyler put her hand on her hip, did the perfect impersonation of her mother's eye roll. "*Caden, please.*"

I laughed. "That mother of yours."

"Well," she said, "are you?"

"Of course," I said.

"That's what *I* said."

I slipped the swimmies onto her arms and finished blowing them up, gave them each a pat even as she rolled her eyes again, this time directed at me.

"Okay, all set," I said.

She walked sure-footed down the sloping path, and didn't even flinch at the temperature of the water, which I knew would still carry a spring chill. As she kept going, the water level remained just over her knees. For a moment I thought she might be able to walk the entire inlet.

But then, in a gasp, she sank fully up to her neck, bright pink swimmies bobbing in the water. She turned around once and giggled.

I heard someone walking down the incline behind me, leaves crunching and sticks snapping. It was impossible to sneak up on anyone here.

My uncle sidestepped carefully down the slope, ice jostling in the tumbler he carried.

"Hi, Roy," I said. Dad's brother was a year younger than him, but had always seemed older to me. Maybe it was his lawyerly way of speaking, or his predictability—the tumbler, I knew, would be full of Diet Coke, his vice of choice—or the fact that he was always dressed for business, even now, in a button-down and khaki pants and brown loafers, thick graying hair slicked to the side.

"That water must be freezing," he said, eyes trailing after Skyler, who was making her way slowly, arm over arm, to the swim platform.

"You don't feel it when you're a kid. It's like magic," I said.

"Guess so," Roy said, taking a sip. He wasn't one for sentimentality, or pleasantries.

"Hazel, listen," he said now, with a quick glance over his shoulder, up to the sliding glass doors, where the rest of them were presumably still sorting through Dad's things. "I want you to be prepared. Caden already came by, saying he wants to challenge the will."

I shouldn't have been surprised. But still—Caden was contesting the will? The tension I felt in that house wasn't my imagination. I wondered if Gage knew. If he approved, even. I felt a jolt of betrayal.

"What did he say?" I asked, voice monotone, ears ringing.

"That it must've been a misunderstanding. That maybe he just meant for you to fix up the house to sell it and split the proceeds with them." It made sense. My father knew I'd be capable of getting us all the best value. But Roy shook his head. "That's not what the will says. If Perry meant that, he would've said it."

Roy stepped closer, lowered his voice. "I'm sure Caden had his own ideas. I think he was planning to make this place his own, even if he had to buy your shares out. I'll tell you the same thing I told him. He can do what he wants, but he's not going to win. It's just going to drag things out."

I'd thought, if anyone, Roy might be able to navigate the nuances of the will—see us through to the other side. Roy and Dad weren't particularly close on a day-to-day basis, but they showed up for each other when it counted.

Maybe Roy understood what my father had been thinking.

I heard a splash behind me, saw the lake rippling around Skyler, who had just jumped from the swim platform.

Now I was the one to lower my voice. "I don't know why he left it to me," I said. Saying, finally, the thing I was sure Caden and Gage were wondering.

"Why not?" Roy said. "You always were his favorite."

"Ha." I rolled my eyes, but smiled. "What do you think he wanted me to do with it?" I asked. It was too big a responsibility. I wished there had been more details, an expectation, an explanation for me, another itemized list he'd left behind.

Roy shifted on his feet, frowning at the dirt on his loafers. "Whatever you want, I'm guessing. Fix it up and sell it, or don't. Turn it into a vacation rental. When the water levels rise again, with a little work, this place could bring in a nice side income."

I stared at the house, and then at him. It needed more than just a little work. Roy lived on the other side of the lake, in a property he'd chosen to rehab slowly over time, instead of moving someplace new. It had taken years, but I'd watched the drab landscaping slowly transform into a peaceful haven—gazebo, hot tub, and all. He must've known what it would take around here.

"Whatever his reasons, he meant for you to have it," he reiterated.

Roy reached a hand out, let it rest on my shoulder, in reassurance. A promise that he was on my side. He looked up toward the porch again. "Besides, I'm sure those boys have access to his accounts. His finances will probably roll over to them automatically. Maybe this was his way of making sure you had something." He patted my shoulder, then dropped his arm and looked up at the deck. "They up there?"

I nodded, swallowed the lump in my throat. "Yes," I said. "Thanks, Roy," I added, as he started up the stairs.

It made sense. Gage and Caden would probably inherit everything that wasn't specified in the will, by default, as the next of kin.

Caden might be a sociopath, but he also didn't lie.

Caden wasn't lying when he told Skyler I wasn't really her aunt.

The men inside that house were not really my brothers.

The man who owned this house was not really my father.

Not in any legal sense.

My mother had grifted her way into the Holts' lives when Caden and I were both almost eight, and Gage was ten. A little more than six years later, she'd grifted her way out, but left me behind. I was fourteen. In place of everything she'd taken, all she'd left me was a letter she'd slipped under the pillow of my bed, inside a single envelope addressed to *Daughter of Mine.*

It was what she'd whisper in the night, when she used to tuck me into bed. So that, when I pulled out the letter, I could see the shape of her mouth, feel the way her whisper brushed against my cheek. *Sleep tight, daughter of mine—*

I'd thought her letter would say she'd be back, or that it would tell me how to meet her later, but there was only a single line inside:

I hope one day you can forgive me.

It was not the first time she'd abandoned someplace in the middle of the night, with no warning.

It was just the first time I'd been left behind.

The most generous interpretation of events was that she found me a good family, wanted something better for me, and didn't leave until she was sure.

The least generous interpretation was that she was happy to keep me around when I was of use, which became less so as I aged. That she played a long game, saw a big take, and found a way to get the contents of two sizable bank accounts and a houseful of valuables all at once, and make off with one less responsibility—freed from the anchor of me.

Or maybe it wasn't a game at all, but an opportunity she couldn't pass up. We'd lived our lives that way—so much of chance was really just opportunity taken.

I remembered the moment Perry Holt came into our lives— we'd all met together. We were renting the detached unit on the property across the street, a fully furnished two-bedroom carriage house, and had just arrived in town a few days earlier, with nothing but our two matching royal-blue suitcases—the same ones that we'd wheeled behind us on every move, year after year. My mother believed in traveling light. That you'd find what you needed when you arrived.

He'd knocked on the door, still in his uniform. There were two boys behind him, both taller than me, wearing stoic expressions. My mother had first tightened her grip on the doorframe. *Can I help you, Officer?*

But he'd just come to offer a neighborly welcome.

Perry, he'd said, though we'd soon learned everyone else called him Holt, last name first. Only my mother called him Perry, like a secret code. But we'd met him together, me at her side. He had crouched down, eyes crinkling, hand held out in an offering. He'd clasped both of his around mine, said, *Pleasure to meet you, Hazel. I heard there would be a new student in Caden's grade.* And so I liked to believe he had fallen for both of us as a unit, and at the same time.

A widower with two sons, a single mother of a daughter. Perry Holt didn't believe in God, but he did believe in fate. Plus: my mother had a way of telling stories, just slightly exaggerated, still on this side of believable. And she had a can-do attitude, finding herself jobs she lacked qualifications for, but promising her ability, if only you'd give her a chance. And people did.

She played on their sympathy, or maybe their weakness, or maybe she didn't see it as a play at all, but a way of survival. She believed she could do it, if only you'd give her a chance. She made deals: *You don't have to pay until you believe it too.*

And always, they did.

She leaned on connections. In Mirror Lake, Perry Holt was the biggest source of trust you could ask for.

When we first arrived, the restaurants were desperate for summer help—we always landed in a vacation spot for this reason. But it wasn't long after she met my father that she heard Roy's company was hiring, and she shoved her foot in that door. And then she kept proving herself until she managed his accounts there too.

The last time I saw her, she was standing at the kitchen window overlooking the lake before I left for school, long green peasant dress brushing her ankles, feet bare. Blond hair straight down her back.

I think of it often, the things she was debating at that moment, staring out the window. How she would justify it to herself. *Take the money and go. The girl gets a better life.*

Other than the trail of destruction she'd left in her wake, it was true—this was the nicest place we'd ever been. Perry Holt was the nicest man I'd ever known.

She'd left me in a good place, with good people, and the truth was, I'd had a good life since.

Look at what I had. Look at what she'd left me. This family, this place, this life—

I turned slowly to the lake now, pulled by something—a feeling, an intuition.

A flat expanse of water, nothing moving, nothing splashing. No shock of color bobbing on the surface. Even the wind was still.

I took a step, twig snapping. "Skyler?" I called.

I was already slipping out of my sneakers, parched earth against my soles, walking closer. I called her name again, my voice tight with panic.

Roy paused at the top step, leaning over the deck rail.

"I don't see her," he said, voice wavering, but he sounded so far away, and I was already stepping into the water.

"Skyler!" I called, waiting for the bob of her head, the wave of her arm.

Nothing but the still surface of the water, the swim platform eerily empty. A ringing in my ears, and a fear—a true bone-aching, breathtaking fear—that I hadn't felt in a very long time.

"Skyler!" I screamed.

I was already striding into the lake, calling her name again and again, so I could barely hear Roy calling for Caden, for Gage, panic rising.

I started to run. I high-stepped it through the silted water, like I'd done long ago. Begging for this to be a game, a joke, nothing but the terrifying prank of a six-year-old.

The temperature of the water, the muddy bottom, the sticks and rocks—none of it registered at first. I couldn't move fast enough, couldn't take in the entirety of the lake all at once. I whipped my head side to side, scanning for movement, for anything.

The steep drop-off came before I was ready for it, my muscles seizing for just a moment while a wave of cold crept up my neck—and then suddenly I was swimming, arm over arm, to the platform.

Hands slapping on top of the wood, elbows digging in, launching myself one leg at a time onto the surface, to the best vantage point. Hoping to see her there, hiding against the far edge, or floating in the deeper water.

Now I scanned the entire inlet from edge to edge. Nothing but water from here to where the inlet fed out to the rest of the lake. The main channel had a current, an unexpected pull, but I couldn't imagine she'd made it that far in such a short amount of time. Still, I hoped. I begged. *Please please please—*

"Skyler!" I screamed, my voice echoing.

"Oh my god," I heard, coming from behind me. "Sky?" I peered back over my shoulder, saw Jamie sprinting across the yard, blond hair wild.

I jumped into the deep side of the lake, then traced the perimeter of the platform, as if I'd merely missed her.

Nothing.

There was one more place, one more hope—

I held my breath and dove underneath the edge of the platform, coming up in the hollow space underneath.

And *there*, two bright pink swimmies, a girl visible between. She floated facedown, hair spread out in a halo.

I grabbed her by the arm, shook her as I pulled her toward me desperately. She flailed, fighting against me. Her head popped up from the surface, and her eyes looked extra wide inside the goggles.

"Oh my god," I said, taking one big gasp in relief. I finally felt the burn in my muscles, the cold in my bones.

Her mouth hung open. I must have shocked her as much as she'd shocked me.

But she was alive. She was fine. "It's me, I've got you," I said. "Skyler, I've got you."

I could hear Jamie still calling in the distance, her voice muffled by water and the edge of the platform. Under here, it smelled distinctly of lake and wood rot, everything exacerbated by the small enclosed space. Even our breathing echoed, everything cocooned and private.

"Hold your breath," I said.

Her arms hooked around my neck as I counted to three and ducked under the platform ledge, popping up on the house side this time.

"I have her!" I called, seeing Jamie already knee deep in the water. "She's okay!"

Jamie's hand went to her heart, but she didn't wait. She kept coming closer, meeting us halfway, just where the bottom of the lake angled sharply upward. As I emerged, I felt the weight of the water in my clothes, and Skyler in my grip.

"I'm sorry," I said, passing her to Jamie's outstretched arms. "She was hiding under the platform. I couldn't see her—"

"I wasn't hiding," Skyler said, as Jamie carried her the rest of the way to shore.

Everyone was waiting, standing in various degrees of shock. Gage, sneakers off beside him. Roy, phone in his hand—ready to call for help.

Caden stared at Jamie and Skyler walking toward him, the blood fully drained from his face. He reached for his daughter, pulling her tightly into his grip, two arms firmly around her back, his eyes wild with relief.

Until finally he turned to me.

"Jesus," he said, lip curling. "Can't even watch a kid for five minutes without losing them, Hazel?"

Not a false accusation.

"I'm sorry—" I said, because what else was there to say? I hadn't been watching. It was the simplest thing, and he was *right*.

"Everything okay?" Nico emerged from the woods where our properties met. He was half-dressed, in gym clothes, barefoot, like he'd still been in bed when he heard the commotion and rushed over.

I didn't know he was living there again.

"We're okay," Roy said, speaking for the group.

Jamie grabbed my arm, just for a second, a quick comforting squeeze. "She's fine. Okay? She's fine." And then, to Skyler, "What did I tell you about staying where a grown-up can see you?"

Skyler pulled the goggles from her eyes, marks still ringing the skin. "There's a shipwreck down there," she said.

Caden frowned. "A *what*?" he asked, pulling back to look at his daughter.

"A shipwreck," she repeated, like it was the most natural thing in the world.

Jamie laughed, like her nerves were finally unspooling. But the sound died out in the silence that followed.

My eyes locked onto Gage's. *A boat?* I mouthed.

Dad used to have an old canoe that had either been stolen or cut loose from the dock in a storm, years ago. But *shipwreck* didn't sound like a canoe. And now I was worrying that something had crashed, sunk, with no one noticing.

If there was an accident called in, I was sure at least Caden would've heard.

"I thought I smelled gasoline last night," I said. "And I definitely heard a motor this morning."

"You were here *last night*?" Caden interjected, latching on to the wrong point.

"We should check," I said.

Gage started unbuttoning his flannel, stripping down to his white T-shirt underneath. Nico stepped closer to the edge, ready to go in as is, it seemed.

"I'm already wet," I said. My soaked jeans were weighing me down, uncomfortable and stiff with water. "Sky, can I borrow those?" I asked, reaching for the goggles.

"This seems like it can wait," Caden said, pulling a towel from the purple backpack, wrapping his daughter inside. "It's probably nothing."

"You're probably right," Gage said, appeasing Caden, even as he opposed him.

It didn't matter that I had already volunteered, Gage and Nico were beside me when I stepped into the water again.

We walked slowly, no longer in a panic. I felt the rocks this time, my sole catching on a sharper edge, ankle rolling in response. Nico reached out on instinct, to right me.

"Thanks," I said, pulling away just as quickly as he dropped his arm.

"You're shaking," he said, frowning, as if he'd just noticed.

But I had been shivering since I stepped out of the water, my black T-shirt clinging, water dripping from my hair, a grime coating my exposed skin.

All I could think of was the hot shower waiting for me after this.

Gage reached the drop-off first, suddenly disappearing up to his neck. I eased in after him, swimming before the ground gave way beneath me.

We made our way slowly and silently to the platform, then ducked under the ledge, all at once, like someone had given a silent count.

I peered down under the surface, and the water in my ears dulled the sounds around me. The water was murky, and dark, and at first I could see only Gage's legs moving beside me. But then, over to the side, I saw a shadowed shape in the distance, caught in a beam of sunlight.

I popped my head up again, taking a breath.

"It's hard to see. But I think something's at the bottom."

"Could just be a rock, or a tree trunk?" Gage said, frowning.

"Yeah," I said. "I'm gonna go down to check."

"I can do it," Nico said, hand reaching out for the goggles. But I ignored him—he may have been the one who ran a dive center in the summer, but I'd gone down to the bottom here plenty of times when I was young.

When the waters were higher, you couldn't touch the bottom when you jumped off the back end of the swim platform. It was always a dare, to see who could make it down, and I was the only one who could. They'd make me prove it by bringing a rock up from the bottom.

I had figured out the trick. Jump in, but catch your breath under the platform. Then grip the chain at the corner and follow it down, down, down. Pull yourself arm over arm, until you reach the cinder-block anchor. Stretch your hands into the mud and muck, find your prize. Then propel yourself off the bottom, break through the surface, fist first, victorious.

They never understood how I could stay underwater so long, and I never told.

Now I gave myself away. I moved over to the corner, where I knew the chain would be hooked, secured to the weightings below. I felt around until I had the familiar metal in my grip.

"Be right back," I said. Then I took a long breath and dropped under the surface.

There was low visibility in the deep, silty water. It had always been best to keep your eyes closed underneath.

If not for Skyler's goggles, I would have.

At first I couldn't see anything through the murk—just shadows and debris swirling up in my path. I followed the chain down, pulling myself hand over hand, until the shadow came into view again.

My hands brushed against the sloped shape of rusted metal. Dirt swirled up as I moved along it. The bottom of the canoe, maybe?

I was running out of breath, about to propel myself to the surface. But then my hands reached a gap—a hollow, an absence. I traced the opening. A window.

My lungs were burning. I reached inside. Felt the curve of a wheel—

I pushed off the object suddenly with my feet and broke through the surface. I sucked in air, pulling the goggles from my face.

Both men stared back in the dim alcove. I gripped the top of the chain again, worried I'd sink without it. I tipped my head back, trying to catch my breath.

"What?" Gage said. "What did you see?"

His eyes were as wide as mine must've been.

"Hazel?" Nico asked, my name a question, a command.

You can't be scared of your own backyard. I tried to cling to my father's words.

And so I kept my voice low, another secret, just for us.

"A car," I said between breaths. "I think there's a car down there."

CHAPTER 5

66 Days without Rain
Sunday, May 19
12:00 p.m.
Precipitation: Zero

I could feel my teeth chattering, and I didn't know if it was from the cold of the water or the nerves.

"Let me see," Gage said, hand held out for the goggles.

"We should wait," Nico said, like he believed me and needed no confirmation.

But I wasn't sure Gage heard. He disappeared under the surface, and I moved to the other side of the platform, giving him space. I drifted through a cold patch—*spirits*, I used to say, to scare Caden.

But now I could only picture what might be down there. A skeleton buckled into a seat. Snakes taking up space in the hollows. I stared down into the dark water, counting the seconds, as if I might be able to catch sight of Gage in the depths. But I could barely see the lower half of my own body.

Had it been too long? I couldn't tell. Time had become distorted, same as the geography of the lake.

I was about to say something, anything, when Gage broke through the surface with a sudden gasp.

"Holy shit," he said, all but confirming what I'd seen.

"I don't think we should touch it," Nico said carefully, cautiously choosing his words.

There was a time, when we were growing up, when we would have thought nothing of trying to solve this on our own. Keeping it to ourselves. *For* ourselves.

I remembered standing inside that hidden closet, taking matters into our own hands, ripping the pictures off the wall—the three of us still the only ones who knew about what we'd found.

"Let's go," Gage said. "I gotta call this in."

We stood close together at the edge of the lake. My hands shook as I wrung my hair out over my shoulder. I could still feel the cool brush of steel under my palm, the sharp edge as I pushed off with my foot.

"Well?" Caden asked.

In response, Gage indicated the phone in his hand.

"This is Detective Gage Holt," he said to whoever picked up on the other end. "I'm at my father's house. I just got out of the lake. Listen. We found another one."

It wasn't long before the cops arrived.

I heard them coming, voices low, rounding the corner of the house, walking carefully down the slope. Gage, wrapped in a towel now, beside Serena Flores, followed by two young men I didn't recognize. I hadn't seen either of them at any department family gathering before. They looked so young—like they must still be in training.

Serena slowed, coming to a stop beside me, hands on curved hips, peering out at the water.

"I didn't know you were back in town, Hazel," she said. I'd seen her briefly at the celebration of life earlier in the week, still in uniform. She'd wrapped an arm around my shoulders then, too choked up to offer any words of condolence.

"Just for the weekend," I said, my voice tight.

"Who found it?" she asked, her dark eyes landing on Gage.

"My niece. Skyler," he said, thumb jutting back toward the house.

"She thought it was a shipwreck," Caden added, monotone.

"It's pretty much right under the platform. The anchor chain is caught on it," I explained.

I felt unsteady under Serena's gaze, and I wasn't sure if it was because of what was happening now, or the fact that she'd always seemed slightly suspicious of me. It was a familiar feeling, being back in Mirror Lake.

This was a different kind of reunion, a different kind of family. A generation of department kids who had come up at the same time. My brothers and me. Nico. Serena Flores, with her sleek dark ponytail and bow-shaped lips. She had been in Gage's grade at school, and dated him on and off since they were in the academy. Both of them were solid and stoic, with similar interests, a shared moral compass.

Mirror Lake was a place steeped in tradition, where multiple generations were born in the same hospital, and possibly under the oversight of the same doctor. Half left the world in the same manner as those who had come before—my father was not the first Holt to succumb to a heart attack in his sixties. Even then, we'd all missed the signs, assumed the fact he'd been cutting back on his shifts meant he was testing out the idea of retirement.

This was a place where sons were named for their fathers. Where daughters wore their mothers' baptism gowns. The department here was just the same—a path was paved for all who would follow. I'd heard Caden referred to as *Little Holt* behind the scenes, and not in a positive way. Like he had pressed someone's nerves the wrong way.

We'd been recruited long before we knew it, in a way. Accompanying our parents to the barbecues, riding in their patrol cars, trying on their uniforms. Hearing the stories they told; hearing the stories others told about them.

I had almost continued that path myself, but it was hard to exist in a role like this when your mother was a known criminal. I instead found that same sense of belonging in the business I'd built with my two college roommates, felt the shared purpose in the investments we made and that shot of adrenaline in the risks we'd taken—the times when we'd taken an old house down to the bones, to the point of no return, and had to find our way back up. I loved the challenge of a project that no one else thought they could turn a profit on: hazards defused, order restored, vision made manifest. It's where we had found our niche.

"You confirmed it?" Serena asked, addressing Gage once again.

"Yeah, I went down to check. Hazel too."

Her eyes skimmed over me, unreadable, before moving on to Nico.

"And no one's inside?" she continued.

"No," Gage said.

But it was nearly impossible to see down there, in the murky water. "I don't know," I said, and Gage frowned, like I'd somehow brought his honor into question. "I just mean, I could barely see anything. It's so dark down there."

I feared that Gage was seeing what he wanted. He hadn't seen a body, but that didn't mean there wasn't one.

Serena checked her watch. "The dive team is on the way, but the salvage company is closed today. They won't be able to get here until tomorrow to pull it out," she said.

"Tomorrow? What if someone's in there?" I asked.

She turned her gaze on me again. "Then I don't think another day is going to make a difference, Hazel."

Nico shifted on his bare feet. "Do you need an extra set of eyes again?" he asked. "I can go get my gear."

She checked her watch for a second time, like she wasn't sure of the decision. Without my father, there had been a change in the chain of command. I wondered who had stepped into his role, and how the rest of the department shook out.

I wondered if she was waiting for her own father, Detective Flores.

But Mirror Lake was a small department; you had to be ready to do it all.

"Should be pretty simple today. But another set of eyes never hurt," she said.

"What?" I asked, his words finally registering. *Again?*

"Nico trained our dive team," Serena said. "He was a volunteer before we got an official group together." Now I understood why he said he'd been held up at the memorial. I'd thought he was stuck at the high school, where he taught biology and earth science. But he was probably called out to assist with the last car.

Even before we found the hidden room in his house, Nico never wanted to follow his father into police work. He was full of questions that stretched well beyond the borders of Mirror Lake. He wanted to know how things worked, with an intensity that made teachers love him, and kids tease him. I supposed it was fitting that both he and I got swept up under Gage's wing, by mere proximity.

Serena started pacing the yard, looking at the dry earth, the patchy grass, the uneven rock—everything untamed and gradually falling into disrepair.

"Notice any tread marks around here recently?" she asked, leaves crunching under her boots.

Both Gage and I remained silent, and I knew it was because neither of us could be sure.

"Not that I've seen," I finally said. "But I'm not here a lot."

"Dad never mentioned, if so," Gage added.

Our father was always involved in some outdoor project: building a fire pit; adding sloping, makeshift steps to fight the erosion; digging out the roots of a diseased tree. I wasn't sure we would have noticed, if there had been.

Serena scrunched her nose, making her seem momentarily too

young to manage this scene. "This is really the only access point," she said, eyes scanning the entirety of the inlet. The rest of the area was surrounded by thick trees, stretching down the slope toward the water. Nico's house didn't have official lake access. Ours was the only place with a backyard clearing that sloped gently into the water.

She was right. I couldn't imagine a car making it through the woods anywhere else.

"What about from somewhere else in the lake?" I asked. "It could've gone into the main channel and drifted this way. The current there can be strong. . . ." This finger of the lake was relatively private—I knew the ins and outs myself, tried to work out where the nearest access point would be—

"We'll know more after the dive team goes down. For now, would you mind if I talked to your daughter, Caden?"

"If it's all the same," Caden said, crossing his arms, "I'd rather keep her out of this. I don't think she really realized what she was seeing. . . . I don't want her to think she did anything wrong."

"I agree," Roy said, speaking for the first time since the police had arrived. "I don't think that's necessary, Serena."

Serena was outnumbered here, at our family home, facing our two cops, our lawyer. She nodded once. "Course not," she said, dark eyes cutting away.

Then she looked me over closely. "The boat bringing the dive team will be a little bit longer, still."

And just in case I didn't catch her meaning, Gage followed with "Why don't you go in and take a shower, Hazel. You're not gonna miss anything."

———

But I did, of course, miss things. I'd been missing things in the blink of an eye, the pause in a conversation, the stretch of a shadow.

I hadn't been watching, hadn't been paying attention, and now look. First my father. Then the car beside the road. And now *this*—another in our own backyard. Like something was spiraling steadily closer. The gravity of the lake, bending everything in its direction—even me.

By the time I emerged again, hair wet but clean, wearing a dry set of clothes, Jamie had left with Skyler. The police boat had made it to our inlet and was currently drifting beside our swim platform. And Nico was out there in the middle of the lake, standing on our platform in dive gear.

I knew him by the way he moved, gesturing his long arms as he spoke to the people on the boat. He was still skinny, like I remembered him as a kid, lying on that platform with his hands behind his head, eyes closed. But he moved with conviction now. More action, less thought.

Eventually, he lowered himself into the water alongside another diver from the boat. They disappeared beneath the surface, and there was nothing for the rest of us to do but watch the water together, and wait.

I tried not to imagine what he might be seeing under there, with more clarity. What nightmares he might've seen in the past, recovering victims from the lake.

Eventually, an orange buoy was released onto the surface of the water, just to the side of the platform. A marker.

The two men emerged from the surface, and Serena's radio crackled.

She took a few steps out of earshot to answer.

"Okay," she said, coming back to our group. "Confirmed, no one visible inside the vehicle." She swallowed. "Also no license plate."

"Just like the other," Gage said.

"Just like," Serena repeated. "We'll know more tomorrow when we get it out."

"Did they check the trunk?" I asked, picturing, again, the gaping mouth of the first vehicle on the side of the road, mud spilling out.

"They'll get it open tomorrow," she said.

I stared out at the water, trying not to imagine the other possibilities. I felt Caden beside me, in a similar position, doing the same. His eyes cut to me, and then away.

"Hazel," Serena said, in the nicest tone she'd used so far today. "There's no reason to think this is anything different than the other one. Seems like a pattern."

Roy squinted out at the lake, like he was trying to read something in the current. "The press is going to be all over this," he said, frowning. I felt my shoulders tighten, imagining them descending on our property.

"We'll do what we can to keep it quiet," Serena said. "But I can't make any promises."

She started walking back up the slope toward her car, the two young men in uniform trailing behind her. Then she stopped, looking down to the lake once more. "We're gonna need to come in through the backyard again, I assume. Is anyone going to be here tomorrow?"

"I'm on shift," Caden said.

"I've got work too, but you have our permission to do what you need to do," Gage said.

"I can take off, if you need," Roy offered after a beat. "Just need to clear a few meetings . . ."

"I'll be here," I said, surprising myself as well as the others, judging by the speed at which they turned their heads.

"We can take care of this, Hazel," Gage said. "You don't need to do this."

"I can stay an extra day," I said. And then, to appeal to his sense of responsibility, "Someone should be here to watch over things."

This place had been left in my care, but none of us had been paying close enough attention. I wouldn't make that mistake again.

CHAPTER 6

By the time the police cleared out, evening was falling. The sun dropped behind the mountains, casting an orange glow over everything, like the landscape was on fire in the distance.

Roy offered to drop Caden on his way, so he wouldn't have to walk back home at dusk. It reminded me of something our father would do.

Nico had rejoined us, in dry clothes, but still smelling of the lake—like something electric and alive.

We sat around the wooden table on the back deck, all of us angled slightly toward the water, where the bright orange buoy bobbed along the surface, out of place and unsettling.

"Let's get out of here," Gage said, abruptly standing from his chair. He stood over me, reached down a hand. "Come on, you've gotta eat too."

I was starving—the last thing I'd eaten was the granola bar I'd found in the pantry when I woke up. In the chaos, we'd all skipped lunch. But it felt irresponsible to go, like we were leaving a piece of evidence knowingly unattended.

Gage followed my gaze out to the water. "Hazel, really, it's not going anywhere," he said with a sigh. And then: "The only food left in the house is the piles of ramen and cans of tomato soup in the garage. And I'd really rather not."

Reflection Point was an establishment as old as the town itself. The dark wood exterior had been aged by the weather; its painted sign had faded to the palest rose. Outdoor picnic tables lined the deck. The parking lot was across a narrow sliver of lake, with a walking bridge leading the way to the main entrance.

Located right across from the police station, Reflection Point was frequented by officers both on and off duty. When we were growing up, everyone knew us here. We had spent a lot of our teen years at this restaurant together, eating at the discounted rate, since our fathers were cops.

I trailed behind Gage and Nico from the parking lot. The drought had turned the landscape more marsh than lake. How much longer until that, too, dried up, and everything before us was an empty gorge? How deep a canyon existed underneath? I tried not to think about all the other things that might be hidden out there, just waiting to be discovered.

Gage weaved past the hostess stand to the bar along the far wall. The main dining area was unsurprisingly full tonight, but there was a free two-seater bar-top against the window, and Gage quickly claimed it, pulling a third stool up from an adjacent table.

The bartender, Felicity, had been my year in school, though we hadn't been particularly close then. I'd gotten to know her more in the years since, as a frequent visitor to the bar myself when I was in town. She was also friends with Jamie, which meant she'd sometimes raise topics she thought I knew about, and I'd have to play it off.

Now her eyes flicked up—took in me and Gage and Nico—and then flicked back down to the glass in her hand.

My shoulders tensed. Could they have heard so quickly? This was a cop place after all. The launch for the police boat was just to the side of their property. I peered around the bar, wondering if news had already started to spread, outside of the station. *Another car found, at the Holt place.*

"I feel like everyone's looking at us," I said to Gage, picking up the laminated menu, though I knew the offerings by heart.

"You're being paranoid," he said. "Want to split the wings?" he asked, as if this were the most pressing concern.

"I could go for that," Nico said.

They both turned to me, waiting for my order. I dropped the menu to the table again. "Isn't anyone curious how a car ended up in the lake behind our house?" I asked, keeping my voice to almost a whisper.

Gage blinked twice. "Of course I am. But we're not going to get any answers tonight."

"It was old, Hazel," Nico added, hands folded together on the table. I could still see the faint lines on his face from the equipment. The pads of his tan fingers were wrinkled and white.

"What did you see down there?" I asked.

He leaned slightly back, then took a deep breath, as if remembering. "It's covered in mud. Definitely been there a long time. Maybe even from before you lived there."

He said it kindly, like a gift.

But my father had built that house when he'd married his first wife, Audrey. Gage and Caden grew up in it. There was no clearing in the trees before that property was built, no way for a car to make it down to the edge of the water—

"Hazel," Gage began, and the way they both kept using my name felt pointed, deliberate. "I know you don't want to hear this, but if it's some kind of scam, which seems increasingly likely . . ."

I stared back at him, jaw tense, waiting. In his defense, he did not finish the sentence. Instead, he let me fill in the blanks, just like everyone else must've been doing.

He looked down, turned the drink menu over in his hands, eyes skimming the list, though I was sure he knew it by heart as well. I waited for him to look up, daring him to say it to my face.

I placed my hand on his menu, lowering it to the table. "If it is, then you think *what*, Gage? She dumped one car off the side of the road, and then dumped another behind our home?" I asked. I didn't worry about the level of my voice anymore. So what if people heard. Apparently, they'd all be thinking it soon enough, either way.

"Actually," Gage said, "I wouldn't be surprised if the one near us was first. It feels more impulsive, more risky. I mean, if anyone found it, it would lead them right back to the house. . . ."

I looked to Nico, hoping he was as surprised by Gage's assessment as I was: there had been a well-known criminal in this town, and she'd lived at the house, and didn't it make sense, then, that she'd dropped one car dangerously close, and then moved on to a less incriminating location?

But Nico's face remained frustratingly unreadable.

I laughed sharply. "Okay, Detective," I said. "You don't even know they're connected."

Gage gave me a hard look. "Seems like a pretty big coincidence for them *not* to be connected. If it looks like a duck and swims like a duck . . ." he began, sounding just like our father. Then he peered around the room, took a deep breath. He shook his head and started again. "It's the same thing. Same MO. No plates. Nothing and no one inside."

"They haven't checked the trunk," I said.

"Have a little faith, Hazel."

"Faith in *what*, exactly?" Faith that my mother, the criminal, for reasons none of us could imagine, dropped a series of cars into Mirror Lake before she pulled a con on those of us left behind?

I continued staring at him, and he raised his arms in half a shrug. "I'm just *saying*. You don't know half as much as you think you do."

This wasn't Gage. This wasn't the way he thought or argued or communicated. This had a whiff of something else, barely contained. Something I'd expect from Caden, maybe. A passive-aggressive undercurrent I'd been accustomed to my entire childhood. A constant feeling of judgment.

Caden and I weren't just *close in age*. We were in the same grade, in direct comparison through report cards and teacher conferences. Our birthdays were three weeks apart in June—mine first, his following, like an afterthought. Dad had often reused the same numbered birthday candles on his cake.

Gage, meanwhile, was two years older than both of us. I'd idolized him from the start, wanting nothing but his company and approval. He gave both generously.

What I had taken, Caden had lost. I had displaced him, with his brother. Maybe even his father. I knew this now. Then, though, I'd seen only that Caden could be tricky, remaining quiet until things inevitably boiled over, and I'd mostly learned to see it coming.

But now Gage had also turned distant. Like maybe I'd finally taken something he'd wanted for himself. Had finally disrupted his life for the worse. And I was nervous about bringing it to the surface—lighting the fuse.

"If you're mad about something, Gage, just say it," I said, voice lowered. Better, always, to see things clearly, to force things into the open.

"Okay, Hazel," he said, finally meeting my gaze, staring back just as sharply. "Here, how's this. If it wasn't your mother, who do you think it was, then?"

Gage pushed back from the table abruptly and headed to the bar to place the order. But he'd made his point effectively. If not her, then I must've been suspicious of someone else. That car was at our house. Did I really want to drag our father's name into this?

"He'll come around," Nico said, breaking the silence. "It was a shock, I think, the way your dad left things. I'm pretty sure it's not you he's mad at." He bumped his leg against mine under the table, in a way that felt both too casual and too intimate. As if there weren't a chasm of history between us.

I swiveled to stare at him, and it took me a second to understand what he was implying.

"You know about the will?" I asked. I wondered if Gage had confided in him.

He let out a single surprised laugh. "Everyone knows, Hazel."

Of course. Of course.

Everything mattered disproportionately in a small town. Your success, but also your failure. *Everyone knows* might as well have been our town motto.

I'd been subjected to it since I was a teenager here.

Everyone knows that I'd had a crush on Nico Pritchard for years, even Gage—who told me it was embarrassing, the way I was always staring at him. I'd felt my entire body flush, unused to being chastised by him. I never knew whether I was embarrassing just myself or my brother too. Or—and this was the very worst option—if my attention was embarrassing Nico instead.

Everyone knows Libby Sharp was a coldhearted con woman, stealing from both her employer and her family before leaving me behind.

Everyone knows your life history here—from where you were born to your family tree, and maybe even before that.

And now *everyone knows* that Perry Holt didn't leave his house—potentially his most valuable asset—to his sons. No, he'd left it to the daughter of Libby Sharp, known criminal, instead.

When Gage returned to the table, I changed the topic.

"Did I tell you about my last big renovation, Gage? The one down by the South Carolina border?" I asked as he placed three bottles of beer on the table between us.

I could still see the tension in the tendons of his neck, but he took the olive branch. "Tell me."

"The contractors kept saying they could feel something vibrating in the walls. Figured it was some loose ductwork, but there was nothing on the blueprints." Nico's eyes were locked on me. Both of theirs were. "Spooky, right?"

"Please tell me this isn't a ghost story," Gage said, taking a sip. He was coming back to me, shoulders lowering, head tipped to the side.

He, like me, needed the satisfaction of concrete answers.

I grinned. "I went over one day to listen, thought it might've been shoddy electrical work. Told them to be careful when they opened up the space. And then, the day they're supposed to take down one of the walls, they spot a leak in the ceiling. Only there's no piping there, and the plumber can't figure out where the water could possibly be coming from."

They were both leaning forward, waiting. Nico's teeth grazed his lower lip, a tell that he was thinking. He used to love the way I weaved a story. I knew how to hook them, and then how to keep them.

"So, I went over again to check out the spot. It was in the corner, half on the ceiling, half on the wall. I got up on the ladder, and turns out it's not water at all," I said, eyes wide. "Honey." I smiled. "We stopped the contractor from opening up the wall just in time. Bees, everywhere. The whole fucking house, it was practically a bee hive."

Nico visibly shuddered, then took a long drink.

"Jesus, Hazel," Gage said, but he was smiling. "Who would live in a place like that after?"

"You'd be surprised," I said.

Gage pulled down the dark driveway, intending to drop me off first. I hadn't left any of the outside lights on, and the Jeep's high beams illuminated the weathered siding.

"Thanks," I said, exiting from my spot behind Nico.

"How long has the window been like that?" Gage asked, leaning forward, palm on the dashboard.

I followed his gaze. The garage window was pushed all the way open—a darkness gaping.

"It was closed last night," I said. I was sure of it.

Gage and Nico both exited the car, walking closer.

Now I pictured animals scurrying around, leaves blown in by the wind. Someone slipping a leg over the sill—

"I think it was Skyler," I said.

Gage shone his flashlight below the window, as if checking for glass. "Skyler?" he asked, spinning back to face me, the glare blinding me.

I put out a hand, to block the light. "Dad apparently showed her how to use it as a way in. I don't think she can reach the keypad," I said.

I entered the code now, and the three of us ducked under the rising garage door. Inside, below the open window, two cases of water bottles had been stacked against the wall, in makeshift steps.

Gage rubbed the dark stubble on the side of his face. "Of course he did." Then he frowned at the door. "But I'm going to check inside, just in case," he said.

"Seriously?" I said. "The whole property was just crawling with cops."

But he ignored me, trying the handle. It didn't budge.

"I locked it," I added.

He pulled out his keyring and let himself inside. Unlike Caden, he made no show of turning over his access. "For my own peace of mind, then," he said.

Gage stepped inside carefully. I wondered if he saw the possibility in everything, the same way I did. If his senses were tuned, instead, to the potential for crime, for violence. The darkness that existed just under the surface of things.

"Slow day at the office, I guess," Nico said, one corner of his mouth rising. He leaned back against the tool bench beside the door.

I pushed the window fully closed, inspecting the surrounding frame.

"You need some help with that?" he asked.

I flipped the latch, then pulled upward, making sure it locked. I wiped my hands together, in triumph. "All fixed."

"Fast work, Hazel," he said, mouth turned up in a flash of a smile—my stomach plummeting in response.

But then Gage emerged from the open door, frowning. "Did you leave the basement unlocked?" he asked.

I shook my head. "I wasn't paying attention. Maybe."

I couldn't remember. I'd been preoccupied by the car under the surface, the police at my home, the way the lake suddenly felt like it really had become a black hole, pulling the past toward it—

"Everything looks fine," he said. "But don't leave anything unlocked. There've been a string of break-ins around here recently."

Nico pushed off the tool bench, frowning. "I thought that stopped."

"I thought so too," Gage said. "But we never caught anyone."

Gage noticed my expression then. "It's nothing, Hazel. Kid stuff. Teenagers targeting empty houses. But still, don't take any chances. This place has looked deserted for the last couple weeks."

"I won't," I said.

Gage ducked into the Jeep again, pulling out the to-go bag. "Since you're stuck here tomorrow, take the food, at least," he said. And then: "Ready, Nico?"

"I can walk it from here," Nico said, standing just outside the open garage. "Probably closer through the yard, anyway."

"Right," Gage said. His eyes slid from me to Nico. He took a tentative step toward his car, like he was worried he was forgetting something. "Call me tomorrow if anything comes up. I'll be working, but I'll keep my phone on."

"I will," I said. "I've got it, Gage."

He nodded once, before slipping into his car.

We watched the Jeep disappear from sight, but Nico made no move to go.

He peered at the sky over the house, a deep indigo—the last remnant of color before full night.

"When did you move back in?" I asked. Last I knew, he was living in a condo complex with a pool and a dock, close to the dive center he ran in summer. The same place where Gage rented a unit.

"Last fall," he said. "My lease was up, and the house needed work before it could be rented for the summer season again. I figured I might as well live in it in the interim, save on rent. And then I decided to just . . . stay. It's quiet. It's big. It's mine."

Except everyone knew what had happened there. His father's death. I wondered how he could stand it, but then, I've wondered a lot of things about Nico in my lifetime.

"I should probably get home," he said, as if it had been up for debate. He took a step back, then another. "Good night, Hazel."

He waved goodbye in the dark and left via the cut through between our properties. As if he had forgotten that he was no longer a teenager, needing to sneak out, and then back in.

I let myself into the house that would soon be mine, following the path of lights Gage had left on. And then I checked each lock, one by one, just in case.

It felt strange to realize Nico had only been across a stretch of woods the night before. That he could've noticed me, turning on the outside lights, listening to the noises out back, when I thought myself alone.

I wondered if he knew someone had arrived at the old Holt house. Or whether it was too obscured through the trees.

Unlike with most people, I could never really be sure of Nico's intentions. Not since that day. Because while he was staring at those pictures on the wall of the murder room when I was fifteen and he was seventeen, I was staring, like always, at him. So I saw the way he looked at them, the way his expression didn't change, as he took them in. Those wide innocent eyes, exactly the same as always.

I had wondered, then, if he had seen the room before. If he'd known it was there and kept the secret for his father. If he would've continued to keep it, if I hadn't been the one to uncover it.

Nico Pritchard provided a mystery in a time when all I wanted was the excitement of one.

Later that same night, after everyone had gone to sleep, he'd knocked on the sliding glass doors of my bedroom, a gentle tap that I could've mistaken for anything, and almost dismissed as nothing. Only the careful rhythm of it drew me closer. And there he was, eyes wide like he was shell-shocked from the day.

Do you think Gage will tell? he asked as I let him inside.

No. I knew Gage wouldn't. He may have had a firm moral compass, but it was rivaled by his loyalty.

I can't get the pictures out of my head, he'd said. And then, solemnly, *He killed himself, you know.*

I nodded. We all understood that, though the police report was more generous in its interpretation of events. There'd been *an accident*, with his own weapon, after he'd heavily self-medicated first. Such things, we knew, could happen.

But Nico came to me that night, instead of going to my brother. He came to me because he knew I would be the one to understand. I, too, had endured a scandal and a tragedy, not of my own making.

In return, I showed him something dark and true about myself. Nico was the only one I ever showed—a secret for a secret. The letter, stored carefully in the bottom of my dresser drawer. I held it out to him.

The blue ink of the envelope, addressed to *Daughter of Mine*.

The last words she ever gave me. The brutal finality: *I hope one day you can forgive me.*

I watched Nico read it, and then read it again. Finally, he looked up. *Do you?* he asked.

No, I said. It was the reason I showed it to him. So he would also know: *You don't have to forgive.*

It was the start of our own friendship, separate from my brother.

When he showed up again, a few nights after the first time, he looked like he wasn't sure why he'd come back. I didn't know either. Whether he wanted to make sure I was keeping our secret. Whether he wanted something else.

But by then I had fulfilled the promise of my mother's claim. I understood what it truly meant to be fearless.

It was a trick, just like everything else. You had to act before you had the chance to feel it. Had to move before the doubt crept its way inside. Jump from the narrow, single-lane bridge. Dive to the pitch-black bottom of the lake. Speak before you think it through.

That's all there ever was to it: impulsively, instinctively act.

I never knew why Nico really came over that night, but it didn't matter. Whether he intended it or not, I fearlessly closed the space between us. I pressed my lips to his, understanding, completely, that this, too, was to be a secret.

CHAPTER 7

The police boat arrived at ten a.m. The salvage crew by noon. The dive team didn't even knock on my door. I wasn't sure who they answered to, but I figured it wasn't to me. Still, I felt there should be some oversight—someone who had the authority to know what was happening. As far as I could tell, everyone still seemed to be assessing what to do.

I wanted to call Nico to ask what was going on—he would know the process—but he was working at the school today. The buoy he'd placed yesterday still marked the spot, a flash of orange on the surface.

I walked out back, down the deck steps, weaving between the emergency workers in matching shirts, huddling together in small groups at the edge of the lake. Serena Flores was stationed slightly uphill, speaking on her radio. She paused when she saw me, then gestured me closer.

"Sorry, Hazel. This may take a while," she said, frowning. "They just got another call out on the lake."

I followed her gaze, then watched as the police boat slowly navigated toward the exit of the inlet.

"Is that Caden?" I asked. He said he'd be working today, but whoever was on the boat was facing away, and I couldn't distinguish their features from the distance, especially in uniform.

Serena shook her head, the edge of her dark ponytail brushing against her collar. "He was swapped out. The department likes to keep things removed by a degree or two, if possible, when things are personal. Prevent any conflict of interest."

But that was a luxury we didn't always have in a town this size, with a police department made up of people who'd grown up together. As it was, Serena qualified as a friend of the family.

The boat engine revved just beyond the marker for the No Wake Zone.

"Everything okay out there?" I asked. I imagined something else emerging from the surface of the lake. Another mystery clawing out from the depths.

"Just property damage. A pontoon ran aground." She sighed, shifting on her feet. "It's a mess out there, honestly. Boats hitting sandbars. Jet Skis cutting it too close. The channels are narrower than people remember." She shook her head. "It's going to get so much worse next week."

Memorial Day weekend. The unofficial kickoff to the summer season here.

I was imagining weekenders from the city arriving at their expensive rentals, when something clearly caught Serena's eye to my side. No, not something—someone.

Alberto Flores. Her father stood at the edge of the yard, overseeing the scene. It didn't surprise me to see him here—there were only so many detectives in the department—but his presence made me nervous. It had been that way since I was a teenager—and it was a feeling I could never quite shake. Even his daughter seemed unsettled by his oversight. She spun one of her silver stud earrings absently, face impassive.

I retreated to the house before he headed our way.

I tried to keep busy with my remote work through the afternoon, waiting for the police boat to finally return.

But then I heard something at the front of the house—a vehicle passing close to the windows. No one had parked in my driveway until now.

I went out front to greet them. A man in jeans and a black T-shirt was smoking a cigarette and peering down the slope on the side of the house. A tow truck sat at the edge of the parking area.

"What's going on?" I asked.

"You the owner of the house?" he asked in response.

"Yes," I said, trying on the role. Close enough. I would be, soon.

"Good. We'll try to keep the damage to a minimum, but . . ." He handed me a clipboard with a disclaimer.

"Are you starting soon?" I asked, signing and returning the paper.

"Who knows," he said. "I just go where I'm told."

It seemed no one had any finite answers, and the day was quickly slipping away.

The landline was ringing when I stepped back inside. I debated ignoring it, letting it go to my father's answering machine, but then figured it might've been full at this stage. One month of telemarketers and people who might not have gotten the news. Or bills that needed paying.

I answered quickly—"Holt residence," I said.

"Hi, hello." A woman's voice, tentative, unfamiliar. "Is this Hazel?"

I held the receiver closer. There weren't many people who knew to reach me at this number. "Yes, who's speaking?" I asked.

"I'm calling from Mirror Lake Elementary. Skyler told me you were staying at her grandfather's house, and well, his number is still down as an emergency contact. . . ."

My head struggled to keep up with this woman's story. I focused on *emergency contact*. "Is Skyler okay?"

"Yes, oh, I should've started with that. Sorry." She cleared her throat. "She's fine. Just . . . her mother hasn't shown up yet. We gave her some time, but . . ." Her voice dropped, as if Skyler were close by, listening. "It's getting late."

I checked the clock. Almost four in the afternoon. We used to be dismissed at three, and things didn't change that often around here. "Did you try Caden?" I asked.

"We did. Went straight to voicemail." Which wasn't unusual when he was working, especially if he was stuck anywhere on the upper level of the bowl, without signal. "Perry Holt was the backup."

"No problem," I said, feeling a lump forming in my throat. "I'll be right there."

Of course, reliable Perry Holt was the backup. Gage would've probably been next in line. Jamie's mother had never been the most reliable adult. It wasn't a surprise that she wasn't listed with Skyler's school.

I tried Caden's cell myself as I started my car, backing out of the garage. Straight to voicemail. Then I called Gage's, in case they were somewhere together—no answer there either. I scrolled through to Jamie and Caden's landline, which I'd stored for emergencies but rarely used. The line rang until the machine picked up, Skyler's high but assured voice: *You've reached the Holts!*

I hadn't called Jamie's cell in years, but the number I had went straight to an automated message box. I wasn't even sure if it belonged to her anymore. By the time I'd finished making the calls, I was just about at the school anyway.

The lot was mostly empty closer to the elementary school side of the property, though I could hear a whistle from the high school fields, and there were plenty of cars on that corner. I caught myself wondering if Nico was still there, or if he was already on the way home.

I had to be buzzed in at the main entrance—a new safety addition since I'd gone to school here. I could see Skyler through the glass of the front office, sitting in a chair alone, eyes turned to the clock. Her face was pinched in consternation, as if she understood that something was amiss.

Her head turned in my direction. Maybe we all had that ability, to know when someone had come for us.

I'd been in the office of the high school once, waiting for someone to come for me too. Wondering if they would. It was the week after my mother left town, and I was a tinderbox. When I was sent to the office, Jamie ditched class to come with me. Still, I didn't know who they'd have called. My mother was gone.

I heard him before I saw him. The squeak of his boots, the jangle of his keys on his belt. The whisper of the other kids in the office with me: *Holt's here.*

The new secretary must've seen his badge and not understood what he was doing there. "Can I help you?" she'd asked.

"I'm here for my daughter," he said, his voice measured. And in that moment, I thought I might never love another human as much as I did him.

Jamie had stood first, always ready to speak her mind. "Mr. Holt, it wasn't her fault."

But he put out a hand, large and firm. "Jamie, go on back to class. This is a family matter." And then, "Hazel? Come on."

The secretary was halfway to standing, gesturing to the offices behind her. "Hold on. You'll have to speak with—"

"It can wait," he said. "Right now I'll be taking Hazel home."

That was the kind of power he had in this town. The way he could make something the truth. No one questioned it. Why would anyone worry about the child left behind with Detective Perry Holt? Who else would they even need to contact, when he was the police? Who would take care of things as well as him? He'd risen to the moment when his first wife died in a terrible biking accident when the boys were just seven and five. There would never be a better man than him. A better father. All those things were true, of course. But the thing that was truer, the thing no one wanted to say, was that there was nowhere else for me to go either.

We drove home in silence, and it wasn't until we were in the kitchen, as he was digging through the freezer for ice, that he spoke. "Care to tell me what happened?"

"Freddy Barker happened." *Your mother forget something on her way out of town?* he'd taunted.

Everyone had seen the pictures. My mother, last spotted on camera at the local bank—withdrawing the remainder of the money from my father's account, after she'd taken everything else. I hadn't believed it until I went to her closet and peered up at the empty spot where our luggage used to be. The two hardback royal-blue cases that had accompanied us, move after move.

Freddy wouldn't let it go. *Hazel, tell us. We're all wondering, what was your cut?* When I tried to walk past, he'd grabbed my arm. But I was the one who left a mark.

"Well, Freddy Barker comes from a long line of assholes," Holt said then. "Nothing new there."

I looked away, embarrassed. Perry Holt never lashed out. Perry Holt conducted himself with calm and composure. Perry Holt drove the speed limit, modeled the type of person we should want to become. He believed that his position came with a bigger responsibility, and he took it very seriously.

"Do you think he'll file charges?" I asked.

He laughed once, deep and sharp. "There's no way he'll want to claim a girl hurt him." Then he examined my fist, a single scratch along my knuckle, where I'd caught a tooth.

"Well, you did it the right way, at least," he mused. "Who taught you how to throw a punch like that? Gage?"

I shook my head. "Jamie," I said, and his booming laugh filled the room, before it set off a fit of coughing.

"Okay," he said, one large hand on my shoulder. "Well, the two of you need to keep your body count to a minimum. They're on to you now."

It was gradual, after. The way I said, *My dad is here. My dad will drop me off.*

He never treated me any differently than his own. It was the one promise, once made, that I never questioned. Maybe Caden did, thinking—or hoping—I'd be sent off to some other relatives. He was the only one who shattered the illusion. *He's not your dad.*

But he said it only once—in earshot of our father—and then he never said it again.

———

The school office now was eerily empty. And when I opened the glass door, Skyler didn't smile—didn't even seem relieved by my arrival.

"Hi, I'm Hazel. Skyler's aunt," I said, approaching the front desk, hoping to channel some of that calm reassurance I'd learned from my father.

The secretary was somewhere between my age and my dad's. I didn't recognize her, but she probably knew our family history, all the same. "Thanks for coming," she said, pushing her sunglasses on top of her curly blond hair, as if she was getting ready to leave as well.

"No problem. Lucky me getting to spend extra time with my favorite kid," I said, grinning at Skyler. Her mouth only twitched in response.

I wasn't asked to sign anything. Even if I wasn't the official emergency contact, small towns, I'd learned long ago, operated on a different level of trust.

The secretary was busy slinging her large bag onto her shoulder and rummaging for her keys. She seemed glad to have this last responsibility of the day off her plate.

Skyler hitched up her purple backpack—the same one she'd used to bring her swimsuit yesterday—and waved to the secretary, before exiting through the door I was holding open.

"Sorry," I called, before letting the door fall shut. Apologizing on behalf of her parents, my family, the situation. I wondered if this happened often. If my dad was a fixture here again, just as he'd once been for the three of us.

I placed a hand on the back of Skyler's head as we walked outside. Then I buckled her into the back seat of my car—were kids supposed to have boosters at this age? I didn't know. It was a short ride, either way.

"Should we stop by your place first?" I asked, unsure of what to do next.

"My mom is never this late," she said, in defense. As if she knew I'd been wondering.

"I can imagine," I said. "Bet it's just a mix-up with your dad, and which one was supposed to get you today."

Her eyes cut to mine in the rearview mirror. She nodded once, face otherwise impassive.

They lived in a narrow, two-story structure with an unfinished basement on a steep slope. The cost of real estate up here varied wildly. Just as the proximity to the lake would escalate a home's value, so would a clear mountain view. But the view surrounding their property was mostly thick trees in the summer, and the highway in the distance in the winter. Roy was right—Caden must've hoped he'd be the one to move into Holt's house, even if he had to buy out the other shares.

The will was probably even more of a surprise to Caden than to me.

Hadn't I continued to be the surprise of his life.

I took the mountain road slowly—it hadn't been fully paved, and the edges were lined with rock, before giving way to erosion.

As I pulled into their drive, I didn't see any other cars out front, but there was a small garage tucked against the side of the house.

I was just putting the car into park when I saw it: the front door to the house hung slightly ajar.

A darkness beyond, waiting for us.

CHAPTER 8

67 Days without Rain
Monday, May 20
4:30 p.m.
Precipitation: Zero

The car idled as I stared at the spot just beyond the door. Nothing moved.

The front curtains to the house were pulled open, so I could see through a series of windows, straight to the back, and into the woods.

There was no sign of anyone inside. Staring at the open front door, I got a sudden surge of *wrong*.

"Stay in the car," I said to Skyler, lowering the windows before turning off the engine.

The afternoon was silent as I walked up to the front porch, my steps crunching the grass, dry and brittle under my feet. The sound of everything was heightened—the wind moving through the branches overhead, the scurrying of a squirrel across the yard.

I rang the doorbell, and the echo made my shoulders tighten. My heart raced in the silence that followed.

I cast a glance over my shoulder once, smiling tightly at Skyler, trying to act like everything was fine.

Then I knocked on the door, pushing it open as I did.

"Jamie?" I called as the hinges creaked. "It's Hazel."

I stepped into their home. I'd been here only a handful of times, and on each occasion, the house had been packed: a Thanksgiving they'd hosted; Skyler's birthday parties; her baptism celebration.

Now the details came into focus. The painted wood paneling, a cluster of artwork on the walls, mixed with family photos. A surprising assortment of furniture, which somehow blended together unexpectedly. *Here* was the Jamie I'd once known, her eclectic tastes slightly refined in adulthood. A peacock-blue sofa, an antique-style lamp, sleek shelving that looked the same as mine, from IKEA. The house screamed *Jamie*, which made it even more unsettling to step through the open door and not feel any sign of her here.

Skyler waited in the car for only about two minutes before she raced through the front door, passing me in the foyer. "Mom?" she called, heading up the steps.

"Skyler, hold on—" I'd wanted to beat her there, spare her the possibilities I'd been imagining.

I pictured Jamie like we sometimes used to find her mother after school, passed out on the sofa or in her bed, with a bottle—or a bottle of pills—beside her.

And then there were the unexpected ways tragedy could sneak up on you: a stroke, an accident.

I took the steps two at a time and found Skyler standing in front of the primary bedroom, peering in. The bed was made, the blinds pulled open. As I stepped inside to get a closer look, Skyler took off for the next room. Then I heard a steady drip of water coming from the bathroom.

I held my breath as I wandered closer. But the only thing out of place was a green terry-cloth bathrobe, dropped haphazardly onto the floor in front of the shower. The sink faucet was still dripping, and I closed it fully now, catching sight of myself in the oval mirror. Dark hair, dark shadows under my eyes, like I was now the haunting, instead of the haunted.

Skyler's footsteps kept racing back and forth, pausing just long enough for her to periodically call for her mother. From the fact she kept moving, it was clear she hadn't found her yet.

I continued checking each room after her, but there was no sign of Jamie.

Back downstairs, Skyler was standing in front of a closed door, peering at the handle. "What's that go to?" I asked.

"Garage," she said, but she didn't make any move to check inside.

I opened the door, and a cool gust rode in with the dark. I felt along the wall until I caught the light switch, bare bulb flickering. The space was empty.

"Okay," I said to Skyler, "she must be out." I forced a smile, hoping to see it reflected on her face.

Just then I heard the sound of wheels on loose gravel. Skyler spun and ran outside, and I pictured Jamie stepping out of her car. A misunderstanding, like I promised. I felt my heart rate slowing. But I stopped dead in my tracks as Caden stepped through the front door with Skyler in his arms. He looked between the two of us, mouth slightly open in confusion or disorientation.

"What?" Caden said, either to me or to her, I wasn't sure. And then: "What are you doing here?"

He was in uniform, cheeks slightly reddened, hair back like he'd been out on the lake, facing the wind. His eyes were wide, watery. I wasn't sure what Skyler had told him, but she had her arms locked around his neck, as if taking solace there.

"The school called me," I said, but his face remained lost and confused, trying to put the pieces together. "They couldn't reach Jamie, or you, and Dad's number was the emergency contact."

A line formed between his eyes, the first sign of age, or worry.

"Why . . ." I could imagine the rest of that question well enough. *Why you? Why are you in my house?*

"Jamie's not here. The front door was open, though," I said quietly, as if that explained what I was doing here.

He lowered Skyler to the floor. "Go make some popcorn, Sky. I'll be right there."

He waited until she had disappeared into the kitchen, the sound of a pantry opening and closing, the beep of microwave buttons.

"Unlocked?" he asked.

I shook my head. "It was ajar. I thought she was home. But I just checked the garage, and the car is gone."

Now the line between his eyes deepened. He lowered his voice. "Did you at least check inside before bringing my daughter into a house with an open front door?" His hand went to the side of his belt, as if on instinct.

"I told her to wait in the car—" I began pointlessly.

But he was off, checking each room, just as I had done. "Caden, I already looked," I said, trailing behind him. But I'd only been checking for Jamie, not signs of someone *else*. He was right. Even Gage had insisted on checking the house before leaving me there alone last night.

Now I took in each room from a different perspective—checking for movement, for shadows.

After his circuit turned up nothing, he grabbed the landline in the den and dialed a number—her cell, I was assuming.

"She's not picking up," he said. The steady *pop, pop, pop* in the microwave picked up speed. The scent of butter filled the room, until it was practically cloying.

I followed Caden as he stepped outside onto the back patio, hands on hips, peering into the woods. In the distance, you could hear the sound of cars on Mirror Highway, somewhere below. Our house was just down there, on the other side of the road.

Goose bumps rose across my arms in a gust of wind.

"She's probably out in a dead zone," he said, and I realized we'd come out back just so Skyler wouldn't hear.

"And missed Skyler's pickup? That doesn't sound like her—"

He turned on me quickly. "Look, Hazel, not that you would know, but it *does*, actually. Not that it's your business, but she can be a little hotheaded after an argument." His eyes drifted away, as if he didn't want to share whatever he was remembering. "She takes off sometimes. As a way for her to remind me of everything she does around here. She's not wrong." Though to me, her leaving like this seemed just as likely a way to embarrass him, bringing their private lives into the public. Which was not at all like the Jamie I'd known.

He moved his jaw around, like he'd solved the mystery. "She'll be back," he said, as he stepped inside. I followed him as he walked straight to the front and stared up the drive, as if he expected her to arrive at any moment. He frowned, and I knew that for all his talk, he had his doubts as well. I wondered what other secrets he wasn't sharing.

"Are there any security cameras?" I asked. "To see what happened with the door?"

It was a stupid question, and he gave me a look that told me as much. Like my father, he didn't have much faith in the newer home-security setups. Dad always said they could be used against you, just as much as they could be used for you—like anything else. And without consistent cell coverage, it's not like you could access footage easily when you were out.

"If she forgot to lock up, the wind could have blown it open," he said, staring off into the trees again.

But now I was thinking about Gage's expression when he saw the open window at Holt's. The way even Nico had known about the break-ins.

Other than the open door, there were no signs of burglary here.

Caden shook his head, then he turned to me. "You can go, Hazel," he said. "We'll be fine."

This was not the time to argue. It was a command, in the guise of something else. I was being dismissed. Something was happening beneath the facade here—a slowly simmering vulnerability. His face was momentarily unguarded—exposed. He looked the same way I'd seen him when my mom left, when he realized she'd taken everything. Not only from me, but from us. She'd betrayed us all.

"Will you call me, please?" I said. "So I don't worry."

He turned to go inside, then raised one hand, but I couldn't tell if it was in agreement or a brush-off.

"You're staying?" he asked.

I nodded. "Just while they handle the car."

"Well," he said, "hopefully it's not too much longer." His meaning was double layered, even now. A cover for having had to share a part of his marriage he'd rather I not know about.

"Bye, Skyler," I called, before walking to my car.

I felt Caden still standing behind me. I wondered if he was just waiting for me to go, before he took off looking for her, trying to convince her to come back to him.

CHAPTER 9

There were vehicles parked on both sides of the road in front of our house. But at least no one else had ventured into the driveway, blocking me out.

In fact, even the tow truck was gone. Maybe they'd given up for the day.

I sent a quick text to Luke and Keira—*Might need to stay tomorrow. So sorry. I'll explain tonight.* We were friends as much as partners: roommates who had taken the plunge and gone into business together after graduation. Keira brought the training in architecture; Luke, the family background in real estate; and me, the vision—the idea. We covered for each other all the time, but I knew they wouldn't make any major decisions without consulting me first. I didn't want to hold anything up.

As I stepped inside the house to drop my bag, my phone buzzed in my pocket almost immediately—Gage.

"Hey," I said.

"Did you call?" Gage asked. He must've just gotten back into range.

"Yeah. Skyler's school called the house. Jamie didn't show for pickup, and they couldn't reach Caden."

"Huh," he said. "Is he still MIA?"

"No, he's at his house now. I just left them there. But Jamie isn't back yet. She's not answering her phone."

There was a long pause where I wondered if we'd lost our connection, before he spoke again. "I'm sure everything's fine. You know how bad the cell service is out here. Hard to track someone down till they turn up."

"I don't know, Gage. It's odd. The front door to their house was open when we got back."

Another pause, as if considering. "You know how Dad was. Always leaving the door unlocked for us. It's a hard habit to shake, when you grow up that way."

"Not unlocked, Gage. *Unlatched.* Open." Like the window in the garage that had him so concerned the night before. "Caden said the wind blows it open sometimes, but he also checked the house from top to bottom, so I'm not sure what he really thinks." I never was.

Another pause. Gage dropped his voice. "Did anything look disturbed inside?"

"Not that I noticed," I said. No, I'd only been focused on finding *her.*

"Hazel, I'm sure it's fine. I'd have heard otherwise." Maybe it was habit, the way he talked to me—placating, dismissive. Always seeing me as a younger sibling, less responsible than he was. Always having to be the mediator between me and Caden. Or maybe this was just his professional tone—measured and calm.

I could imagine him showing up to take the statement of a panicked homeowner, hearing their story, trying to put them at ease. Believing in the good of this place, first of all.

An engine was rumbling in the distance, a churning of gears, drawing me to the window. "Hold on," I said.

I opened the back slider and stepped outside. A line of people in and out of uniform stood at the edge of the lake.

The tow truck was near the bottom of the yard, facing the house, engine rumbling. Slabs of wood had been set up in a makeshift ramp, trailing from the side of the house down to the water.

"Gage," I said. "I think it's coming up." I ended the call before he could respond. And then I descended the steps.

I pushed my way through the crowd—fire team, dive team, police force. There were a bunch of other people I didn't recognize, and I worried some might've been here just to watch. I spotted Nico among them, still in his clothes from work.

Serena stood at the very edge of the lake, boots just touching water. Her father was standing at the top of the yard, taking everything in. Like a position of command, leaving the smaller logistics to his daughter—and watching to see how she did.

A sound I'd never heard before was coming from the lake. Like something fighting to stay below. The water bubbled in defense, like it was trying to hold on to its prize. And then suddenly the top of the vehicle emerged.

Someone cheered, though Serena quickly turned to them, frowning. We had not, after all, confirmed that there was no one inside. I felt my chest tightening, my fingers trembling—anticipation, more than fear.

Nico was suddenly beside me, pressed up to my shoulder—closer than we'd been in years. I felt myself leaning into his gravity.

"It's definitely been there awhile," he said, voice rough, mouth close to my ear.

The tow truck paused, the car halfway out, while two men partway in the water repositioned the chains attached to the hood of the car.

I heard the flutter of a camera, saw a man a few yards behind me taking photos with a long-range lens.

"Excuse me," I called as I strode toward him.

He had a ball cap, bright blue eyes, nondescript clothing. His expression was friendly and open.

"This is private property," I said. He blinked at me, looking around for someone in charge it seemed. "Mine."

He dropped the camera. "I thought this was an empty house. . . ."

"You thought wrong."

Serena must've noticed our conversation, because she quickly joined us, her uniform changing the expression on the man's face. He turned to leave before she could tell him to go.

"Sorry about this," she said, frowning. She faced the crowd and cupped her hands around her mouth. "If you're not part of the operation, you need to leave. This is private property."

The yard fell silent. Several people looked to one another before slowly peeling off, slinking away up the slope.

I gave her a small smile of thanks. I was glad I had stayed to oversee things.

Eventually, the gears of the tow truck began to grind again, and the chains pulled taut against the vehicle. The water continued to churn, but the car was finally moving.

"Here it comes," Nico said.

And suddenly, the car wasn't just a hypothetical but a reality. It continued to emerge, inch by inch, coated in mud and rust, just like the other one. The windows were either down or broken, and water poured outward from them. Eventually, it was hauled onto the makeshift ramp, where it came to rest, sitting at an odd angle.

A woman in a police uniform started taking pictures, circling the vehicle. I walked closer, to get a better look. Confirming there were no plates.

Just like the other car.

Another uniformed officer reached into the window with a gloved hand, unhooking the latch to the glove compartment. It opened with a sudden thud, water and mud pouring out. He reached inside and carefully pulled out a pile of disintegrating papers.

He frowned, turning them over. "Looks like they're maps."

"No registration?" Serena asked.

"Not that I can see. But nothing's really legible," he said.

"Okay, bag it all up anyway."

"Was there registration in the other car?" I asked Nico.

"No," he said. "Nothing. It was totally empty. They have no idea where it came from still."

No one argued as I pressed closer. The seats were filthy, and it seemed the seat belts were not engaged.

Alberto Flores stepped into the scene then, approaching the vehicle. He looked at me briefly as he passed. His eyes were the same shape as Serena's, but hooded, lines radiating outward through his deep-tan skin.

Serena was suddenly in front of me, blocking my view. "We're going to open the trunk," she said, arms forward, as if guiding me back.

A man with a crowbar approached the vehicle, but disappeared behind a crowd of officers who blocked my view.

I heard the creak of the trunk, the yawn of the door. Everyone was leaning forward, peering inside. I kept my eyes on Al Flores, trying to guess what was inside by his body language, but he remained perfectly still. He didn't reach for a phone or a radio.

Serena quickly turned around, gave me a shake of her head. She mouthed: *No one.* I felt my shoulders finally relaxing.

"Just like the other," Nico said. "Exactly the same."

Except. Not quite.

A man was pulling something out of the trunk. A rectangle, covered in mud. Too small to have a body stuffed inside. He set it on the ground, and then pulled out a second. Same shape.

I started moving closer, feet sinking into the muddy bank, like it was pulling me in.

"What is that?" I asked, even though I thought I knew.

"I think maybe it's luggage?" Serena said.

The sides of my vision went blurry.

"Hazel?" she said, one hand on my arm. I felt myself pale, felt the blood draining from my head. "It's okay. There's no one in there."

"What color are they?" I said, my voice sounding small and far away.

"What?" she asked, like she hadn't understood the question.

Nico was suddenly beside me. "Hazel, what's the matter?"

"That luggage," I said, "what color is it?"

"I don't . . . it's covered in mud," he said.

But one of the younger officers had run a hose down from the house and was beginning to clean off the car.

Serena nudged his shoulder and nodded toward the bags, as if sensing something in my expression.

The water ran clear over the luggage, cutting a line through the muddy surface. I knew it before I saw it. My knees buckled.

Two hardback cases. Royal blue.

I stepped back, almost tripping, until Nico caught me by the elbow.

I was sure that under the layers of mud and rust, the car would be white.

Both, I knew with certainty, belonged to my mother.

PART 2

MOTHER

CHAPTER 10

67 Days without Rain
Monday, May 20
6:30 p.m.
Precipitation: Zero

The day my mom disappeared, I didn't realize anything was wrong. I saw her at breakfast on Friday morning, and left her where she'd stood at the kitchen window in that long green dress when Gage drove the three of us to school, as if it were just a regular day.

I was fourteen, preoccupied with my own life—the math test I hadn't studied for; the injustice of my curfew; my growing infatuation with Nico Pritchard. I had Gage drop me off at Jamie's on the way home from school, and figured he could relay the information to anyone who asked—I was no longer at the age where I thought I needed permission to stay over. I issued statements instead of requests. Our house was a constant stream of people coming and going, especially when Holt was out on calls during the evening shift.

Jamie's mom let us order pizza twice, just because Jamie had a crush on the delivery driver. She let us sleep on a trampoline in the backyard under the stars, armed with an array of flashlights to ward off the nocturnal animals. Jamie's mom let us all call her Sonny, and she let Jamie take her car at night—or else she didn't notice— even though neither of us had a permit yet.

We'd drive around the loop, crawling slowly by the homes of our classmates, and end up parked at the overlook of the Barrel, an alcove of the lake situated between a semicircle of cliffs at the end of a hiking trail. There was a clearing in the woods with just enough space for one car, hidden from the road. We'd sit on the cliff edge, feet dangling over the water and rocks below—like some metaphorical precipice. It was a place for secrets, protected by the dark and the trees, frequented only by the two of us alone. Confess something over the cliff, and you could imagine it falling to the lake below, swept up in the current—gone. No evidence left behind.

Years later, it would be where she told me about her and Caden.

It wasn't until Sonny dropped me off on her way to work a shift at the motel on Saturday afternoon that I started to realize something was wrong. The presence of the three extra cops in the kitchen didn't tip me off—that was a common enough occurrence at our house. Nicholas Pritchard was here all the time, and it was usually a welcome sight. A hint that maybe Nico was here as well. I thought nothing of the way he was leaning back against the fridge, or the way he stood suddenly, refocusing, when I entered the room. I barely noted the way the others were gathered around the table, with photos spread out in front of them.

No, my first clue was the way Holt glanced up from the table, dark circles under his eyes—that look of surprise to see me standing there. His mouth half-open, a series of rapid blinks when I said hello.

"Hazel," he said, "have you seen your mother?" His deep voice cracked at the end. Something out of character. That's what threw me off-kilter: His voice. His expression—both pleading and confused.

"What?" I asked, walking closer, trying to process the question, his demeanor, the tone of his voice.

The other men, Alberto Flores and Pete Henderson, stepped back from the table, as if making space to invite me forward. Neither of them offered a joke, or the over-the-top hello that I'd come to expect from my father's team.

The photos before them appeared to be from our local bank branch and seemed like they had come from security footage. I recognized my mother from the overhead angle, in the same green dress I'd seen her in the day before.

"She's at the bank?" I asked, not understanding.

"She's *gone*," Caden said, arms crossed, from the other side of the room. He'd been standing at the edge of the living room, watching in silence. He pointed to the table, his hand shaking slightly with rage. "That's the last time anyone saw her. Yesterday afternoon. She took everything and left."

I peered around the room, confused. Everything seemed to still be here: the mugs in the china display; the pictures on the mantel; me.

I headed straight for their bedroom closet, even though I heard Holt calling after me. The closet was a mess, her clothes in disarray, like they'd been pulled from the hangers in a rush. I couldn't tell what was missing. Then I stood on my toes, peering up, but I could already see the absence. The place where our two pieces of luggage had once been stored.

Even before I found that letter in my room, those inadequate final words—that was the moment I understood that it was real.

It occurred to me only later that they'd been surprised when I turned up the next day.

That Holt and the other detectives, and probably Caden too, must've assumed she'd taken me with her—maybe even that I'd been in on the whole thing. But after the meticulous way she'd planned things—draining the accounts from work slowly over time, so as not to tip anyone off before the final step of her escape—the fact that I was left behind was obviously a well-thought-out intention, instead of an oversight.

The fact that I was still here turned her actions colder, more criminal. She'd stolen from Roy's business. She'd taken not only her own jewelry but Holt's first wife's too—whatever she could get her hands on, in a rush. And she'd drained all that remained in Holt's account on her way out of town. The investigation would reveal that my mother had bought a gun in the weeks before, but she hadn't had to use it. She took everything of value without raising any alarm, until it was too late.

Gage and Caden were understandably angry. But I couldn't quite muster the right emotion or response. I wanted to feel that same fury and betrayal, but I couldn't pull it to the surface. It felt like the air had been knocked from my lungs—a sudden and distinct lack of gravity. Just like the time I'd gotten lost in the grocery store when I was young, and instead of frantically searching the aisles, I'd desperately held on to the edge of a shelf, metal digging into the crease of my fingers.

Now I was staring at those two suitcases pulled from the back of my mother's car, and that feeling had returned. I couldn't get my bearings, and I needed something to ground me.

"Those are my mother's," I said, to everyone, to no one.

I turned to Nico beside me, and felt myself reaching for him, fingers closing on the fabric of his shirt, knuckles brushing against his stomach. "That's her car."

His face shifted slightly, a moment of skepticism or doubt. He opened his mouth to speak, but something over my shoulder caught his attention.

"What's going on?" Gage asked, jogging down the hill. "Is everything okay?" He had dark circles under his wide eyes, and I thought he of all people would understand when he saw it. He was sixteen when my mother left. Old enough to remember the details, to recognize the specifics.

I released Nico and gestured to the car in front of us, to the suitcases still dripping before us—that shock of blue. My arms were shaking, and I couldn't still them.

"What is it?" he asked again. How could he not see? But maybe my mother's disappearance hadn't been the turning point in his life that it had been in mine.

Serena stepped between us. This time, it was only me she addressed. "Hazel, are you sure?"

"Sure about what?" Gage asked. But Serena kept her gaze on mine, placing a steady hand on my shoulder, as if she could feel me losing contact with the here and now.

"I'm sure," I said. And then I turned to Gage, extended my arm. "That's my mother's car."

He blinked twice, and then his gaze slowly slid over to the vehicle at the edge of the lake.

I waited for him to take it in. I waited for him to catch up. To arrive at the same conclusion, with the same dizzying, horrifying fear—that maybe my mother had never left at all.

His throat moved, and he looked back to me, mouth slightly open, asking a question. The alarm in my eyes must've been answer enough.

Finally, jolted into action, he assumed the role of taking charge. "Is someone going to open those?" he asked. A statement, in the form of a question.

Al Flores stepped between us and the scene, frowning as we pushed closer. "Serena, why don't you take them inside."

"Open it," Gage said, gesturing to the luggage. The force behind his voice reminded me of when we were young—when I knew, like always, he would be on my side. *Hazel won. I saw it.*

"Get back, Gage," Al said, in a voice that left no room for discussion.

Gage backed up only a single step, taking me with him. "This is our house," he said, throat moving, eyes wide. "We have every right to be out here—"

"You're right," Al said, "it is your house. So step back and let me do things the right way."

Gage peered around the group, seemed to notice that everyone was now staring at us, instead of the car.

Serena's deep brown eyes were wide with anxiety—something I'd never seen in her. I suddenly didn't want to know what she was so worried about discovering inside. "Please, back up, Hazel," she said.

As if what she really meant was: *Don't look.*

I'd been expecting to see my mother's clothes. The way she folded them into perfect squares, tucking the socks into empty gaps, maximizing every inch of space. Plenty of her clothing had still hung in her closet; I'd assumed she'd left with only the essentials. Or maybe the luggage was used for the jewelry she'd taken. Possibly stacks of cash she'd siphoned from the accounts.

But it was clear that Serena was worried about something else. Something darker she'd once witnessed.

"Gage," I said, in question—in terror.

Suddenly I was fifteen, stepping into a hidden alcove tucked behind a closet, unaware of what was waiting for me. I was seven, spending my first night in the basement alone, staring out through those large glass doors while the wind blew in from the lake, rattling the frame—

"Okay," Gage said, voice breaking. He placed a hand on my arm, guiding me away.

I trudged up the yard, casting glances over my shoulder—Nico was trailing behind us, and the car still lay at the edge of the lake, the hood of the trunk agape, monstrous in everything it represented.

We didn't go inside. We stood at the end of our upper-level deck, overlooking the scene. The dark water was unnaturally still. A surface of secrets.

A row of people stood in front of the car, as if they were trying to maintain some semblance of privacy. But from my spot above, I could see Al Flores crouching down in the mud, reaching for the zipper.

Another body shifted, cutting off my view.

"Can you see?" I asked Nico and Gage, standing on either side of me.

"No," Nico said, but Gage remained quiet. Time moved slowly as we waited for some indication from the scene.

Eventually, Serena peeled back from the group and gradually walked toward us, eyes down at her feet.

I felt Nico's arm go to my back, his fingers firm on my waist. I felt myself holding my breath.

She stopped just below us, tipping her head up, shading her eyes. "They're empty," she said.

Relief flooded my body. But I didn't understand. I didn't understand why my mother's empty luggage was in the trunk of her car, at the bottom of the lake behind our house.

"There's *nothing*?" Gage asked.

Serena shook her head, then took the steps up to the deck. "Let's take this inside, okay? The crew here has a lot to process before they can take the car."

I only realized I was shaking when I tried to slide open the back door, saw my fingers trembling against the grip.

Inside, the air felt different—heightened, buzzing—but I couldn't tell if it was us or the house. Gage closed the door behind him, but I remained almost pressed up against it, staring out.

"Hazel," Serena finally said, voice low. "Do you have any pictures?"

I stared at her, unsure of what she meant. "Of my mother?"

"They're gone," Gage said quietly, sparing me from having to say it. They'd been thoroughly removed from the family albums and mantels and walls—a painstakingly careful excision. Though I was sure she must've still existed in digital images, stored on computers and phones. I hadn't looked.

"I meant of the car," Serena said. "Or the luggage."

I shook my head. "I don't think so." But it had been a long time since I'd checked. "What about on the bank footage?" I asked. It was the last place she was seen—emptying our account before leaving town. Surely her car would've been picked up in the parking lot.

She nodded. "I'll have to check the old file. See if they pulled any images from the lot. And if so, whether they kept them."

"A lot of maybes there," Gage said, arms crossed.

"Gage—" I began. I didn't know what to do from here. My mind wasn't connecting the dots. "Why is her car out there?" I needed him to make sense of things, just the same as he used to do with my physics homework.

He put a hand out, placed it on my shoulder. "I think, if she didn't want to be found, it makes sense that she would've dumped that car. It would've been an easy way to track her, caught on camera, just like you said. She'd want to get rid of it. She had a plan."

My throat constricted. Of course she had a plan. A plan that didn't involve me. Had she managed to push it into the lake, letting it drift downhill in neutral, before heading for the bank, so she could slip out of town, untraceable?

"But why the luggage?" I asked.

"Why anything?" he said. "You've spent years trying to figure out why. Why she left you. Why she did this to us."

I nodded, welcoming the company of his understanding.

Nico remained silent, neither agreeing nor disagreeing, staring out the windows, watching the scene out back. His expression never changed: large brown eyes carefully taking everything in; mouth downturned in contemplation, as if he was still trying to work it through himself. Knowing him, he'd speak only when he was sure.

"Gage, Nico," Serena said, "I need to speak with Hazel alone."

Gage took a beat before saying, "Right. Okay, sure." It was obvious he was not used to taking orders from Serena, even when she framed them as requests.

They returned to the deck, and then it was just me and Serena in the kitchen, both of us hovering awkwardly around the table. The place I'd once seen my father and hers looking at those security photos of my mother. The place I'd first learned she was gone.

Then, like now, I'd been interviewed alone. Holt had brought me to the station, where it was Alberto Flores who had asked Holt to leave the room.

That day, Al was hard and serious. How quickly he had switched from my dad's friend, Serena's father, who grilled burgers and hot dogs in an apron for anyone who showed up each Sunday. He did things by the book, and he did not seem to care that I had been a victim in this as well.

Tell us about your mother, Hazel.

He asked me about where we had lived before—*all around the Carolinas*—what had brought us here—*a fresh start*—as if the entirety of our six years here was all part of the scam.

I was fourteen years old. It was half my lifetime.

Do you know where she would go? Any people from your past? Who she might call?

No, no, I don't know. We moved frequently. She never went backward, only forward.

I could sense Al's growing frustration, barely contained in the way he flipped the pages in front of him. The questions kept coming: *What did she do for work before? Why did you have to leave your last home?*

I don't remember. I don't know.

These were lies, of course.

I didn't tell him about the last man we left, or that we'd done it in the middle of the night. I didn't tell him we moved from vacation town to vacation town because she said there would always be work. I just wanted to get out of that room as quickly as possible.

I'd imagined Holt on the other side of the one-way mirror. And so I turned to it, staring at my own reflection. My hair was dark, where hers was blond. But, I knew, we had the same oval face, same high cheekbones, the same sharp profile to our nose. I only noticed in pictures, but it was obvious to anyone who looked at us that I was her daughter. It was too easy for them to see me as an extension of her—whether I wanted it or not.

Please, can I go home? I said, to the mirror. *Please, Holt, can I come home?*

I stared back at my reflection, holding my breath, until the door suddenly opened, and Holt ended the interview.

I was not a cooperating witness. But it wasn't for the reasons they thought.

I didn't want her to get caught, it was true. But not because I wanted her to escape. In that moment, I just didn't want her *back*. Didn't want to have to come face-to-face with her and the fact that she'd left me. The fact that she'd chosen something else, and didn't want me to be part of it.

I was fourteen, *just a child*. I was fourteen, *old enough to know better*.

I was fourteen, and didn't teenagers know—didn't they practice it, even—how best to keep secrets?

"I want to show you something," Serena said now. She kept her voice low, as if Gage and Nico were still too close, on the other side of the glass doors. I wondered if they could still hear us.

She pulled out her phone, which had a relatively large screen, and set it on the table between us. There was a picture on the display, and it took me only a second to recognize it. The photo was of the first car pulled from the water—the one I'd driven past earlier in the week, when it rested on the side of the road. Only now it was cleared of the mud and grime, so I could see the streaked paint job underneath.

I bent over the table, drawn closer.

"Have you ever seen this car before?" she asked, almost at a whisper—like a secret meant just for me.

The vehicle had been set on a clearing of asphalt. She scrolled through a few pictures from different angles. Some were taken close up, focusing on details: the shape of the window opening, the Buick symbol set into the hood. The car was brown, maybe—but that could've been the age, the rust.

"No. I don't think so. That car," I said, gesturing to the back-yard, "we had it when we moved here." We'd driven into town with that same luggage, even.

Serena stood at the window, and then turned back to me. She leaned on the table, fingers blanching white from the pressure points, a sharp contrast to her dark maroon polish. She had a thin gold band around her thumb. "What do you think happened to your mother, Hazel?"

I knew she was asking something more. What I might've known that I hadn't said back then. I wondered what her father might've told her about that first interview.

I'd had a lot of time to think about it since. I sat down at the table, leaned back in the kitchen chair. "I think something must've caught up to her." Something from our life *before* we moved here. Something that might've been the reason she ran. What else could possibly justify it? Leaving this life she'd built? Leaving me? "Something that made her desperate enough to do it. To take what she could and run." It had always been the two of us against the world, before Holt. As I grew older, the only way I could rationalize it to myself was by believing she'd done it to keep me safe.

I raised my eyes to hers, and watched as she waited. Like she knew I had a secret. Something I never told. "We left someone else once."

She sat slowly, carefully, like she was worried about disrupting the moment.

"Do you remember his name?"

"Joe Lyons," I said, watching as Serena wrote his name in her notepad. I remembered easily, even after all this time, because of the lion head tattoo on the back of his shoulder—the way an eye peered out from the edge of his sleeveless shirts, like it was watching me. "We lived with him for a year, maybe, in Carston Beach, down in South Carolina. She went by Beth then."

I imagined he was the reason she started going by Libby, once we arrived here. That Mirror Lake was a place to hide, with its boundary of mountains protecting us from the outside world, and its lack of cell service, like we were cut off from the past that was looking for us.

Here, Beth Sharp had eventually transformed into Libby Holt, her past wiped clean. But what if he'd found her?

"Did you tell anyone this back then?" she asked.

She knew I hadn't. "I didn't think it back then." I felt my jaw setting. I was twenty-seven now. Thirteen years had passed. I had become a different person.

But now the car in the yard was messing with my head. The luggage. I couldn't piece together the right story.

"Can I ask you a question?" I asked.

"Sure," she said, folding her hands together on the surface.

"Was there anything I don't know about? After she left, I mean. Any sign of her at all, in the investigation?"

I had never once asked my father if there had been any updates. I didn't ask him if he had searched on his own. I didn't ask him what he thought happened. We rarely discussed her, as if she were a topic too dangerous to bring into the open. I worried about what would come with it: the logistics of our custody situation; my own allegiance.

Serena glanced over her shoulder at the men outside. She shook her head, leaned closer. "From what I remember back then, no. There was nothing." I imagined she had listened to her father telling stories at the dinner table, just as I had. "No credit cards. No leads or sightings that ever panned out." She swallowed. "She vanished completely, like a ghost."

I nodded.

Serena drummed her fingers on the table, the slender ring tapping against the wood. "I want to ask you again, Hazel. What do you think happened to her?"

It was a question no one had asked me—not then, and not ever since. Not what happened, but what might've happened *to her*. I had never imagined it was a possible question.

"I have no idea," I said, shaking my head. "I've gone back to it, over and over, and there's nothing. No warning. No signs." I swallowed, picturing the way her father had interviewed me back then. "People here think I must've known what was coming, but I didn't. I swear it."

It's why I didn't come back to Mirror Lake after college. I couldn't build a life for myself here, in her shadow. Not even protected by Perry Holt.

I thought again about the letter she'd left. *I hope one day you can forgive me.*

How much deeper did my mother's secrets go?

I had been built by my mother's absence. Had grown out of its shock. The worst thing I could imagine had happened, and surviving it was the thing that had finally, fully made me truly unafraid.

My mother abandoned me in the most public and shameful way. She took what she could, and she left everything else behind. She believed in traveling light, I knew. That you would find what you needed when you got to the next place. Maybe the car, the luggage, were all part of a ploy, like Gage believed. *Maybe, maybe.*

And yet.

She was not a bad mother. She wasn't resentful or selfish or cold. If I let myself think back to the times before—and sometimes, *sometimes* I would—I'd remember the parts of her that had long been buried by the aftermath. She was full of life and optimism. She was incredibly resourceful and confident. Even Gage and Caden had grown to love her. She'd had a way with them both, becoming what each needed, in turn. She gave Gage the space he needed, and Caden the attention he'd always desired. She never missed a sporting event, or a school activity, for any of us.

Really, the only terrible thing she'd done was leave.

But what if she hadn't?

By the time the car was finally removed from the yard, most of the emergency crews were gone. No one was treating this as a crime, that I could tell. Or maybe the evidence was just being relocated to a new site, off our property.

I watched from the window as Gage followed Serena to her cruiser. They seemed to be arguing—or rather, *he* seemed to be arguing. His frustration at being held at a distance from the investigation was evident in his demeanor.

Nico stood just outside, hands deep in his pockets, eyes on the tow truck as it pulled my mother's car into the dusk.

Both of them turned at the sound of the front door. I hitched my weekender bag onto one shoulder, hooked my backpack onto the other.

"You're leaving?" Gage asked, standing at the edge of the drive.

"Yes," I said, carrying my things to the car. I was out of clothes. Out of time. Out of patience and understanding. Out of reasons to stay.

"I think that's a good idea," he said. "There's nothing left to do here but wait."

"Will you call me with any news, please?" I asked, dumping my bags into the trunk.

I felt myself cracking. I needed to get home, to reorient myself. Remember who I was, before I grabbed on to the wrong thing, desperate for a sense of gravity. The story I had told myself about my life seemed suddenly too fragile. The past had started clawing out from the earth, rising from the water. Even the walls of the house felt off.

"I'll let you know the second they tell me anything," he said, a muscle twitching at the side of his jaw. "And Nico can keep an eye on the place for us."

Nico's teeth caught on his lip for a second before he nodded. "I'll keep an eye out, Hazel."

I locked up carefully with Caden's key—remembering Gage's warnings about the house appearing deserted. I checked the back windows, the back doors, the basement. Everything seemed secure.

Then I left, driving in the same direction the tow truck had turned, wondering if I'd catch up with it, have to follow this haunting image all the way back to the highway. But the road was blissfully empty.

I was halfway home when I glanced in the rearview mirror and caught a flash of purple in the back seat. Skyler's backpack, left behind in the search for her mother.

But the road opened up before me, like a sign. My eyes drifted shut for just a second—maybe two—and I imagined a different scene, in a different time. My mother, eyes forward, hands gripping the wheel of a strange vehicle.

Deciding not to think about the things pulling her back. Deciding, instead, to keep going.

CHAPTER 11

Just before midnight, the block surrounding my apartment appeared deserted. I lived in the unit above the office where I worked with Keira and Luke—and the entire building was completely dark. The area was bustling with activity during work hours, but most everything shut down by late evening.

This had been the first big property we'd rehabbed together, a proof of concept, and we'd sold it with the promise of a long-term lease—us.

I had figured I would practically be living here during the re-model anyway. We had all put everything into it—our money, our time, ourselves. It was our first risk, and every morning when I woke, I was reminded of that thrill, and that success.

But now I stared up at the dark uncovered windows, and the dark storefront below, and felt an unsettling absence.

I understood the pull I'd felt to rush back here. It wasn't for someone—it was for some*thing* instead. The car in the lake, the luggage in the trunk, the timing—there were just too many questions, and I needed to still them, to quell them. I needed to pull the letter from the safe, where it had remained since I first moved to Charlotte.

I lugged my bags and Skyler's backpack up the steps to my second-level unit, dropped them just inside the entrance to the open floor plan, and went directly to the high shelf of my bedroom closet.

The safe was not unlike the model we'd gone through in my father's office.

Mine contained the same types of items: passport, birth certificate—the paperwork that defined who I was. Details spelled out under an official seal. *Father: Unknown. Mother: Elizabeth A. Sharp. Date of Birth: June 3, 1996. Place of Birth: Richland County, South Carolina.*

And below, a manila envelope containing an item that defined me just as much: the letter my mother had left behind, tucked underneath my bedroom pillow.

Over the years, I did, sometimes, look for her. First, I waited for signs: a ringing telephone, the call suddenly dropped; an email from an unknown address ending up in my spam folder; a stranger who knew my name.

But then, late at night, I'd sit at the old desktop computer, trying variations of the names she might use—*Libby Sharp; Beth S. Holt; Liz H. Sharp.* When she disappeared, the people of Mirror Lake stripped her of the Holt name, referring to her only as a Sharp. But part of me wondered if she'd kept it for herself. Used it. A stepping stone to the next iteration of who she might become.

I'd even tried the towns we'd left before, their names pulled from my hazy memory, despite what I'd told Al Flores. I'd had to memorize them at each school I attended: East Andover; Carston Beach. A string of coastal towns, before she'd finally disappeared into the mountains of Mirror Lake.

There, she must've believed, was a place no one would go looking.

I wondered now if things would've been different then if Holt had only asked me directly. His style was well-known through-out town. He didn't have to push. His presence alone enough to make you confess. I'd heard stories of him pulling people over, leaning his large forearms through the open window, with a look of vague disappointment. *Sorry, Holt,* they would say, heads hung low.

We all make mistakes, he'd respond, driving them home instead.

If only he had asked what I'd thought, what I might've believed. Maybe we would have found something—a thread to pull, before she got too far from our grip.

The only thing I ever found—or thought I'd found—was a postcard that once arrived for me in my college mailbox, my name and address printed on a label. A picture of a beach at sunset, a single palm tree, from a town on the coast of Mexico. As if maybe she'd been keeping tabs on me, and wanted me to know it too.

I'd looked up the location after, and imagined her there, in another vacation town, as another version of herself. Liz or Lizzy. Maybe Eliza.

But five years had passed by then, and I'd become someone new. Someone who had pulled herself out from the shadow she'd left behind. Who had risen above her mother's terrible legacy.

I never went looking. Still, I'd kept the postcard, just in case—tucked it in that same manila envelope.

I pulled the packet from the safe now and brought it to the kitchen, which had the best lighting at night. I tipped it over, letting the contents fall onto the long white countertop. The tattered post-card, the orange glow of a fiery sky.

And below it, the letter.

The blue ink on the torn envelope, in that large, familiar print. The oversized *D* in *Daughter*. The curve of the *M*, and the way she'd underlined *Daughter of Mine* so emphatically, like a command.

Inside, the lined page of loose-leaf paper was folded in thirds, details lacking. That same blue ink could've come from any of the pens in my desk in the hallway, where I imagined her pausing to scrawl the note before tucking it under my pillow. *I hope one day you can forgive me.*

The police didn't know about this letter—not then, and not now. No one knew, other than Nico. If they had, I was sure it would only bolster Gage's interpretation of events.

I closed my eyes, trying to imagine any other outcome.

What Gage said made sense: she'd dumped the car on her way out of town. She was going to disappear. This note was proof. The postcard, a confirmation that she'd succeeded.

Everything else was just details.

I felt my heart rate settling, gravity returning. But I couldn't put the letter away; I didn't want it out of my sight. I reread it, until I could see her clearly, in that green dress, hovering over a piece of lined paper, wondering what she could possibly say. Knowing, maybe, that no words could ever be adequate.

I imagined her on a beach somewhere, setting foot in a new town—a new story, a new name.

I fell asleep with that letter on my bedside table, like it was the grounding I had been searching for. I sunk into sleep, fast and sudden. An anchor, racing for the bottom.

That night, I dreamed of water, of darkness, of drowning.

I dreamed of my mother floating facedown, blond hair splayed around her in the water, mouth open.

I dreamed of her screaming my name.

CHAPTER 12

I woke feeling unsettled, like I'd forgotten something important.

Two nights away in Mirror Lake, and suddenly the high white ceilings with the dark exposed beams, the clean lines and large windows of the place I now called home, had started to feel unfamiliar. I had woken expecting the sliding glass doors, the soft light filtering through the trees, the lake visible in the distance. The view out the windows now was a stretch of buildings with the occasional trees, instead of the other way around.

It took me a long moment to orient myself: *I'm in Charlotte. I'm in my condo. I'm fine.*

I'm home.

The envelope was still on my bedside table—except it seemed different in the stark daylight. Like something haunting. Not something grounding me back to my current life. But like something had followed me back here, instead.

I got ready quickly, trying to shake the feeling loose.

At the kitchen window, I could see Keira's red hybrid Toyota parked along the curb—which meant she probably knew I was here too. The parking spot that came with my unit was clearly visible from the street, through a grating of contemporary steel bars.

The sidewalk below was teeming with activity, like always at this time of day. But I couldn't settle into it, find my footing. A horn jarred me. And when I spun around, the white, contemporary lines inside seemed to disappear into one another, so that I couldn't find the dimension.

I closed my eyes and clasped the letter in my hand. But I couldn't clear the buzzing in my head. Like something was fighting to be noticed, to cut through the distance—

"Knock knock," I heard Keira call from the lower level, instead of coming up the flight of steps to actually knock on the door.

I shoved the letter into my purse on the kitchen island and opened my apartment door.

Keira stood at the base of the white stairwell, hands on her hips, a sea of windows behind her. A cascade of long braids trailed halfway down her back. She'd grown up not far from here, understood the history of the area in a way that gave us the confidence to invest. Keira always seemed boldly confident—in a way that sometimes reminded me of Jamie. Today, her red blazer popped against her darker skin tone, and she wore name-brand heels, even though it was generally just the three of us in the office.

Keira and I had been randomly paired as roommates our freshman year—if there was anyone who knew me better now, I couldn't think of them. I still considered our room assignment one of the great fortunes of my life—up there with meeting Perry Holt.

"How'd it go?" she asked, in a gentle tone, as if she could read enough in my expression.

They found a car out back in the lake. It belonged to my mother.

"My dad left me the house in the will," I said. It was as much a shock as anything else, and seemed a safer place to start.

"Just you?" she asked. Her heels echoed in the stairwell as she took a few steps up.

"Just me." I gestured for her to join me, as Luke peered around the corner, wide-eyed. I guessed he'd overheard.

Keira and Luke had probably arrived together. They were now officially a couple, after years of dancing around it—but it also changed the way we operated as a business together. We'd taken a hard line on it. Decisions required three people.

We'd begun when we were all living together in our off-campus apartment our final year of college and were kicked out of our unit due to renovations. We ended up having to take whatever was available—a shitty rental house I could not believe hadn't yet been condemned— and we spent the rest of the year imagining all the things we would do to fix it. Until suddenly the questions became less hypothetical and more specific—*How much would it take*—and Keira was drawing up plans, and I was setting us up as a business with the state, and Luke was asking his family for an initial investment loan.

I've since decided this shared confidence was the most essential quality in business: the confidence to try; the confidence that you had something to offer, that you had a vision worth seeing through.

The more you believed, the more you could convince others to believe too.

The only issue the three of us ran into was that we each thought our role meant we had the final say. Luke, because of his connections and capital, and because he was *good at money*—his words, though I suspected that was just because he'd always had it.

Keira, because she knew the ins and outs of the work itself. She was objectively the smartest and most technically skilled of the three of us.

Me, because it had been my idea, and my business degree that had gotten us started. But also: I had an affinity for details and a proclivity for suspicion. I did things carefully and by the book— permitted, permissioned, unimpeachable. I understood, more than anyone, that you were nothing but your reputation. I had modeled myself off Detective Perry Holt, beyond reproach.

We worked hard. Threw ourselves into it. Blurred the lines

between business and personal. We were turning a small but consistent profit, and we loved the life we were leading.

"What are you going to do with the house?" Luke asked as he followed Keira up the steps. He had a distinct drawl that seemed to work in his favor in meetings—either as some membership code or an unexpected play. His father was a well-known developer in the Charlotte region, and his name carried a level of respect—just as the Holt name did in Mirror Lake.

I held the door open for them both. Luke's cheeks were flushed, making me wonder if he'd been out in the sun. But with his Irish complexion and red hair, it could've just been from taking the stairs or having a hot drink.

"I don't know yet. I might send you some pictures, Keira, see what you think?" I couldn't imagine keeping the house now; how could I ever stand in the backyard without picturing that car emerging, monstrous, from the surface?

"Yeah, of course," she said.

"Did you see the news yet today?" Luke asked, cheeks flushing even deeper.

Ah, there it was.

I closed my eyes, shook my head.

"Another car found in Mirror Lake?" he continued, as if I didn't know. "For such a small town, it's sure in the news a lot these days. . . ."

He was right. Most people in Charlotte knew of Mirror Lake from their weekend getaways, their hiking excursions. A picturesque postcard. A place they passed on the highway.

I sat down on the edge of my gray couch. "I know. Trust me, I know. It was right behind my dad's house. That's why I had to stay. They had to pull it out through our yard."

Keira's deep brown eyes widened as she sat beside me. "Oh god. Why didn't you say?" I couldn't tell whether she was hurt by the omission.

"It's all so surreal still," I said, as explanation. "I can't really believe it."

I should've told them the rest then. Maybe if Luke wasn't here, I would have told Keira everything. But it was still too new, too fresh, too unexplainable. And ever since they'd gotten together, I couldn't help but think of them talking about me after, by themselves. Dissecting my life without me there. As if I were an outsider to my own experience.

"Do they know what it's from?" Luke asked.

I shook my head. "Gage seems to think it's all part of an insurance scam."

But why would my mother drop her own car? It didn't add up. Didn't fit the *pattern* everyone was talking about. The car. The suitcases. My mom. She'd left no trace, let alone filed some insurance claim.

I wanted to believe him, but there were too many moving pieces.

"Jesus," Luke said, peering down at us, arms crossed.

Keira gestured toward the purple backpack with the sparkles on the floor beside the couch. "Well, this is new," she said, trying to ease the tension in the room. "Anything else you need to tell us?"

"Skyler left it in my car," I said. "I need to call them."

Keira and Luke shared an unreadable look. Something had developed when they finally committed to each other. Some new language I couldn't quite decipher. Maybe I should've been more wary. But this was a situation I knew well. I had found myself a third wheel in so much of my life. There was always the chance that I could be cut out on my own, so I had learned to make myself indispensable, tethered to the core—living, even, in the same building where I worked.

I always had trouble with boundaries, both my own and those of others. I didn't want to give anyone the chance to decide on me. It was easier to remove the element of choice for them.

Keira stood and smoothed the sides of her black dress pants. "We'll be downstairs, Hazel. But take your time. Let us know how we can help, yeah?"

I nodded, then gave her a small smile. "Yeah," I echoed.

It was after nine, which meant Skyler would probably be at school, if they were trying to keep things normal. I tried Caden's cell, but it went immediately to voicemail, which could've meant anything. Either he was out on lake patrol or somewhere along the upper levels of the bowl, out of range.

I called the landline to their house, just in case.

A woman answered, but it didn't sound like Jamie. "Holt residence," she said.

"Who's this?" I asked.

"Um, may I ask who's calling first, please?" she asked, a sense of self-righteousness in her voice.

"This is Hazel. Caden's sister. Skyler's aunt." I wasn't sure which carried the most weight.

"Oh," she said, changing her tone. "Hi. I'm Layne. Just babysitting today."

I frowned, the room hollowing out. "Jamie's still not home?" I'd been hoping she'd returned the night before. Assuming it, even, since no one told me otherwise.

"Guess not. Caden called and asked me to watch Sky today. She's not feeling well."

In the gap of conversation, I heard a cartoon in the background, something loud with peppy music.

"Can I talk to her?" I asked. I figured if anyone knew the truth, it would be Skyler. If Jamie had come back and left again, she would know. And if not, I wondered if Caden had given her an explanation that he wouldn't give to me.

There was a short pause. "She's up in her room right now. I think she's sleeping."

I still heard the cartoon in the background. I didn't know if she was lying to me, but there was no way to push the subject over the phone.

It was possible Caden had advised this Layne not to let anyone speak to Skyler, in person or on the phone. He could've been protecting her—by now everyone in town probably knew she'd been the one to discover the car.

No doubt lots of people were poking around, trying to get answers, just like me.

I couldn't help thinking about my mother, instead. How easily she had slipped away, without a trace.

"Do you want me to leave a message?" Layne asked, after a long stretch of silence.

"No thanks," I said. "I'll call him on his cell."

I hung up, and the room buzzed. Something wasn't right. Something had happened, yes, but I couldn't shake the feeling that something was *still* happening.

I had missed so much with my mother, and my father—both of them gone without warning, when I'd been busy doing something else. I desperately hoped it wasn't happening to Skyler now. But I remembered that cold feeling when I'd brought Skyler home and stood just inside their empty house. The feeling I got seeing the front door hanging ajar.

I called Gage's cell, and fortunately, he answered immediately. "Did you make it home okay?" he asked as greeting. His steady, calm demeanor made me think that maybe I'd had it all wrong.

"Yes, I'm here," I said. The static on the line let me know that Gage was currently on the move. It sounded like he was wearing earbuds that were picking up the wind.

"Has anyone heard from Jamie?" I asked.

"What?" he asked, through another crackle of static.

"Jamie. Did she come home?"

Silence. I thought the line had dropped. But then I heard another crackle. He must've been standing perfectly still, thinking. "I assume? No one said anything to me. I saw Caden this morning when he got to the station."

"You didn't ask?"

"No," he said, drawing out the word into a question. "I did not

ask my brother if his wife came back home after a fight, Hazel."
Like it was the most ridiculous thing he could imagine. "It's pretty
busy around here, if you haven't noticed," he added, with an edge
to his voice. But then, I imagined his workload had just increased,
with the loss of my father. There were only a handful of detectives
in the department, and they needed to cover a large range of inves-
tigations.

Gage and Caden's relationship wasn't strained, but it also wasn't
as close as their shared profession would lead one to believe.

I had been the wedge that came between them, according to
Caden. How many times had he stormed out of a room, disgusted
by his perception of a Gage-Hazel alliance. Something formed with
the intent to oppose, to outnumber.

Now they had different goals, different lives, moved in different circles. Though Caden was only two years behind him in age,
it didn't seem like he was looking to become a detective anytime
soon. He seemed to prefer the lake as his domain—issuing citations
to intoxicated boaters, answering calls for assistance—and then
leaving work behind at the end of his shift.

"Is Caden there with you now?" I asked.

"No, he's not here with me."

"I called his house, and there was a babysitter. Someone named
Layne. Skyler didn't go to school."

"Hazel," he said sharply. "For god's sake, leave him alone. We
have real cases we're trying to work here. I've got a runaway kid.
People who are *actually missing*."

I jolted—at both the information and the tone.

I was not used to being reprimanded by Gage. Our father's will
had changed things. We weren't playing the right versions of ourselves.

"A kid?" I asked, picturing Skyler suddenly, wandering down
the road, alone.

"A teenager. Left in the middle of the night, and no one's seen
him since. His parents are in a panic."

"I'm sorry," I said, because he was right. He had a responsibility that stretched beyond the borders of our family now.

He sighed. "I really think you're worrying about nothing, Hazel."

"Okay," I said, rubbing my temple. He wasn't wrong. But I had also learned, long ago, that when you don't pay close enough attention, you can't see the signs.

"Look," he continued, tone softening. "We're all shaken up over the car. These things have a way of distorting everything. Sometimes, when I'm working a case, I can't help but see it in everything. During that string of robberies a couple months back, I'd come home, sure things were missing when I'd just misplaced them. It got in my head."

But I thought it was still in his head. The way he saw the open window to our garage: a sign.

Now I thought of Caden's place again—an empty house. An opportunity. The front door, left open, like a calling card. And now I was seeing a string of people suddenly disappearing from Mirror Lake, without a trace.

I stared at Skyler's backpack, frowning. Maybe this was causing the issue—something tangible, weighing on me. A piece I'd accidentally brought back with me, that I'd have to eventually return. "I just want to be sure she's okay," I said.

"I'll talk to him when I see him," Gage said. "I promise."

I had to get out of this room, away from the backpack, away from that letter. Leave Mirror Lake in Mirror Lake. I joined Keira and Luke downstairs, taking a seat at my normal workstation.

But I knew I'd interrupted something by the way they fell to silence. Their desks were across the aisle from each other, and their typing echoed through the open space.

Keira paused, looked up. "Should we do a project update?" she asked.

"Farrow Road is almost complete," Luke said. "Everything on schedule." He picked up his mug and walked around the desk, leaning back against the edge, ankles crossed.

But I couldn't even get through half of Luke's update. His words weren't registering. Instead, I was seeing Jamie at the celebration of life, telling me about their weekend plans to clean out the house. Jamie in our kitchen, looking through the pictures from our childhood. Jamie running into the lake, screaming her daughter's name.

I stood abruptly, chair legs screeching against the concrete flooring, stomach twisting, pulse pounding.

"I'm sorry," I said. "I'm sorry, I have to go back. Something's not right."

Keira and Luke shared a look that convinced me they'd been talking about me before I joined them.

I tucked my laptop under my arm. "I'll work from there. Please, send me anything I need to do. Or call me. I just, I need to be there right now."

Keira stood up, placed her hands on both sides of my arms. "Go," she said. "Luke and I have things covered here."

I nodded, my brain already three steps ahead. Packing a new bag, loading the car, feeling the bends of Mirror Highway as I made my way back.

I didn't explain what had me so shaken.

I had never told anyone—not even her—that when my mother left, I didn't once question it.

And eventually, the anger had come, in a full-on flood of rage. I'd gone through every photo album, removing her from our past, piece by piece. I'd purged every picture I could find around the house, and burned them in the fire pit my father had built in the yard.

I still remembered the scent of singed plastic, her blistering image, and the cloying smoke—the air growing hazy over the lake, with the little that was left of her. If my brothers knew it was me who had done it, they didn't say. None of us mentioned her after that. None of us wanted to pull her to the surface again.

It was only years later when I started to search. And even then in only the most perfunctory way.

But I didn't follow any possible trail. It hadn't occurred to me that maybe she'd wanted me to. Too much time had passed by then, if so.

And all along, that car had been in our backyard, and I'd missed it.

My god, I had missed so much.

I pictured Jamie lying on the trampoline, shining a flashlight up at the sky. Jamie driving her mother's car in the night, pulling into the overlook, feet dangling over the edge of the Barrel. And then later, Jamie trying to tell me something—*I'm seeing someone, Hazel. He makes me happy*—

And now: Her house, eerily empty. Her daughter, unwell. And the knowledge that I hadn't asked enough questions the last time someone had up and left.

It was too late, now, to trace the path my mother had taken. It was too late to understand why she'd done it.

But this—whatever it was—this was still happening.

I owed her. I owed them both.

Caden was right—my dad *was* always trying to get me to come home. He'd left me the house. And now I thought I understood what he meant by it.

A message. A promise. A warning: *Come back, Hazel. Look. Find them.*

CHAPTER 13

68 Days without Rain
Tuesday, May 21
12:00 p.m.
Precipitation: Zero

told no one I was on my way. I didn't think anyone would understand the intention behind the action, and didn't want them conspiring to guess what it might be.

I'd been gone too long, and I couldn't decipher the undercurrents of the relationships anymore. But I was still well aware that, in a small town, every interaction carries weight. Everyone cares more. They know more.

They remember more.

They doubt and distrust more.

This time I stopped on my way in. I wasn't sure how long I would be in town—whether it was one night or two—but I stocked up on bread and cold cuts, coffee, muffins. The essentials to see me through the workday in the house.

As I approached the town, horse farms gave way to signs for fishing trips, scenic boat rides, canopy zip lines. And then, suddenly, the mountains appeared in the distance. In the daylight, they were the first sign of home.

The lake gives us our name, but it's the mountains that make us. Cars have to be equipped for it. We learned to bike on the terrain, honing our muscles, just as we learned to swim in the lake, testing our endurance. We waited at bus stops in the wildflowers on the side of the road, where there was no shoulder. And in the winter, we sledded down backyards, between properties, barely escaping the trees.

The town was really more rocky slope than coastline, more trees than water, more hiking than fishing. But we were named, as things often were, for the focal point at the center instead.

I knew exactly where the boundary for the township of Mirror Lake began—well before the welcome sign. There was a slight deviation in the pavement, if you knew what you were looking for, where the road had been paved—or not—in different periods of time.

There were houses on the winding lanes that branched out from the road here that all had Mirror Lake in their mailing addresses, but were considered, by those inside the bowl, a separate area. *The wrong side of the sign,* Jamie used to joke.

Jamie had grown up in one of these clusters—a collection of single-lot homes designated only by a group of mismatched mailboxes out on the main road. She used to bike to our house, until Holt had noticed and demanded someone give her a ride instead.

He'd often do it himself, if her mother couldn't. Sometimes he'd send a patrol car for her—the benefit of having a father on the force.

Both of my parents preferred that we spend time at our house, and Jamie seemed all too happy to agree. But to me there was something uniquely appealing about her place, with the freedom to make our own rules, and the lack of parental oversight.

On impulse, I veered abruptly at the set of familiar mailboxes, taking the narrow dirt road as it sloped upward, until it ultimately branched out into different offshoots, each leading to a separate lot. If Jamie had left home, she might go to her mother's. Maybe I could find her for myself, instead of relying on Caden or Gage.

It had been a long time since I'd been out this way. I had no idea if Sonny even still lived up here, but I'd heard nothing about her leaving. I'd seen her the few times I'd been to Jamie's for an event—Thanksgiving, Christmas morning—but I hadn't really spoken to her in years. Our interactions were surface level and fleeting.

The community wasn't too different from how I remembered. But it seemed duller, smaller. A combination of the brown of the woods and the wear of the structures. Here, tucked out of sight, nothing had been flipped or rehabbed for the visitors.

I maneuvered my car over a series of roots that had pushed through the road, swerving to avoid the rocks and branches encroaching from the edges, and suddenly I could imagine the street gone. A year or two with no upkeep, and it would be overtaken by the mountain.

Sonny's house was the last on the street, set farthest back in the woods, like a secret.

It was a one-level beige cottage, with siding that had somehow turned darker over the years. The branches of the surrounding trees now hung so low that it looked like they'd be a danger in a storm. Maybe if the landscape were green, it would've been like something out of a fairy tale. But as it was, the house seemed more like something slowly fading into the brown landscape, being swallowed up by the woods. I couldn't tell if anyone was home.

There were two folding chairs on the porch, with a hand-painted wooden design over the front door: a burnt orange—the rising sun. It was the only flash of color in the landscape, other than the red handles of a bike, leaning up against the side of the porch. I wondered if it had been Jamie's from long ago. I couldn't bring the details to the surface.

I parked the car and stepped out, crunching over leaves and gravel. The front door to the house was open. Only a screen door remained closed, torn at the top right corner, just below the rising sun.

Sonny had always kept the door open, no matter the season, believing fresh air was the cure for all ailments, from a cold to a hangover.

As I approached, I saw a figure moving inside, coming closer—seeming to move in mirror image to me. It paused at the screen door, staring out.

The only sound was the pebbles and gravel kicking up in my wake. Whoever was inside remained standing behind the screen, a still silhouette. She did not open the door or call out to me—either in welcome or in question.

"Sonny?" I asked, taking the first uneven step up to the porch.

Finally, the screen door creaked open, and Sonny Varino stood at the threshold, dressed in a set of pale green scrubs, the uniform for the motel where she'd worked for as long as I could remember.

"Well, look who it is," she said, stepping out onto the porch. Her voice had turned raspier, but Sonny was still skinny and tall, a combination of sharp edges and freckled skin. Her hair, something between curled and slept-on, was currently a shade of copper instead of blond. The lines around her mouth had gotten deeper, and her eyes appeared smaller, more hooded. I couldn't tell whether she was tired or she'd just aged more swiftly than I had anticipated. An unlit cigarette dangled from her hand.

"What brings *you* back to this neck of the woods?" She cocked her hip and leaned into it, and I caught a flash of Jamie, doing the same.

"I'm looking for Jamie. Wondered if she was here."

She laughed once, looked over her shoulder, peering back into the house, like she was searching for her. "Jamie doesn't come out this way anymore. Why are you really here, Hazel?"

"Because I don't know where she is. Caden said they had a fight and she took off. I don't think she's been home since early yesterday."

Sonny stared at me for a beat, swaying gently. She had always moved like this, slightly languid and unsteady, which made it hard to tell whether she was under the influence or not. As if sensing that vertigo, she sat on the top porch step, pulled a lighter from her pocket, and lit the cigarette in her other hand.

I sat beside her, in mirror image. I did not wait for invitations. I'd learned early that it was best not to ask for permission. To plant your feet and act like you belonged.

"Heard Holt died," she said. "I would've come to the memorial, but I had work." She ended with a hard *k*, as if to drive the point home. She stared into the trees, eyes slightly narrowed.

I nodded, scanning the woods, wondering if there was something she was looking for out there.

Then she pivoted to face me. "Heard you got the house too," she said, leaning one arm on her knee, planting her chin in her hand, and blowing smoke out the side of her mouth. "Wouldn't your mother be proud." She smiled.

She'd never seemed to care for my mother, and I believed the feeling was mutual. As if they could each see something in the other—a different path, an *almost*.

I wondered if something had happened between Jamie and her mother—a strain, or a specific reason she didn't come around. Or if Sonny's behavior had finally caught up with her.

"Have you heard from Jamie, Sonny?"

She waved her cigarette absently. "I hear *about* her more than I hear from her."

Growing up, Jamie had been fiercely loyal to Sonny, despite everything. She was the reason that Jamie wouldn't leave for college with me.

I'd tried to convince her to apply for the financial aid. We could be roommates, I promised, and Asheville was only a little over an hour away. We had been lying on the trampoline out back, imagining the future. At least, I had been. But she'd said I didn't understand, that it still cost something, and not all of us had a Holt backing us. *It's just me and Sonny*, she'd said, and I wondered if she was thinking about her mother left all alone, instead.

I couldn't quite fathom this new breach between them. Or maybe Sonny was just playing me.

"You don't seem surprised," I said, wondering what she might've known that she wasn't saying.

"It's a pattern, don't you think?" she asked.

A pattern with the cars. A pattern of behavior.

"Wives, leaving the Holt men?" she continued. "Your mother, Audrey. God, I don't even remember the name of Roy's wife, that marriage was so quick."

I shook my head, stuck on the piece that didn't fit her pattern. "Audrey didn't leave. She died." I had never met Audrey Holt, but I lived with the tragedy of her death all the same—knew how it had impacted not only her sons but our father. She'd lost control of her bike on the loop of Mirror Highway, while going too fast down a hill in the dark, and collided with a tree head-on. She hadn't been wearing a helmet. Her children were only five and seven years old.

It was part of our shared history—the reason Holt didn't want Jamie riding into town on her bike. The reason he always, *always* reminded us to be safe on the roads.

Sonny rocked slowly, one arm hugging her knees. "Oh, but she was going to, though."

"How do you know that?" I asked.

"Well, I know the signs, don't I?" she said, with a harsh laugh. Jamie's father left when she was five. He would swoop back into town every couple of years, only to leave again at the first sign of responsibility. "But if you don't believe me, ask your uncle." She winked.

It was a surprisingly good idea. As the owner of the only family law practice in town, Roy probably had a finger on the pulse of what was happening beneath plenty of marriages. He might even know something about Caden's.

"And also," Sonny added, "*why* does someone go biking in the dark? A question no one saw fit to ask. Like it's irrelevant. People don't like asking the hard questions around here."

Something stirred in my stomach.

No, they didn't. Neither had I.

"Audrey loved those boys, though," she said.

"You knew her?" I asked, surprised. The things I knew about Audrey Holt were limited to the way she'd been remembered by her children: kind and funny, smart and beautiful. And because she was dead, there was no one who would say anything otherwise.

"Used to. Before she became a Holt, at least. She grew up right around here, with me." Her smile widened at my expression. "Oh, you thought she was something different?"

I shook my head. But maybe that's why she'd never cared for my mother, and vice versa. My mother had taken the place of a person she used to know.

"It doesn't look good, does it? To lose two wives? Not good for your image at all. But somehow, he prevailed."

"It was an accident." A bike in the night, a tree. "And my mother conned him. Took everything."

I was taking the bait.

Sonny was always smarter than she liked to pretend. She had successfully weaved the conversation away from Jamie. She knew something, I was sure of it.

"Where's your car, Sonny?" I wondered now if Jamie had ditched hers, taken Sonny's—a safe escape. Like it seemed my mother had done.

"What use would I have for a car? I don't have a license any-more." She laughed, and I didn't know if it was at me or herself. "Don't believe me?" She leaned closer, and her breath smelled of cigarettes and something sharper. Up close, I could see the veins under her skin, the red lines in her eyes. "Ask your brother." She grinned, like it was a running punch line.

I tried to imagine one of them pulling her over, asking for her license, having her walk a straight line, pass a sobriety test—

She sniffed. "I warned her, you know. Being a Holt isn't all it's cracked up to be. But I guess I don't need to tell you that."

"You warned who? Jamie?" Maybe that, then, was the source of strain between Jamie and her mother.

Sonny shrugged with one shoulder, so I could see the jut of her collarbone, a galaxy of freckles covering her exposed skin. "I always thought that girl was bigger than Mirror Lake. Didn't want to see her stuck here, tied down. The Holts aren't going anywhere." She tapped the ash off her cigarette, watching as it fell to the dirt. "I *told* her she didn't have to get married."

I grimaced, sucking in air through my teeth.

She laughed. "Yeah."

I hadn't understood it either at first. They were twenty-one. Jamie had gotten her associate's degree, but Caden wasn't even finished with school. They would be living off her income alone, as an assistant manager at Reflection Point.

I'd been a bridesmaid, along with Felicity and some of Jamie's new friends I didn't know well. The bridesmaid designation, I thought, was probably because of my father. It wasn't even formally asked of me. Caden sent me the link for the dress. A package arrived in the mail with a bracelet and a piece of stationery that said *Thanks for being a bridesmaid!*

We had all gotten ready downstairs in the church. Jamie commented that she'd had to alter her dress. She smirked and said that at least her boobs looked amazing. I stood on the outskirts of the in-joke and pretended I understood. It was the champagne toast that finally tipped me off. The sparkling cider that had been poured into her glass alone. Skyler was born before the year was out.

"But, as I'm sure you know, my Jamie doesn't like to be told what to do. Never did." She smiled, like she was proud of that fact.

It was part of the reason, I had later decided, that I was wrong: she and Caden did make a decent pair. Both honest in their critiques. Neither afraid to use the sharpest tool at their disposal. I imagined Jamie would hold her own with him.

Maybe she was. Maybe she was using the sharpest tool at her disposal, right now. Leaving him so publicly, with no explanation. Leaving him holding the pieces of their lives.

"I just can't believe she'd leave Skyler behind," I said.

Sonny turned to stare at me, eyes roaming over my face, so that I felt my cheeks flushing red. Of course, kids were left all the time. I had just thought Jamie was different.

"Do you know what happens, Hazel, if you take a child from another parent?"

I shook my head.

"Kidnapping." She took another drag from her cigarette. "Lord knows she's smart enough not to take a child from a *cop*. That's not going to win you any friends in a custody battle. And *definitely* not around here."

A noise from the side of the woods jolted me, like someone was out there. My head whipped around, and I stared into the trees.

I noticed her eyes drifting off in that direction too.

"Animals, Hazel. You've been gone for too long. I know it's easy to forget, after moving to a city. But we live in the woods here. You couldn't imagine the things I see sometimes when I come home after working a night shift."

Sonny stood then, one hand on her knee, trying to hide a grimace. I recognized the move well, from my father—both of their bodies worn down by their physical jobs.

I reached a hand for her elbow to help, before deciding better of it. "Sonny. If you know where she might be . . ." I began, hoping she'd pick up the thread. Maybe I was worrying for nothing, like Gage had said. But the only way I'd be sure was to hear it from her directly.

Sonny narrowed her eyes, taking me in. "What exactly are your intentions here, Hazel?" Then she turned for the house, done with me, with this. "Jamie can handle herself. She doesn't need you chasing after her. Or me, for that matter."

I expected her to do *something*. To act. To be her mother. Help her. Protect her. But hadn't I learned by then that mothers were not all they were cracked up to be either?

"What if she does, Sonny," I said. "Do you know where she would go?"

She looked at me for a beat, as if debating, and then thinking better of it. "This place is her world. Where else would she possibly go?" She stepped back, hand on the screen door, still staring out at the woods. "Heard they pulled your mother's car out of the lake. That true?"

I nodded. "Yeah, seems like she dumped it on the way out of town."

She whistled. "You believe that?"

"What?"

Her eyes searched mine. "I'm asking, do you believe it? Do you believe that's what really happened?"

I tried nodding, but my body felt frozen. "What do you mean?"

"I mean, it seems to me that not everyone makes it out of Mirror Lake so easily." The screen door cried as she pulled it open. "Honestly, Hazel. You're lucky you did."

My skin was covered in goose bumps from the breeze that had cut through the trees, or the impact of Sonny's words, lingering.

———————

I took Sonny's guidance to heart, whether she'd intended to give it or not. *Where else would she possibly go?* I inched past the motel where Sonny worked, scanning the lot for Jamie's car. Then I took the long way around the lake, driving past the Inn. Both lots came up empty.

I didn't know who her close friends were here anymore—what other place she might seek solace. And I had promised I'd wait for Gage to check in with Caden.

I pulled into the garage again, beside my father's truck. I was surprised one of my brothers hadn't taken it by now. I assumed the will stipulated that everything else would go to them.

I carried the groceries inside, and quickly emptied them into the fridge, hoping they were still good.

There was a scent to the house. Something faint and unfamiliar. A remnant of panic. It was a feeling I'd once gotten at an abandoned property—the final time I'd visited one alone. Something that lingered from the people who had last been inside.

Everything here had still been locked up, but I couldn't shake the sense of another presence. I paused, taking in the house. The drip of a faucet. A trail of dirt in the hall. The light over my father's chair, on again.

It was all easily explained: we could have dragged the dirt in from the backyard; washed up in the hall bathroom; forgotten a light switch.

But there was just enough doubt for me to want to check the house, like I did when I saw Jamie's open door. I went room by room, before finally concluding that the feeling had just been left behind from the panic and chaos of the day before; the people in and out of the house; the way I'd left, anxious for home.

As I turned off the light over my father's chair, I wondered if there was an electrical issue with the house. Then I noticed the clock over the stove, flashing midnight.

A power surge, then. Something wreaking havoc on the old appliances. Possibly caused by all the commotion in the backyard the day before. Maybe they'd used the outside outlets for part of the operation, overloading the electrical panel.

I reset the time on the stove, then caught sight of the list on the side of the fridge again: *Check basement. Check garage. Check crawl space.*

I opened the drawer beside the fridge, where he'd always kept a collection of pens. I pulled out a red one now, adding to his list: *Check the breakers.*

Then I threw myself into the house, tackling my own to-do list first, cleaning the kitchen, disinfecting the surfaces, trying to bring an order to the chaos—so that I could take pictures to send to Keira tomorrow, for her professional opinion. I spent the afternoon wiping away the years of purpose and wear, until I could see the bones underneath.

When evening fell, I made dinner, heating up a microwave

meal. I still hadn't heard from Gage, and whether he'd checked in with Caden yet. The longer I went without a call or a text, the more anxious I became.

Tomorrow, I decided, if I hadn't heard, I'd go check the house on my own, once I knew Caden was at work.

Somewhere out back, I saw a light on the lake, flashing on and off. Another boat, just beyond the inlet. The police? Or the press, trying to get more pictures?

I circled the house, turning the lights off one by one, watching until the boat finally drifted out of sight.

———————

A bright light woke me, coming from outside. Much too bright to be the morning sun.

I had to lift my arm to shield my eyes as I sat up in my bed, staring out the double doors. At first I wondered if it was that boat, parked down at the edge of the water. But the beam was too strong. Like headlights, shining straight in.

All I could picture in my half-waking state was a car emerging from the lake, alive, engine rumbling, a hazy shadow behind the wheel—

I stood and approached the windows. The light was directly over the back of the house, shining down, illuminating the lower-level patio and surrounding yard, stark and bright.

I had to squint just to look at it—it seemed like backyard flood-lights had been installed.

I couldn't remember anything like this in all the times I'd vis-ited. And then, as I stood there, it abruptly turned off, and left me staring at my dim reflection in the glass.

I backed away, confused, wondering if this could be part of the electrical issue. I tried my bedroom lights, a quick flash on and off—they seemed to be working normally.

Then the floodlights turned on once again, and a sudden garish white halo exposed the concrete patio. I stood in the middle of my room, watching. And then, a minute later, darkness fell again.

A motion detector?

Maybe set off by the trees, swaying in the wind. Or a cluster of dead leaves, swirling across the ground.

Had I slept through it over the weekend here? Or was there something different about tonight?

I stood perfectly still, peering out into the darkness, until it triggered on once more. This time, I caught a flash of movement—a shadow, at the edge of the halo, quickly disappearing into the dark.

I stared at that circle of light, and then at the place the shadow had just been—farther down toward the lake.

Someone was out there.

Something just outside the circle of light, watching back.

CHAPTER 14

I grabbed my phone and strode quickly out to the rec space, where I had the best view of the backyard. I stared again at the border where the light gave way to shadow, waiting for something to happen.

Then I slid open the back doors, stepping into the cool night. I was still barefoot and in loose pajamas, and I could feel the cool and gritty concrete just outside the sliders. The decking overhead cast everything beyond the patio in shadow, blocking the stars and impeding my long-range visibility.

"Hello?" I called, standing in the halo of light thrown by the motion detector.

I heard only the sound of something buzzing in the trees, crickets in the grass, the water gently lapping against the dirt in response.

"This is private property," I yelled into the night. Imagining that man with his camera from the day before, thinking this was an abandoned home. Imagining the boat I'd seen out there earlier in the evening, just waiting for a chance to explore. Imagining worse.

I listened for sounds from the lake—footsteps on the old dock, or a boat knocking against the wood planks in the current.

But the only noise came from the decking right above me—a creak of wood. Like the deck was straining against the edge of the house in the wind. Only right now, the air was perfectly still.

I twisted the flashlight upward, but couldn't see anything through the wood slats. I remained unmoving, listening—glad I had the phone in my hand.

Suddenly I heard footsteps in the woods, off to the side of our yard, where the trees grew thicker between properties. I spun quickly in that direction, but couldn't see anything beyond the halo of light.

And then I thought: maybe it wasn't a person at all, but an animal. Just like Sonny had warned me. It had been too long since I'd lived in the woods; I was no longer accustomed to the things that roamed in the night.

But something was moving out there. And I was at the disadvantage—exposed, while the other remained in shadow. I turned off the flashlight app and stood still for so long the lights above me turned off, bathing everything in darkness.

The footsteps started up again, and I clapped loudly, hoping to scare it off. Then I backed away, palm out for the handle of the door to the basement.

And then a voice came from the direction of the woods. "Is someone out here?"

I took a step forward, triggering the lights again. I knew that voice. "Nico? What are you doing out here?" I asked.

"The lights kept turning on," Nico said, arm out to block the glare as he exited the woods. "I thought I heard shouting. I didn't know it was you."

He appeared in gym shorts and a white T-shirt and sneakers. His hair seemed more disheveled than normal, and his skin looked a little overexposed and pale in the glare of the floodlights.

We had asked him to keep an eye on the place, and, like all things, he took the request very seriously.

I peered into the trees behind him, frowning. I couldn't see anything but shadows crisscrossing into the distance. "You can see that far?"

"Well, I could see the light flashing. It's pretty intense."

It was. I had to squint just to take him in now.

"It's new, isn't it?" I asked. I couldn't recall an automated light outside my window over Christmas, or any time before. I felt sure it would've woken me, if so.

"I've only been staying here since the fall," he said, joining me on the pad of concrete. "So I can't say for sure."

"You've noticed it, though."

He shifted on his feet. One of his shoelaces had come untied. Or had never been tied, as if he'd slipped them on in a rush. "Sometimes. I assumed it was for the bears. You know how they can get after hibernation. Desperate for anything left in trash cans. We have a light like that over our front trash area, for just that reason."

I nodded. They would do anything to get into the garbage, pulling latched doors off hinges, scattering garbage across the street. So Holt had put our trash enclosures at the end of the driveway, up on the edge of the road.

Still, I wouldn't want bears roaming around the backyard either, rummaging for anything they could find.

"Something else triggered the motion detector," I said. "It wasn't me."

He took a step toward the house, like he was imagining what might be out there too. Then he looked back to me, in my pajamas, barefoot on the concrete.

He ran a hand down his face, disoriented. "I thought you left. I had no idea you were staying here."

"Yeah, well, it was a surprise to me too."

There was another rustling sound down by the edge of the water, and Nico and I both turned to look that way. We couldn't see anything while standing in the light, and I had no intention of stepping outside the perimeter now that I was imagining a hungry bear out there, watching us. I frowned, then slid the door fully open behind me.

"Are you coming in?" I asked. Not exactly an invitation. Not exactly the absence of one either. It was always a dance, with us. A dare. I rubbed my hands over the goose bumps on my arms, the leftover adrenaline buzzing through my limbs.

He tipped his head to the side. It had been so long since we were alone together, like this. But it always felt comfortable when it was just the two of us.

When we were younger, that first year, I believed we had kept things a secret. But Gage must've sensed it anyway. Maybe from the cadence of our conversation, an intimacy in the rhythm of it. A look passing instead of a word. The way I'd do anything to make Nico laugh—the flip and flash of his smile like a shot of adrenaline. And while Gage was willing to share his father, the same couldn't be said for his best friend.

It was something I could only understand years later, when Jamie started seeing Caden. A surprise that came with a sting. That something that had belonged solely to me was in danger of changing.

Gage must've said something. Must've warned him off. Must've given an ultimatum, or talked some sense into him, something like: *She just turned sixteen.* The morality of it all, so Gage-like. He wouldn't have listened when Nico said, *No, it's not like that.* Not exactly.

But that was all in my head, anyway. For all I knew, it was more curt and boy-like: *Are you messing around with my sister?*

God, no.

Either way, Nico had capitulated rapidly and without warning near the end of that summer, and I had never quite gotten over the shock of it. After my mother, I should've grown accustomed to the feeling of being cast aside, developed some foresight, some inner warning system, some deep buried instinct that *You will be left again.* But I was destined to repeat the same fate, again and again.

The truth was, I had believed Nico would be more careful with me. I'd thought that he of all people would understand. But I had put too much pressure on the idea of him, when he was only seventeen himself, and fighting his own demons. So I had forgiven him, just as I had forgiven myself, even if I hadn't quite forgotten.

Nico followed me inside now, whistled slowly when I turned on the rec room lights. He was staring at the far wall, with the series of mirrors, reflecting back slivers of his face, his upper arm, my dark hair.

"Love what you've done with the place. How very gothic."

I laughed. "I can't take credit. That was Holt," I said.

"He didn't have your eye."

"The mirrors are the least of the issues here," I said.

"It's not so bad," he said, hand on the dark green wall, like he could feel the structure underneath, solid through the years. "No bees," he said, and I laughed at him.

He pulled his hand away abruptly, rubbed it against his athletic shorts, as if he were still imagining it. "Please tell me that's the worst thing you've ever seen."

For a moment, I got a flash of the pictures on the wall of the murder room. But if he was thinking of that at all, his face gave nothing away.

"The bees were bad. But termites can be worse," I said. The damage they could do under the surface. You could be standing next to a wall with absolutely no support, not realizing the whole thing could collapse at any time. "People don't realize how often a house could be primed to kill you."

He laughed quickly, the way we did at the absurd. His smile, the game changer. And I wanted more. Wanted to draw him in, and keep him here.

"The worst project, though," I said, "was the haunted one."

"Hazel, don't," he said, covering his face. "I can't take it."

"Okay, science teacher, explain this to me, then." We were circling each other, moving slowly around the room. "We took down the wallpaper in the bedroom of this old colonial that had been abandoned for years, falling to disrepair. And there was literally writing scratched into the wall. *Help us.*"

Even now I couldn't fight the chill.

"Did you call the police?" he asked.

"Yeah, they thought it was probably a joke. But I don't know. Even the workers were weirded out, said they could feel some sort of energy." Our contractor wouldn't even set foot in the room.

"I'm trying not to think about it," he said, staring at the walls of the basement. His reflection caught in the center mirror—eyes wide, but with a small smile.

"The truth is," I said, "most of the issues you can see, those are just surface problems. Easy, honestly. If you can see it, you can fix it. It's the things you don't see that can really hurt you."

He walked around the room, taking things in slowly, in his careful way. Touching the brass frame of the center mirror, running his hand across the top of the dusty computer monitor. His gaze caught on my open bag in the hallway outside my room. I wondered if he could sense my mother's letter—I'd brought it back with me, tucked safely between the layers of clothes. "How long are you staying?" he asked.

"Honestly, I'm not sure. I just feel like I have to be here right now." In the light of the rec room, I was hyperaware of the thin pajamas I was wearing, the distance between me and Nico; the distance between us and the bedroom.

"I get it," he said. "Maybe while you're here, you could come take a look at mine? Make sure it's not primed to kill me?"

"Sure. Just let me know when."

"Whenever you want. I keep a key in the same place as always."

"Jesus, are you trying to get robbed?" Nico used to keep a spare key for himself in the backyard, under a loose slate tile on the edge of the patio. It made sense, when he spent half his time out on the lake in a bathing suit, with no convenient place to store a key. But I remembered what Gage had said about the petty thefts that had been occurring a few months back—kid stuff, he'd said. Nico was a high school teacher. If it *was* kids, I could see his place becoming a high-value target for a dare.

"Well, I don't go around telling most people, Hazel," he said.

The way we tiptoed around each other, the inevitability of it . . . It was a game we'd been playing for over a decade. Part of the thrill. Sometimes I thought it might be the part we both preferred.

"Are you seeing anyone, Nico?" I asked. The truth was, I didn't care. If being left was the low, an ungrounding, then being chosen was the high. The rush of gravity. The free fall of a roller coaster, racing for the ground. No matter what the damage might be after.

Over the years, he'd dated a string of very nice girls who looked at him like he was steady and reliable and responsible, and could never imagine him slinking through the night, letting himself into a home, uninvited.

"No, Hazel." He smiled, though I didn't understand how he wasn't serious about someone by now—he was always so serious about everything.

"Me neither," I said, not that he'd asked. Since our business had taken off, dating had turned complicated and sporadic. I couldn't mix the people I met through work with my personal life, and yet those were the only people I had time to see. Recently, I'd become something of a project for Keira—she continued to set me up with people she knew. But nothing lasted through the first sign of trouble. I left things quickly and without hesitation or regret.

"Does anyone else know you're here?" he asked. That smile again—bridging the time. More than a decade, reduced to a moment.

I almost answered that I'd told my friends I would be here, but I knew that wasn't what he was really asking. I shook my head. "Just you. Just us." A secret, just like we both liked it.

We liked it best when I had to sneak him in. When he had to creep through the yard, undetected. When he had to cover my mouth. When we knew someone might come down the basement steps at any moment.

Sometimes back then, when I was home alone during the day, I'd swim out to the platform and wonder if he was watching. I'd lie back and close my eyes in the summer sun and listen for his footsteps in the yard, the subtle disturbance to the water the moment he entered the lake. The careful arm-over-arm swim until his weight disrupted the balance of the platform, and my stomach swung with it.

The way he'd look toward my house, listen as I'd say *no one's home*, before kissing me, tasting like summer.

Now, as he followed me back to the room that was too small even as a teen, and the bed that was definitely too small for grown adults, I could be more honest with myself.

This was a pattern, and a predictable one at that. We came together in times of high emotion. Of exposed vulnerability. When I felt adrift, and I knew what I needed was a grounding. And I believed it was the same for him.

The first time was after his father's death.

The second, after Caden and Jamie's wedding my junior year, but wasn't that just a cliché—it stretched through my final years of college, in the gaps of time when I'd be home. By then he was working at the school and lived on the other end of the lake. And when I told him I was moving to Charlotte after graduation, he'd only nodded, made no remark about *us* or coming to visit.

He wasn't leaving, and I wasn't staying, and there was nothing secret about driving the two hours back and forth between here and there.

The last time was two years ago over his spring break, when he came to Charlotte for a concert. He texted me out of the blue. I invited him to see the project we'd recently flipped—our first big, lucrative success. We were all riding that high. I offered him my couch, which made him laugh. He'd come out and met my friends, even—which he hadn't done in college. And he told them, after the third round of drinks, that I had once accidentally broken a window with a baseball. But I knew he was wrong. *No, that was Caden.* Back and forth we went, until I pulled out my phone without thinking, laughing. I knew Gage could settle this, and I was still smiling as I scrolled to his number.

Nico had put a hand on mine, firmly. A reminder. A warning. *He doesn't know I'm here.*

I jolted, surprised, before hanging up. *Aren't we a little old for this?* And then, without thinking: *Do you always do whatever my brother says?* But it came out sounding like a dare.

Don't you? he'd countered.

On the way back to my apartment, I'd pushed. *Maybe you should go now.*

It was just another dare, I knew. But he drove off that night without looking back.

And it turned out he could bring me down from a high as easily as he could bring me up from a low. The great equalizer.

What I wanted to tell him: *Did you know I loved you then? Did you know you were the second person to break my heart?*

But I'd never said anything. It was like neither of us knew how to take the second step. Hindered by our history, bound by our secrets. I had learned, since, to protect my heart a little more closely. To hold back a little more deliberately. To proceed with caution and care. We didn't work long-term because, I believed, we were both more interested in the secret.

We loved the idea of the unknown, more than the known.

"Do you hear that?"

Nico sat up in the dark, shirt in his hands.

My dreams, whenever I was back in Mirror Lake, felt too close to reality, so that it always took me an extra second to be sure. To process what was real, and what was not, in bright flashes: *Nico, in my bed. His face just over mine. A whisper that he'd missed me. That he always missed me—*

A loud, high-pitched series of beeps broke through the memory, and then silence again.

"Is that the smoke detector?" he asked, slipping off the side of the bed that we'd long since outgrown. The beeping cut through the house again, loud and jarring. He dressed quickly, a rustle of clothes, a stumble for shoes.

I imagined loose wires in the walls, sparking. A tangle of cords in the insulation, fraying. The dangers hidden under the surface of the house.

But the noise was periodic—not the continuous high-pitched alarm of a fire.

"Batteries," I said, slower to wake and get moving.

He frowned. "Better check to be sure."

I stood beside him, disoriented. I grabbed my phone and took the steps up to the main level, slightly nauseated by the late hour, trying to determine the source of the beeping. He turned on the hall light, and I instinctively closed my eyes.

No smoke. Nothing burning.

The smoke detector in the kitchen was beeping periodically. The one down the hall was echoing on a delay. The clock over the stove was flashing again, like there'd been another power surge.

"Do you have batteries?" he asked. The smoke detectors here were old and hardwired; they'd continue this way until I addressed the offending unit.

I pulled out the utility drawer, rumbling through old pens and utensils and loose batteries. "Just double-A, triple-A." I groaned. "No nine-volt."

His eyes went to the clock over the stove. "What time is it? I didn't bring my phone. . . ."

"Three in the morning," I said, checking mine.

Now he was the one to groan. "I have to be up in two hours."

"Go," I said. "Save yourself."

He stared back at me, like he was debating something.

The thing about a first love was that you told them everything.

All the secrets, all the parts that made you into who you had become. Before you boxed them up, stacked them away. But they still had them: all the pieces that you eventually learned not to share with others, from experience.

He crossed the room, one hand sliding to my lower back, pulling me to him. "I'm really glad you're here, Hazel," he said, before lowering his mouth to mine. A little slower than earlier. A little more deliberate.

The other thing about a first love was that they became the point to which all others would be compared, and found lacking.

He pulled back at the next series of beeps, cringing.

"Seriously," I said, hands on his chest. "Go." I gave him a playful push—a permission, this time, to leave.

I watched as he slowly eased out the back doors to the deck, as if he were trying to avoid detection. He waved once before sliding it shut. The floodlights caught him as he crossed the backyard, and he paused, looking around, before realizing that he was the trigger.

He slipped out of the halo of light, and disappeared into the night, like a ghost.

CHAPTER 15

The periodic beeping was cutting through each of the rooms, in a delayed echo. All of the smoke detectors were in on it now, in different rhythms.

Through the kitchen windows, the sunrise crested the mountains in the distance, casting an eerie orange glow over everything. A boat appeared anchored just outside the entrance of our alcove, and I leaned closer, watching it for a moment, as it rocked back and forth in the current. Someone fishing, I thought. Or were they staring at the house?

I backed away, imagining them watching me, peering out.

I was growing paranoid, and the noise hadn't helped.

I dragged a kitchen chair over to the nearest smoke detector, and balanced precariously on top. I wasn't sure which device was the main culprit, but I wanted to check how many batteries it took—I'd probably have to replace them all, to be safe.

But when I pulled the detector down, wires still connected to the ceiling, I was confused to see there was nothing at all inside. The single battery compartment was empty.

I moved down the hall to the device outside the office, unscrewed it, and frowned. No battery.

I checked them all, one by one. On the main level, none of the smoke detectors had batteries inside. I thought that's what usually kept them from beeping, but now I wondered if it was just another power surge that had kicked the chain off.

In the basement, there were two smoke detectors. The device in the rec space was also missing a battery. Last, I stood on the edge of my bed to check the one in the bedroom. Here, there was a single 9-volt battery connected to the unit. It was the only one still intact.

At least I knew exactly how many to buy.

My father always said if you wanted to find someone in Mirror Lake, all you had to do was drive around the loop. You were bound to run into them, either coming or going.

Even off the main road, it wasn't easy to go unnoticed. The roads forked and narrowed and dead-ended. People took note of unfamiliar vehicles. There was no way I could swing by Caden's place to check if Jamie was there without someone seeing me go by. I needed to wait until I was sure he would be at work—preferably out on the lake, with an additional layer of distance between us.

But the Country Store should be opening right about now. At least I could tackle the smoke detectors in the meantime.

Just as I passed the front windows, keys in hand, I noticed a car pulling in to the top of the drive. I couldn't tell who was inside, but I knew enough to recognize who it wasn't: it wasn't my brothers; it wasn't a police car; it wasn't anyone who had liberty to be here.

The driver's side door opened as I walked up the slope to investigate. A loafer; khaki pants; hand on the doorframe as he pulled himself out.

"Hazel?" Roy asked, squinting, his sunglasses on top of his graying hair. "I didn't know you'd be here." He took a tentative step, as if he could tell something was off by the speed of my stride.

"Oh," I said, slowing to a halt. "I thought you were someone snooping around." I gestured behind me. "I thought I saw a boat out there last night. And there's another one sitting at the edge of the inlet right now."

He sighed, then closed the car door behind him. "I heard there might be some folks arriving in town. The news of a second car was bound to draw some amateur detectives out there." He rolled his eyes. "Buy a piece of sonar and suddenly everyone's an expert. Let me know if you need me to send someone a letter."

"Thanks," I said. I wasn't sure how much impact that would have, considering his letter heading would be for Holt Family Law, specializing in divorce and various estate issues. But I'd take what I could get.

I looked again at his car, still idling. "Were you coming by for something?"

He gestured to the black mailbox beside him with our house number displayed in gold reflective stickers. "I've been stopping by to check the mail, couple times a week. Keep it from overflowing. Make sure there's nothing important."

"Oh, thanks," I said, momentarily taken aback. How easy it had been not to think of all the logistics involved in a death. The people who had to be told. The bills that had to be paid. The services that had to be canceled.

Roy had experience. He had temporarily moved in here after Audrey died, to help my dad and the boys get through. He'd cooked dinners, handled bills, kept things moving until his brother could restart his life. I assumed this was why both Gage and Caden had closer relationships with him than I did. He'd been here in that time of vulnerability. He'd seen them through the worst of it. Got them all back on their feet. I preferred thinking that, to the alternative: that Roy had never viewed me as family himself.

Either way, he was keenly aware of the logistics involved in situations like this.

I thought of the batteries in the smoke detectors that needed to be replaced, and the electrical system that seemed to keep overloading. "Hey, Roy, the power bills, stuff like that. How are they being paid right now?"

"Should be automated from his account. At least I'm assuming he has it set up that way. I haven't seen any past-due notices anyway. It's generally easiest just to let that ride until everything transfers after probate. You're not responsible for the bills until the house is yours, Hazel."

I nodded. "Are you sure the payments are going through, though? Will things get shut off if not?"

He opened the mailbox and pulled out a stack of envelopes, flipping through them. "You can check for yourself, if you want. Just call the companies, give the account number." He handed me the stack. "Worst case, we just get things turned back on after the transfer."

Except I was staying here, in this house. And right now I needed power and Wi-Fi, at the bare minimum.

I took the stack from his outstretched hand.

"This could take a while, Hazel," he said, not letting go of the mail. "If Caden goes forward with his challenge." He swallowed, looked off to the side. "In my professional opinion, he's not going to win. But it is going to slow things down."

I nodded, then pulled the stack from his grip.

"What I'm saying is, he might not take too kindly to you staying here in the interim."

"I wasn't planning on advertising it," I said. Anyway, Caden had given me his key. I didn't see how he could use this against me after the scene he'd made of placing the house key on the entryway table.

Roy raised an eyebrow. "How long, do you think, before he notices?"

I understood. It had taken Roy just over twelve hours. It wouldn't be long before everyone in town found out.

The Country Store was still run by the same family who owned it when I was in high school, and a boy in my grade named Austin

Mahoney had worked here most summers, for his parents. Now there was a younger kid behind the register, but with the same soft, rounded features. His eyes were bright blue, and he was hunched over a fishing magazine that bore the same symbol as his ball cap.

He barely looked up as I passed.

I paused on the way up the first aisle, noticing a collection of *Private Property* signs tucked into a magazine display case. I picked one up—I assumed they were in high demand in our area, considering they kept them stocked. It was understandable, with the large wooded lots and the way the lake touched the shore in sections that seemed to have no houses. There were trails—both officially marked and not—that wove through the woods, stretching up the bowl. No one could be sure where a property line began. It was easy to wander, to cross over, to explore.

A sign was often an effective deterrent.

I made my way to the battery section, taking the only packets of 9-volts on display.

"I'm going to need some more of these," I said, sliding the two packs across the countertop.

He grinned, revealing a slight gap between his front teeth. "Smoke detectors?" he asked.

"How'd you guess."

"It's the one thing that has people coming in either first or last thing, looking for nine-volt batteries." He pursed his lips, before twisting off his stool. "Let me check."

He disappeared into the back room, just as someone else came through the entrance.

I turned to see Nico, dressed for work, carrying an insulated mug in one hand, his phone out in the other.

He paused when he saw me standing there, smiled a small, secret grin.

"Hazel," he said in greeting, and my heart immediately plummeted to my stomach, same as it did when I'd come home from college and wait for him to stop by, in the guise of visiting my brother. Watch as he slowly made his way closer—shaking my father's hand, laughing at something Gage said—a slow-motion game, a lesson in practice and patience. Eyes finally sliding over to me, one side of his mouth lifting, eyes sparkling—*Hazel*, he'd say, just that single word, just like that. I'd have to bite the inside of my cheek to stop the ridiculous smile.

I felt myself doing that now, but smiling all the same.

"Morning necessities," he said, raising his mug, then heading for the coffee dispenser beside the counter.

I held up a pack of batteries. "Stocking up."

The kid emerged from the back room with an armful of batteries. "It's your lucky day," he said. "How many of these do you need, exactly? Oh, hey, Mr. Pritchard." He drew the *hey* out, in a level of casual familiarity.

"Levi," Nico responded, placing two coffees on the counter and handing Levi a ten, before sliding one of the cups my way.

Levi glanced quickly from Nico to me, then back to the register.

"I hope you finished your homework," Nico said, taking a sip of his coffee.

Levi lifted the magazine to show the biology worksheet below. "Done," he said.

Nico dropped the change into the tips jar beside the register, then turned for the door. "See you later," he called.

For a second I didn't know which of us he was talking to, and Levi smiled broadly at me, slow and knowing, like a Cheshire cat.

———

In the end, I left with four packs of 9-volt batteries, a three-pack of *Private Property* signs, and a mediocre coffee that I did, in fact, need. I'd probably have to come back within a day for more supplies, once I got a good look at the house. But this would do for now.

It was obvious that this place would slowly fall apart without oversight. I'd seen it happen so quickly on older properties. First, it would be the smoke detector batteries. Later: pipes rusting, roots pushing into the foundation of the house. How easily something could cause a spark. A gas leak. A water leak.

And without power, it could get even worse.

I let myself in through the front door, and the light over my dad's chair was on again. I frowned, reaching over to turn it off, then decided to unplug it from the wall. It was unnerving me, especially after the story I'd told Nico about the haunted remodel.

At the base of the outlet, I saw the issue. The light was on a timer, the dial slowly ticking down. I laughed out loud, nervous energy dissipating into the room. It must've been scheduled to turn on in the night, to give the illusion of someone sitting in the front room. And with the power surges, it had shifted off schedule.

I added the batteries to the smoke detectors, one by one, until finally, blissfully, the beeping subsided. I felt my shoulders lowering, the tension seeping out of my neck muscles.

I passed the rest of the morning by taking pictures of the house for Keira, earbuds in, letting the music drown out the desolate silence.

I stepped out back to take photos of the lower level, since the light was always most stunning there in the morning. But the yard, usually a selling feature, was torn up from both the drought and the activity. There were plywood boards left behind by the tow company, and deep gouges where the tires of the truck had drifted into the yard. At the edge of the lake, a depression in the mud marked the spot where the car had emerged, clumps of sludge left behind in its place.

It was still early, and the sun glared off the lake in an orange misty haze, like I could almost see the water evaporating. I took a picture of the view, cutting out the damage to the yard.

At least the boat from earlier was gone. But as I watched, two blue kayaks drifted by the edge of the inlet. I slowly lowered my phone, tracing their path. I was growing paranoid—couldn't tell whether they were just on a morning workout or trying to catch a glimpse of the latest scene. Maybe both.

I removed my earbuds, as if I might hear the low hum of their conversation. But there were just the familiar sounds of morning: the birds in the trees; a squirrel jumping from branch to branch, shaking the leaves overhead; the gentle splash of an oar, or a fish.

I spun and took a few shots of the house and deck with my phone, then continued inside.

The rest of the house was easy to photograph, now that the surfaces had been cleaned. I took a shot of every living space, bathroom, and bedroom.

After texting Keira the photos one by one, I checked on the bills. If we *were* going to flip it to sell, I'd need to start calculating the real expenses.

I found the latest electrical bill in the pile of mail. It was due next week, and I hoped, like Roy said, that my father had automated payments set up. I was also hoping he still used the home computer for personal use, since his work laptop wasn't currently in his office upstairs.

The old desktop had somehow still been on when I arrived. But judging by the labored whirr of the computer tower now, I wasn't sure whether it would boot up at all. An error message popped up, warning of prior improper shutdown, asking if I'd like to recover previously in-use items. I clicked yes and hoped for the best.

Slowly, programs opened up, coupled with warnings that progress had not been properly saved. I couldn't believe he still used this old model. But that was very much like him, sticking with the tech he was most comfortable with. We couldn't even get him to carry a personal cell phone, instead using the unreliable combination of his radio, his department-issued work line, and the home landline.

Right now I was incredibly thankful for his habits. And for the fact that he'd bookmarked his most visited pages and never cleared his cookies, so that usernames were already filled in. All I needed were his passwords. I knew he'd left the list in the safe. I'd looked over Caden's shoulder, shared his disbelief that he'd used almost the same combinations for everything. But Gage had taken all the paperwork from the office.

I tried it now, *Mirror Lake*, his birthday. Then his birthday plus *Mirror Lake*. Neither worked.

A flash of movement jarred me. When I looked up, it was only the mirrors, reflecting the outside. The empty patio, the steps. The trees, the lake. Everything appeared still.

Maybe a bird or another animal had crossed the frame.

Sitting here, where my father so often had, the mirrors suddenly seemed intentional. Set up five-across for a wide view of the yard and the lake behind him.

I started to wonder if my father, with his light on a timer in the den and motion detector in the back and mirrors positioned to show the outside, even when he was facing away, had been growing paranoid. As if the burglaries Gage had told me about had also been eating at him—making him wary of things that weren't there.

The floodlights alone could make anyone jumpy. I'd imagined so many dangers outside the circle of light before Nico showed up.

I opened my father's personal email now, and thankfully, I was automatically logged in. His inbox was completely empty. I wasn't too surprised that he was an inbox-zero personality. Or that he'd set up filters for junk mail. Now that I knew I had access, I clicked the *forgot password* button for the bank, and used the email to reset it myself. I'd tell Gage later, so he could update the spreadsheet.

Then I was in.

He had both a savings account and a checking account. But both balances seemed worryingly low. If his bills were being auto-paid from here, they might not all clear.

I felt my back teeth clenching. Of course, Gage and Caden had moved the money already. Of course.

Hadn't Roy warned me? The boys had direct access, probably through linked accounts. The house was the only thing left for me, and Caden wanted his hands on this too.

I wondered how long they had waited before raiding the accounts.

I opened the checking account, and saw that the bills had

successfully been drafted from here last month. Just enough money to do so, it seemed. There would not be a second month of success. I'd have to talk to Roy.

But I didn't see a large transfer of money going out, after his death. Nothing to indicate that the money had been moved.

Instead, there were increments of money being withdrawn in cash, month by month, before he died. It seemed like he took the maximum amount, whenever he could.

I opened the savings account. Money transferred over to the checking almost as quickly as it went in from his biweekly salary direct deposits.

I exited out of the account, disturbed.

Did Gage and Caden already know? Had they checked the accounts immediately, and realized the truth?

At the time of his death, our father had nothing left. Nothing but an old truck in the garage, and this house.

Maybe when Gage said that *everything's in the house*, he meant the value, not the list of information and assets.

Perry Holt had slowly and methodically paid off this house, and it was ours.

Except now it was only mine.

CHAPTER 16

I was searching the accounts again, top to bottom, when another flash of movement crossed the mirrors. I spun around, then stayed perfectly still. Word of the break-ins was getting into my head too. Gage had said it was just kid stuff—empty homes—but school was currently in session.

I turned on the television in the rec space, letting it play the local news.

Upstairs, I flipped on a few lights and turned on the television there too, so anyone who might be sneaking around would know: *This house is occupied.*

And then, while passing the back doors, I *did* see people, trying to pull a small motorized boat closer to the dock.

Judging from the way the boat hovered, rocking, I was guessing they had almost run aground. Our dock barely stretched over the water now, and I knew how quickly the drop-off went from shallow to deep, and vice versa.

I grabbed the *Private Property* signs I'd just purchased and jogged down the deck steps, my sneakers echoing on the space below.

They must've seen me coming, striding down the slope of the

yard. But they didn't stop until I was standing just before the edge of the dock.

As I approached, the passengers came into focus: a man and a woman, both fit and towheaded, the type that made it seem they spent their year out in the sun, surfing. The woman had her hair tied back in a long French braid and wore a dark, short-sleeve wetsuit. The man wore a T-shirt scrawled with script that I couldn't quite read.

He had a recording device in his hand, and he seemed to be pointing it right at me.

"This is private property," I said, staking the sign into the mud, for impact.

"The lake isn't," the man called, from yards away. Like I hadn't witnessed their attempt at docking. They were now drifting beside the swim platform.

"This is," I said, gesturing to the disintegrating wood of our dock. The black, rotted edges had become visible, and I wasn't sure if it was safe to walk on. It was another item to add to the list on the fridge: *Check dock.*

"And *that* is," I said, gesturing to the swim platform. I had a feeling that was going to be their next attempt. "This cove is only for these private residences," I said, which wasn't entirely true, legally speaking. None of us could claim ownership of the lake. "Are you *taping* me?"

He made a big show of raising his hands, the device still in his grip. "We weren't taping *you*, but you kinda walked into the frame all on your own."

The woman stepped out from the captain's chair. "Was it you who found the car here?" she asked. There was a waterproof camera strapped to her upper arm, wrapped around her wetsuit.

Now I fully understood why Caden would keep his daughter inside, away from the questions of strangers, prying for details.

"Not me," I said.

The man looked to the house and squinted. "Do you live up there?"

I nodded, not because I wanted him to know where I lived, but because I wanted him to know I was in charge here.

His eyes trailed across the property. "Who else lives there?"

I almost took the bait, but years of living alone in a city had wizened me to the leading questions of strange men.

"None of your business. As I said, these are private residences."

He raised one single, arching eyebrow, as if I were the one acting suspiciously.

"I can get you the number for our lawyer, if you'd like. You can take this up with him. His name is Roy Holt."

The man raised his hands, as if I had accused him of stealing something, instead of trying to anchor to my platform, my dock, in order to check out the secrets underneath. He had just attempted to trespass, and I'd caught him in the act.

"We're doing a public service here," he said. "If there are more cars hidden in the lake, shouldn't people know something dangerous has been going on around here?"

I wasn't about to tell them that the car they'd found here was left behind by my criminal mom when she fled. Or that my brothers—both cops—believed the first was just an insurance scam. I didn't even blame these strangers for their assumptions. Hadn't I pictured it myself? A body strapped into a seat, or stuffed into a trunk? Someone who had tried to free themselves, desperate for the surface?

"There's nothing else here," I said. "The police boat has already been through."

"Did they look around? Or were they just here for the thing someone told them about?" the woman asked. They spoke in the same cadence, the same leading tone. Siblings, I decided.

I didn't answer, but I rolled my eyes. The truth was, I didn't know.

"Because," she continued, picking up steam, "the police aren't gonna go searching for a problem. They'll pick it up after you find it for them. That's it."

She gestured to the bucket behind her, beside the gear I hadn't noticed. "There's plenty out here they haven't found."

"What's that?" I asked, picturing the other boat I'd seen this morning. I'd assumed—hoped, even—that they'd just been fishing.

"Fishing magnet," she said, smiling wide, her teeth bleached white. "You'd be amazed, the things people pull up."

"The things people dump in the lake, she means," the man added, with an equally toothy smile. They could really pass for twins. "Like no one will ever find it."

I shuddered, imagining what else they might be looking for. What else they might uncover.

"And who are you, exactly?" I asked. They seemed about my age, if that. The cameras made me nervous.

"Miles," he said, and then tipped his head to the woman. "Amber." Then he gestured to the logo on his shirt. "Water Hunters."

Roy had warned me about this. It hadn't taken long at all.

I guessed that they made some web series or social media clips. The woman dipping into the lake to show what lay underneath, the man providing commentary from above. Both of them pulling up old objects that had long since been discarded, in some amateur treasure hunt.

"Let me just ask you this, and then we're gone," Amber said. "Aren't you worried about who might be living next door to you?"

I let out a laugh, but it came out shaky. I forced a smile. "I know exactly who lives next door to me."

She smiled, wide and knowing. "That's what everyone says, before they don't."

And in her knowing smile, I saw pictures hanging inside that hidden room next door. I saw a man who had been consumed by something. And then I wondered about those photos again, maybe for the first time in all the time since we were kids. I had assumed they were from crime scenes from his prior job. And suddenly, in a rush of goose bumps, I imagined something else: photos he had taken himself.

The twisted limbs. The hair splayed in dirt. A trail of blood—

How well had I known Nicholas Pritchard? He was Dad's partner up until the day he'd died by suicide. He'd been like family. A big personality—loud and jovial. And suddenly I wondered: Was someone investigating him before his death? Did someone *know* what he was hiding?

I shivered, imagining something much darker and violent and criminal in those pictures. Something maybe only Gage and Nico had understood then.

But my next thought was that it had nothing to do with my mother, or the cars. It couldn't.

My mother had left me a note.

She had withdrawn money from the accounts. She had taken any jewelry she could get her hands on. She was not some victim of a Mirror Lake serial killer.

These Water Hunters were searching for something that didn't exist. Nicholas Pritchard was dead.

"There aren't any victims here," I said.

"No, there aren't any victims *found*," she said—as if that's what they were actually looking for. "Yet."

Images from my nightmare returned—the lake, the dark, the halo of hair, and my mother's terrible scream. The past, reaching out for me—

"Stop," I said abruptly. I needed this to stop right now. "Hold on." I took out my phone, then aimed it in their direction. "Stay very still."

"What are you doing?" Miles said, holding out a hand, to block the shot.

"Just getting some footage for my lawyer, so he can reach you later. Seems only fair," I said, gesturing to the camera in his hand as well.

"Jesus, fine," he said, starting the engine, the boat revving as he turned it around.

Amber remained facing me—or facing the house—as they

sped away. Ignoring the No Wake Zone, drawing attention. They wouldn't get very far like that.

I staked another *Private Property* sign for good measure—this time just at the edge of the woods, between my house and Nico's. Then I left, the television still on inside.

Gage still hadn't called me, but I understood he had pressing issues he was dealing with. I drove toward the station, hoping to see Caden's car, before swinging by his house and checking in myself.

The headquarters of the Mirror Lake Police Department was a low brick building, set at an intersection on Main Street, with two walls of glass windows, and a lot full of cars mostly visible from the front. There were generally only a dozen or so people full-time on the force, in various roles, and I could probably still name the majority of them. I'd probably gone to school with half of them.

But I didn't see Caden's car in the lot. He usually left it here, then walked to the police boat launch across the street, beside Reflection Point. But I didn't know his schedule. I didn't want to risk it. I decided to grab lunch at Reflection Point across the way while I waited—there were other people in town who knew Jamie, who might've heard more. My brother wasn't the only one who could find out the truth.

Felicity was working behind the bar, where an older man already had a beer and sandwich in front of him. He was turned away from me, watching the television overhead, but I recognized him immediately. The scruffy salt-and-pepper beard, ruddy cheeks, the exposed skin of his arms right on the cusp between sunburned and deeply tanned: Pete Henderson. He had been in our house the day my mother went missing. He'd officially retired not long after.

Felicity greeted me curtly as I took the seat a few spots down from Pete, then slid a menu in front of me. Her nails were painted a matte pale blue, almost matching the color of her eyes.

Felicity kept her dark hair deeply parted, sleek straight, choppy at the edges. Her left arm was covered in a sleeve of colorful tattoos. As usual, she was wearing black jeans and a black muscle tank, but I wasn't sure if that was just the uniform.

I ordered a Coke and a grilled cheese, the specialty for those in the know, and tried to think of how best to broach the topic of Jamie.

The noon news update featured a young woman with a microphone standing at the curve in the road near the missing guardrail, Mirror Lake stretching behind her. Felicity changed the channel, then handed the remote to Pete. "Please, find something else," she said.

Pete registered me beside him. "Hiya, kiddo," he said, face splitting into a warm smile. "Good to see you back in town."

Pete had always been the softest of the men I knew in the department. There was probably a reason my interrogation hadn't fallen to him.

I lifted my hand in greeting. "Good to see you too. I missed you last week." I couldn't remember seeing him at the celebration of life. But it could've just been me, slinking around the edges, the sea of people in uniform blurring together.

"Well, I was sitting at this very spot," he said, and then laughed. "Figured I could celebrate Holt just as good from here. If he'd made it to retirement, I'm sure he would've been right here beside me." He raised his glass toward me now, as if in toast.

Felicity smiled warmly at him. "My very best customer."

Eventually, Pete settled on ESPN, which all agreed was the best alternative.

"I ran into Sonny yesterday," I said to Felicity. "She told me she lost her car."

Felicity's eyes widened. "Lost her license anyway. Jamie drops off groceries."

"Oh, I got the impression they weren't really speaking much."

"Well, she is her mother. Despite the circumstances."

Something twinged in my side. I took a stab now: "My brother pulled her over?"

Felicity didn't answer, using a new customer as an excuse to slip from the conversation. I knew it was because her rule as a bartender was to listen, not to spread gossip.

Pete leaned his thick arms across the bar. The backs of his hands had turned weathered, a series of pale scars cutting through the deeper tan. "Can you believe that? Little Holt." He shook his head—a familiar refrain. "Your father would've never. No family discount even." He gave me a knowing smile.

If Felicity tried to avoid gossip, Pete was the opposite. "Though can't say he's wrong, exactly. I passed Sonny's bike in the parking lot of the ABC liquor store this morning. Old habits die hard." He laughed to himself, then picked up his empty glass. "Not that I should talk." He gave me an exaggerated wink, before calling for a refill.

Felicity deposited my plate of grilled cheese in front of me, and I breathed it in—along with a sense of peace and nostalgia. "Have you heard from Jamie recently?" I asked, picking up a steaming half of the sandwich.

"Um, not for a bit, no. She doesn't work here anymore. Not in ages." She stopped sometime after Caden officially joined the department, and she could be home with Skyler.

"No, I know. I was just trying to catch her for lunch today."

Felicity looked up sharply. "She's meeting you *here*?"

I shrugged. "I don't know. I only have her landline in my phone. I'm not sure if I have the right number for her cell. Can I check?"

She hesitated for a beat, before sliding me her cell with Jamie's number pulled up. Then she went to help the new customer across the bar. I checked it off my own—it was indeed the same. I tried it again now, but it still went straight to an automated voicemail.

While Felicity was turned away, I checked the most recent

texts or calls to Jamie as well. They hadn't been in touch in quite a while.

I placed Felicity's cell back on the other side of the bar, but not before I saw Pete watching me closely, eyes cut to the side.

I opened my mouth to say something, but then his gaze drifted over my shoulder.

Serena and Al Flores walked in to join a group in uniform in the main dining area. "Here comes the lunch crew."

I didn't see Caden with them, but it hadn't occurred to me that he might pull into the lot and catch me here instead.

Al veered in our direction, greeting Pete with a hand on the shoulder, reminding him about the Memorial Day barbecue this weekend. Then he turned to me, mouth in a tight smile, in a way that made me wonder if he'd come over for me primarily. "Always nice to see you, Hazel. Everything going okay at the house?"

I nodded, not wanting to make any small talk.

"If you're still here this weekend, you know where to find us."

I'd spent plenty of long weekends over at the Flores property, before my mother had disappeared.

Al unfolded a piece of paper. "Felicity," he called, smoothing it on the counter. "You know the Falkner kid?"

She paused for a second. "Max, right?" Al Flores nodded. "I know the name," she continued, "not the face."

"Senior," he said. "Just turned eighteen. Parents haven't seen him since Monday. Didn't realize he was gone until they went to wake him up for school yesterday morning," he said.

Felicity leaned over the bar top, frowning. "Haven't seen him around here, Al," she said.

I stared at the photograph, the dark shaggy hair and straight teeth, the baby-fat cheeks with the dimple. Al Flores looked to Pete, then to me. We both shook our heads.

So this must've been what had Gage so occupied. Max Falkner. *People who are actually missing*, he'd said.

"Runaway?" Pete asked, straightening up, wiping the corners of his mouth. Like the case gave him a spark. A jolt.

"Possible, but he left just about everything behind, if so. He's supposed to graduate in a couple weeks. Not a bad student, from what I hear."

They called him a kid, but he was eighteen, and the rules were a little different after that. He was entitled to leave. But small towns worked differently; plenty of the officers in the department probably knew the family personally.

"Mind keeping this around?" he asked.

"Sure," she said, sliding the page across the bar top.

"If you hear anything, give Gage a call," he said, tapping the counter between us. "It's his case. We're just helping with the canvassing."

I motioned for the check as Al joined the group around the corner. Pete tipped the rest of his new drink back. Unlike my father, he had gotten out as soon as timing allowed. Spent his days fishing in the mornings and drinking in the afternoons, catching up on gossip from the civilian side.

"Do my brothers usually come here for lunch too?" I asked Pete.

"Sometimes," he said. "Depends."

I had to leave before Caden found out I was here. How long before either Al or Serena mentioned it in passing? *Just saw Hazel at Reflection Point.*

Felicity slipped into the kitchen again after I signed my check, and Pete grinned. "You're not the only one trying to stay under the radar. Little Holt and Felicity, they like to pretend they don't know each other now," he said, lowering his voice. "Which only makes it more obvious." He winked.

I pushed back from the table, but he reached an arm out, his cold, callused hand circling my wrist. "Also, hon, Jamie doesn't come here anymore." He smiled tightly, as if to let me know he was on to me.

My stomach sank at his implication. The sudden lack of texts between Jamie and Felicity. The strain between Caden and Jamie. Rumors of an affair had made it as far as Pete Henderson.

Maybe Jamie leaving was a simple thing, after all. Something even her mother understood.

She'd caught them. Or at least heard the rumors around town, felt the eyes of people watching—knowing. And so she'd left, abruptly and publicly, for him to pick up the pieces.

But she'd left her daughter behind, and she didn't tell anyone where she was going. As if she had reason to be truly afraid. No one had heard from her since, that I could tell.

Her phone was off, as if she didn't want to be contacted.

Or as if she didn't want to be traced.

On the way, before I lost service, I tried their landline—no one answered.

I wove off the main drive, cutting up the bowl, taking the circular, unpaved road toward Jamie and Caden's house. I parked right in front of the entrance, and grabbed Skyler's backpack from the passenger seat. There were no cars out front, but I couldn't see into the garage.

The curtains were pulled closed, but I peered between a gap before knocking—the house seemed dark.

I rang the doorbell, then held my breath at the silence.

Nothing.

I tried the door handle, but it was locked. I hoped maybe the back would be open, but I also wondered whether Skyler might've carried a house key in her backpack.

The main compartment held only a few printed-out coloring pages and a sheet of stickers. Two pencils with push-on erasers shifted at the base.

I unzipped the smaller front pocket, reaching my fingers into the corners. There was nothing inside but a loose paper clip and a wrapped piece of candy. And something that felt like an index card. I pulled it out and saw that it was a picture instead.

I recognized the scene immediately, in the drive of the front yard I knew so well. Two small children, Caden and Gage, were sitting together with their mother, the lake stretching behind them. She must've taken it from my house, when she and Jamie were looking through the pictures—

The sound of wheels on the unpaved road made my heart race, and I quickly turned in that direction, hoping the car would drive on by. No such luck. I rushed to tuck the photo in my back pocket. Then I smiled like I'd been waiting for them. I held the backpack out as a gesture, or excuse, as Caden, and then Skyler, exited his gray Honda sedan. Though he was in uniform, he must not have been at work just now.

Caden's steps didn't falter as he approached, and part of me wondered if he'd known I was here. If there was, indeed, some sort of camera set up that alerted him.

Skyler didn't run toward me either.

"Go on inside, Skyler. I'll be right there," he said. He unlocked the front door and pushed it open, and Skyler kept her head down as she skirted inside. She looked pale, blond bangs damp and clinging to her forehead.

My gaze trailed after her, something both unsettling and familiar in her demeanor.

"She left this in my car," I said, by way of explanation.

He frowned at the backpack in my hand, then took it from my grip. "You drove all the way back to bring this by?" Incredulous, as he had every right to be.

"I called the house yesterday, but your babysitter picked up. I was worried."

"Skyler hasn't been feeling well. I took off this afternoon to take her to the doctor. He said there's some virus going around school." He shifted his jaw back and forth, gaze locked on mine, like he was daring me to question him. "What else can I do for you today, Hazel?"

"I stopped to see Sonny on my way in."

His face didn't change. If he was surprised, he didn't show it. Instead, he stared back, unblinking. "And why would you do that?"

"I thought Jamie might be there. But she said she hasn't heard from her either."

"Jamie wouldn't go there. She told Sonny to clean up her act, and she wouldn't. She doesn't bring Skyler around anymore."

"Yeah, I heard she lost her license. I'm sure that went over well."

He tipped his head slowly to one side, eyes slightly narrowed. "After she got her third DUI."

Maybe it really was simple: Skyler was sick; Jamie left because of an affair; and Sonny wasn't worried because she knew.

"Look, I just want to know she's okay. She seemed fine on Sunday, and then . . ." I trailed off, letting him fill in the blanks. "What happened, Caden?"

"I would *love* to know that too." He took a step closer, veins in his neck clearly visible. "The only thing that changed here is *you*, Hazel. *That's* what happened. So you tell me. Because I would really like to know what the fuck you said to my wife—what lies you told to make her angry enough to leave."

"I didn't say anything, but I heard about *you*—"

The door creaked open, and Skyler poked her head out. He took a step back, unclenched his fists, remembering himself. Skyler's sudden presence seemed like the only reason he didn't say anything else, didn't *do* anything else. The levels of his anger were so high.

Her eyes cut briefly up to her father, before sliding away.

"Can I have a lemonade?" she asked. And suddenly, I knew what had unsettled me about her demeanor. It wasn't that she was acting sick, or even afraid. It was the silence, the stillness. Something I'd felt only once before: when you were too young to know what you could—or should—say.

Caden nodded, and she pulled the door shut behind her again. I stared at the space she'd just been, something stirring in my gut.

Wrong. Everything here was wrong. Caden was lying to me, and Skyler knew something too. Everyone was keeping secrets here.

Maybe that was the thing that bound us all.

Caden's fingers drummed against the side of his leg. A fidget. A tell. "You're very good at telling stories, Hazel. No surprise. You learned from the best. I wonder what you told my dad to get him to leave you the house."

I shook my head, steeled my nerve. "I know you're contesting the will." Everything out in the open, then.

"Your mother was a con artist, and you're just like her."

"My mother's car was just pulled from the lake behind the house!" I shouted, knowing Skyler could probably hear me. "Has it occurred to you that maybe you were wrong about her too?"

"I can't tell whether you're really that naive or doing this intentionally." He shifted a step closer. "I could *never* tell what you were up to. I just know that you've been in the business of taking from me since the day you walked into our lives."

Something prickled at the back of my neck, telling me to *move.* There was something simmering under the surface in him. Something he'd always been very, very careful to keep hidden. But I could feel it now, threatening to come out. If Skyler wasn't right inside, I wondered if it would.

I wondered if Jamie had felt it too.

I strode to my car quickly, relieved I didn't hear his footsteps following behind. My arms were shaking as I took the turn away from their house, wishing I could drive faster over the unpaved section of road.

The adrenaline was still coursing through my limbs when I pulled into home, and my heart rate didn't subside until I had successfully closed the garage door behind me.

When I stood, I heard the crinkle of the photo, wedged into my back pocket.

I pulled it out now, looking again. Why had Skyler—or Jamie— hidden this away? Was it the image of Audrey Holt? There weren't that many around our house anymore, but I knew Caden had some at theirs.

Audrey had that same rounded face as Caden and Skyler, but raven-dark hair, like Gage. I could see pieces of her in both of them.

This couldn't have been the best picture Jamie found, though. Audrey had been looking to the side, talking to Gage. She was leaning her hand down—

I was too busy looking at *her* to see it at first. The place her hand rested. On the brown hood of a car that her children were sitting on.

Her hand grazing the Buick symbol.

The photo started trembling in my grip.

I'd seen that car before. I recognized it now from the images Serena had shared in my kitchen, asking if I'd ever seen it before.

It was the first car pulled from the lake.

CHAPTER 17

This car in the photo—it had belonged to Audrey Holt.

But Audrey had died in a biking accident. There was no reason for this old car to end up in a lake.

Everyone kept mentioning a pattern, a trend, some connection between the cars—like it had the whisper of something dangerous. I'd thought I knew better.

But it did.

Because if there was a pattern, it was this: the cars of Perry Holt's two wives had both ended up in Mirror Lake, and one way or another, both of them were gone.

What was it Sonny had said? *It doesn't look good, does it? To lose two wives?*

No, it didn't. And neither did this.

I sank into the nearest kitchen chair, heart pounding, head spinning.

Not my father. *Please*, not my father. He had always been the only one to choose me, when presented with far easier options, over and over. I'd barely had time to come to terms with his death— clinging to the memory of him everywhere I could. And now I felt like even those were slipping through my fingers.

He raised me like his own.

He was such a good man.

He left me this house—

My mind rebelled, unable to reconcile the evidence with the man. I was jumping to conclusions. Growing paranoid, just as my father seemed to—in this house, with the motion detector flood-lights and the steadily growing collection of mirrors.

It was the isolation. Without other people here, there was an unsettling feeling that the walls were closing in, that the dimensions were off, and nothing was exactly where it was supposed to be.

This was just a random picture. A single photo of a brown car with a Buick symbol. There must've been a million cars just like that. It didn't have to be hers.

It didn't have to be the pattern.

Anyway, wouldn't one of my brothers have looked into it, after it had been pulled from the lake? Serena had showed me pictures from every angle. It had been well documented. I was sure every-one at the police station must've seen them. They were probably circulating through town.

And yet Serena said they still had no idea who the car belonged to. No one had said anything. No one had raised the possibility.

But I remembered how Caden had raced over to the site, once the picture came through on his cell. A memory triggered from an old photograph? A question. As if he, too, needed to see it for himself.

I remembered driving past him on the way out of town, where the freshly exposed car had rested on the shoulder of the road. The mud on the side of his pants, as if he had been pressed up against the vehicle, looking inside. Looking for something . . . some proof?

I wondered if maybe he found it.

———

Was *this* the thing that had changed for Jamie? Not a fight with Caden about an affair. Not something I had said. But this picture, which she'd found in our house. I remembered the moment I'd snuck up on her, making her jump. The way she'd turned the image facedown.

She had recognized it too.

Had she taken it to show Caden? Did she ask him about it?

All I knew for sure was that she'd seen the picture, and now she, too, was gone.

It made me leery, cautious. But if I went to Serena with this before I was sure, it would look foolish, reckless, impulsive. Combative.

There was only one person who had talked about knowing Audrey well. Who implied she knew more about her than most— that she'd been unhappy, looking to get out. I wasn't sure whether it was an act or not, but I believed Sonny might be the one person who might remember. And if they had indeed been friends, maybe she had pictures too.

———

I drove toward Sonny's house again, but as soon as I pulled up the dirt road, my stomach sank. The bike that had been resting against the side of her house was gone, and the front door was latched shut.

I knocked, just to double-check, but there was no response. Just the unfamiliar noises in the woods that kept pulling my attention. A rustling. The sound of a branch breaking off and falling somewhere inside the tree line.

I circled the house, in case she was out back. There was still a small patio there, though it seemed long neglected, with weeds pushing up through the bricks. In the clearing of grass behind it, the remnants of the trampoline remained, though there was a layer of dried leaves over the top that no one had bothered removing. I doubted the springs were in any condition to still be usable, after being exposed to the elements for so long.

Three metal chairs were set at odd angles around the small patio table, so that I could imagine everyone abruptly standing and leaving, just a moment earlier. A collection of beer bottles was gathered between them like a centerpiece, with an ashtray beside.

The back door was closed, all the curtains pulled shut.

I didn't know Sonny's hours—but Pete said he saw her bike at the ABC liquor store earlier, and she had mentioned what she saw in the woods coming home after night shifts. I couldn't just sit on her front porch until she came home.

Back inside my car, I found a pen and wrote a quick note on the back of my grocery receipt.

Sonny—Please call me whenever you get home. I left my number and signed my name, and wedged it into the screen door beside the handle, hoping she'd see it.

Just before the sign for Mirror Lake, I pulled into the lot for a long white rectangular building. Mirror Lake Motel offered a convenient location at a discounted rate. The lake wasn't in view, but the sign was. Like an *almost.* Just like everything else outside the bowl.

Sonny had worked here ever since Jamie and I were in high school, and she still wore that same uniform when I saw her yesterday. I scanned the lot for her bike, but there were only a handful of cars and two motorcycles, all lined up against the curb. I entered the lobby, where a young woman with bluntly cut dark hair was sitting behind the registration desk. Her bangs hung low enough to move when she blinked.

"Help you?" she asked, barely looking up from her phone, as if full sentences required just a little too much effort.

"Is Sonny Varino working?" I asked with a friendly smile. "I was hoping to catch her here."

But the young woman didn't smile in return. Just shook her head slightly back and forth. "Not today," she said, monotone.

"Okay," I said, drawing out the word. There was a time I would've recognized most of the young people in town, but I couldn't place them now. Not the boy at the Country Store, and not this girl either. "If you see her, can you tell her Hazel was looking for her?"

"Sure," she said, eyes drifting back to her phone. If she knew who I was, she made no indication either.

I drove around the loop of Mirror Highway twice more, trusting my dad's mantra that you just had to circle a few times to find whoever you were looking for, but I didn't see any sign of her. She could've been at a grocery store, at a bar, at a friend's. Could've been down the street at a neighbor's. Could've been looking for Jamie, even. It was almost dinnertime—she could've been anywhere, and I had no idea when to expect her back.

Later, in the dim light of my father's kitchen, the photo of Audrey Holt stared up at me from the center of the table. I leaned over it, as if some extra understanding might come from it now. Then I took a picture with my own phone and zoomed in on the image to see if I could pull any extra details to the surface. But the photo was grainy in higher magnification, the Buick symbol distorted.

A gentle knock at the front door jarred me. I hadn't heard a car pull up, or seen headlights flooding through the front windows.

I felt myself stepping carefully, not wanting to make a sound until I knew who was out there.

Peering through the gauzy curtains of the den, I saw a paper bag of food in someone's hand. And then Nico, shifting into frame.

I opened the door, confused—surprised. My pulse, like always, kicked up at the anticipation. Like I was fifteen again, hearing him outside my back door. Before I remembered to hold myself back, to be careful, to remember.

He grinned slowly. "In the mood for Marty's?" he asked, raising the bag. I could smell it from across the threshold, and a wave of hunger washed over me from nowhere. Such was the magic of Marty's famous chicken.

"Always," I said, holding the door open for him. Meaning it. I followed him back into the kitchen, where he emptied the food and paper plates onto the countertop.

"Figured I should come around front instead of lurking through the woods." He cleared his throat. "You were right, you know. We are a little too old for this."

It was the closest he'd come to an apology, after the way we'd ended last time.

"Well," I said. "Look at us now." The closest I'd come to accepting.

He reached a hand for my arm, pulled me gently toward him, like he was trying to bridge the chasm of time between us.

Maybe this was it, a Step Two. But it was coming at the very worst time, when the entire axis of my world had come off-kilter. I hated the idea that it was this vulnerability that had drawn him back to me. I pulled away slightly, grabbed cups from the cabinet. I could feel him watching me carefully.

"I have a meeting tonight, back at the school," he said, serving us both. "But I wanted to swing by before. Not just, you know, in the middle of the night when I see your backyard lights flashing." Then he pointed to the ceiling. "Though I see you've got the smoke detectors handled. Very resourceful, as always."

I grinned. "You've got a school meeting at night? What kind of clubs are you running in the dark?" I teased. I grabbed a wing off the plate on the counter. My fingers were immediately covered in a thick honey glaze. There was no way to eat this gracefully.

He rubbed the stubble on the side of his face. He hadn't shaved in a day, maybe two. "One of my students is missing," he said, busying himself at the counter, piling his plate with food. But I saw the concern in his expression. Maybe he'd come here for himself, as much as for me. "We're trying to figure out what we can do. How we can help."

"Not a runaway?" I asked, leaning against the counter, facing him. "I heard he was eighteen."

He paused, ran a hand back through his hair, and leaned against the counter, mirroring my position. "His friends are freaked out," he began. "Not a good sign." I nodded, urging him on. "Some of them didn't come into school today. Spent the entire day searching the woods."

I shuddered, appetite gone. "What are they afraid of? What do they think happened?"

"That's just it," Nico said, frowning. "I don't know. I don't know what they think is out there, Hazel."

I stared back, wondering if we were imagining the same things. Flashes of limbs, twisted. Hair, splayed. Something moving under the cloak of darkness—

Nico shook his head, pushing off the counter. "Come on, I didn't mean to bring the mood down."

We took the plates to the table, but I had to force myself to eat. The atmosphere had shifted, but it wasn't just because of what he'd shared. It was the fact that suddenly I was imagining a new trend: People, disappearing without a trace. Jamie. Max Falkner. Something dangerous and alive, seeping around the edges of Mirror Lake.

"What's that?" Nico asked, head tipped toward the single photo on the table.

My fingers were too messy to pick the photo up myself. He used his elbow to drag it slowly closer.

"Did you know Gage and Caden's mom?" I asked.

"No," he said, shaking his head. "Not really. We moved in not long before she died." He paused, frowning. "God, they were all so young."

He kept staring, large eyes slowly blinking. I waited to see if he'd notice anything in the image, but he didn't seem to see the details. But I felt him leaning closer, as if he could sense something niggling at the back of his mind too.

"It looks like the first car pulled from the lake," I said, voice low. "Don't you think?"

He looked up at me, then back down, taking it in. He had been on-site that day, helping the dive team pull it out of the water.

"I don't know. I really don't. It was a Buick, but . . ." He raised his gaze to mine. Careful, always so careful.

"Yeah," I said. "I don't know either."

He pushed the photo away again, before taking another bite. "Are you going to ask Gage?" he asked.

"Maybe. He already thinks I'm paranoid." But I knew if I showed Gage that picture, I'd be accusing our father of something. How far did his compassion truly go? I didn't want to find out. Not until I was sure.

Then I shook my head, trying to find a way back to the fact that Nico was here, and he'd brought dinner, and seemed to be trying to apologize for our past. "Tell me, Nico. What's the craziest thing you've ever found on a dive?" I raised a hand between us. "Other than the cars in the lake, obviously."

That at least got the ghost of a grin. He leaned back in the chair, thinking. "A knife," he said definitively.

"Like a dinner knife? Or a weapon knife?"

"A weapon knife. Definitely. Serrated edge. Military style."

I pictured the boaters with fishing magnets, trawling the bottom. "Here?" I asked, gesturing toward the lake.

"No, it was on a shipwreck dive, during college. Everything was old—ancient—rusted and fragile. But in the middle of it, there was this knife, shiny new. Totally out of place." He shook his head. "I used to think about it all the time—what had brought it there. If it fell out of someone's pocket by accident. If someone dropped it there, on purpose." He turned, smiled at me. "Or if it's just one of those mysteries of the ocean. Currents and luck. A moment in time."

"Huh," I said. I placed an elbow on the table between us, leaning closer. "Did you take it?"

"No, Hazel, I didn't take it."

"I bet it's still there, buried under a new layer of sand and debris. And in a thousand years, someone's going to discover the site again and believe everything came from the same era of history. Pirates on sailboats from the 1800s armed with military-grade weapons from the twenty-first century."

"Did I ever tell you," he began, smiling, "that I'm fascinated by the way you think?"

We were cleaning up from dinner when my phone rang. I quickly washed my hands in the sink and rushed for my purse—hoping it was Sonny.

But it was Gage's name on the display. I turned to show Nico, before answering.

Nico smiled tightly.

"Hazel, I told you I'd handle it," Gage said as greeting.

"Hello to you too," I said, drying my hands one by one on the sides of my pants.

"I was just over at Caden's. He's pretty pissed." A pause. "Said you practically ambushed him."

I closed my eyes. "I just *dropped by* to return Skyler's backpack. How is that an ambush?"

"I don't know—accusing him of lying about his wife being missing?"

I groaned. "I didn't mean . . . But Gage, it's a little strange, don't you think? No one's heard from her, and no one can reach her? He has plenty of resources at his disposal, but he doesn't seem at all concerned?"

Silence from Gage. And then: "You always think the worst of him. He is concerned. He is. But Hazel"—he dropped his voice—"this is not the first time she's left him. So she's keeping a low profile. So what? You know what it was like growing up with Dad. Anywhere you went, word got back to him. You know?"

I did. *Heard you and Jamie were out for a joyride last night*, he'd once said casually, over dinner. Someone had noticed us driving around the loop, or seen us parked out at the Barrel, and reported it straight back to him.

"He could've just told me that," I said.

"Really? Because you sneaking around his house puts him in such an open and friendly mood." Now he was teasing instead of reprimanding, and I felt myself relax.

"I wasn't sneaking. I was standing right there at his front door."

A pause. "He thinks you were inside."

"I definitely was not." Though I would've been, if only I'd had a way in.

"I didn't even know you were back," he said. As if accusing me of something too.

"I'm working remotely for a bit," I offered, then looked up at Nico, who was emptying our plates into the trash.

I have to go, he mouthed, gesturing for the front door.

I nodded, waved a small goodbye.

"Well, if you're still here tomorrow," Gage continued, "why don't we all get together for dinner. Clear the air. Okay?"

Nico's hand grazed the end of my hair as he passed.

"Okay," I said. "And Gage?" I looked down at the photo on the table. At that very young boy, smiling over at the mother he was about to lose. "I'm sorry. I am."

By the time I was ready to get to bed, my house still smelled like honey-glazed chicken. I tied the garbage bag where Nico had dumped the remnants of dinner, then took my phone with me out to the front. I turned on the outside light, but still used my flashlight to guide the way up the drive.

I did my best to make as much noise as possible, humming a tune, kicking up rocks as I walked, so that I would not surprise any hypothetical bears nearby. I felt Nico's words, like a chill in the air—*I don't know what they think is out there*—and started moving faster.

The trash enclosure required two hands to unlatch. I set the bag down to get the lid up and over, then paused. I'd expected it to be empty. And it mostly was. But at the very bottom, something glinted off the light of my phone.

As I leaned forward, a chill worked its way from my neck to my toes.

A collection of 9-volt batteries was scattered along the bottom of the garbage bin. As if someone had been inside the house last night and removed them while we slept.

CHAPTER 18

There were a lot of things out in the woods that you couldn't always see in the dark: hikers, hunters, campers. Bears.

They didn't generally come inside your house.

I stood hovering over the garbage can, counting the batteries, trying to talk myself down, to stop jumping to the worst conclusions, to keep the paranoia from carving out a place inside my head.

But then I thought again of the open doorway at Caden and Jamie's house, the way he stared off into the woods, like he was searching for someone.

I backed away slowly, listening to the woods, then raised my phone to my ear.

"Yeah?" my brother answered, like we were still in mid-conversation.

"Gage," I said, unable to hide the fear in my voice. "I think someone's been in the house."

"What?" he began. "What happened? Are you still there?"

"Yes, I'm out front. I'm . . . I'm not sure." I stared down again. "Last night, the smoke detectors started beeping. There were no batteries inside."

"I'm not following, Hazel." His voice was tight and fast—not at all like the calm I had imagined him projecting to a panicked homeowner.

"I'm staring down at a garbage can full of batteries, Gage. Like someone took them out while I was sleeping."

Silence.

"You mentioned some break-ins, kid stuff. What exactly have they been doing?" I asked.

"That's not . . . No, that's not the MO. It doesn't fit." He paused. "It could've been Dad. Maybe they were acting up before he died. I don't know if anyone's taken the trash up for collection."

I nodded my head. "Okay," I said, feeling my heart rate slow. It didn't have to be someone in the house last night.

Wasn't it just as likely my father had removed the batteries before he died, and no one had seen fit to check the trash since, bring it out to the main road for curbside pickup? Wasn't it just as likely the smoke detectors were functioning fine while connected to the electric system instead, until the power surge?

It was, it was.

I wanted to believe it so badly.

"Look. What I was telling you about before: they were breaking into empty homes. Taking little things. *Moving* things. Nothing valuable. I really think it was just pranks. Why else take that risk, but steal nothing of value?"

I thought of the risks we used to take at the same age, on a dare. Jumping off the edge of the guardrail, into the deep. Sledding headfirst on the lid of a garbage can, through the trees. I could imagine it, in a different season, with a different mix of personalities: *I dare you—*

"How were they getting in?" I asked.

I heard him breathing on the other end. "Doors and windows left open, we think. Just make sure you lock up. These aren't criminal masterminds, Hazel."

I ended the call, disjointed. Feeling the memory of a presence inside that house. Not just when Nico had arrived, but *before*. The lights flashing outside in the night. And the feeling I got when I'd arrived back in town yesterday, like something was lingering—

The landline was ringing as I closed the door behind me and turned the dead bolt. I took a step into the foyer, but it fell silent. I waited, wondering if whoever had called would try again. It was too late at night for telemarketers or bill collectors.

The last time I'd answered a call on the landline, it was the school, asking me to pick up Skyler.

Who else knew I was here? Nico, on the way to his meeting? Felicity, who had something to tell me after all?

Curiosity got the best of me, and I decided to check the voice messages on the dial-in service. The code was the same as it had been growing up, and it was immediately obvious no one had checked them since his death.

The first message began with an automated time stamp: *April twenty-third, 10:02 a.m.*

I held my breath. It was the day he died.

Perry, you there? Give us a call when you get this, please. The captain, looking for him, when he didn't show up for work. I sank into the nearest chair, transported back to that day. Since my father didn't carry a personal cell, they'd tried this line before Caden came over to check in.

I deleted the message, and braced myself for what was to come next.

But it was mostly just telemarketers or scams. The calls slowed as the weeks passed. And then another voice I recognized, in a message dated *May twelfth, 12:15 a.m.*—Pete Henderson, in the middle of the night, words slurring. *Good to hear your voice again.* And then another pause, voice quieter. *I'm sorry, old friend.*

It almost did me in. Pete, drunk dialing my father's mailbox, just to hear the sound of his gravelly voice again. How many people here had loved him. He'd left a hole not only in our family but in this town. I saved the message, on impulse.

One new message, the automated service announced: *May twentieth, 6:07 p.m.*

At first there was nothing but dead air, and I almost deleted it.

And then a voice: *Hazel, are you there?*

The room chilled, everything focused down to a point.

Her voice, soft and familiar. It was Jamie.

Jamie, on this answering machine, calling for me—like her voice had reached across the distance, pulling me back.

Please, she said, voice small and quiet. *Do you still have Skyler?* I heard her breathing, slightly frantic. Panicked. *I need to go. Someone came into my house. I was in the shower, and they walked right in. I swear the door was locked. There was no car. But whoever it was, they must've had a key.* Her voice picked up speed, becoming almost indecipherable. *It's not safe for us. For any of us. I don't know who to trust, Hazel. Please bring her to me. Bring her and meet me . . .* Her voice drifted off, and then she was back, voice so close I could imagine her mouth almost pressed up against the phone, her hands gripped tight. *Meet me tonight at our spot.*

———

Our spot. She had to mean the Barrel. The overlook.

I listened to the message three more times, desperate for details.

It's not safe for us. For any of us.

She'd called at some point when my mother's car was being pulled from the lake. I'd already left Skyler with Caden. I'd missed her, and I'd driven back to Charlotte.

And now I was picturing her there, at the clearing overlooking the Barrel, waiting for me in the night. Waiting, and thinking she couldn't trust me now either.

I was right—something was wrong. Something was happening here. I'd missed her, and another two days had passed. Jamie had tried to meet up with me, and now she was gone.

But maybe she left something for me—another piece to follow.

A trail, if only I looked for it this time.

The clearing for the overlook wasn't visible from the road. There wasn't a sign or even a noticeable entrance. The shoulder of the road gave way to a patch of dirt—a gap through the trees. I pulled my car in, a cleared circle opening up just past the tree line.

My high beams pointed over the cliffs, disappearing into the darkness beyond. I turned off the engine, stepped out of the car, leaves crunching, twigs snapping. The wind rushed through the trees, and it sounded like the woods were alive.

There was nothing quiet about this spot.

I stepped closer to the edge, where a trail continued on my left, heading upward. To my right, another trail continued to the base of the lake—but there was a chain hung between trees, with a sign, blocking the path. I shone the light from my phone: *Danger. Keep out.*

Beyond, I could see the dark path sloping steeply downward. Long slabs of rock in a set of makeshift steps, which had slowly succumbed to erosion. And directly in front of me: the dark expanse of Mirror Lake.

In other spots around the lake, there were breathtaking views befitting the name—where the stars and mountains reflected off the water, in perfect harmony—and then there was *this*, where the landscape fell away, like the black hole I'd always imagined it to be.

Even now I felt I could whisper a secret over the edge, and it would be caught up in the vortex, sucked under the surface.

Standing near the edge, I could hear the sound of something out of place carried from below, echoing off the curves of the surrounding landscape. Water lapping against rock, in the current. And then a periodic thud. I strained to see over the edge, hand gripping a branch beside me. With the water so low, this wasn't a dangerous jump anymore. It was a death sentence. I felt the shift in balance, the wave of vertigo, and backed away.

Instead, I maneuvered around the chains, taking the steps

slowly down toward the bottom. I moved carefully, hands wrapping around branches, bracing against trunks as I passed. Until I reached a bend and could see into the center of the Barrel.

I shone my light, and could just barely make it out: an old canoe, tipped on its side, caught between a log and the rocks. In the water around it, a collection of beer cans bobbed. Other debris, pushed this way in the current, was caught in the tide pool.

"Hello?" I called, just in case. But only my voice echoed back.

I turned the light back toward the path, and the beam caught on an object just off the trail. A reflection, under a pile of dead leaves. I crouched before it, brushing off the surface.

It was a disposable camera. My light had caught on the flash in the corner.

Probably a hiker, or a sightseer, from long ago. Who even used these anymore, when we had phones constantly at our disposal? But I took it with me as I made my way back to the top.

I'd just stepped over the chains when a light shone directly in my eyes. I put an arm out on instinct to block the glare.

"What are you doing out here?" a man's voice asked.

I blinked rapidly, trying to clear the spots from my vision. Below the light, I could make out dark boots, dark pants, a gear belt—a familiar uniform.

A police officer.

"Can you lower that, please?" I asked, turning my own light in his direction instead.

He obliged, his features slowly coming into focus. Cropped hair, squared jaw. He looked so young. I recognized him as one of the officers who had worked with Serena. The name on the upper left side of his chest read *C. Melvin.*

"What are you doing out here, Hazel?" he asked again, and his use of my name was unsettling. We'd never met. But he'd been at our house when we discovered the car. Watched as we pulled it out of our yard.

I thought he must've been a friend of Caden's, the one he

mentioned at the memorial—*Mel's trying to send pictures*. He would undoubtedly report this right back to Caden in the morning.

Jamie's haunting voice on the message echoed through my head: *I don't know who to trust—*

"I used to come out here a lot, as a kid," I said. "To think."

The arc of his flashlight caught on the camera in my hand. "And take pictures?"

"It's my favorite spot," I said. "No one else ever seemed to know about it."

"It's not a safe place," he said. "You shouldn't be out here alone." Which sounded suddenly like both a warning and a threat.

I couldn't figure out how he knew I was here. My car had been tucked out of sight. I didn't even see his patrol vehicle. "What are you doing out here?" I asked.

He frowned. "We've got a missing kid," he said. But it sounded like a cover. It sounded, instead, like he had followed me here. "You should go home."

"I was on my way," I said, gesturing to my car.

He followed me and watched as I backed out of the clearing. I passed his patrol car, parked along the side of the main road, just before he'd reached the clearing.

As if he knew exactly what he'd find inside.

I couldn't talk myself down. The call from Jamie. The batteries in the trash. The feeling of someone in the house when I'd returned yesterday. A cop following me out to the Barrel, watching me. Not paranoia. Not at all.

I didn't sleep downstairs in the basement. Instead, I curled up on the couch in the den beside the front door. And I left the television on, so no one would mistake this for an empty house.

The truth was, whoever it was, I think they knew I was here. And I didn't think they cared.

I kept jerking awake, disoriented, wondering if something had startled me. But it was just the laugh tracks from the midnight comedy reruns, the music from the commercial jingles.

Eventually, I made my way back to the china cabinet, craving a shot—or two—of my father's old liquor, like I had the first night. Something to settle my nerves, take the edge off.

I grabbed the same bottle as last time, and then paused. The box with my father's personal gun was still tucked behind it. Caden had forgotten to take it, in the chaos of finding the car.

For a moment, I thought of bringing it with me to the front room, slipping it under the couch. Just another layer of protection.

My father had taught me to shoot. But he'd also never wanted me to own a gun. Said they were all—every one of them—most likely to be used against you. Which made me wonder why he had this, and if there were more, hidden around the house, that I hadn't yet found.

In the den, I resettled into the worn chair instead. I felt the impression of my father in the leather below. Imagined him watching me now, in this room. *You're a step behind, Hazel.*

The light on the automated timer. The mirrors on the basement wall, with the wide view out the window. The motion sensors out back.

He knew, of course. He always knew—whereas I was too slow on the uptake—when there was something to truly fear.

CHAPTER 19

By the time morning came, I was exhausted, like I was nursing a hangover. The first thing I did was check the house, top to bottom, for signs of entry. Everything was locked up, just as I'd left it.

But this house had been breached. Just as Jamie's had. Of that I was sure. Something had happened, and I'd missed her. I should never have left Mirror Lake. I imagined, instead, receiving the call, meeting up with her. Bringing Skyler to her, and leaving together.

But whatever she feared, it was enough to make her leave, with or without Skyler.

The camera I'd found last night sat on the entryway table. There was a small chance it was hers, left behind—a trail, for me to follow. But when I checked online for one-hour photo locations, there were no options. Apparently, developing film was a dying art. I'd have to mail it out, wait a week. A dead end.

I thought once more of Jamie's call, and wondered if she'd tried again. If the hang-up from last night was from her reaching out—hoping I would answer this time.

I took the phone bill down to the basement, to my father's

old computer. Between the paperwork and his email, I was able to access his account and scroll through the recent incoming and outgoing calls.

Last night's call had come from an unknown number. My pulse quickened, imagining it was Jamie, maybe. Lying low, trying to stay hidden—to stay safe.

I scrolled back farther, wondering if her original call had also come from an unknown number. Or whether she'd turned on her cell instead.

Monday, at 6:07 p.m. A number was listed, but when I pulled up Jamie's contact, it didn't match.

She definitely hadn't called from her cell.

On impulse, I called the number now. It rang five times, and I was on the verge of giving up, when it finally clicked over.

Hiya, it's Sonny. You know what to do.

I pushed back from the desk, adrenaline coursing through my limbs. Sonny had lied. Of course Sonny had lied. She had known exactly where Jamie was. Jamie had called from her house on Monday night.

I grabbed my bag and stuffed the photo of Audrey's car inside.

I was about to kill two birds with one stone.

I drove out to Sonny's with the sun glinting off the cars in front of me.

It was going to be a bright one. Hot and dry, the earth thirsty and brittle as I pulled up the dusty lane.

I didn't see her bike leaning against the siding.

But the front door was open.

She must've gotten my note, but hadn't bothered calling. And now I knew it was because she had something to hide.

"Sonny?" I called as I walked up the front steps. I knocked on the screen, where it shook loosely against the doorframe.

"Hello?" I called again. I strained to see anyone inside, but could see only the shadows of the wall partitions and furniture shapes. "Sonny, come on!" I was getting irritated—at her, and at myself. I'd let her talk me in circles, take me for a fool.

Then I caught sight of a figure on the couch, facing away. Curly hair, head resting back—asleep.

"Sonny?" I said again. "I'm coming in."

How many times had Jamie and I found her like this, passed out on the couch, not quite making it to her room?

The door creaked as I pulled it open, and the house felt stale.

Inside, school photos of Skyler hung on the walls, slightly off-kilter.

Sonny was sitting slumped gently to the side. I placed a hand on her shoulder as I said her name, trying not to startle her.

I needed her awake and focused. I shook her by the shoulder, and she slid farther into the couch. "Sonny," I said sharply, frustrated and desperate.

I rounded the curve of the sofa—her eyes were open, fixed on empty space. Mouth slightly ajar, slack. Everything was unnaturally still.

A wave of cold panic swept over me in a rush.

I screamed her name louder, like I'd seen Jamie do once. The one time she looked genuinely afraid. I shook her again, more violently.

"Please," I said, when nothing happened.

A noise came from the back of my throat. *No no no no.*

I tripped backward, hand shaking as I pulled out my phone, thankful for the single bar of signal.

I pictured Caden walking into my father's office—*Dad? You awake?*—seeing his feet up on the desk, eyes closed. The chill and horror slowly setting in.

It took me three tries to dial 911 successfully, my hands shaking with more adrenaline than I'd ever had to contain.

"Please send help to Sonny Varino's house. Paradise Lane in Mirror Lake. Please, she's not breathing."

I noticed, then, the orange vial open on the end table. There was no label—I had no idea what she'd taken. I didn't know what people did in these situations.

I started opening cabinets, searching, in vain, hoping that there might be some Narcan in the house. I had no idea if she kept it, or whether it would even work for her now, but didn't know what else to do.

I tried the medicine cabinet, the refrigerator, moved around the fresh groceries: fruit, juice, milk, eggs, freshly sliced deli products. A container of chicken salad from the grocery store I'd passed on the way into town.

I couldn't help picturing Jamie dropping these off, like Felicity had told me. But there was nothing that could help her mother now.

Finally, the siren of an ambulance grew closer.

I ran back to the couch, placed a hand to her neck, her skin eerily cold.

I was too late. She was gone.

I'm sorry, Jamie.

Through the screen, I watched an ambulance pull in, and then another car, following fast on the heels of the EMS team: my brothers.

But I couldn't meet them outside. I couldn't leave her alone.

Not Jamie's mother.

All these mothers in Mirror Lake, never making it out of town.

Hadn't Sonny warned me of that, just a couple days ago?

I should've been more afraid from the start. It wasn't a strength but a failing of mine, that I wasn't. I should've understood what she was saying. *Do you believe that's what really happened?*

Sonny had known. She'd tried to tell me.

Two cars in the lake, and my father, the only thing that connected them.

But I couldn't forget the way he'd looked when he saw me standing in the kitchen the day she'd gone missing, genuinely shocked that I was still there.

He'd left me the house. He'd had nothing remaining in his bank accounts, and the house went to me. What was he trying to make up for?

I don't know who to trust, Hazel—

I stood in the entryway, frozen, as a team of people filed into the house. I waited for my brothers to find me here—waited for their looks of surprise, like I'd once seen on my father, long ago.

For years, Perry Holt had been the only one who had chosen me. I believed it had been from a deep and powerful love. And now, suddenly, I was faced with the shock that maybe it was not because of that at all.

But maybe because I was a piece of evidence left behind instead.

PART 3

SONS

CHAPTER 20

Sonny Varino was dead. Obviously dead. Confirmed by the medics as soon as they'd arrived on the scene.

And now a woman was photographing the couch where she'd sat, the pills beside her.

She turned the camera toward the front door, and Gage pulled me to the side, out of frame. At the edge of the porch, the tree branches dragged across the overhang, like a cocoon.

"Did you touch anything, Hazel?" Gage asked.

"Of course," I said, eyes wide and burning. My god, I'd touched everything. The furniture, the cabinets, her. "I was trying to *help*."

He ran his fingers back through his hair, obviously frustrated. He stepped even farther from the door, the wood of the sagging porch creaking under our weight. He shot a glance toward the front lawn, where Caden was currently pacing back and forth with his phone to his ear.

I wasn't sure if he was prevented from being inside because she was his mother-in-law, or if he just preferred it this way. And then I wondered if he was picturing our father again, legs up on the desk, eyes closed—

"What were you even *doing* here?" Gage asked, pulling my attention back to the present.

But how could I tell him? How could I even begin to explain?

Jamie found a photo of your mother's car, and she called me to meet her on the line from this house. I missed her, and now she's gone.

Jamie was missing, and Sonny was dead, and something was happening here—

"I saw Sonny a couple days ago. Came to check in . . ." I said, sticking to pieces of the truth, letting him fill in the rest of the story for himself.

My brain felt like it was working on a delay, like I'd woken in the middle of the night, disoriented. It was the lack of sleep. The slowly creeping paranoia of the house, and the feeling of people watching me, following me. The image of Sonny slumped over on the couch—

How late had I been? *Maybe if I'd come back earlier. Maybe if I'd searched harder yesterday, looked for her bike. Maybe if I'd asked that girl at the motel for her number . . .*

His mouth set into a firm line. "Please tell me this isn't about Jamie."

I said nothing. I knew better than to lie to him. Gage was a strong observer. It made him a good brother growing up, and a good detective now.

I don't know who to trust—

Nothing I said to Gage now would stay private. It would be part of the investigation.

But Gage had missed something, when that first car was pulled from the lake. And I didn't know whether it was intentional. Jamie was afraid of something, and as far as I knew, she hadn't told her husband.

"Dammit, Hazel," he said. He sniffed, then looked over his shoulder at Caden again. "Go home. Someone's probably gonna need to stop by later, get your official statement on how you found her. But don't let it be here."

As if he was saving me, like always, from a confrontation with Caden.

A low hum of voices carried from beyond the screen door, and I strained to hear what they were saying.

"What happened?" I asked. "Do they know yet?" The crew had been inside for a while. There must've been some sort of initial assessment.

"What was always going to happen," he said, letting his eyes drift shut. "Those pills beside her—they came up positive for fentanyl on the test strips."

As if her past made this a preordained outcome, and everyone had just been counting the days. All of us, in our designated roles, playing our assigned parts. But I couldn't shake the feeling that *I* had somehow set this in motion. That I had precipitated the end, or sped it up. Had I made her worry? Driven her to overdose?

"We'll reach Jamie," he said, hand on my back, guiding me toward the steps. "Hopefully before she finds out about it from someone else."

But they wouldn't, and he had no idea. She was gone. She'd been spooked, and fled town, and now no one could reach her.

There was a crowd gathering along the other side of the dirt road. Neighbors standing on the edge of the woods, between properties. Some were texting or taking photos. Others stood solemnly, hands in pockets, watching quietly. No one came forward to ask what had happened here. It was like everyone agreed that her habits were bound to catch up with her one day.

"Go," Gage said, just as Caden ended a call.

As if I needed to move, before something caught up with me too.

———

Even though I understood the problem with towns this size, I fell right into the trap. News like this needed an outlet. It couldn't stay bottled up—it needed a place to go. It wasn't because Mirror

Lake was full of gossips. On the contrary. It was because everyone here was connected by friend or family, in varying degrees, and had a right to know. And there were only so many people who would hear before it reached a critical mass, in a self-perpetuating cycle.

The first person I called from the car was Nico, but his cell went straight to voicemail. I was sure he was teaching, and that school protocol meant he'd need to keep his phone off when he was in the classroom. Still, I sent a text while I lingered with the engine running: *Did you hear about Sonny Varino?*

I waited for the message to show as delivered. But it didn't.

I started driving, my reflexes just a beat too late. I couldn't find the right rhythm—jerking the car to a stop just before the intersection with the main road, tires screeching as I accelerated too fast onto the main highway.

I was haunted by the unnatural stillness of Sonny's house. The way she'd been slumped over on the couch, so obviously not asleep, her body seized up, and the fear, still tingling in my fingers.

I couldn't shake the feeling that I was a step behind, or that something was catching up with me. Something that Jamie, too, was trying to outrun.

If there was a trail to follow, I had been too slow. I was already three days behind.

The picture in my purse was dangerous. Who else would know the truth?

Just after passing the sign for Mirror Lake, I saw the entrance to my uncle's law office. The long brick building was positioned between the ABC store and a locally owned café. Holt Family Law shared the location with an insurance company and a real estate office, like a convenient one-stop shop.

If there was any place with a finger on the pulse of family news, it was here. How many people had come in for a consult, just to begin to figure out their options? How many were preparing to file, catching the other party unaware? Who else would be able to confirm what happened to Audrey Holt's car after her death?

I greeted the secretary at the front desk—the place, I imagined, where my mother had once sat. This woman had deep brown eyes behind wire-rimmed glasses and dark hair pulled back into a high bun. I couldn't tell whether she was twenty or forty. If she knew who I was, she didn't let on.

"Can I help you?" she asked, brown eyes looking even larger behind the lenses.

"Hi," I said. "Is Roy in?"

"He just got back. He had a morning appointment. . . ." She picked up the phone, but I ignored her, wandering straight down the hall to his closed office door.

I knocked but let myself in at the same time. Roy was standing before his dark wood desk, removing his suit jacket. His mug had left a water ring on the surface. "Hazel," he said, his gaze drifting behind me, as if surprised I'd bypassed his secretary on my own. And then, with a line forming between his eyes: "Is everything okay?"

I shook my head. "Sonny Varino is dead."

"What?" he asked, hands pausing as he draped his jacket on the back of his chair. "What happened?" He blinked twice, like I'd caught him by surprise. I'd forgotten that he'd probably grown up with her too. That I was breaking the news of a death, abruptly and without consideration. I remembered the gut punch from Gage's call: *It's Dad—*

I shook my head, words stuck in my throat. "Sorry, Roy. Overdose, I think."

He frowned, then nodded solemnly, as if agreeing with all the rest. "Such a shame," he said. "Poor Jamie." My stomach twisted at her name.

"Roy, can I show you something?"

I pulled out the photo from my purse, placed it on his desk. He picked it up carefully between his thumb and pointer finger. His nails were down to the quick. "Oh," he said, corners of his eyes tensing. "This is an old one." He frowned. "Did you find this in the house?"

I paused, then nodded.

"That car," I said. "Do you see?"

I held my breath, waiting to see if he did. He tipped his head just faintly to the side, before his eyes shot up to mine. I felt a surge of adrenaline—someone, then, who saw it too.

"Audrey Holt drove a Buick," I said, needing him to confirm.

"Yes," he began, as I watched the understanding dawn on his face. "It was her car. Have the boys realized this?"

I shook my head. "I don't think so. Not yet." But I didn't know what Caden believed or knew. He'd rushed over to the scene, when the first picture came through.

"You stayed with them at the house, though, after her death, right? My dad said you'd come to help. Do you remember what happened after she died?"

He pursed his mouth, thinking. "I don't. God, that was so long ago. Another lifetime. I didn't stay there all the time, Hazel." He took a slow breath in before continuing. "And you know, those were some dark days. I was working to get sober then. We helped each other—I needed them as much as they needed me."

"I didn't know," I said. All of these versions of people who had existed before were strangers to me. "Do you know what happened to this car?"

He stared at the photo again, then shook his head. "I guess if I thought back to it, I assumed Perry sold it. It wasn't like he needed a second car. And he always drove the truck."

I lowered my voice then, asked the thing I'd come for, after all. "Was it true that she was going to leave my father?"

His gaze became sharp, firm—like I'd crossed a line. "Why are you asking me that?"

"I figured you might know." I gestured to his office. The only family law office in town.

He replaced the photo on the desk, and frowned. "I wasn't in private practice yet then. I was still at the prosecutor's office."

My heart sank. "Sonny said . . ." I shook my head. She'd gotten it wrong. Close, but not quite.

"Sonny said *what*?" he asked carefully.

But I switched gears, before he shut me out entirely. He still might know something useful. "Roy, is Jamie filing for divorce?"

His mouth fell to a flat line. "You know I can't tell you that, Hazel. Even if I knew anything."

"She left, you know. Caden said she'll be back. But no one can reach her. Gage mentioned she's left him before. I figured you might know the truth."

"Are you saying you don't believe Caden?" he asked, speaking the words slowly and deliberately.

"I'm saying he wouldn't tell me the truth if I asked. He's so angry with me."

Filing a challenge to the will. Telling Gage I'd ambushed him— that he suspected I had been in his house, even. Like he was seeding a story to use against me later. And maybe he was.

I wonder what you told my dad to get him to leave you the house.

As if he were trying to find a way to undermine my claim, take it back.

Roy sighed, coming around the desk. In some ways, he was so much like my father: the same large stature, the same imposing frame. But in other ways, he was so different—he'd moved to family law, he said, because it was far more lucrative, for far less headache. "I don't know what you expect me to say here. You're understandably shaken up. Let me get you home."

"No," I said, hand up. "I'm fine. I can drive." I just wanted someone to tell me something real and true.

This was the part of my job I was usually best at—the people, the talking. It wasn't some hard skill you could put your finger on, like the finances or the architecture, but something that got results, all the same. A trait, I had to admit, that I had gotten from my mother.

Out there, it was a strength. But, in this one place, I had forgotten how nervous it made people, like they were seeing someone else standing before them, weaving a story—or pulling one from them, instead.

"You're shaking," he said. He put his hands on the sides of my arms, not unlike how my father might have done. I imagined their own father doing the same with them. An inheritance of mannerisms. How much we had all been molded by the people who came before.

"When Caden found your dad . . ." Roy looked off to the side, frowning. "He was shaken up too. He wasn't making any sense. So take a breath, Hazel. You need to give yourself a minute. Two, even." He gave me a knowing look. "Take some time. Before your mind starts spiraling." He patted my arms again, in an approximation of comfort. "I promise you, that boy wouldn't hurt her. There was a time, I'm sure, that you would've known that too."

But the truth was, I didn't. I didn't know what it was supposed to be like, growing up with siblings. I'd lived the first seven-plus years of my life as an only child, before our families merged. And when we did, it was too sudden, a clashing of personalities, instead of a blending. But I was used to adapting, by then.

Gage had been my way in. I'd proven myself a good partner for him—I was naturally athletic, and just as impulsive to try whatever he suggested. I *could* do whatever he claimed—I wanted to. I could beat his friends in a race. I could swim faster than Caden. I could hold my breath longer, stay quiet longer, keep secrets longer. But the more I grew attached to him, the more distant Caden became.

Where Gage helped with homework, Caden would misplace it. While Gage waited for me, Caden would happily slip away and leave me behind. If I made their father laugh, he'd make sure my mother was preoccupied by his needs in turn. It wasn't overt, never something truly harmful, but he seemed to take pleasure in causing me discord and frustration.

And he got bolder the older I got. He'd once locked the door behind me after I snuck out to see Nico in the night—as if he wanted to get me in trouble. I'd had to sleep in the backyard, curled up on the patio, and wait for my father to leave in the morning. So no, I did not know, I really didn't, what he was capable of now. Did any of us?

CHAPTER 21

There was a police car in front of my house when I pulled in. As Gage had warned me, this hadn't taken very long at all.

I wondered whether Caden had followed me back home in his cruiser.

"Hello?" I called, stepping into the early afternoon air.

I tested the front door, just to make sure no one else had let themselves inside, but it was still locked, just as I'd left it. I circled down the slope of the side yard, following the tracks of the tow truck damage, listening for anyone else. My hand trailed along the base of the house that extended below the main level, a cooler concrete, coated with grime.

Serena stood at the edge of the lake, hands on her hips. She seemed to be staring at a boat that lingered near the entrance of the inlet. As she stood there, it slowly motored out of sight. As if her presence alone had deterred it.

She spun as I approached, hand going protectively to her hip, like she'd been bracing for something else.

"Yikes," I said, hands held up. We were all so jumpy here. So untrusting.

"I've been looking for you," she said, eyes narrowed, like I owed her an explanation of where I'd been. I felt as if the entire department had been watching me, following me.

But I was just as jumpy. Shaken and disoriented by the day's events. "Was that boat in the inlet?"

"Not when I got here," she said. "Looks like they were fishing. But I wouldn't be surprised if they're amateur investigators, searching for evidence." She frowned, narrowing her eyes, as if she could still see them. "I can't tell you how many calls we've gotten the last few days, of things they've been pulling out of the lake. Junk, mostly. At least they're doing a public cleanup service."

"What are they finding?" I asked. I pictured magnets hanging from the edges of boats, dragging along the bottom. Knives and bullets and strips of metal, pulled from the depths. A graveyard under the surface.

"Utensils, mostly. Someone found a bike last night—looked to be in pretty good condition. Probably some angry kid, in a fight."

She sighed, then stared up at the sky. "Heard it might finally rain this weekend, at least. Hopefully that'll clear them out of the lake."

That was the first I was hearing of it, but I hadn't been paying much attention to the weather forecast.

"Can we go inside to talk?" she asked, while I was still staring out at the water.

"Sure," I said, leading her up the deck steps, using my key to let us in the back sliders. I was glad to have her beside me. Something was happening at this house. I felt the paranoia seeping inside. The batteries in the smoke detectors. Lights on timers and new motion detectors and mirrors, mirrors, lining the walls.

Something my father must've felt too.

If Serena noticed me cautiously taking in the house, she didn't let on. I did a quick assessment of the space, but everything seemed just as I'd left it.

Then I felt her looking around the room too. As if something had struck her as off. Her boots resounded on the hardwood floor, a slow pacing.

"I'll try to make this easy," she said, pulling out a kitchen chair, the legs scratching against the floor. "I know it must've been a disturbing scene. But I'm here to get your statement about how you found Sonny Varino."

"I already told Gage," I said.

"I'm afraid you're going to need to tell it again, to me," she said, taking a seat.

I joined her at the table, laying out the basic facts. That I went by to see if Sonny was home this morning, and her front door was open. That I could see her through the screen door, sitting on the couch. That I thought she was sleeping. Or passed out.

"And what were you doing at her place this morning?"

I paused. "Jamie's gone," I said. Not sure, still, who I could trust—especially after her frantic phone call. The fact that she must've fled town when I didn't show. "I was trying to get in contact."

Serena tipped her head to the side and blinked slowly. "Jamie's gone," she repeated, as if she'd already heard.

I nodded, waiting to see if she'd add anything else—some insider information I might not have known. But Serena remained quiet, waiting for me to fill the silence instead.

I raised my arms in an exasperated shrug. "Is it true that Caden has been seeing Felicity Sterling?" I said it fast, before I could talk myself out of it. Every line felt like an accusation—a case I was steadily building against him.

Her eyes raised slowly to mine. "He was definitely not seeing Felicity Sterling."

"Pete Henderson said—"

She rolled her eyes. "*Pete Henderson* spends his days fishing and drinking. He's not a reliable source, Hazel."

"He's there all the time. At the bar. Said it's obvious."

She closed her notebook, leaned back in my kitchen chair. "What, exactly, did he say?"

"That Little Holt and her try to avoid each other now, which only makes it all the more obvious."

She let out a laugh from half her mouth. An exasperation. "Jesus, Hazel. He means *Gage*." And when I didn't respond, she added: "Little Holt? He looks just like your father."

"Oh," I said, reimagining the scenes. Walking into the restaurant with Nico and Gage that first night out, and Felicity looking down. Avoiding not me, but him. Had Gage been in the restaurant during lunch yesterday too?

At home, *Little Holt* would've meant Caden—both in age and in stature. It hadn't occurred to me it could've been anyone else.

"Honestly, I always thought you and Gage would end up together," I said.

She shook her head emphatically. "No, that ship has well and fully sailed," she said. She took a deep breath before continuing. "I grew up with a man like that. At some point, you realize it's not really what you want for yourself anymore." But then she smiled. "Makes for good detectives, though."

But Gage was nothing like the man who had interviewed me, all those years ago. Alberto Flores was firm and unyielding and exacting. He did not care that I was a child, that my mother had left me, that I was alone and ungrounded and lost.

And then I realized, *Little Holt* had taken Sonny's license away. Gage, not Caden.

I couldn't reconcile the way others talked about Little Holt. The slight tone of derision.

So maybe Gage was a little too by the book. But he was just like our father, trustworthy because he wouldn't bend the rules for anyone, not even family.

Maybe others didn't like the speed with which Gage had risen. The exacting way he followed the book, modeling himself after our father. How many people had he outpaced in his rise?

"You know, you and Caden, you're kind of the same," Serena said now, drumming her fingers against the table in a subtle rhythm.

She must've seen my active recoil.

"A little hotheaded, act before you think."

"We're not—" I said sharply, and she raised an eyebrow.

She grinned. "All gut and impulse, but it doesn't mean you're wrong." She leaned back casually in the chair, crossing her legs at the ankles. "Honestly, I'd rather it this way. It's much easier to deal with, out on the surface. What you see is what you get."

But I didn't agree.

Caden might *seem* straightforward on the surface, but he was always stirring up discord, in a vortex from below. I thought Caden was quieter in his intentions, the way he'd told Skyler that I wasn't really her aunt.

"I know this isn't the best time," she continued. "But I've also been meaning to talk to you again about your mother. And now seems as good a chance as any."

"Okay," I said. I folded my hands together, bracing them under the table.

"You should know, I managed to track down Joe Lyons." The name made my shoulders tighten, the room buzz. I got a flash of that lion tattoo, his sharp, toothy smile—even after all this time. "He owns a shop called Lyons Garage, still out in Carston Beach," she continued. "Real piece of work, but claims not to have heard from your mother since she took off with a family heirloom diamond ring."

My heart sank. "I didn't know that," I said. I'd thought we'd left because of his outbursts. His anger. The danger, simmering under the surface of him. Maybe both things could be true.

"Why would you?" she said. "You were a child." She uncrossed her legs, leaning forward. "But I don't know if he would've confessed to that part, if he had anything to do with her disappearance. He seemed both surprised and not, when I told him she's been missing for thirteen years. Like it made sense to him, that she'd done it again."

Another confirmation of the pattern. My mother, the thief. Perpetrator instead of victim. A reputation she couldn't shake.

"I want to ask once more, Hazel. Have you ever heard from her, *ever*, since the day she disappeared?"

Serena was very good at interviewing. A style between my father and hers—something all her own. She gave you an opportunity. Pulled it out of you. Leaned close and made you think she'd believe.

"Maybe once," I confessed.

"Maybe once?" she repeated, with a slight widening of her dark eyes.

"I got a postcard, when I was in college. Thought it might be from her."

"Where was it sent from?" She opened her notebook again.

"Some tiny town on the coast of Mexico. I looked it up after. El Cuyo."

Serena's hand hovered over the page, but she didn't write it down. Her face shifted subtly. "I know it, actually."

"You've been there?" What were the chances?

"I have . . ." she began. She tucked the pen and notebook away. "Pete Henderson has a little place there. He lets us all use it. Maybe he told your mother about it once."

Or maybe I was wrong. There was nothing that indicated the postcard had been sent from her. Just wishful thinking. A story I'd told myself—one that I wanted so desperately to believe.

I shook my head. "It wasn't signed," I said. "I guess anyone could have sent it."

Serena stood from the table, brushed her hands over the sides of her hips, smoothing her uniform pants. "Thanks for your help, Hazel. And it's a good thing you showed up when you did. Sonny Varino had already been dead a day."

I stared up at her, confused. "No. No, she wasn't."

She tipped her head to the side, standing over me. "No? I've got someone from the ME's office on scene who seemed pretty sure, judging by the state of rigor mortis."

"No," I repeated, emphatically this time. "I stopped by yesterday evening, and she wasn't home. The front door was closed. I left her a note."

She frowned, taking out her notepad once more. "When? When exactly?"

"Sometime around dinner. She wasn't there." But according to what Serena was saying, she'd already been dead. It didn't add up.

She remained perfectly still, like she was thinking things through, slipping a puzzle piece into place. "Why did you leave her a note?"

For a second, I debated lying, letting her believe some other story—something about Jamie, or Caden—without me at the center. I locked eyes with her for a beat, two. "I wanted to show her something," I said quietly. "I wanted to ask her something." Maybe I was naive. But Serena had let this interview go both ways. She'd given, as much as she'd taken. She'd listened. She'd promised.

"What did you want to ask her?" she said carefully, as if understanding there was something here.

I swallowed. "Can I see the pictures from the first car again, Serena?"

"Sure." She pulled them up on her phone, then placed the cell on the table in front of me. She stood behind me, so close I could hear her breathing as I scrolled left and right through the images.

A Buick. Brown. The bigger details seemed right, but the car had been through so much. It was impossible to truly identify from the photos.

I handed the phone back to her, then pulled my purse onto the table. "Do you think . . ." I began, reaching into the bag, ". . . that this is the same car?"

I handed her the photo, watched as she held it carefully at the edges, avoiding fingerprints.

My phone chimed in my bag, but I ignored it, keeping my gaze on Serena.

I registered her looking closer, holding her breath.

"That's their mother in the picture," I said. "This is her car." Roy had just confirmed as much.

She didn't answer. "Can I take this?" she asked.

I nodded.

"Serena," I added, as she turned for the front door. All gut and impulse. Acting before I thought it through. "My brothers don't know."

I watched Serena see herself out. Hoping she, too, was stern and by the book, like her father. Thinking how closely we were molded by the people who had come before us. Forging ourselves forward either in their path—or in resistance to it instead.

I waited until she was out of sight to pull out my phone, hoping against hope that it was a message from Jamie.

But the text was from Keira. I tried to drag my mind back to work, back to my real life.

She'd sent a thumbs-up for the photos of the house, then added a message.

I'm going to send these to FK with some thoughts, she wrote. He was our usual general contractor. *See if he can give us a ballpark range without going out there.*

Then, a second text: *Can you retake the ones from out back, though, without someone visible inside? You know he's superstitious. He's going to think it's haunted . . . Xx*

I had to read her message three times to understand. I'd sent two pictures of the back of the house. I looked at them now but couldn't see anything in the windows. Must've been a trick of the light or a smudge on her screen.

But I pulled the images up on my laptop to see what the issue was.

She was probably looking at them this way, enlarged, assessing everything, counting windows and doors and rooms.

I scanned the back of the house, and then froze. Beside the windows to the lower level, behind the grating of the crawl space vents, I saw it. A shadow.

The angle of the morning light, maybe.

I clicked to the next photo. The shadow had moved just slightly to the side.

Either an animal—a large one, capable of reaching the upper grates—or. *Or.*

Someone had been inside, looking out.

CHAPTER 22

Was I imagining things? Was *Keira*?

Was something *still* there, hiding below the house?

Kids, everyone kept saying. Kids, breaking into abandoned homes. But some petty thief or prankster must've known this house was occupied. I was standing right there, in the backyard, taking pictures. What were they *doing* here?

I listened to the house—the ticking of the grandfather clock, the hum of the refrigerator. The sounds of home. I'd been particularly attuned to the noises from above: a creak in the floorboard; a rustling in the vents; the beeping of the smoke detectors.

I hadn't given a second thought to what might be below.

Now I searched the house slowly, room by room, with my phone in hand. I stepped into every hallway alcove, every bedroom, checked the closets, even.

The house appeared secure, exactly as I'd left it. There was no sign of anyone else.

A figment, then. My imagination, creating monsters from nothing.

The shadow in that picture—I wouldn't have thought anything of it, if Keira hadn't pointed it out.

It could've been something inside the crawl space that cast a shadow from above. Or a raccoon, a trapped animal, walking along the sill, or along some shelving I didn't know existed inside.

There was one way to be sure. And I needed to be sure—especially now.

I went out the back and descended the deck steps. To the side of the basement sliding glass doors, a low wooden door led to the crawl space under the house.

I'd inspected so many houses this way, ducking in after the contractor before deciding to invest. The biggest risks were often exposed in the underbelly—in the level of moisture, evidence of mold, cracks in the foundation.

There was a padlock on the latch here, rusted along the border from years left in the rain. The numbers stuck as I moved them. I tried Dad's typical passcode—his birthday, which he also used for the garage. No luck. Then I tried Gage's birthday; Caden's; mine. Nothing.

I wondered how long it had been since the lock had last been opened. Maybe it was rusted on the inside, gears stuck.

I trudged up the side of the house and let myself into the garage, looking at the supply of tools my father kept in the house. Along the back wall, a hammer hung from a peg board, beside a wrench. Underneath, there was a familiar orange toolbox, the same one he used whether dropping a cable to connect a television or replacing a long board on the dock.

Now I carried the old toolbox with one hand, and the hammer in the other. He didn't have anything that could cut off the padlock, but the low wooden door was attached by hinges—and those I could pry off with a screwdriver and hammer.

I'd done it before. Abandoned properties often had old locks, forgotten codes, doors that had become wedged shut as the walls resettled. And the small crawl space doors never provided the same security as the entry points to the main home. The hinges here were on the outside.

The first hinge pin came out easily. But the second was stubborn and stuck. I tried bracing my feet against the concrete and pulling at the wood, but it didn't give. I had to reposition my angle and keep swinging the hammer, jamming my thumb, scratching my knuckles, until finally the second pin popped loose.

By the time I pulled the door open, I was sweating, and a line of blood trailed down the outside of my hand where it had scraped against the wood. I wiped it now against my jean shorts, and crawled through the opening below the house.

Inside, the earth was covered in a blue tarp to protect against moisture and mold.

It had been on his list beside the fridge: *Check crawl space.* I lifted my shirt over my mouth, just in case he knew something I did not.

Even though it was daylight, I had to use my phone to illuminate the space. The grated windows along the upper wall didn't let in much sun or air.

It felt colder under the house, and I was surprised I could stand up once I was through the door. Above me, ductwork and cables ran along the beams, tracing the rooms of the house.

Next to the entrance, to the right, there was a spot where old recreational equipment apparently went to die: an old kayak that I hadn't seen in years, covered in spiderwebs; two tangled fishing rods and a tackle box; a blue bike tipped over onto its side, handles askew.

I walked along the space against the back-facing wall, where the window squares in the concrete faced the outside. This was the spot the shadow had been. I was tall enough to see out, and to fit my hand through a tear in the last window grating.

There was a small corner of metal that seemed like it had been pulled slightly away, just big enough for a small animal to make its way inside. A squirrel or a chipmunk. Snakes. I shuddered, checking the uneven footing under my sneakers. The tarp rose and fell with the terrain. Anything could've been burrowed under there.

Maybe it was an animal, climbing the walls. . . .

The ground sloped below my feet as I made my way deeper into the space, so that I could touch the main level of the house above me. I used the flashlight to guide the way. In the back corner, there was a set of crude wooden slats in the shape of a rickety ladder, leading up to the ceiling.

I tried to figure out where I was in relation to the house. One of the boys' bedrooms, I thought.

Jesus. I wondered if others knew about it too.

I had to put my phone away to climb. I pressed my fingers into the square above the steps, and it gave, easily lifting with a slow creak. Beyond, the wooden hatch led into an equally dark space. I pushed through and shone my light around, trying to orient myself.

Four narrow walls. A rod above me. A door in front.

A closet.

I climbed up and opened the door, then found myself in the entrance of the guest bedroom—what had once been Caden's room. It still had his full-sized bed, his dark wood furniture, a collection of his baseball trophies.

I thought I caught a flash of movement out the window, but by the time I whipped my head in that direction, it was gone. I pressed my hands against the glass, peering out: nothing but the sloping, uneven terrain.

The pictures were messing with my head.

Carefully, I descended the steps from Caden's room into the darkness to close everything up again and secure the house as best I could. As I stumbled through the crawl space exit, I caught a whiff of smoke, the faint scent of something burning, out on the lake.

There was a no-burn notice, but if visitors had started arriving for the long weekend, they might not know. They might not care. They might not understand how quickly something could catch, and spread, especially now. Dead leaves blowing across the dry landscape, embers seeding, flames growing.

I picked up the broken door and attempted the code for the lock again, this time trying the one date I'd forgotten: Skyler's birthday. Immediately, it clicked open.

Of course, Dad. Why was I not surprised.

I had done too much damage to the hinges to reattach the crawl space entrance, so I maneuvered back inside and wedged the door into place behind me. Then I pulled the old, cobwebbed kayak in front of it. It wouldn't do much to stop someone—I'd have to get new hinges, a new door maybe—but it would be enough of a message to tell them: *I know.*

And then, in the spot where the kayak had just been, my flashlight swept over something in the corner, where the tarp had been pulled up.

Something red, catching on the light. I poked the tarp with my toe, exposing something hard and rectangular.

I sank to my knees—it was a red box.

I pulled the tarp farther aside, brushed the dirt from the corners. This was a small jewelry case. What was it doing in the crawl space of the house, hidden below a kayak, tucked underneath a tarp?

I opened the top—the few items inside were kept safe in a ziplock bag. Holding it up to the light of the window, I thought I could make out a delicate gold band. A bracelet with a teddy bear charm.

My heart raced.

These hadn't been my mother's. But the bracelet looked familiar. I believed these were some of the pieces of jewelry that once belonged to Audrey Holt. Pieces that hadn't been taken after all.

Pieces, instead, that had been hidden—buried—in the corner underneath my house.

My phone chimed in my hand, making me jump—as if someone was watching me *right now*. But it was just Gage.

EMERGENCY FAMILY DINNER.

He must've finally left the scene.

Another text came through immediately after: *7pm at Caden's. Ok?*

I responded with a quick thumbs-up, though there was nothing okay about this place, this house, this family.

Jamie had fled, believing something was after her. Her mother was dead. There were cars in the lake, and pieces of jewelry that had once belonged to a dead woman hidden in the darkest corner of my house.

It felt like the truth was trying to finally break free, on its own. Rising from the water, clawing out from the dirt.

A mechanical whir sounded from the corner, and I shone my light in that direction. But it was just the HVAC system, coming to life. Recirculating the air in the house.

I shuddered, imagining someone else in the spot I now sat. Listening to the sounds from above. With access to the heart of the house's functions. At home with the darkness.

I couldn't get out of here fast enough.

I took the jewelry case and climbed back up the ladder, into Caden's closet.

Who else had access to this crawl space? Who else knew about it? Whoever had been in here yesterday must've listened to my steps overhead, then watched me take photos of the house.

And now I was picturing the way those two people on the boat—the Water Hunters—had drifted near my house with their video cameras, asking who else lived here.

I'd thought it was a probing question about me, but now I was thinking it was something else.

As if they'd seen something that I hadn't.

I set up my laptop on the kitchen table and tried to track down the man and woman who had almost trespassed onto my property yesterday.

When I searched their names—*Miles, Amber, Water Hunters*—a small YouTube channel popped up showcasing their familiar tanned faces and bleached-blond hair.

Their bio read: *Siblings, investigators, adventurers.*

Their episodes were organized by location. It seemed they traveled the southeast, following the news of people both missing and found.

Their most recent video was called: *Mirror Lake, episode 2: See the site of the second car!*

I opened it immediately.

The clip began in the dark, with nothing but the sound of a boat engine. The beam of a small light faced forward, and I recognized the entrance to our inlet as they quietly churned into the area.

These must've been the boat lights I'd seen out back that night.

Now the light focused on Amber's face as she narrated.

"Somewhere in this quiet cove, a second car was pulled out of the depths. As you can see, it's a sleepy section of the lake." A pause. I heard the gentle lap of the water, could almost feel the rise and fall of the current. Behind her, I saw my own house, the lights on in half the windows.

It was eerie to see it from their angle, knowing I was just inside. I paused the video, wondering if I could catch a glimpse of myself. But the footage was too grainy in the dark. "We'll be back in the morning to see what other secrets this cove holds. But for now, imagine how this car could've possibly ended up here." She raised one eyebrow and the camera scanned the dark cove once more.

The video transitioned straight to the daylight, wind blowing in Miles's hair as he held the camera to record himself. "And here we are in the daytime. We'll see if we can get a better look at anything we missed."

Then the perspective cut to Amber's camera as they approached the dock at my house. "The only obvious way in is from this property," she said.

"Whoa, much shallower here," Miles said, grimacing at the

238 · MEGAN MIRANDA

camera. "The car must've been found a little farther out. By the swim platform, maybe. Amber, see if we can tie up over there."

The video then panned from my house to the surface of the lake.

One more cut, and the boat was out of the inlet, speeding away in the main channel. "Homeowners were *not* happy to see us there," Miles said confessionally, holding the camera super close to his face. His hair blew backward, making his bright blue eyes seem even wider, knowing. "Wonder what they don't want us finding." His smile grew. "Stay tuned for the next episode, when we finally go under the surface."

I groaned. They'd be back, they said. But there were no other episodes posted.

I wanted to see the rest of the video they'd taken. I knew they had me on tape marching down to the edge of the lake with the *Private Property* sign in my hand. Knew they had our entire interaction recorded. I guessed my threat of legal action prevented them from posting it.

I glanced out the window now, expecting to see them drifting on the water. But the lake remained eerily empty and dark and still.

The information section below the video had a note that said *Send us your tips!* with an email address.

I opened my own email and sent them a message with the subject line: *Second car tip.*

> *Hi, my name is Hazel Sharp. We met briefly when you tried to dock at my house yesterday. I was hoping to see the rest of your footage from that day. In exchange, I do have a tip for you. I know who the car belonged to.*

I pressed send, and then stared at my email, as if expecting an immediate response.

While I waited, I clicked their earlier video: *Mirror Lake, episode 1: See the first car site!*

This video opened with the two of them sitting on the edge of their boat, with the curve of the road behind them. I knew exactly where they were, had jumped off the rocks in the distance behind Miles's head myself, years earlier.

After an introduction from Miles, Amber took over. "We haven't been able to get much information from the police. But lucky for us, we have the man who found the first car with us here today!" The camera then scanned over to the man who had been just out of frame, beside Amber.

"Can you introduce yourself to us, tell us how it happened?" she asked.

"Sure thing," he said, and I saw that same rounded face, scruffy salt-and-pepper beard, guileless grin. It was Pete Henderson, his hat pulled low, squinting against the morning glare off the water.

A fisherman, the news had said. But Pete Henderson was many things. He was a cop first. He was a friend of the family. He had been my father's partner. He was with us in my kitchen the day my mother was discovered missing.

"My name's Pete. I was out fishing, like I do every morning. I was at a new spot—right here—" He gestured around him. "Wanted to check it out. And, well, my boat ended up almost right on top of it."

"Not a lot of people seem to fish here," Amber said, panning the camera around the empty curve of water.

"No," Pete continued. "Since it's right up on the road, it doesn't get a lot of action. But I'm retired, I've got time. I launch from Derry Pier, and pass by this site every day. I got curious. I'll try anything once." That smile again.

She nodded, urging him on.

"Anyway, I was just about to drop the anchor when I saw it."

"Did you know it was a car?" she asked.

"I thought it might be. Just because of how close it was to the road."

The camera panned up now. There was a series of bright orange cones, lining the curve.

"Long time ago, there wasn't any guardrail there," Pete contin-ued. "The township put one up about fifteen years back. It's only gone now because they had to remove it to pull out the car."

"Any idea whose car this was?"

"Nope," he said. "Just that it must've been here for a long time. Since before the guardrail was installed. So, fifteen years, at least."

Pete's face remained a flat line, eyes on the camera, like he was looking right at me. And I had to wonder what the chances were. He had been my father's partner before Nicholas Pritchard moved to town. In the Audrey years. What were the chances he would be the one to find that car?

What were the chances, now, that he would talk to me too?

I didn't have any contact information for Pete Henderson, and his name was too common to narrow down online. I knew I could probably find him at lunch, down at Reflection Point. But that wasn't the best place to go asking questions you didn't want others hearing about.

Instead, I went down to the basement, to check my father's old desktop computer, where he'd remained logged in to his email. I figured he might have Pete's personal contact information stored in an address book.

His email account was still empty, except for the message from the bank, resetting the password. Mine would've become overrun with junk mail by now, if nothing else. I checked his address book, but couldn't find a Pete Henderson.

I tried entering Pete's name into the search bar instead, hoping an old email might pop up or, at the very least, a contact address.

Nothing.

But then, as I was watching, a notification popped up for a new email.

It gave me the sense of him still being alive, somehow. Still able to receive messages.

The message was from a banking address, and the subject read: *REQUESTED ACCT STATUS.*

While I was still staring at it, the bolded message suddenly turned lighter. And then, seconds later, it disappeared entirely.

"What?" I said out loud.

I refreshed the inbox, but nothing happened. I checked the trash and spam, but everything was empty.

A chill worked its way down my spine, raising the hairs on the back of my neck.

Someone was in this account, right now. Someone had seen the email come through—read it, and deleted it immediately.

Someone else was monitoring this account, receiving notifications as messages came through, and deleting them.

Which meant they had probably seen when I'd reset the banking password. They knew someone else was looking around.

I wondered if they knew it was me.

A flash of movement in the mirrors jarred me from the screen. I stared, eyes burning, waiting.

Then I turned for the back doors, peering out. I slid them open—the scent of smoke was stronger now. Like it had wafted over the lake, settled in our inlet.

I frowned, walking toward the water.

Something was burning—a haze hung over the backyard. A crackle. A spark.

But it wasn't coming from the other side of the lake. It was here.

CHAPTER 23

70 Days without Rain
Thursday, May 23
3:30 p.m.
Precipitation: Zero

There was a small blaze growing in the fire pit that my father had built. The dry leaves curled and crackled, throwing off orange embers. I raced for the hose before one of them jumped to the yard—catching, spreading.

I doused the flames, until the pit sizzled to smoke. My arm shook with adrenaline as I sifted through the remnants, trying to find the spark. The pit was nothing but a sopping mess of soaked leaves and debris.

And there—at the edge of the circle—a cigarette.

Serena's, maybe, while she waited for me in the backyard, growing impatient, trying to settle her nerves? How long had it taken for the glowing ember to become a flame?

I didn't want to think of the other possibility, but I couldn't shake it from my mind. Not after seeing that photo. The feeling that someone had not only been out here but had set this fire intentionally. During a drought, with a no-burn notice. As if they had intended to do damage.

As if they had intended to harm.

A sound came from the side of the house. A scramble of footsteps in the dry landscape.

I dropped the hose and took out my phone instead, ready to call 911—

"Hazel?" a deep voice called. "Are you out here?"

Nico appeared from the corner of the house, and I tucked my phone away, relieved but still tense.

"You didn't answer the door, but I saw your car in the garage . . ."

I noticed him pause briefly, taking me in. I was dirty and dusty from being under the house, and probably had remnants of blood on my shorts.

His mouth hung slightly open. "I got your message. I heard at school, just when I was leaving. You okay?"

I shook my head, the images flooding back. Sonny, on the couch. The stale house. Her cold skin.

"I was the one who found her," I said.

His face fell. "Oh my god," he said. Here, then, was the comfort I hadn't gotten from Gage or from Caden.

He stood on the edge of the yard. And in that quiet space between us, I remembered that he had been the one to find his father. And that Caden had found ours, in the room just inside. How many of us were seeing those images now? How long would they haunt us?

Nico walked toward me, and I lowered my head straight to his chest, could hear his heartbeat through his button-down shirt, steady and fast. He didn't ask what I had been doing out here beside a sopping-wet fire pit, or why I was covered in dirt and sweat. As if it all made perfect sense to him. As if I did, even.

"Nico," I said, pulling back, "do you really think it's just kids? The break-ins Gage was talking about?"

His forehead creased slightly, like he was thinking it through. "It *was*. It definitely was. A fucking game to them. A joke. A dare. So reckless." His eyes drifted around the yard, into the trees. "It goes like this: Someone takes an item from the house—like proof. They pass it to the next. And then that person has to put it back and take something new from the house. Until someone in the chain finally chickens out." He rolled his eyes. "They're lucky they haven't been shot, honestly."

He seemed to know far more details than Gage had shared. "You know who it was?"

His face remained stoic. "I have my suspicions. But no, not *definitely*. Names get thrown around, but it doesn't mean it's true." He sighed. "But people talk, in class, in the halls. . . . I'm pretty sure it's over now. No one's talked about it in a long time, like they've lost interest." And then, eyes drifting up to the house. "Is something missing here?"

"Honestly, I wouldn't even know if it was. I was just thinking of the motion detector lights. The smoke detectors . . ."

He laughed. "I don't think that would count. But it's possible your dad put the lights up because of that, yeah. It's all the town was talking about a couple months back. No one was ever arrested for it."

"Did you ever tell Gage? That it was a game? Who you thought it was?"

He shook his head once, then again. "If I was wrong, I'd lose their trust—all of them. And there are bigger things that can happen around here, other than dumb teenage shit. . . . They need to know there's an adult who will listen." He sighed. "It's one thing if I was sure, but I'm not. So no." One side of his mouth quirked up. "Of course, it would be a different story if they broke into mine."

"They wouldn't dare."

"No," he said. "Truly, they wouldn't."

Kids, I told myself.

But I thought Nico was wrong; maybe it was kids who got smarter and stopped talking about it.

Kids, finding their way into a crawl space, with an access point to a closet.

Kids, lucking out and taking something, in a dare. Needing

to return it again later. Lights turning on as they ran through the night.

God knows I'd done worse when I was their age, just to feel like I could make something happen.

He checked his watch and grimaced. "I wish I could stay," he said. "But I'm running after-school lessons at the dive center. If there was anyone else I could call in . . ."

Nico's return to Mirror Lake after college wasn't primarily for the house, or even for the teaching. It was for the lake.

Here was a place he could build his dream. The things under the surface, or beyond the reach of the human eye. It's what first took him away from this place—the drive to see more, to explore—and then it was the thing that brought him straight back.

His father's money had all gone to him—not just the house. And he'd used it, along with his connections here, to establish the Dive Bar—which was not a bar at all, but its reputation lured people to it all the same.

Even the police had apparently partnered with him.

"Come with me, Hazel." He said it abruptly, definitively. "You should get out of here." His eyes drifted to the lake again, the swim platform moving with the current. "I don't think hanging around by yourself is good for you."

"I can't. I have to meet my brothers for dinner," I said. And then: "Can I show you something first?"

———

Nico followed me back inside, up to the kitchen, where I'd left the red jewelry case.

"You found this in the house?" he asked, as I opened the case for him.

"I found it *under* the house."

I felt his eyes taking me in again—reassessing the dust, the dirt, the blood.

He reached his hand out for the plastic bag, but didn't quite touch it.

"I think these belonged to Audrey Holt."

His eyes shot to mine, but he didn't respond.

"My mom didn't steal these. They weren't taken, but they were hidden." I left the rest unspoken: That if this part wasn't true, what else was a lie? Was the rest of her jewelry still here, hidden somewhere?

"Have you shown anyone else?" he asked.

"Just you," I said. *Just us.* The mantra of my youth. Maybe longer. But I had started to worry that this mantra was blinding me. Keeping me from seeing the things that might be dangerous.

I kept hearing Jamie's warning—that she didn't know who to trust—and I was afraid anything I told Gage would make its way straight to Caden.

The crawl space hatch was in Caden's room. I imagined him using it, sneaking out into the night, undetected. I imagined him hiding things under the floor of his closet that he didn't want found.

Nico paused at the exit before leaving, reaching for the disposable camera on the entryway table.

"You too?" he asked.

"Me too, *what?*"

"Seems to be a new trend around here. Kids at school, carrying them around. Using them instead of phones. Like they're rebelling against modern tech." He shrugged.

"I found it outside," I said, being careful with the details. "I really wanted to see what was on it, but I can't find a place that can develop the film anytime soon."

He frowned. "I know someone who might be able to," he said, looking up. "A friend." He cleared his throat. "A colleague. Teaches art, has a serious photography habit. She turned the art room closet into a darkroom, even."

His eyes drifted to the side, which made me think she hadn't been just a friend or colleague.

But this camera was the last thing left behind in the place Jamie said she'd be. "Take it," I said now. "Please."

I took a long shower, trying to wash away the memories of the day. The horror of finding Sonny on her couch. The photo of someone inside my house. The unsettling realization that there was an access point through that crawl space.

Nico was right: I had to get out of here.

I saw the sign for Reflection Point on the way to Caden's, and figured I had just enough time to stop in and look for Pete.

Reflection Point was as crowded on a Thursday evening as any weekend. A line of people waiting for seats stretched out the door. It was a different crowd from midday, when the tables were occupied by the cops.

When last I saw Pete Henderson, he'd implied he was here more often than not.

Inside, I bypassed the hostess stand and veered into the bar area. Every table was taken; every seat around the bar too. But no Pete.

Felicity caught my eye when she looked up from pouring a drink. She waved me closer, to the edge of the bar.

"Hey," she said, raising her voice to be heard over the laughter of the group beside her. "Did you hear about Sonny?"

"Yes." I didn't tell her I was the one who found her. "Have you seen Pete?"

She mixed a drink in a shaker, then peered over at me again. "Not since yesterday," she said. "But he sure is popular today. Serena was in here asking for him too."

I was checking my phone as I crossed the bridge back to my car, so I almost missed her. Serena Flores.

She was out of uniform, sitting against the base of a tree—staring out at the water. Probably on the same schedule as Caden, officially clocked out for the day.

"Serena?" I called. As I approached, I saw she had a sandwich to go, wrapped in paper.

She looked up, didn't object as I crouched to sit beside her, angling between the dry roots of a tree. "Did someone tell you I was here?" She looked over her shoulder, toward the department headquarters—the glass windows, the feeling of eyes staring out from behind the reflection.

"No, but I need to talk to you," I said, lowering my voice, wondering what she'd think of the jewelry case under the house. If it would change her understanding of my mother's disappearance. "I think I found something."

"There's nothing in there, Hazel," she said sharply, cutting me off. She turned to me abruptly, her dark eyes searching mine.

I couldn't keep up. She seemed to be somewhere else, in the middle of another conversation. "Nothing *where*?"

"The old file. Gage and Caden's mother. There were photos taken at the accident scene, referenced in the report, but they're gone now. The only thing left is a brief summary." She looked me over closely, like she was debating telling me. "The report said it was an accident. That she hit a stationary object."

A stationary object. Sounded like words chosen carefully.

"Can you ask your dad?" I asked.

She nodded slightly, on a delay. But it made me wary. That maybe I'd been wrong about her, and she had been forged in contrast to him instead.

"Pete Henderson found the car," I said.

"I know that," she said.

I suddenly wondered if she had been looking for him in order to question him.

"He's my godfather, did you know that?" Serena asked.

I swallowed, shook my head.

"Practically family," she added. "*Everyone* here is, whether I like it or not. This is my family. Every time I think about leaving, I think of another reason not to."

I didn't like how Serena was talking. Like she was drawing a line, pulling back. Reminding herself where her loyalties truly lay.

"This is your family too, Hazel." A warning.

Serena reached into her messenger bag then and pulled out the photo I'd given her. A young Gage and Caden, their mother, that car. She studied it closely, then handed it to me.

"I don't think it's the same one," she said, without looking at me. "You should hold on to this."

I took it from her, understanding fully what she was saying. What she had decided.

"Serena—"

"You need to stop," she said, ending the conversation. Ending this. She stood and walked away, head lowered, back toward the station.

There was no one here I could trust. Who would choose the truth over our fathers and brothers and friends. A legacy, bestowed on us.

As if she'd thought she wanted answers, and then realized, suddenly and vehemently, that she did not.

And that maybe I shouldn't either.

CHAPTER 24

When I rang the bell, Roy let me inside.

"You made it," he said, like it had been up for debate. Like I'd come from any farther than a half mile down the road.

The house was alive with noise. Not at all like the solemn, tense atmosphere I'd thought I'd be stepping into. I heard my brothers in the kitchen, the sound of Skyler's laughter. A baseball game in the living room, the cheer of a crowd.

On the walls lining the hallway, Jamie had hung family photos. I was surprised to see even I was up there, in a family shot from their wedding. Another where I was holding Skyler at the baptism. She had photos of Sonny, and one of Caden and his mother, facing each other, from when he was a baby.

I paused in front of it now. It was black-and-white, obviously a studio shot. She wore a bracelet with a teddy bear charm, and his chubby baby finger was hooked on to it, like it was a toy.

I felt a chill, though the house was warm: the bracelet, I was sure, that I just found hidden in the crawl space of my house. This was where I'd recognized it from.

"Coming?" Roy asked, jarring me back to the present. "Come on, this is supposed to be a peace offering."

"From who?" I asked. Since Gage sent the text, I didn't think this was really Caden's doing.

I floated down the hall, untethered. All I'd ever wanted was this, like Serena said—this family. The people who took me in and treated me as their own.

My heart rate had slowed, instead of speeding up, like my body was conserving energy. Like it could feel something coming.

Someone was watching Dad's emails, deleting them. Jamie had called me in a panic, and now she was gone.

Who could I possibly trust? Everyone here was connected not only to one another but also to the police. Pete had discovered the first car. Caden and Gage had not pointed out that it could've belonged to their mother. Serena returned the photo to me, washing her hands of it.

When I rounded the hall corner, I saw Skyler standing on a stool beside Gage, making a salad, while Caden tended to pasta on the stovetop.

My brothers were both good cooks. It was another thing Perry Holt had taught them. The two of them now moved through the kitchen with ease, acting like everything was normal, probably for Skyler's benefit.

I made myself smile. "Feeling better, Sky?" I asked.

She turned and grinned, holding a set of salad tongs, oozing dressing. She still looked a little tired, eyes puffy and skin faintly pale.

Though it could've also been because of the news about her grandmother.

"Hi there," Gage said, coming to greet me with a hug, like we hadn't just seen each other earlier at the house of a dead woman. And then I realized the reason, as he leaned in to whisper. "Skyler doesn't know yet. He doesn't want to tell her without Jamie here."

I tried to keep my breathing still, to lower my shoulders. Play at normal.

"Beer?" Caden asked, pulling one from the fridge. He held it in my direction, like an offering of something else. Maybe this was the olive branch—a bottle of beer and a home-cooked dinner.

"What's the emergency?" I deadpanned, taking it from his hand.

"Let's eat first," Roy said, cutting his eyes to Skyler.

Having Skyler around always helped bridge the divides between us. Over dinner, she narrated the baseball game for us, interjecting her thoughts on the umpire's calls, to Caden's obvious delight.

When I asked about school, just to fill the silence, she told us how some of the kids acted like they could read but were just faking, with a roll of her eyes so similar to Jamie's, it seized my heart.

She climbed into Caden's lap when her plate was mostly empty. She seemed drained, as if dinner had been work for her too. Maybe we were all pretending here.

"Why don't you go on upstairs, Sky," he said, looking at the clock. "It's a school night. Shower, teeth, bed."

She seemed hesitant to leave, like she was afraid of something too. Eventually, Caden stood, setting her on the floor beside him. "I'll be up soon to check on you," he promised.

We waited, not talking, until we heard the pitter-patter of her feet up the steps, and then the sound of the shower above us turning on, water rushing through the pipes.

"Hazel," Gage began, like he'd been waiting all this time. "This week has been very trying, for all of us." Chastising me, like he was my father. "We need to have a plan."

I blinked slowly at Gage, then at Caden. This was what we were here for, then. A talking down. "A plan," I repeated, confused.

Gage took a drink, then continued. "There are all these outsiders around who want information. Roy said they've been by the house, even?"

I set my jaw. "On the lake, yeah." I guessed now was not the time to tell him I'd just emailed them, offering information in a trade.

"We have to leave it to the department to sort through, Hazel. Not go around setting other people on edge."

Caden grunted in agreement. "Like Sonny," he said, not even looking me in the eye—his implication perfectly clear.

"Jesus, Caden," Gage said, just as I dropped my fork to my plate with a clatter.

"*Me?*" I asked, always rising to the moment with him.

Caden raised his head, looked me straight on. "Wherever you go," he said, even-toned, stabbing a piece of chicken, "chaos follows."

His aim was sure. Wasn't that my fear? That everything had been fine—or, at least, normal—until I turned up at her house? It's what Caden had said from the start. Everything was fine with Jamie until I showed up. Everything was fine with Sonny. *I* was the only thing that had changed. . . .

"Enough," Roy said, hands out. I was right—he was here to defuse the tension, to act like the adult, because Caden and I couldn't exist together without reverting back to teenagers, or worse.

I pivoted to Roy, deciding to find another outlet for my anger. "I thought you said this was a peace offering. What the hell am I even doing here?" I asked.

"Your father," Roy cut in, hands still up. "This would kill him. The way you're all acting toward each other. The things you're doing to each other."

"Hazel," Gage began again, leaning forward, getting straight to the point. "You can't go telling people Jamie's gone, like you're accusing Caden of something."

My gaze slid from one person to the next to the next. I remembered the panicked tone of Jamie's voice in that message. The fact that someone with a key had come into her house.

There were only so many possibilities.

"Sorry," I said. I wasn't going to argue. I didn't want to. Didn't want them to know what I knew.

"That's it?" Caden asked.

"What else do you want me to say? I'm *really* sorry, Caden."

But the discovery of Jamie's message had only doubled my suspicions. And I wasn't about to stay quiet. Luckily, I wasn't the only one looking anymore. She was Sonny's next of kin. It wouldn't be long here before things reached a critical mass.

"Okay, look," Gage cut in, "please keep this between us, but we're pretty sure Jamie went to visit her father. Got witnesses who tell us as much. We've called the department in Knoxville to send people out to Heath Varino's last known address."

"What?" I said. "Knoxville?"

I considered the possibility that Jamie had fled for Tennessee, to her father, whom, last I'd known, she'd rarely heard from, outside the occasional holiday cards.

Caden nodded slowly, in agreement.

But I thought they were lying to me. All of them.

"Look," Roy said, hands folded on the place mat. "There has to be an amicable way to handle the house."

I stared at him, eyes burning. Hadn't he been the one to tell me that Caden was going to contest the will? That my father meant for *me* to have it?

Did they know there was nothing else left?

Did they know that *I* knew?

"Handle *what*, exactly, about the house, Roy?" I asked. If this was where they wanted to go, I was going to make them spell it out.

"It might be best to consider a simple division of assets. To think about what, exactly, your father intended—" Roy said.

I kept my gaze focused on Roy. Is that why he was here? "Is this a negotiation?" I asked. Because if so, I knew how to run those. I was very, very good at them.

"We're trying to understand what Dad wanted. That's all," Gage said.

"It seems obvious what he wanted," I shot back. "That's the point of a will."

"Hazel, please," Gage said, head in his hands, like I was giving him a migraine.

"Can I get a copy of the will, Roy?" I asked, pivoting to my uncle. Gage had found a copy in the safe, but it seemed he'd taken it for himself.

"We all know what it says," Gage said.

"I want to see it," I said, eyes boring into his. "That's my right, isn't it?"

"Of course, Hazel," Roy said, voice calm and level. "I'll drop one by the house tomorrow morning on my way to work. Okay?"

I could've laughed out loud. This family emergency—this desire to make a plan—it was for them. It was only for me to stay quiet while they figured out how to take the house from me.

"I'm not discussing it anymore," I said. "So you can all just stop."

"Seriously, Hazel?" Caden asked, voice rising, anger evident. "Do you really think he intended to leave us with *nothing*?"

The room fell silent. Just the drone of the ball game, and the sound of Caden's hand slapping down on top of the table.

Oh, they knew. They knew there was nothing. They knew I knew it too.

Someone was inside that email account, watching. Watching me in there, and watching me out here . . .

"Dad?"

Caden cringed, and we all turned in the direction of the voice. Skyler stood at the base of the stairs, in a turquoise pajama set, wet hair dripping straight down her shoulders.

"Are you ready for bed?" he asked, trying to soften his expression, to shift the tenor of the room. But it was too late. Even Skyler must've felt it. Her wide eyes darted around the room.

She held a book in her hand. "I wanted to see if someone could read this to me."

I stood abruptly, needing to get away from them. Before I said something I didn't mean. Before I said something I *did* mean, but couldn't take back.

"I would love to," I said, hands on her shoulders, guiding her back up the steps. "Come on, Sky."

They called their good nights after her, but it was all too forced, and too late. Skyler was no fool.

———

Upstairs, I couldn't hear what the others were saying, but their voices carried—a low hum, a new plan forming. I tried to clear it from my head. Focus on just this. Skyler had been through enough in the last week—and she didn't even know about her grandmother yet.

She slipped into her bed with the purple sheets, and I scooted in beside her, resting against the headboard.

Her room was a sea of purple and horses, from the comforter to the stuffed animals to the walls. When I'd been through the house on Monday, looking for Jamie, her room was practically spotless—everything organized into cubbies and drawers. Now her toys and books were spread in a layer across the floor. Her hamper was overflowing, clothes heaped into piles around it.

Jamie's absence could be felt in every aspect of the house. But it was felt in this room, most of all.

She handed me the book, and it was obvious she'd paged through it many times before. "I can read, you know," she said.

"Oh, I know," I said.

"I just like it better when someone reads it to me instead."

I patted her hair, let her rest her wet head on my shoulder, while I read a story about a girl and a horse in a fantasy world, with no danger, and no loss.

I closed the book and tucked it on her shelf. "Grandpa got that for me," she said.

"He has good taste," I said, before catching myself on the use of present tense.

I turned away and started organizing her room. It was the least I could do for her now.

She watched me as I picked up the books and piled the toys into bins. And then she watched as I picked her clothes up off the floor. As I scooped up the last items—the shorts and T-shirt I'd seen her wearing on Monday—a folded-up envelope fell to the ground.

I dropped the clothes, staring.

Words in familiar, slanted handwriting stared back up at me.

Daughter of Mine.

I felt a scream building in my chest. A panic, quickly rising to the surface.

Skyler sat up in bed, looking straight at me.

Slowly, I bent to pick it up, my hands trembling as I did.

"Skyler," I said, trying to keep my voice steady and calm. "What is this?"

Trying, desperately, to control my reaction. But my ears were ringing, and the room felt too hot, and I could hear my heartbeat echoing inside my skull.

"My mom left it for me," she said. "I found it in my backpack when I got to school."

I swallowed dry air. Tried, desperately, not to panic, realizing the envelope had been inside her purple backpack on Monday, before I picked her up.

I stared down at the script. It looked almost identical. Except for the color of ink, which was a deep and bleeding purple.

The envelope trembled in my hand as I peered inside, but it was empty.

"Was there something inside?"

She nodded. Her eyes drifted to the open bedroom door. She lowered her voice. "I'm not supposed to tell." The secret she was keeping. A child, trying to navigate the unknown. Unsure what she could tell. *Who* she could tell.

"Sky," I began, slowly and carefully. "This isn't from her. This isn't her handwriting."

I heard the warnings again of the people who had arrived on the boat. Two cars, and didn't I wonder who lived beside me? Their implication, which I'd laughed off, pushed away: a serial killer in Mirror Lake.

Gage and Caden's mother. My mother. Her mother.

Someone was coming up the steps, and I eased the door shut quickly.

"She's coming back," Skyler said, in stubbornness or desperation. Her eyes, I noticed, were slowly filling with tears.

I nodded, the room on fire.

"Please," I said. "Show me."

She climbed out of bed and pulled open her jewelry box. A tiny ballerina spun around, music playing a little too slowly, like it needed a battery.

She lifted a plastic friendship bracelet and a necklace with a unicorn pendant, placing them aside.

Then she removed the felt bottom of the jewelry box, exposing a lined piece of paper, folded into a square.

"She's coming back," she said, placing it in my hand. "She promised."

I unfolded it carefully, with trembling fingers. Wondering if the message in this *Daughter of Mine* envelope would be the same: *I hope one day you can forgive me.*

And it was. It almost was.

But here, the message stretched on, down the page, purple ink, slanted handwriting:

I hope one day you can forgive me for this.
We have to go. It's not safe for us here.
Pack light. Bring only what you need. I'll be back for you tonight.
We're being watched.
Don't tell.

CHAPTER 25

W*e're being watched.*

Don't tell.

"Your mom sent you to school on Monday with this in your backpack?" I asked Skyler, trying and failing to control the waver in my voice.

She blinked, eyes welling. "My dad brought me to school," she said.

There was a creak in the hall—someone at the top of the steps, coming this way.

"I need to take this, Skyler."

"You won't tell?" she said, in a question. Big blue eyes suddenly spilling over.

"I won't," I said. That much, I could promise.

I saw myself out. Brushed by Caden in the hall, standing just outside the door, like he'd been about to come inside.

Ignored Roy in the kitchen, and Gage trailing after me into the night, calling: "Let's not leave things like this, Hazel—"

I had to get back to the house.

I didn't understand how there could be two letters. One for me. One for Skyler.

I'd only ever told Nico what I'd found, after his father died later that year. When he'd told me something dark and true about himself, and I'd done the same.

But I'd kept the letter in my safe—a piece of my core. An absence I'd grown from for more than a decade.

I drove straight home, pulled all the way into the garage, then sat there listening to the ticking engine, breathing in the scent of gasoline, my father's truck beside me. In the dim overhead light of my car, I unfolded the letter again and read it once, twice, three times.

I'll be back for you tonight.

I went inside, locked the garage door behind me, and slowly flicked on the lights, like a trail to follow—like my father had always joked.

My letter was under a layer of clothing inside my suitcase, and for a moment, as I reached through, I was afraid it was gone. How easily things tended to disappear around here. Money and people and things.

But my finger brushed the edge of the manila folder that I kept the letter in, along with that postcard, for safekeeping.

Side by side, the envelopes looked so similar, other than the color of ink. The same curl of the *g* that I recognized as my mother's. The size of the *D*, the angle of the *M*.

They had the same idiosyncrasies. The same spacing. The same emphatic line under the words, even, in a way that felt almost eerie.

Maybe the purple one seemed more rushed—like it was scrawled swiftly in the dark. Maybe the pen strokes were heavier in the blue. Maybe. But the differences were subtle.

I stacked the envelopes together, slipping one behind the other, and held them to the light. In the glow of the desk lamp, the words lined up, letter for letter.

They were *too* close. In a way that felt unsettling instead of natural. An uncanny valley of pen strokes.

As if, I realized with a start, one had been traced off the other.

But it made no sense. I'd had this envelope, and this letter, inside my safe in my apartment in Charlotte. It had never been out of my possession. How could Skyler's letter be so close to the one that had been left for me?

I took pictures of them, side by side.

My phone showed that a new message had come through, and I opened it, hoping for the video from the Water Hunters.

The message was indeed from them, but there was no attachment. The message was short and succinct: *You first.*

I'd promised a tip about the second car, and it seemed I wasn't going to get the video without it. Gage had warned me to keep things quiet, to let the police sort it out, but I'd seen what the police here did with the things that made them uncomfortable—burying them instead of digging. Being careful never to disrupt their sense of security—or the legacy of the ones who had come before.

It was time for everything to come out, for the ruse to collapse under the weight of our own history.

It was time.

The car belonged to my mother, I wrote. *She disappeared thirteen years ago. Her name was Libby Sharp.*

I sent the message and waited. And while I did, I tried to make the pieces fit. Thinking of who might've had access to my letter. Why they would've done this. What they *wanted*—

I took the lined pages and placed Skyler's longer letter over mine. The words similarly lined up.

And then, with a sharp intake of air, I switched the order. Laying my short letter over the longer one instead.

I felt my knees buckling, the room swaying.

What if the letter under my pillow was not the original version? The one in Skyler's backpack—what if *that* was the original, instead?

I felt a wave of something unfamiliar rolling through my gut. The satisfaction of discovery, the horror of what it meant.

It wasn't Skyler's mother who had planned to come back.

It was mine.

CHAPTER 26

She had been coming back for me. And someone had stopped her. Dumped her car behind our house. Erased every trace. Made it look like she had planned an escape and left me behind.

I pictured a shadowy figure in the house. Creeping down the steps to my bedroom, finding the letter left behind for me—forging a different one in its place. I'd never had a chance to see the original, because I'd stayed at Jamie's that night instead.

I closed my eyes and saw that familiar last image of her, standing at the kitchen window, staring out at the lake. For so long, I wanted her to turn around, *tell me the truth*, say it to my face.

But the truth was not what I'd always believed.

She never imagined—never planned—that she wouldn't see me again.

What had happened next? She'd gone to the bank and taken out the money. She had planned to come back for me. . . .

Had she made it back to the house that night? Had she looked for me? Gone into my room and called my name? Did she think I'd found her warning, but didn't want to go?

Had Jamie found the original letter somewhere in this house? Found it in my father's things, as she was boxing them up, emptying drawers, organizing the closet?

While my brothers and I were in his office, tallying his personal paperwork, she'd been in his bedroom, with Skyler.

And later, while I'd been out back with the police after the discovery of the car, Jamie was inside, keeping Skyler away from it. What had she uncovered in that time? What had she understood?

She must've been afraid.

Afraid enough to hide this letter away inside Skyler's backpack, for safekeeping. Until Skyler accidentally took it to school the next day.

My father must've had it in his things . . . which meant that he must've known the truth, at the very least.

The story he had woven for my life. The event that had molded me, that I'd risen beyond. I'd been forged by his lie.

And then I did scream. Something from the depths of my gut, muffled by the walls.

It's not safe for us here, she'd written.

It's not safe.

We're being watched.

My phone suddenly chimed—as if I were *still* being watched. And hadn't I felt it? Eyes, in the house. Eyes, on the road. Eyes, finding me at the Barrel. A web of whispers, threading through town.

But it was just another email from the Water Hunters. There was no message inside, only an attachment for a video, marked by the date and location:

CarSite2 - Wed AM.

I could tell by the lack of steady focus, by the casual chatter in the background, that this was—as requested—the raw footage from that morning, taken from Miles's camera. It was jerky in his hand as their boat sped into our private cove.

While he narrated their arrival, and then Amber gave the overview of the story, I kept my eyes glued to my father's house in the background, whenever the camera would pan that way. I kept pausing the feed, looking for something I had missed before. Something near the crawl space entrance, maybe.

But the only thing I saw was the second-level door of the kitchen sliding open, and me, walking down the steps.

"Oh shit," Miles said. "She looks pissed."

"Keep going," Amber said, as they pushed back from the dock, aiming for the swim platform instead. "We have every right to be here."

I saw myself marching down the slope of the yard, staking the *Private Property* sign into the earth. I saw myself call out to them, arms moving dramatically, with unrestrained anger.

And then I paused the frame. The house was too far in the background, and Miles had been moving the camera, but I saw it: the image of someone else quickly climbing the deck steps.

My entire body went cold.

The siblings on the water had seen it too. Someone else, entering my house. Entering in the easiest way possible—I'd left the back door open.

I scrolled back and forth, trying to get a clearer view of the person. But whoever it was became a blur of dark colors, nondescript clothing. Dark pants. Dark shirt. Maybe their hand was on the rail. Maybe their head was tucked down. But every time I zoomed in, the image pixelated and distorted.

Nothing, except for the fact that there was another person here. And they had gotten inside.

Now I stood in the middle of the basement hall, perfectly still, listening to the silence.

How long had this intruder been inside? Had they checked what I was up to? Had they been there, still, when I came back, after chasing the boat away? Had they watched me, followed me, biding their time, and waiting?

Could they be here *now*?

I tried to clear my head, watch again. Focus on the way they moved. Could it be a kid? They looked so confident. They didn't pause—they *committed*, and they moved.

My eyes were growing strained, and everything had started to blur. I paused the video at a sudden flash of reflected light. Something near the middle of the body.

Something shining from the waist.

I pushed back from the screen, my heart pounding. The dark pants, the dark shirt. Something hanging from a belt. My best guess: a police uniform.

I'd checked the house from top to bottom, but I hadn't known about the crawl space entrance until this morning. How many other access points were there?

I thought of my father's list again: *Check basement. Check garage. Check crawl space.*

As if he were warning me.

I pulled at the two sets of sliding doors of the lower level, making sure they were secure, first in my room, and then in the rec space, where my reflection stared back at me from the series of mirrors lining the walls. Like my father had been trying to keep an eye on something *out there.*

Careful, so careful, not to let it inside.

I had to get out of here. My mother had tried to warn me, from the start: *It's not safe for us here—*

I didn't recognize the way my spine had stiffened, and my ears were ringing, and the way my head felt untethered, my thoughts disconnected from time. And then I realized: I was afraid. Well and truly afraid. Afraid, after watching that video of someone sneaking into my house.

After seeing those two letters, and realizing someone had copied my mother's note, and left a forgery for me instead.

Afraid about what really happened to my mother that night, and angry—furious, really— that I'd spent all this time so readily believing the lie that had been crafted to explain her absence.

Afraid that Jamie was gone because of what she had uncovered.

Afraid that I had drawn too much attention, and now I would be next.

It was after midnight, but I couldn't stay here. Couldn't be in this house, not with those letters and the person on the video feed, walking brazenly through the back doors.

I texted Nico, but he didn't respond. I called, but his line just rang until I was sent to voicemail. He was probably dead asleep. I knew he had to be up early in the morning, but he was the one person who would understand. The last person left in Mirror Lake who I trusted. Who would tell me if I was seeing things clearly. Who would make sure I wasn't jumping to conclusions, my mind clouded by fear and grief and shock.

I wanted to cut through the woods between our homes, the quickest distance. But I knew the second I crossed the concrete pad out back, the floodlights would flash, drawing attention.

I heard my father's warning—*Hazel, the lights!*—and knew instinctively that I should stay in the dark, so that whoever might be hidden out there, watching, couldn't see me.

So I could have the upper hand.

I eased out my bedroom slider, staying close to the wall, careful not to trigger the motion detector. I traced the edge of the patio until I found the plug box and pulled the cord free.

I held my breath and took a silent step forward, to test the trigger.

See, Dad? I thought, as the yard remained bathed in darkness. *I'm paying attention.*

No one could follow my trail now.

I locked up the entrance behind me and pocketed the key—making sure everything was secure.

And then, under the safety of darkness, I stepped out into the night.

CHAPTER 27

moved quietly through the woods, pausing every few steps to make sure I wasn't being followed.

I could hear the lapping of the water against the shoreline, the wind rushing through the leaves above, and then skittering across the ground in a delayed echo.

The moon shone brightly, reflecting off the surface of the lake, but I couldn't see any other lights out on the water.

It was just me and the night, and I felt my heart rate slowing, a feeling of comfort and safety in the geography of this place I knew so well.

I waited for my eyes to adjust, and moved by memory through the woods, until I knew I had crossed onto Pritchard property. Here, the slope had been graded with steps built into the landscape, edged with logs, coated with slate and gravel.

The terrain was uneven and dangerous if you didn't watch where you were going, and I discovered that there'd been a hand-rail added in the years since they'd first lived here. Probably a safety necessity for when they were renting out the property.

I kept my grip on the wooden rail now, as I made my way up the back slope, toward their house.

All of the windows were dark. The living room and kitchen were on the base level, along with the primary bedroom. The other two bedrooms were upstairs, facing the front.

At the edge of the patio, I knew, was a loose tile, where Nico kept the spare key.

I pried the piece of slate up quietly, and I closed it in my grip, easing the slate gently back into place.

How trusting he had always been.

I let myself in through the back door, hinges squeaking as I pushed it closed behind me. Safely inside, I let out a sigh of relief. I'd made it this far, unseen.

I didn't want to spook Nico either. So I flipped on the dim light over the kitchen table and saw his white sneakers, bottoms coated in mud, beside the door.

I kept moving through the house, stopping at the primary bedroom on the lower level. It was dark inside, the curtains pulled tight. The door was open, but I knocked anyway, then waited a second before calling his name.

No response.

I shone my flashlight around the room. But the bed was empty and the comforter pulled up, tucked neatly below plush pillows.

Maybe he still slept upstairs in the room that had been his growing up. I moved by muscle memory now—how quickly all these things came back. It was always like that with Nico. The grounding I needed. A reminder, of something true.

Hand on the banister, fourteen steps to the second level, his room first on the right.

I stood in the entrance now and could see the glow of his phone charging on the bedside table.

"Nico?" I whispered. I took a step into the room, but no one stirred. I ran the flashlight along the bed. Empty.

Back out in the hall, I headed to the only other bedroom upstairs.

Something brushed my shoulder, and I jumped, hand out. But it was just a string—dangling from the ceiling. I looked up, light from my phone held in front of me.

The attic entrance was open, access panel hanging down from its hinges, the cord dangling in the middle of the hall.

The attic steps weren't lowered—I couldn't see inside. Just a darkness, beckoning.

Two more steps to the last bedroom, though I couldn't imagine Nico sleeping in there. It was the guest bedroom. The place his father had stayed before the divorce. The place where we'd once found that secret room, tucked behind the closet.

But as soon as I stepped inside, I knew he was there by the steady rise and fall of his breathing, a familiar rhythm.

"Nico?" I said softly, taking another step inside, the floor creaking below me.

I directed the light onto the bed, where I saw the shape of him, asleep on top of the sheets.

I registered the moment his breathing changed. He pushed up slightly in bed.

"Hazel?" he asked, voice rough with sleep.

"Yes." As I began to move closer to the bed, the beam of my flashlight arced across the room. And then I froze. Felt that cold, cold fear that had started at my own house, and that I couldn't quite shake.

Along the far wall, beside the closet, there were pictures. Pictures taped together, taped up, dark and haunting. Pictures I'd seen once before, years ago. The pictures we'd torn from the wall and thrown away. That Gage had dumped in the trash on the way home.

I took a step back, grasping for balance.

Another step.

"Hazel, wait," he said, bed springs creaking as he rose, following me.

I backed down the hall, nearly tripping over myself in the dark.

"Please," he said. "Let me explain." He kept coming, swift and assured. It was the first time he'd ever chased after me when I'd left. The first time he tried to get me to stay.

His hand groped my wrist, just as I reached the stairs. Fingers closing tight and firm. "Please," he said again, his body trembling. "It's not what you think."

I stood there, balanced between his body and the empty stairwell. I couldn't tell whether the fear coursing through my body was for this moment or for the discovery of that letter. As if I were in shock.

"I need you to look at them," he said, when I didn't answer. His hand relaxed on my wrist, and he took a step back, waiting.

My head was buzzing with anticipation. I thought I could trust him. That I saw underneath the surface of everything—

I felt something tingling across my skin. Like time had contracted, and I was suddenly both the girl who had first discovered that room and the adult coming back to it.

Sometimes, when I thought back to that night—the way we scrambled so quickly to get the pictures down; the way Gage made me promise never to speak of it again—another possibility would briefly cross into my mind, in a fleeting, grasping moment:

There were two people living in that house.

Which meant there was a chance that secret room belonged to Nico, instead.

Maybe the question had always kept me at a distance. Or maybe the mystery had kept me coming back—that I could never be sure what existed at the heart of him. Only that he saw something in me that drew him closer too.

And so, even now, I followed him back to that room. As if I might finally understand something not only about the pictures but about time, about him, about myself.

Isn't that what I'd always wanted? To find the mystery inside, and unwind it?

He flicked the light and a yellowish glow came from the bedside table. I saw the imprint of his body on the comforter—where he must've fallen asleep. And then the trash bag on the floor that he must've rescued, years earlier, from where we'd dumped it on the way out of his house. He must've stored it in the attic, for over a decade.

And then I saw the pictures.

This time, I made sure to look at *them*, instead of him.

They were not quite as I remembered. In my mind, they had been more violent, brutal. Limbs bent unnaturally. Blood pooling. Hand reaching out desperately in a lifeless state.

But up close, against the wall, the images were a little flatter. And I finally understood that they were all of the same woman, just from different angles. A close-up of her hair in the dirt. Her limbs, scratched, but sneakers on her feet.

An arm stretching away from her body, bracelet broken and caked with dirt, instead of blood.

"Oh," I said, standing closer, so that my face was just inches from the last image.

"You see it?" he asked. Needing me to say it, to confirm.

I reached a finger out to the photo, which had been torn in half, taped back together.

I traced a line down the bracelet to the charm of the tiny teddy bear, tucked into the dirt.

I'd seen it in a picture hanging from the wall of Jamie and Caden's house.

And I'd seen it earlier today, in the jewelry case under my house.

"I see it," I said.

He nodded solemnly, and I could see his throat moving as he swallowed. "The scene of the accident," he said, pointing to a wider shot.

Not a crime scene. An accident scene.

"Are these police photos? They're missing from the official file at the station," I said, remembering what Serena had told me. "Serena said they were gone."

His gaze slid back to the wall. The pictures existed here, and here alone.

"I'd always thought she hit a tree," he said, face contorted in confusion.

I felt a thrumming in my chest, a rush of adrenaline. A puzzle piece sliding into place. "Me too. But no," I corrected, remembering the detail from the file. "She hit a stationary object."

Close your eyes and see it now: A brown car, stationary in the road. A bike, coming down the hill too fast. A crash.

"My father," he began, voice breaking on the word. "I think he was investigating yours," he said, not looking at me.

I nodded. It must've been Nicholas Pritchard who had taken these photos from the file. Hid them out of sight as he quietly investigated his partner.

Sonny was right—you couldn't lose two wives. Someone would start asking questions. It seemed that someone had.

And within the year, Nicholas Pritchard ended up dead. *An accident*, the report had claimed, though we all thought we understood better: that it was a suicide.

But what if it wasn't?

I understood then how my father had kept the crime rate low and his cases closed for so long here. It was the fact that nothing was designated as a crime. There were accidents, disappearances, suicides.

Anything at all but murder.

"My mother was going to come back for me," I said, speaking the words aloud for the first time. "I was coming here to tell you. To show you." Something dark and true about myself, once more. "There was a different letter. Someone copied it. But only part of it."

I pulled up the images on my phone. He looked down at the photos, then back up at me, eyes wide and unflinching. I wanted to sink deeper into them, understand what he was thinking.

"What if she never made it out?" I said, at a whisper. "What if she's been down there, all along." I gestured toward the back of the house, toward the dark, dark surface of the lake—

"She's not," he said, but it sounded like how I'd promised Skyler her mother was coming back for her—a lie, because it was the kind thing to do. Or maybe just the easier thing.

He eased onto the edge of the bed, sitting down, but looking up at me.

"You know what's the worst thing I see, when I'm called out on a search?" he asked.

I thought of the things I'd told him—what we'd found hidden under the surface of a house: *words scratched into the walls, hidden under wallpaper; bees inside the hollow spaces; secret rooms that had to be pried open*—

I didn't know, now, if I wanted to hear it. But he continued anyway, voice dropped lower.

"It's what I can't find. Searches can take days. And sometimes people are still swimming on the surface, with no idea what we're doing out there. Drinking beer, diving off the edge of the boat. And all along, there's a body tangled in the branches underneath."

I shuddered, closing my eyes.

"The worst thing, though, is eventually they come up. As long as it's not too deep or too cold. They always do, Hazel. They come up, all on their own. It's much, much better if we find them first."

"How can you stand it?" I asked. "Going back to a place you've seen such terrible things." He still seemed to love the water.

"The dead," he said, "they're as much a part of this world as the living. They're not something to be afraid of."

But I *was* afraid. Afraid of what we might find out there one day. The thing I had never known could be out there—that was the worst possibility.

"She's not there, is what I'm saying. She's not," he repeated.

But he couldn't be sure there wasn't a body—bodies, even— weighted down, the work of a cold, cold killer. He'd just said so.

"They should search the rest of the inlet, though, right? To be sure?"

"There's nothing there," he said, eyes closed. "I promise. I've seen every inch of it."

I tipped my head to the side, just as he opened his eyes, something very dark suddenly alive between us.

"When," I asked.

"Hazel," he said, like a warning. Like a plea. Like he was trying to take it back.

"*When?*" I repeated.

He looked away, rubbed the side of his face. I watched him, so carefully, until he turned back to me. My eyes were burning, waiting.

Show me something dark and true.

"I started dive training just before college, remember?" He waited for me to answer—to stop him, maybe. But I wouldn't.

No, I thought, even as I could feel it building. Even as I wanted it, needed it, to be pulled out into the open.

"I remember," I said. He'd spent early mornings driving out to the old dive center halfway to Asheville, logging hours. He'd gotten his own equipment, hauled it around in the back of his car.

That summer, when we were together, if he wasn't with me, he was probably in the water.

"I wasn't supposed to dive alone. I knew that. But I wanted to practice. To see everything." That was always like him. The curiosity driving him. Pulling him from this place, and then bringing him right back to it. "I went down there."

My heart was beating so loudly inside my head, I was convinced he could hear it too.

Don't, I thought. But instead I said, "What did you see?"

"Something," he said, very quietly. So quietly, I knew he would never speak it again.

I shut my eyes, shook my head. "You knew it was there?"

That's why he didn't go down to see the car, with me and Gage. He already knew what we had found.

How many years had he kept silent?

"You knew my mom's car was behind the house," I said, needing to be sure. "All this time?"

"I knew *a* car was behind the house."

My eyes widened. "What else did you possibly think it could be?"

He raised his arms up, in a shrug, or in confession. "I thought my dad had *done* something, Hazel. You saw those pictures on the wall. I thought he had . . ." He trailed off. He thought his father had hurt people. Hurt *her*.

"I thought *he* was being investigated. I thought that's why he did it."

I shook my head. Of all the things, both dark and true, that he could've confessed. "A decade," I said. That's how long he'd kept the secret. And all that time, I might've known my mother hadn't left me. "How could you not tell me? How *could* you?" I asked, rage growing in the place where the fear had once been.

How could *anyone* do these things? Questions I'd been asking my entire life. *How could you leave me. How could you hurt me. How could you—*

"How could you ever be with me, if I had told you?" he said. "If you thought my father had hurt your mother?" He stared at me, imploring me to understand. But I couldn't. "You looked at me like I was a drug, and I loved you, and I couldn't say it. You thought she left, and you were *happy* here. And the longer I didn't say anything, it slowly became something I never could. I tried, but I couldn't do it. I thought it would ruin you." He shook his head. "I know it was the wrong thing, Hazel. Trust me, I know that now."

I was going to be sick. All the secrets I'd told him, and no one else. Believing he had done the same. But he'd kept this, for himself—and his father's legacy. The way he had pulled back at the end of that first summer so suddenly, without warning, leaving me confused and adrift. His darkest, truest secret.

"I knew you would never stay here," he said. "That once you

were gone, you could never truly come back. And I also knew I could never leave."

Like the car was a tether, holding him there. The perceived sins of his father that he'd kept hidden all these years.

Both of us, growing from a lie.

"But, Hazel," he said, even as I was backing away. "Those pictures on the wall, I've never gotten them out of my head. That hair, that hand, the bracelet. I was wrong." His voice cracked. "My father. He didn't do anything wrong."

As if that was the most important piece of information here. And maybe it was for him. An absolution, for the both of them.

I had thought my father might've been investigating Nicholas Pritchard. But I'd had it backward. *After* my mother disappeared, Detective Pritchard was investigating my father. Something didn't sit right with him. Not with the story told about my mother. And not with the story told about Audrey.

Nico took a step forward. "I know you well enough to know you won't forgive me for this." He didn't bother apologizing.

I had thought I wanted answers. I thought I wanted to know. I thought I wanted to understand what lay at the core of him, and us, and everything around us.

"Well," I said, my voice scratching against my throat, every word an effort. "You were right about one thing."

And then I left.

This time, I did not hear him follow.

CHAPTER 28

71 Days without Rain
Friday, May 24
3:00 a.m.
Precipitation: Zero

The Mirror Lake Motel was the last place I thought I'd end up when I returned home this week. It was certainly not the place I could ever have imagined I'd feel safest.

But I kept hearing my mother's warning: *It's not safe for us here.*

The motel lobby was empty in the middle of the night, but there was a sign beside the phone, designating a button to press for assistance. I checked over my shoulder, out the small front window, imagining a car pulling up. Following me. Knowing what I had in my possession.

That letter from my mother. Proof, that something dark and true had happened here. Proof, that it was *still* happening.

The same woman who had been here when I was looking for Sonny emerged through the back door. Her long bangs hung into her eyes, and she wore matching loose light blue pants and a T-shirt that might've been pajamas, but maybe not. From the way her eyes appeared hollow and bloodshot, I thought I'd woken her. I wondered if she lived on the premises.

She staggered slightly when she noticed me, but she asked no questions. She didn't even want my name. Maybe she took pity on me because of the way I stood there—shaking, looking over my shoulder, in the middle of the night. Maybe she'd seen other people arriving like this.

"Pull your car around back," she said, handing me a key but not making eye contact. "There's a curb. You'll have to go over, but it's fine. There's a parking area back in the trees. You'll see it."

Her hand brushed mine briefly as she handed me the key. Our eyes locked, just for a moment.

"Thank you," I said.

My room faced the woods, and my car was tucked out of sight in an empty clearing. No one would see me here from the road. No one knew where I was.

But I couldn't still my mind enough to sleep. Couldn't shake the pictures from Audrey Holt's accident, hanging on Nico's wall. Couldn't stop thinking about my mother's letter—hidden from me, for years, by my father.

I didn't know who was left to trust here.

I needed a grounding—something or someone to hold on to. That's why I'd raced over to Nico's in the night. It felt like I was circling something dangerous, spiraling closer. Getting pulled deeper and deeper, and losing myself in the process.

I opened my phone and sent Keira a text. I knew she kept her phone on Do Not Disturb through the night, so I didn't worry about waking her: *Sorry for the middle-of-the-night text. Just wanted to check in. Things are getting strange at the house. I didn't know anyone was inside that day until you pointed it out in the pictures. So I'm staying at a place nearby called the Mirror Lake Motel. Just wanted you to know where I was.*

The unspoken part, which I hadn't wanted to add: *In case something happens. In case I disappear.*

Who would come looking from outside Mirror Lake, if not for Keira and Luke?

There was only one person who seemed willing to talk about anything real here. Who seemed willing to share secrets, instead of keeping them.

Pete Henderson, fake-whispering gossip at the bar. Pete, interviewed on camera by the Water Hunters team. Pete, the tie to the single postcard I'd received—the only possible sign of my mother, after. And he'd said exactly where I could find him this morning.

<hr>

Derry Pier was one of the few public access points on the east side of the lake. It was now the only one usable after the water level at Gemma's Creek had gotten so low. It was rustic, in terms of amenities. A dirt parking lot in the trees. A handful of port-a-potties lining the perimeter. A concrete ramp, backing into the lake.

There was a wash station beside it with a hose and a basin, but now a handmade sign hung on a wooden post, due to the drought, warning: *DO NOT USE.*

It was barely sunrise—a gray sky lightening—but I pulled into the lot just in time to see a truck backing a trailer into the water. Pete Henderson stepped out of the truck, engine idling, to tie his boat to the edge of the dock, before revving back up into the parking lot.

The air felt charged, but I didn't know if it was just from my lack of sleep or the early morning hour.

Today was the start of the long weekend. People would be driving in, ready for their vacation. But something hovered, heavy and ominous, over the mountains. There was no orange glow, no pink haze. Nothing but a colorless void at dawn. Like the lake was a black hole, no color escaping.

I knew Pete saw me coming by the way he looked up and paused, before grabbing the tackle box and rod from the bed of his truck.

"Pete," I called, so he would know I was here for him.

"Hazel," he said, face hidden under the brim of his hat. His stomach hung over the waist of his khaki shorts, and his calves and arms were a deep tan, even this early in the season. "Surprise seeing you out here this time of morning."

He hadn't been at my father's memorial, opting to stay at the bar instead. And now I noticed the shiny pickup truck, the shiny boat at the dock, and wondered how he had come into money to support his early retirement, his vacation home—if this was where the cash from my father's empty accounts had been going.

Because of what he knew.

"You found the first car," I said, stepping into his path.

The trees cast long shadows across the lot, so that he stood in a pocket of darkness, expression unreadable.

He stepped to the side, a small smile under the brim of his hat. "That's no secret, Hazel."

I sidestepped into his path again. "I think you knew it was there."

Now he did stop, peering back up at the main road, like he was expecting someone else to arrive at any moment.

"Would you care to join me, Hazel?" he asked, gesturing with his rod toward the dock. "It's the best way to spend the morning, before the lake gets busy."

I paused for only a moment, considering. "Okay," I said. I fell into stride behind him, wondering if I should be more afraid. But he'd once been my father's partner. *Another type of family*, my father always said.

He heard things. He knew things. He was willing to talk. And my car was in the lot, with his. It was no secret where I was, if someone came looking.

"Oh, and Hazel," he said, pausing. "We don't bring phones out there." He turned to face me. "It's supposed to be relaxing out on the water. Phone calls, texts, that's not relaxing at all. Besides, things get wet out there. Damaged."

I didn't know if this was a threat. Pete wasn't dumb—he'd been part of the police department for decades before his retirement. He knew conversations could be recorded. And it seemed like he was offering me something now, in exchange for the promise that it wouldn't lead back to him.

Answers. The truth.

He peered at me from under his hat, eyes in shadow, like he was waiting for my decision.

"I'll meet you down there," I said, heading back for my car. I locked my phone inside, heart pounding, while he watched. There were no other cars in the lot yet.

I walked slowly, hoping someone else would pull in, notice me here. Proof of life. Place last seen.

By the time I made it onto the dock, Pete was pulling a cooler full of ice down into the boat. He reached a thick hand up for me, and I took it, a point of balance as I stepped down from the dock. The water level was lower than anticipated, and it was a long, unsettling drop down to the boat platform.

Pete put a second hand out to brace against, and the boat swayed with the change of balance. "Got it?" he asked.

"Got it," I said, taking a seat beside the cooler.

His gaze kept drifting up to the parking lot. Another car finally pulled in, but he quickly started the engine, pushing away from the dock.

As if he were doing something he shouldn't. As if, as much as I wanted to be seen, he did not.

I held my arms across my body as we started moving, preparing for the bite of the wind, the splash of the water, as we cut our way into the main channel.

I peered over the edge of the boat as he rounded a bend. The surface of the water was dark in the morning hour.

He headed to the spot where the first car had been pulled from the depths. Where he'd sat with the Water Hunters, narrating what he'd found. As if he intended to repeat the performance with me.

Here, the water fell to shadow, shaded on three sides by mountain and trees. Nothing was visible through the surface.

Pete turned off the engine, letting us drift as he opened the cooler. He pulled out a Bud Light and offered one to me. I put up my hand, to pass. If anything, I needed caffeine.

He shrugged and popped the top, the only noise the sizzle of carbonation before he took a sip.

"You know how many times I used to pass this inlet?" he asked, leaning back in the seat, gazing out at the water. "Every day. Every day on the road. And now every day on the water. Every day, since I've been retired, I think to myself, *There it is*."

He lifted his head to face me, though his features were still in shadow, like everything else. "It should've never been there," he said. And then he leaned forward, arms on his knees, a secret, just for me. "He's dead now, Hazel. It seemed like it was time."

I was right. Pete had found that car on purpose. Reported it *after* my father's death. Set everything in motion. I thought back to the voicemail he'd left. *I'm sorry, old friend—*

"Were you blackmailing him?" I asked.

"Now hold on," he said, standing abruptly, the boat shifting with the sudden change in weight. "Why would you think that?"

I placed an arm on the back of the seat, steadying myself. "This boat. Your place in Mexico. The early retirement," I began, for starters. I did not mention the lack of money in my father's accounts— the amounts going out, each month.

Pete frowned. "I'm an only child. Inherited everything from my parents when they passed, God rest their souls. Never had children of my own. So I have a little cash. I have a little freedom. I allow myself the odd indulgence. You really think . . ." He shook his head. "You've got it wrong, kid. I would never hurt him. I'd do anything for him. Just like he would for me." He seemed to notice he was hovering over me, and lowered himself back to his seat.

I tried to understand what he was saying. "You helped him?"

He nodded once. "He asked me for help, and I gave it. That's how it worked with us. No questions. If anyone had come asking him about the car later, he could say he didn't need it anymore. That it was stolen. Sold. Given away. Whatever."

"I don't get it," I said. "I don't understand why he'd have to hide it, if it was an accident." *A stationary object*, the report had said. A tree, I had been told. But she'd hit a car—her own car—instead.

Pete cut his gaze to me. "Really? What do you think happens when a woman is leaving her husband. When she rides off on a bike in the middle of the night after a fight, like she's trying to escape, because he took the keys to her car. And then he follows her, to bring her home? It doesn't look good, Hazel. Even I could see that." He lifted his hat, pushed back his graying hair, lowered it again.

Hadn't my father always said that if you wanted to run into someone in Mirror Lake, all you had to do was drive around until you found them?

"But you believed him?" I asked.

He tipped his head. "He didn't keep secrets from me. Told it to me straight. Didn't try to make it pretty. Said he'd gone around the loop to find her, to stop her. Spotted her on a side street and parked in the middle of the road where she'd be coming out, like a game of chicken. And she didn't—couldn't—stop in time. I'm not making excuses for the terrible thing that happened. He made a wrong decision, and then another, and it ended in tragedy. He became a different man after. You didn't know him before."

He was right. I couldn't imagine the person he was describing. He only existed in the time before I met him.

"He was terrified he'd lose those boys," he continued. "And hadn't they already lost enough? Who was going to raise them, if not him? As much as I loved your father, I wasn't exactly cut out for the role." He gave me a small smile.

"Why was she leaving him?" Sonny was right—had told me as much, about the trend of women leaving the Holt men. She always knew more than she let on.

He paused, frowned. "That, I couldn't tell you."

It was another secret I wondered if Roy knew. All the secrets he must've kept for my father—but he hadn't answered when I asked him directly. Clinging to the bonds of family, above all. But wasn't I family too?

"So, you dumped the car?" I asked. Was that it? Evidence destroyed, like it had never existed? Like everything here that was ugly and inconvenient—covered up, dumped in the lake, buried in a crawl space.

"Not at first, no. It seemed like it was going to play out exactly like the report said—as an accident. A tree, maybe. The car just sat there in his garage. But if you knew what you were looking for, you'd see it. Someone in the department started asking questions. Said we should've interviewed the boys, even. But hadn't they been traumatized enough, without making them relive it again?" He looked at me, waiting, like he was asking me to agree.

I nodded. I remembered being dragged down to the station after my mother disappeared, questioned like a suspect.

He continued. "Enough time had passed by then that it seemed logical he would've gotten rid of the car. She was gone, and they didn't need it anymore. So, I helped him."

I could almost understand it. A simple thing to do for family. She was gone, and what good would come from the truth?

"Gage and Caden—do they know?" I asked.

"About the car? I don't think they were really old enough to realize it was missing."

Not before it was raised from the lake. Not until Caden recognized something about it in the photo, rushing over to see if it could possibly be the same one from their old family albums—

"No. Do they know what really happened that night, I mean?"

He opened a second beer, the crack of the top cutting through the quiet morning. The boat creaked as it rocked in the current.

"Well, I'd think they'd have to," Pete finally said. "They were in the back seat."

He took a long drink while I sat there, frozen, taking in what he was saying. The absolute horror of it.

They were *there.*

"I'd assume they were both old enough to remember it," he continued. "As much as I wish they didn't."

My father had always driven a truck, but that night, he'd driven her car. Because he'd taken the boys with him, to stop her.

I closed my eyes and saw that photo of Gage and Caden and their mother, sitting on the hood of the car. How young they'd been. Five and seven. I imagined them now, eyes wide open, peering out into the night. Those images on Nico's wall—

Another boat sped by, the wake radiating outward, tipping us violently. Pete stood up, restarted the engine, moving us through the waves.

"Who else knows?" I asked as we idled.

He turned around, one hand still on the wheel. "Can't say I ever got around to asking. I assume Holt made sure the boys understood the importance of keeping it quiet. But the older I get, the less I like secrets. They eat at you. Destroy you from the inside out."

"Pete," I said quietly. Afraid, suddenly, of the answer to the question I was about to ask. "Do you know what happened to my mother?"

He paused, but only for a second. "No."

"Did you know the second car was hers?"

"I have heard that, yes." His gaze drifted away. "But I didn't know. I swear. I thought she left. Same as everyone else."

"She thought it wasn't safe here," I said, hoping he could tell me why.

"Like I said, I've seen what secrets can do to people and I want no part of it. I've kept my fair share when I've had to—but I do not keep them for the dead." He dropped his voice. "Secrets kept that long, they grow tendrils. Holt made his choice, but no one else should have to suffer for that, don't you think?"

As if he were trying to stop the spread by revealing it. Pulling the car out of the depths. Cutting off its power. But it had taken on a life of its own. Had he not anticipated the risks? It was too late to stop anything now.

One more thing. I had to know. "Pete, I got a postcard once, from where you have a place in Mexico. I thought, maybe, it was from her."

He shook his head emphatically. "No, no," he repeated. "I only bought that place about eight or nine years ago—it was well after she up and disappeared. You thought I tipped her off, sent her down there?"

But that wasn't what I thought at all anymore. Did someone notice I'd been searching, and send me that postcard to throw me off the track?

"Serena said some of the guys have used it. Who else has been there?" I asked. I couldn't bear to spell it out: *Do you think my father hurt her?*

He frowned, then laughed. "Everyone, Hazel." Then his face changed, as if he understood what I was looking for. What I was asking. "That department, it's the only family I have," he said, in an echo of Serena's warning. I would get nothing else from him now.

"I'm ready to go back," I said, shaking. I wanted to get out of this boat. Out of the scene that was running through my head. My brothers—the absence they had grown from. The horror they had witnessed that night, in the back seat of the car.

All of us here, emerging from moments of violence.

"That seems like a good idea," he said, angling the boat back toward the pier.

I had thought my father owned this town, but now it seemed like Mirror Lake had owned him instead.

As we approached the pier, another boat was launching into the water.

"Hi!" a woman called, too cheerful, waving to Pete.

As we got closer, I recognized Miles and Amber, heading back out onto the lake. Amber in a wet suit, Miles with the camera. They turned to watch as we pulled into the pier. I felt their eyes on me.

"Did you get the video?" Amber asked, eyes darting between me and Pete, in question.

I nodded, then pulled myself up onto the pier. I had told them everything I knew. I wanted to warn them it wasn't safe to go digging. That it was best to leave the secrets to the lake.

"Careful out there," Pete called, peering up at the sky. "Won't be too long now."

"Won't be too long for what?" I asked.

He tipped his head to the side. "Can't you feel it?" he asked, a smile slowly spreading. "The rain is coming."

I stared up at the sky, a gathering haze. A darkening shelf approaching from the mountains.

"You should think about heading home, Hazel," Pete advised, standing below me.

"Yes," I said. "I'm leaving."

"Another good idea." Pete tipped his hat, then angled away from the dock once more. "You always were the smart one."

CHAPTER 29

My phone was buzzing with missed calls as soon as I got back to my car and turned it on. I had several messages from both Keira and Luke, each growing more frantic. Keira must've woken to my text from last night, and not been able to reach me.

I quickly called her back, and she answered immediately. "Oh my god," she said. "We were just about to get in the car to come find you."

"I'm okay," I said. "I'm sorry I scared you. I'm coming home."

"Right now?" she asked. I could hear Luke in the background, asking follow-up questions.

"Soon. I just have to fix a door on the house, and then I'm leaving. I promise. I'll call as soon as I'm on the road."

"Okay," she said, hesitating briefly. "Just know if we don't hear, we're coming for you."

"Got it," I said. "And, Keira? Thank you for checking on me." I'd been worried no one would notice if something had happened to me. That I was running out of people who would care.

There was only one other car in the lot for the Country Store when I stopped in for supplies. I had wondered if I might cross paths with Nico at this time of the morning, but I seemed to be the first customer on-site.

Levi briefly looked up from his catalog when I entered, then back down, circling items on the glossy pages.

"I need a padlock," I said, marching up to the front counter. "Hinges. And something that can work as a door for a crawl space, if you have one."

Levi looked up again, eyes widening, fully taking me in this time. I knew I sounded slightly frantic. Which was exactly how I felt—I made no point of hiding it.

"Also, security cameras," I said, leaning both hands on the surface.

Cameras, to know who was coming into that house. Cameras, for proof.

He dropped his pen, letting it roll across the counter. He shifted the catalog over the top, facedown.

"Okay," he said. His throat moved as he swallowed, and his hand faintly trembled. He didn't make eye contact as he stood from his stool. "Let me see what's in the back."

He disappeared into the stockroom, and I drummed my fingers on the counter. Then I twisted the catalog, to see what was worth hiding from me. Like the whole town was in on some conspiracy, and I was the only one on the outside.

But it was just fishing gear. I shook my head to myself—the paranoia had taken over, tainting everything.

But then I saw the pen that had rolled underneath, gold catching the gleam of the overhead light.

I picked it up, shaking—with anger, this time.

"Hey, Levi," I called. "What's your last name?"

"Huh?" he asked, poking his head around the corner from the stockroom.

"I mean, you're a Mahoney, right?" Like all the ones who had come before, owning and working at this store. Sons following in their fathers' footsteps.

"Yes, ma'am," he said, disappearing again.

"So nothing that starts with an *H*, then."

He slowly stepped fully into the doorway, a padlock in his hand. His eyes drifted to the pen in my grip, where the letter *H* was engraved on the side. A gift I'd given my dad for Father's Day, years earlier. The pen currently missing from his office.

For a second, I thought this kid would take off running, but he shook his head instead. "No, ma'am."

I held the pen up, so I was perfectly clear. "Where'd you get this, Levi Mahoney?"

He swallowed again, face paling. "I found it."

"I think you took it, Levi. I think you've been inside my house."

That image of someone creeping up the steps. Eyes in the crawl space. A secret way inside.

"No, listen, no," he said, speaking faster than I'd heard before. "It was one of my friends. A stupid dare. I'm just supposed to get it back inside."

His eyes shifted around the store, as if one of these friends might be there. As if they might save him.

I was right. The game hadn't ended.

"And how did *your friends* get into *my house*, Levi?"

"The garage," he said sheepishly. "There was an unlocked window."

"I know what you've all been up to, Levi. Take something and return it until someone chickens out, is that right?"

He blinked rapidly, like he was debating his options. "We knew it was empty, we didn't think it'd hurt—"

"But it wasn't empty."

He walked closer now, more emboldened by his defense. "No, it *was*. After Holt—" He cleared his throat. "After Detective Holt passed on. No one was there."

"What else have you taken from my house, Levi Mahoney?"

His eyes drifted to the entrance again. He lowered his voice. "I'm sorry," he said. "The gun, that was stupid. My friend, he was getting more reckless. I tried to stop it. It just kept getting worse—"

"The *what*?"

His eyes widened. He'd thought I knew, and now he was caught. "The gun in the garage? It was stupid dangerous, I know that. I told him that. I brought it back right away, left it on the table. Right by the pictures. Figured someone would know what to do with it that way."

He said it like I should feel grateful to him for this act of responsibility. But I was still stuck on where they'd found it.

"The gun was in the garage," I repeated.

"Yeah. We were looking for a key. We didn't realize the door was already *open*." He rolled his eyes, as though unimpressed—either with my father or with his friends.

The wooden box had been locked with a silver key, the gun resting on a bed of maroon felt inside. I'd found it on the kitchen table, assumed it was my father's personal weapon.

"Where, exactly?" I asked.

"In the corner. Under the food. I'm sorry, it really got out of hand—"

I shot him a look, cutting him off.

It made no sense. Why would my father have hidden away this weapon? He was meticulous about safety. It should've been in his office, or on him, or in a safe. Stored safely and responsibly.

"I'm going to take this now," I said, raising the pen between us.

He nodded quickly, like he was just glad I wasn't calling the police. "I swear, I was trying to bring it back. I went by when we were out on Monday night, but someone was inside. I saw the lights. Someone behind the window, peeking out. Spooked me. I guess it was you." And then, quietly, "I'm really sorry, ma'am."

I pictured floodlights turning on in the night. The feeling that someone had been outside. Serena, poised with her hand on her weapon, like she'd heard something—

But I hadn't been there Monday night. I'd been home in Charlotte, and had carefully locked up behind me when I left. Now I was remembering that feeling when I came back on Tuesday. The dirt in the hall. The dripping faucet.

Someone else had been inside while I was gone.

I stepped outside the store with a new lock, a set of hinges, and a pair of wireless cameras, staring out at the gray sky. Pete was right—the wind had gotten hot, dense with humidity. I tipped my head back, and a big thick drop fell on my forehead, like a blessing.

I felt the earth, calling the rain closer. The lake, a vortex, pulling everything back home.

My windshield kept misting over as I drove home. Not enough to use the wipers, just enough to coat the glass in a thin film.

At the house, there was a package on the front steps, sheltered by the overhang from the mist, my name in block letters across the envelope.

Like Roy had promised, a copy of the will was inside. He'd included a handwritten note, to meet him for lunch at the café by his office.

I took it inside and read the details. It had been notarized at the bank, years earlier. But it seemed like my father had created it himself, with an online program. I thought how easily Caden might be able to contest this, wondering if I'd played a hand. How precarious my claim might seem.

The specifics in the will itself were as Roy had said—the house in Mirror Lake was to go to one Hazel Sharp, born June 3, 1996.

But then I got to the next line. The part that must've shaken the foundation, turned everything completely toxic.

The contents of the house were also at the discretion of Hazel Sharp.

I thought of everything inside the boundaries of this property.

Every picture. Every memory. Every item of furniture. The truck in the garage. The gun, even.

And then I remembered how Gage had asked me for Dad's wedding ring, when I'd found it. Like he was asking for my permission.

Because he was. According to the will, he *needed* it. Everything here was mine. They had hoped to clean it out without my oversight. Hoped I wouldn't notice, until it was too late. Even Roy had shown up that day, in on the plan.

But once I was here for the memorial and Jamie told me their plans, everything changed.

I wondered if she had seen the will too—if she knew they were planning to do something they shouldn't. If she'd been trying to right it.

I passed through the house, seeing everything in a new light: Mine. For me to decide.

Why, Dad?

I went out to the garage, where Levi said he'd found the gun.

I pushed aside the stacks of food I'd teased my father about, saw the gap between the concrete pad and the wall. Just enough space to wedge a box.

I needed to see that gun now. I returned inside and opened the china cabinet, pulling out the box, and fishing the key from the cup on the upper shelf. Then I brought it over to the table and opened the top.

My mother had bought a gun. I'd learned this during the investigation into her disappearance. She'd bought one, but hadn't needed to use it. If my father had another weapon, he would've left it on the itemized list for us to find together—the responsible thing. No, this wasn't his.

This gun must have belonged to my mother.

I wondered if she'd come back home for me, armed, for her protection. If it got turned on her instead—

Why was it *here*? A small case of jewelry, in the crawl space. A gun, in the garage. Pieces of evidence, spread hidden around the house.

Everything's in the house.

I turned around, walked slowly to the refrigerator, where a note still hung from the side.

Check basement. Check garage. Check crawl space.

As if he hadn't been double-checking the entry points to the house but telling me something instead. Leaving a trail, for me to follow.

Check basement.

I walked down the steps slowly, looking for any crevices or alcoves that I'd failed to notice. I pulled the furniture away from the walls, ran my hands under my mattress, stripped the cushions from the couches.

Where, Dad? A wave of grief washed through me as I looked around the room. From the realization that I could never ask. Never get an answer. Never hear him calling after me again, *Hazel, the lights!*

I checked the entertainment console, emptied drawers, looked up at the lights. Used the contents of my father's toolbox to dismantle a hollow end table. I caught a glimpse of myself, looking disheveled and erratic, in the series of mirrors. I was out of breath and sweating, growing desperate. I couldn't stand to see the mess reflecting back.

I took the first mirror off the wall, placed it gently on the floor, ready to move on to the next. But behind it, the wall was a patch of white, instead of the mossy green I'd painted it long ago.

I ran my hand over the spot and felt the roughness of the drywall patch covering the area.

My hands started to shake with a wave of adrenaline.

I took down the next, and the next. Five mirrors, hung over a series of drywall patches, lining the wall. I started laughing, delirious and unrestrained.

He left me the house. He left me that list. Told me exactly where to look.

A gun. Jewelry. The truth.

I thought of my brothers, afraid to dig any deeper. Nico, hiding his suspicions.

All these sons, covering up for the sins of their fathers. Keeping their secrets, without even asking for the truth.

All these things they didn't truly want to know.

Daughters, though. Daughters are different.

I picked up the hammer and swung.

PART 4

DAUGHTER

CHAPTER 30

Friday, May 24
10:00 a.m.
Precipitation: Trace

Money.

Money in plastic bags, coated in plaster dust.

Money lining the walls of the basement. The most dangerous thing I had ever seen.

I didn't understand. I'd thought my father had been draining his account for some sort of blackmail payment. But from the amount I had uncovered, it seemed he'd been taking it and storing it in the walls.

There was so much.

Enough to fill a section between wooden beams, and then move on to the next, and the next. An inheritance, hidden behind my own reflection.

I felt like he had left me a message with this house, and the instructions in the will. *Hazel will know what to do.*

But I didn't. I didn't know what he wanted. Why not just *tell* me? Why leave it for me to find instead? The gun, the jewelry, the letter Jamie had uncovered—it was enough to cast the blame on anyone.

It was enough to incriminate himself, even.

Or maybe the money was a payoff. Hush money. *Please, Hazel. Keep quiet. Let the past die with me.*

How much was my mother worth?

I couldn't figure out what had suddenly changed here back then. If it wasn't a con, what had made her want to run, after so long?

We have to go. It's not safe for us here.

Had she figured out what had happened to the first Holt wife? According to Pete, there wasn't much to tie my father to it—unless one of his sons told what they'd seen that night. They'd only been five and seven.

Or maybe it had nothing to do with Audrey at all.

There was only one person I knew that my mother had feared.

The eye of the lion, visible from the back of his shirt. The tremble of her voice in the middle of the night was something I could still remember, as she scooped me out of bed.

Shh. Don't make a sound. It's time to go, daughter of mine—

We hadn't looked back. It had been so long. But maybe he'd found us. It was a lead that Serena had started to pursue, before she shut down on me.

———

It wasn't hard to find a number for Joe Lyons. His business was listed with the town, and a man answered on the first ring.

In the background, I could hear the whir of machinery echoing.

"Lyons Garage," he said, the syllables of his last name stretched out, in a thick drawl.

Some voices come right back, a visceral memory.

"Joe Lyons," I said.

"Yeah?"

"I'm calling back from the Mirror Lake Police Department," I said. He'd seemed willing to talk to Serena. He probably wouldn't feel the same sense of responsibility toward me.

"Well, isn't this a treat," he said. "But I already told you everything." He said it like a taunt—undermining, undercutting. "And I've got some real work to get back to."

"You're going to have to tell me again," I said. "I'm trying to corroborate my partner's report."

"Well, as I told *your partner*, some guy called me up, a long time ago, asking about Beth. Sorry, *Libby*. Asking if we were still married."

"Were you?" I asked, my heart pounding. I didn't remember them getting married at all. But it was possible. An elopement—opportunity taken, moment seized.

"Yep. Second biggest mistake of my life. The first was not catching her when she bolted." He laughed, and I could hear a rattle in his throat.

I was shocked that he was willing to tell a cop this.

"You told him that you were still married?" I asked. "That you didn't know she was leaving you?"

"Sure did. I told him how I woke up one morning and she and her kid were just gone, with my grandmother's heirloom ring. No trace of them. I told him to be careful. Sounds like she went and pissed someone else off."

"Did he give you a name?" I asked. I wondered if my father had done a background check when we moved in—or whether the call had come during the investigation after she disappeared. But until I'd given Serena his name, no one in the department seemed to know about Joe Lyons.

"Can't say I remember, if he did."

"Perry?" I asked. "Holt?"

"Maybe so, maybe so," he conceded. And then: "I hope you find her. I hope she pays."

I ended the call, shaken, as if I could still feel him, lingering in this room with me.

Be careful, he'd told the man who had called him—my father? And then he'd shared exactly what my mother had done.

Not just a warning.

In someone else's hands, I feared it had become something else: The promise of a pattern. A plan.

Someone was at the door.

I hadn't heard a car arrive, but it was hard to hear from the lower level. Still, I crept up the stairs carefully.

The floorboards creaked under my feet. A black sedan I didn't recognize was parked out front. Someone waited on the stoop, just out of sight.

The doorbell resounded again, making me jump. My hands fumbled for the lock, and I cracked the front door, peering out.

Alberto Flores stood on my front steps, tucked under the overhang.

"Hi," I said, surprised to see him here. The outside smelled of rain, and I could feel the humidity, slick in the atmosphere.

"Hello," he responded. "May I have a moment of your time, Hazel?"

Al wore a dark sport coat, dark pants. He did not bother with pleasantries.

I swung the door open.

"You seem busy," he said, eyes skimming me quickly. A fine coating of white dust clung to my knuckles. "Sorry for showing up unannounced."

I wiped them against my pants. "Just starting to fix the place up," I said, hoping he didn't ask to take a look around.

"This won't take long," he said, closing the door behind him. He walked with slow, steady strides down the hall, into the kitchen. Then he pulled out a chair, and gestured for me to take the one across from him.

He'd been here many times over the years. It always brought me back to the day my mother had been discovered missing. Every time he spoke to me now, I felt his suspicion. My world, cracking open as he watched.

Outside, the sky had darkened, so that it felt like dusk, instead of morning. A fine mist had started clinging to the windows, fogging the glass.

"Sonny Varino only made three calls between Monday and Wednesday afternoon," he said, folding his thick hands on top of the table. "One on Tuesday afternoon, to the place she worked, calling out sick. Another just after, to an untraceable number. And on Monday evening, she made a call to you. I'll be honest, I did not realize you were in contact."

But the call on Monday had come from Jamie. She'd been at Sonny's, before heading over to the Barrel, to meet me.

"I wasn't here on Monday," I said. "I didn't get it."

I didn't trust his reasons for being here. I wondered if they were looking for Jamie here. "The call was almost a minute long," he said, eyes boring into mine. As if there were something I wasn't telling him—again.

"Like I said, I wasn't here on Monday. I went back to Charlotte after the car was removed from our yard."

"And yet," he began, unfolding his hands, "here you are again."

"It's my home," I said. I willed myself not to rise to the bait. "An untraceable number. What does that mean?"

"Probably a burner phone. We assume it's Sonny's dealer. There are enough calls going out like that to see a pattern." His gaze didn't leave mine the entire time he spoke. "I'm sure you know, she's had a lot of health issues over the years."

I nodded. She'd had a bad back since I knew her, and she still seemed to be in pain when I saw her last.

"But the vial we found beside her, it's not a prescription," Flores continued. "Someone sold her those pills—they were laced with fentanyl. Whoever it is will be liable for her death, if we can ever find them."

It occurred to me then that he was asking me something.

"You don't think it was an accident, then?"

He kept watching me. "You tell me. I saw the notes from Serena's interview with you. You told her Sonny wasn't at home when you went by on Wednesday night. Doesn't match with the estimated time of death."

"You think she died somewhere else."

He paused for just a moment. "I think your account doesn't match the facts."

The hair on the back of my neck stood on end. He thought I was lying. That I'd lied then, and I was lying now.

"Did anyone find her bike?"

"Not sure."

I imagined her dying somewhere else, and brought home. The door left open, so she'd be found. The scene staged.

"Everyone keeps acting like her death was expected," I said. I shook my head. "I didn't realize anyone was looking into it."

"We try, here, whether you believe it or not. We really do." He stood then, smoothed the front of his coat. "I've always done my best. I hope you know that."

Did I? I thought of Serena, handing the photo back to me, telling me to stop. "It doesn't seem like many people really want to find the answers," I said.

He checked the time on his phone, not making eye contact. "Your father, I am sure, did his best to protect you when he could." He slipped the phone back in his pocket. "That's how it is, when you have kids. It's a hard habit to shake, no matter how old they get."

I followed him to the front door, his words processing on a delay.

Alberto Flores had told his daughter to stop.

He paused at the exit, one hand on the knob. "If I was your father, I would probably tell you to have a safe trip back to Charlotte, Hazel."

"I'm going," I said.

He wasn't the first one to encourage me to leave today. But it was the first time I lied in response.

CHAPTER 31

Friday, May 24
1:30 p.m.
Precipitation: Steady Rain

I stuffed the money into trash bags, then hid them in my bedroom. But there wasn't much I could do about the holes in the walls or the chunks of drywall and white powder littering the carpet.

I was late meeting Roy for lunch, but he was lucky I was showing up at all. I was no longer interested in his advice, but I thought he might have answers—about what had happened with my father, and my mother, all those years ago.

I felt *so close*, like I had found all the pieces and just needed to slip them into the right order.

The rain was really coming down now, washing the debris down the mountain slopes, across the road. A river of twigs and leaves, like the landscape was shifting as I watched.

By the time I pulled into the lot, circling past the ABC store, I already had a missed text from Roy, asking where I was.

Just parked, I responded, slipping into the spot beside his car. The café was a small converted home and had no parking area, so I had to jog from Roy's office to the building next door.

He was already seated at a second-floor table, pressed up to a windowsill, watching the traffic.

310 · MEGAN MIRANDA

He stirred the ice in his soda with his straw, eyes to the window. "Here they come," he said. It was the holiday weekend, and a trail of cars had started winding around Mirror Highway, many of them stopping at the liquor store on the way to their rentals.

Then he turned to me. "I'm sorry how things went last night, Hazel," he said, wiping the corners of his mouth with the cloth napkin. It seemed he'd grown impatient and had already eaten without me. "You got the will, I presume?"

"I did," I said.

I picked at the basket of bread at the center of the table, unable to muster an appetite.

"It's strange, right?" I asked.

"It's unusual wording," Roy conceded. He was acting like a neutral party, but I couldn't forget how he'd sided with my brothers. "I think that's what has Caden so riled up. That, and the fact no one else knew Perry even had a will. Perry did that all on his own."

"He knew he wasn't doing well," I said now. "He must've hidden it from the rest of us." He'd been getting his affairs in order, just in case. I wondered if anyone else had noticed, tried to convince him to see a doctor.

Roy sighed. "Well. You know how he was. Protective, to the core." Now he reached into his bag and pulled out a file. "I just want to help. To work something out, for all of you."

I didn't move to take it. Just stared back at him, anger rising.

He'd brought paperwork with him. As if they'd planned a settlement after I'd raced out of there last night.

But I would not be steamrolled by the three of them.

It seemed like everyone wanted me out of here. Alberto Flores, Pete Henderson. Someone in a police uniform, sneaking around the house. Starting a fire in the pit. Taking out the batteries of the smoke detectors. The message was pretty clear: *Leave.*

How many people could that possibly be?

"I don't think Caden has a leg to stand on here, Roy. I'm pretty sure he's been messing around in the house. Fucking with me." He lived just across Mirror Highway, up the slope of the bowl. Could make it on foot in no time, if he chose.

Roy frowned. "He wouldn't."

"He's trying to get me out. I have proof."

"Proof?" he asked.

I had learned this from my mother. Weave a story. Play your cards. Make them believe.

"It's on camera."

He raised a single eyebrow. "Perry has a *camera*?"

"Not Dad. Someone else. From the lake." So he would know: I'm not the only one who knows. "They caught him sneaking into the house."

He folded his napkin, placed it on the table. "Well, maybe not exactly *sneaking*. It's technically not yours until after probate. . . ."

"You're on his side," I said, sounding like a child again.

"No, Hazel. I'm on your father's side. I have a soft spot for Caden, sure. Always have. He was such a sad little thing when he was young. Used to have these terrible nightmares."

My stomach dropped, remembering how Caden used to wake up screaming, after we moved in. Then, I'd been told it was night terrors—and he eventually outgrew them. But now I knew the horror he must've been seeing: A bike in the night. Tragedy, heading straight for him. I pictured his wide eyes staring through the window, one small hand out, trying to stop it—

Now I stared at Roy, wondering if he knew how dark my father's secrets truly were.

I thought of the money in the walls, the jewelry case in the crawl space, the gun. And suddenly I wondered whether the money was just another piece of evidence.

"How much did my mother take?" I asked him now.

He froze, cup halfway to his mouth. "I don't know. Your father didn't share all the details with me, exactly."

"No," I said. "From you. From the business."

He swallowed, then put the cup down. "Maybe ten thousand

over time. It had been going on for a while. I didn't realize, since she handled the accounts."

"Did you report her?"

He leaned back in his chair, ran a hand over his graying hair. "Your mother, she was complicated. I know you were too young to really know what was going on. But I need to tell you, I've always blamed myself. I confronted her, you know, about the business accounts—once I finally noticed. I think it's what made her run. She was worried Perry would find out."

There were a lot of things she didn't want Perry to find out, I realized.

He shook his head. "Afterward, your father insisted on making it right. Believed it was his debt to pay. Took him a while, but he did it. It was important to him."

Now I wondered if there was a different reason—born from guilt, instead of responsibility.

"I found some things in the house," I said. "Some things that don't look good for him."

Roy tipped his head. "What sorts of things, Hazel?"

It was too hard to say it all. I'd have to admit it, say it out loud. And I wasn't ready. "You heard about the gun they said she bought?" I asked. The one I now knew was for her protection. Because she was scared of something.

Of someone.

"Yes, I remember."

I leaned across the table, lowered my voice. "I'm pretty sure I found it. Why would she leave it behind?"

He paused, thinking it through. "I don't know," he conceded.

"Do you know, did Dad ever go down to Pete Henderson's place in Mexico?"

His forehead creased in confusion. "Mexico? What does that have to do with anything?" he asked, then laughed. "But I doubt it. You know how your father was, liked to keep close to Mirror Lake. Like this place couldn't function without him. I think it was in his head. He was like that, even as a kid." He rolled his eyes, but I could see the affection underneath. "Only time I heard about Mexico was for some surprise thing for Caden, before he got married. Some bachelors' trip. But I don't think Perry was there. It was just the boys."

Caden and Jamie had gotten engaged when I was in college. Gotten married during my last year . . . "Who went?" I said, voice stern and serious.

"Why are you asking this, Hazel?"

I had to finally say it—because I believed it. Because it was true.

"I think someone killed my mother."

He stared back at me, body frozen. I got a sense of him, then, as a prosecutor. Stone-faced, giving nothing away.

He dropped his voice to a whisper. "You've got to be careful with an accusation like that, Hazel."

The rest of the café was too quiet. If my words echoed, I didn't care. The secrets were killing us here, and I needed to pull them to the surface.

"You think I *want* to believe that? Trust me, I don't."

"The boys are not gonna take too kindly to something like that." From the set of his jaw, he wasn't either.

My phone rang—I saw Nico's name on the display, and quickly silenced it. I wasn't ready for any apology.

But then a text came through: *Hazel, I'm sorry. I know you're angry. But please pick up the phone . . .*

"Listen," Roy was saying, but I was too focused on the new message coming through my screen:

I brought your camera into school. We're developing the photos.

I'd almost forgotten about the camera I'd found when I was out looking for Jamie. After our fight last night, I didn't think Nico would make it a priority. But he was. Of course he was.

Are you still at school? I responded, at the same time he was writing.

Yes. Can you get here?

I stood abruptly. "I have to go," I said.

"Hazel, we're not done discussing—"

"We are, Roy. He left this for me to handle. Not you. And we're done here." I pushed the folder back his way. "Whatever this is, I'm not interested."

CHAPTER 32

Friday, May 24
3:00 p.m.
Precipitation: 1–2 Inches per Hour

I called Nico on speakerphone as soon as I got in the car. "I'm on the way," I said. "What's going on?"

"Listen," he said, voice low—almost to a whisper. "I shouldn't be calling you. But I thought you had a right to see this." The connection started to cut in and out as I drove. "The police are already—"

The call dropped. I didn't know if it was me or him. Whether it was the unreliable cell service or the weather, or if he'd just hung up.

The wipers beat frantically as I crawled along Mirror Highway. It only got worse as I climbed the streets up the bowl, as if I were pushing against nature, moving the wrong way.

Finally, I parked at the high school and sent a quick text: *I'm here.*

The high school hadn't changed since we were students, a decade earlier. There was the corner of the lobby where I'd meet Jamie in the morning, before making our way to class. There was the front office, where Holt once came for me. I passed the familiar doors for the gymnasium, before seeing Nico standing out in the hall, in front of the art room door.

He barely made eye contact. I still felt the sting of betrayal, the shock of last night hanging between us.

And then, as I rounded the corner, he put out an arm, blocking the way, and leaned closer, sharing a secret. "She called the police. I wanted to wait. But they're already here."

I turned to look at him slowly—trying to understand what he was saying.

He shook his head. "It's better if you just see."

The classroom was empty but smelled faintly of chemicals. He led me to the closet and knocked twice.

"It's okay now," a woman's voice called.

Nico took a deep breath, then opened the door, which was draped with a heavy black curtain from the inside.

The closet glowed red from a lamp on the counter, a haunting shade. I saw the woman first—the soft red catching the curls of her hair, the narrow slope of her chin, the thin bridge of her nose. Wide eyes, sliding between me and Nico.

"This is Carly," he said.

She nodded, and then I clocked the other person. Square jaw, buzz cut. Officer Melvin.

He was staring at the series of pictures now strung from a clothesline over the counter.

The hairs on the back of my neck immediately stood on end as I took them in.

Faces, eyes closed, arms thrown over a head or out to the side. Everything in shades of red. I looked again, carefully this time: A series of people in bed, asleep. And in the corner of each image, a terrifying pattern—another sliver of a face, turned to the camera.

An eye, peering out from a dark ski mask.

Whoever the camera belonged to, he'd been sneaking into homes, taking photos as people slept. Capturing himself in the image, as proof.

I shuddered, imagining this masked man inside my house. Seeing Nico and me, sleeping. Snapping a picture of us together. A bare arm, a shoulder, our faces side by side. A moment of intimacy, captured and exploited.

But these faces all belonged to strangers.

"That's Charles Diamond," Nico said, one finger reaching out to the last photo hanging from the line, askew.

"Holy fuck," Officer Melvin added. Then he pivoted to me. "Where did you find this again? Out on your property?"

"No," I said, feeling Nico's head whip my way. Maybe we were both good at keeping secrets. Maybe *that's* what drew us together. That we knew exactly what the other was capable of, and recognized it, in ourselves.

"I found it on the trail, at the clearing by the Barrel," I said.

Officer Melvin's throat moved, a gradient of red slanting across his skin. "Where I saw you Wednesday," he said. "Then?"

I nodded. I felt my face burning, indecipherable in the eerie glow.

"I've seen a bunch of students carrying these around," Nico said, voice low. Knowing, perhaps, that he'd been wrong. The game wasn't over.

The game had only changed. I remembered what Levi said about his friend—growing more reckless. More dangerous. Judging by these pictures, that was an understatement.

The art teacher—Carly—was leaning over a bin of liquid, staring down at the final image she'd processed. Whatever she saw had stilled her movements.

I stepped closer. What could possibly be worse? I could only imagine it was me and Nico after all.

But there was only a single person in the last image, and she was wide awake.

A blur of hair. A hand, reaching out. Eyes wide open, mouth caught in a state of shock and fear. Darkness surrounding her.

It was Jamie's face staring out from the picture, rippling in the tub of liquid. Her arm, stretching toward me. Reaching out and desperate for help.

I grabbed on to Nico's arm, pulling his attention. I heard him suck in a breath just as Officer Melvin turned to me, eyes wide and haunted.

He quickly backed out of the darkroom, relaying a message over the radio, but I followed him out, the change in light disorienting, overexposed.

"We need to get a boat out to the Barrel ASAP," he said, facing away. "I'm heading there now."

I turned back to the room, to see if Nico had heard. He was facing our way, hands gripping the edge of the counter, bathed in red.

Behind him, Carly had just finished hanging the final image, and Jamie's face stared back at us all, a vision of terror.

I closed my eyes against the glow of red, and saw her in the night. An altercation. A kid in a mask—

A horde of high school boys, slinking through the woods while we slept.

And now it had ended in a shocking moment of violence.

A noise escaped my throat, just as I felt the presence of Officer Melvin behind me.

"Don't touch those," he said, pointing at the photos hanging in the darkroom. "Someone will be back for them." And then he spun for the exit.

I grabbed on to his arm, making him pause.

"Is Caden on lake patrol?" I asked.

Officer Melvin frowned. "Not sure."

I pictured Caden as a small child, staring out the window of the car, the horrors he had witnessed. The tragedy he was about to see. His wife, this time—

"Stop him," I said, racing for the exit. "Please, stop him."

Nico was right behind me out of the parking lot. We were first on scene from the road—closer than any of the other patrol cars, though I could already hear the sirens approaching from the distance.

Officer Melvin was just exiting his vehicle as I rushed past him, into the clearing.

"Wait!" he called, but I didn't. I heard the rain hitting the trees, the lake below, like a cascade. The trail beyond the *Danger* sign was slippery and unstable, water flowing over roots and rock, racing toward the bottom.

Everything, going back to the lake.

I lost my footing twice, and had to brace myself against a tree before coming to my knees at the bend—where I could finally see into the Barrel.

The canoe was still there, tipped on its side, knocking against the rocks in the rain.

I had to go down another level before I could see the police boat positioned close to the shoreline. And a single man in a dark raincoat hanging over the edge.

"Caden!" I called, trying to stop him.

He peered over his shoulder, confused. But I was too late. Suddenly, I could see it all.

A body—the stark and final horror of it.

Everything was dark: The pants. The shirt.

A ski mask, pulled over a face.

I jerked back, surprised.

Nico stumbled down the path, meeting me at the curve.

"That's not . . . it's not Jamie," I said.

He followed my line of sight and sank down, crouching in the mud, head in his hands.

My hand went to his shoulder.

A student was dead. A kid.

I had thought the masked man in the photos had done something to Jamie—that he'd pushed her to her death, over the Barrel, into the lake.

But it was *his* body down here, and her face in the photo, wide with shock and panic.

She'd been waiting for me, and he'd been sneaking through the woods. Lives converging in the dark. She'd already been in a state of panic—paranoid, after someone had snuck into her house. Someone, she must've thought, who was after her. Someone who'd come for her, and she'd reacted.

And then, either in horror or fear, she'd run.

I was waiting by my car, trying to stay out of the way, when I saw Caden coming toward me on the side of the road, talking to Officer Melvin. Nico and I had given our statements—about the camera, and the photos now hanging in the school art closet.

A crowd of teenagers had started to arrive, and I saw Nico with them, trying to keep them back—knowing him, he was probably trying to explain, to comfort them.

A hand suddenly gripped my shoulder, forcing me around.

"What the hell are you doing here?" Caden asked, cornering me against the car. "Melvin said you found a camera and it looks like Jamie was . . ." He drifted off, not wanting to say it. Not wanting to think it. He was angry, so angry, and finally, he had a place in which to focus it.

I pushed him back, so I could get some space. "I didn't know—"

"I would've found a way to protect her, Hazel! What the fuck did you do?"

This time, the arrow struck, straight and true.

What *had* I done?

Solved a crime I didn't know existed. Got to the wrong answer, the very wrong place.

He leaned close, voice dangerously low. "I want you out of our lives."

"Oh, I got that message, Caden. I've gotten it loud and clear, all fucking week."

"I don't know what you're talking about," he said.

"Really?" Now I was the one to step closer. "You're on camera, you know, sneaking into the house." I said it loud, so people would hear. I didn't care anymore.

"It's not *yours*. Not yet. You can't just sell it. You have no *right*—" he hissed.

"I grew up in that house too, Caden! As much as you wish I had also disappeared." I gritted my teeth, thought I saw him flinch. "You never saw me as family, not like Gage."

He laughed, something mean and forceful. "*Gage* treats you like a goddamn pet. *Jump*, he says, and you ask how high. *Run*, he says, and you do—without ever pausing to think why."

I shook my head, hand grasping for the car door handle behind me.

I could feel the anger radiating off of him, his face close. "Roy said you'd agree to a settlement. I'll buy you out. Whatever it takes. I want it, Hazel. I want it for my family. Not for the money . . . I was born in that house. My mother—" He choked, stopped. "I have lived my entire life in a five-mile circle from that house. It doesn't make any sense that he'd leave it to you. Not unless you did something to force him. Told some story."

"Caden!" Serena called, from the other side of the road. I didn't know whether she needed his help or if she had witnessed the way he was leaning over me, coiled to snap.

In that moment of distraction, I threw open the car door—escaping both the rain and him.

CHAPTER 33

Friday, May 24
4:30 p.m.
Precipitation: Steady Rain

t wasn't far from the Barrel back to the house. But I paused where the road intersected with Mirror Highway. Thinking of Jamie, running.

A man in a mask, sneaking up on her in the woods.

Where would she *go*?

Back to my house, to see if I was still there? I closed my eyes and could picture her there: Finding it empty, sneaking inside—washing away what had happened, in a panic. Leaving a trail of dirt in the hall; a dripping faucet. The person Levi had seen inside, looking out. Who had felt—or known—she was being watched.

And then what?

Not knowing who she could possibly trust. Maybe not even me.

Had she thought I had given her away? Told someone about the message? Sent someone to find her?

The fear must have seized her.

Sonny's words echoed in my head. *This place is her world. Where else would she possibly go?* She knew the truth then. She knew, and was keeping her secret.

Al Flores had confirmed it, even. Sonny had made a call on Tuesday, to the motel. It must've been after I'd shown up at her house, looking for Jamie.

Whoever had talked to Al, claiming Sonny was calling out of work, had lied.

Sonny knew Jamie was in trouble. She knew where she was hiding.

When she dialed the motel that day, Sonny was calling her daughter.

I burst through the door of Mirror Lake Motel, startling the woman behind the counter. I knew I was a mess: covered in rain and mud, like I'd been sprinting through the woods, trying to escape.

How willingly she'd protected me, when I'd turned up in the middle of the night, needing help.

"Are you—" she began, standing.

"I need to see Jamie," I said, and her eyes widened for a beat, before her face shut down.

She stood, arm out, gaze flitting around the room, as if checking for anyone else who might've heard.

"Please," I said, hands pressing into the counter. I'd brought the rain in, could feel it dripping down my bare legs, onto the floor. "I know she's been here."

"Sonny Varino," she began. "She was family here." I could see she wasn't about to budge. Telling me something instead: *We protect our own.*

I closed my eyes, shook my head. "Tell her . . ." I sucked in a breath, and it sounded like a wheeze. "Tell her I'm sorry. I thought something had happened to her and . . ."

This woman was still staring back at me, waiting. Waiting for the things I didn't want to say.

I took a breath. "Tell her Max Falkner was just found dead at the bottom of the Barrel."

Her hand shook as she slowly brought it to her mouth.

"They have the camera he had with him that night. A picture of Jamie was on it."

She didn't say anything. Just grabbed my wrist and pulled me around the counter, out the back door.

She took me around the back to a second structure and slid open the garage, revealing a blue sedan and a red minivan—Jamie's car. Hidden out of sight.

"It's me, I'm coming up," she called, leading me up the steps. My heart beat wildly with anticipation.

She took out her key but didn't need to use it. The door swung open at the top of the steps, and there was Jamie.

My breath left me in a rush of relief. I had imagined the very worst, and now she was *here*, standing before me, alive.

I enveloped her in my arms, not thinking of the rain and the mud, my body trembling with relief. But Jamie remained rigid and tense.

She pulled back, eyes wild with panic. "Is Skyler okay?"

"What? Yes, she's fine. Skyler's fine."

Jamie raised her hand to her face, her eyes searching mine. She was in a pair of oversize sweats, and there were dark circles under her eyes. Her nails had been bitten down to the quick.

"Jamie, sit down," the woman said.

Jamie backed away, almost stumbling to the L-shaped sofa. She perched on the edge and shook her head, like she already knew.

Her eyes drifted shut, her face crumbling, as I told her anyway.

The woman—whose name I learned was Anna—brought Jamie a steaming drink. "Okay, it's going to be okay," she was saying, though we all knew it wasn't.

Anna turned to me, frowning. "We didn't hear that Max was missing until Wednesday."

Jamie pressed her knuckles to her mouth. "I didn't want to be-lieve it. But Anna called in a tip just in case, after the police came by with their missing person notice. She told them she had seen someone in the clearing over the Barrel. But there was no news after. They hadn't found anyone. I thought it was okay." Her throat moved. "There was a man who had chased me, and I thought he was still out there."

Her eyes were wide and pleading, like she was begging me to believe. To understand.

I thought back to Wednesday night, when Officer Melvin had found me there. I'd assumed he had followed me. But he was fol-lowing up on the tip instead. And he *had* found someone there: me. I'd told him it was my favorite place. He must've assumed it was me who had been spotted there. There was no need for him to keep searching, until he saw the pictures hanging in the darkroom.

"Jamie, I'm so sorry," I said.

"Why are you sorry?"

"I missed you. I missed the call."

Like Caden had said, all of this would've been different, if not for me.

"And your mother."

She flinched, her face a wave of emotion.

"Hazel," she said then, leaning forward, like she'd forgotten everything that had come before. "Someone came in the house. I found something in your dad's things. I think they were there for it. . . ."

"I have it," I said. "It was still in the backpack."

She nodded. "The letter. Is it what I think?"

I nodded back, slowly. "I had never seen it before."

"I'm sorry," she said. Because she understood, too, what it meant: My mother had been coming back, and something stopped her. She wasn't okay. "Someone knows I found it, Hazel. There were only so many people who could've noticed. But I don't know who else they might've told."

I thought back to that day, cleaning out the house. "Do you think it was Caden?" I asked.

She stared back, eyes watering, shaking her head. But I wasn't sure what she was saying no to. She dropped her head to her hands for a minute, and then raised it again. "Okay." She turned to Anna, pushed back her shoulders. "It's time to call the police."

"Jamie," I begged. "Call Caden. Please, tell him first." No matter what had happened between them, he should hear it from her.

"You'll make sure Skyler's okay, right?" she asked.

"Of course. But, Jamie, they're going to understand. It was an accident."

"I ran," she said.

"You were afraid. You didn't know."

But she shut her eyes again, like she was trying to hold everything back.

I knew she would never forgive herself.

CHAPTER 34

The lights were on inside my father's house, and Gage's Jeep was parked in front of the door.

I had no idea how long he'd been here.

Outside, the landscaping had seen some damage. The wind and rain had knocked down dead branches. The ground was coated in a layer of them, so that it was almost impossible to tell the drive from the surrounding yard. As if the house were being consumed by the surroundings.

"Gage?" I called, walking through the garage door entrance.

Silence.

I kept moving through the house, calling his name.

And then I heard him answer from below. "Hazel?"

My heart sank. He must've seen the wall. The hammer I'd used to open it up. There was so much to explain.

When I rounded the bottom of the stairwell, I came face-to-face with all he had discovered. He stood in the middle of the rec space, shell-shocked. Around him, the bags of money from my room were at his feet. One had been torn open.

"What the hell is this?" he said quietly. I'd never seen him like this before—like he was on the cusp of something, trembling with either adrenaline or fear or anger. Not when we'd found the murder room. Not even when he'd called me home with news of our father.

"I was going to tell you. To explain. How long have you been here?"

His eyes were wide and unblinking. "I heard they found Jamie and stopped to tell you. I was on my way over to the school. The students and teachers are all there, for some vigil. I need to interview them, before the rumors start mixing with the facts." He spoke, as if in a trance. "Why are there holes in the wall, Hazel?"

"Dad hid his money here. He emptied the accounts."

He shook his head, not understanding. "And where did you find *that*?" He gestured to the jewelry case.

"In the crawl space. I think Dad hid it too." *Evidence*, I wanted to say. *Evidence, that my mother's disappearance was not what it seemed.*

"I don't understand," he said. And then, in a quiet voice, "That was mine."

"*What* was yours?"

"That jewelry case. It was my mother's. I'd kept it in my closet after she died. They were just a few of the sentimental pieces. I didn't think anyone knew I had it. It was the only thing I had left of her," he said. "I don't know why . . ." He trailed off.

Why my father hid it in a crawl space.

I needed to show him everything. "Listen, Gage. My mother bought a gun before she left."

"I know that."

"The gun is still here. Dad kept it hidden in the garage. She didn't take it with her. Gage, I don't think she made it out," I said, the truth of it seizing my lungs.

His eyes cut to me slowly. I wondered if he had already suspected this. "Please, Hazel. He's gone. Don't do this."

Like Pete told me on the boat: *He's dead.* What does it matter now?

But it mattered to Gage; it mattered to all of us. His name—the most valuable thing any of us had left.

"Gage," I said quietly. "I think he wanted me to know." A confession, hidden inside the walls of this house. "My mother left me a letter, and he found it. . . . Let me show you."

But when I reached my hand into my luggage, searching, there was nothing.

I tossed the clothing aside. No envelope. No letters. Not the real one, and not the forgery either.

Gage said nothing.

I turned around slowly, realization gradually dawning.

What was he doing down here? What had he been looking for? What *else* had he found?

Oh no. *Please*, no.

"What did you do?" I asked.

"Please leave it alone. He's gone. It's over."

But it wasn't. "Someone killed my mother!" I shouted. A chill ran through me. "Was it you?"

He jolted back, like I'd struck him. "Was *what* me?"

I couldn't ask it. Couldn't believe it. "Did you leave me that letter? Gage, did you trace her note, and leave me that letter instead?"

He didn't respond.

"How *could* you?" I said, but I was yelling now.

He threw his arms out to the side. "I came looking for you that morning. I found the note on your bed."

I could see him at sixteen, just as he explained. Picking up the letter, reading her warning. "It's not *safe for us here*?" he continued. "It sounded like she was scared of Dad. Like she knew . . ." He trailed off, looking away.

"About what happened to your mother?" I finished.

He stared back at me, stunned. The room felt charged—everything so close to the surface. All the secrets we kept. "Caden

332 · MEGAN MIRANDA

must've told her," he said. "Dad made us *promise* never to say it. But Caden was only five. He had nightmares—everyone knew. He was never the same. He doesn't always think things through."

I shook my head. "He shouldn't have asked you to keep that secret. You were just kids." But now I was imagining my mother, hearing the truth from Caden—afraid, and deciding to run.

"He wasn't a bad person, Hazel. You know that."

"Of course I know." There was a time when I would've forgiven him anything.

"Libby was gone. She'd left you that note, claiming she was coming back, but it was obvious she wasn't. It looked bad for him. So I took it. I took the note. That's all," he said. Like he was just doing the reasonable, responsible thing.

"Except, you didn't just take it. You left me a fake. You let me *believe*," I said, my throat tight with tears.

"I let you believe she was safe somewhere. Is that really so terrible?"

My hand went to my mouth. "You thought he hurt her too."

Gage, protecting his father. The Holt name, his legacy.

He didn't answer directly. "I kept it, in case we ever needed it. It's evidence, I understood that. I kept it safe. But then I came over one day after I got my own place and he'd turned my room into his office. Didn't even ask, just did it. I couldn't find half the things I used to own."

He took a step closer, so that I could hear the rasp of his breath. "He didn't say anything about it, Hazel. If he found it, he didn't say a thing. Why else would he stay silent? I thought he must've destroyed it."

But he'd hidden things in this house, left them for me to find . . . after he was gone.

Such a good father.

Such a good man.

"Hazel, he's dead," Gage said again, arms out—pleading with me. "Please, let it go."

But now I didn't know what he was asking me. Maybe I'd had it backward again.

I couldn't believe that he had hurt her and wanted me to know. Maybe my father, as his final act, had framed himself to take the fall. But who was he trying to protect?

My eyes rose to his.

"You," I said. "He thought it was you." My father would have done anything to protect his children.

I looked at the bags of cash at my feet now. Blood money. As if my father were begging me now: *It was me. Please, say it was me instead.*

"No, Hazel. No." He said it emphatically, eyes wide and desperate. But now he was looking around the room, as if seeing everything through a different filter.

"You were looking for the letter at Caden's house," I said. "You knew Jamie found it."

"I heard her the day we were cleaning out the house, asking Caden if your mother had left a note. She didn't sound like she believed him." The fight that had kicked everything off. The thing Caden thought I'd told her, to get her to leave him.

Everything was coming out now. A dam, failing. The answers, breaking free in a powerful, dangerous rush. "You went into her house looking for that letter," I said, understanding what must have happened, to scare her that day. "And when Jamie freaked out, you framed it like it was the kids you'd been investigating—leaving the front door open."

How long had I revered Gage, idolized him? Thought he followed the letter of the law to a T, unyielding and unbending?

He stepped even closer, hands up. "I didn't know Jamie was there, I swear it. I rang the bell. She didn't answer. I just needed to find it. Destroy it. He's dead, and it shouldn't exist anymore."

He was still acting like he was protecting his father, alone.

"Everything that happened to Jamie after—it's your fault. She thought someone was after her, Gage! She wanted me to bring Skyler to her, but I was too late. She was terrified, and Max Falkner snuck up on her in the woods in a mask—like someone was *still* after her. He's dead because of you!"

"I never meant for—I didn't think she'd *run*! I panicked, Hazel! What was I supposed to say?"

"Please, Gage," I said, but I didn't know what I was asking for. All these answers—none of them were what I wanted.

Over time, my father had found the pieces—a letter, the jewelry case, the gun—and he thought he understood what had happened here. A trail, leading right to Gage.

What must he have thought, all those years later, about his son, now a grown man? An officer in the Mirror Lake Police Department, like him. Did he look at Gage and think, *We all make mistakes*—because he had once done so himself? Did he believe he was to blame because of the horrific night that had been seared into their memories? Did he think he had created him, from this terrible act of violence? That he had raised a monster?

Gage was seeing it too. The realization of who his father had thought him to be.

"He thought you killed her, Gage. He's trying to protect you, even now. Beyond the grave." I choked on the words, knuckles pressed to my teeth.

Gage was coming untethered at the realization—the very worst thing. And I was suddenly terrified of what he would do to keep this secret too.

"I didn't, Hazel. I swear it. Please, believe me."

Run, he'd say, and I'd sprint. *Jump*, he'd say, and I would. *Believe me*, he said now—and my god how I wanted to believe him.

But I'd come this far. "Tell me, Gage. Did you send me that postcard in college?"

I stared at him, believing I could read it on his face. The tightening at the corners of his eyes. The tensing of his jaw. I saw the truth before he said it.

"You were home for Christmas, and I saw you searching her name on the computer. I just wanted to give you some closure."

I shook my head, backing away. He had crafted the lie. The lie from which I had grown. Forging myself in resistance to my past.

"How *could* you?" I yelled.

"I wanted you to be happy. You *were* happy. Even after everything—"

"You think I was *happy*? Happy to believe my mother left me behind, like I was *nothing*?"

"I thought I was protecting him," Gage said. "We'd done it before. We weren't supposed to talk—"

"Get out," I said.

"Hazel—" He reached for me, but I couldn't look him in the eye.

"Out!" I yelled. I was shaking with rage. It was more than an ungrounding. It was a devastation. I felt like a black hole, pulling every terrible thing toward me. Every horror. All the things I thought I wanted, the darkest truth.

He left me then, hands out, a last proclamation of innocence.

But the letters were gone. He'd taken the only proof I had. The trail back to my mother was dead.

Gage had taken it all. But he'd left the money behind—like a trade, a bribe, a plea.

For your silence. Like father, like son.

I didn't know if I could believe him, as much as I wanted to.

Even my father thought him capable of the darkest thing I could imagine.

My phone chimed while I sat there, and I hoped it was Gage, after everything. Coming back, apologizing, promising I had it all wrong. Ready to explain it in a way that made sense.

But the note came from Keira: *Are you on your way? The weather's so bad here. Be careful.*

I sat on the floor of the room, raw and broken. My family, gone. All of them, strangers to me.

There was nothing left for me here. I knew how to do it: *Pack light. Move fast. Take only what you need. Don't look back.*

The rain started to come then, fast and powerful. A second wave. A second surge.

I loaded my bags into the trunk.

I removed the gun from the china cabinet, to secure safely on the way out.

Then I took one more trip for the money downstairs—and all the lights went dark.

CHAPTER 35

For a moment, I was completely disoriented. The dark inside, the dark outside. Rain, hitting off the roof, so that I felt like I was under the surface—

And then, a light. A flash out back, so fast I almost missed it.

A boat, out in this weather? Lightning? I listened for the sound of thunder, but couldn't hear anything through the rain.

I walked closer to the back doors, peering through the curtain of darkness, trying to see out onto the lake.

One more flash—closer this time. In the side yard. The glow of a flashlight turning on and off quickly—as if to see the way, but remain undetected.

And then: a bolt of lightning. A figure in a dark raincoat, before darkness fell again.

My shoulders tensed, but I wasn't afraid. Not anymore. I knew now who had been sneaking around the house. I texted Caden while staring out the window, into the night: *I see you out there.*

Nothing.

He had been so angry earlier, and now, he must be furious—so very furious. Jamie must've turned herself in to the station.

I opened the slider and stepped out onto the back patio, sheltered from the rain. It fell around the perimeter in a curtain. I could barely see anything.

I tried calling him now—to listen for a ringing phone in the night. But the rain was too loud, or his phone was on silent.

"Caden!" I yelled.

I stepped closer to the edge of the patio, hand on the post. My text showed as delivered.

One more try: *Grow up. Stop hiding,* I wrote.

And then a sound from behind, in the house. I spun around just as the glass door slid shut.

I lunged for the door, but the lock clicked into place. "Seriously?" I called, pounding the side of my fist into the glass. But I couldn't see his face. Could only see the dark shadow of his raincoat moving through the lower level.

I'd finally ruined his life. Taken everything from him. And suddenly I wondered what he planned to take from me. Would he destroy this place? Burn it down to the ground, if it meant I couldn't have it?

I wondered if anyone would even believe me. No one here wanted to dig. Not really. Serena had shown me as much. Not without proof. And proof had a way of disappearing around here.

I had to get inside before he did something dangerous and irreversible. Before he took down everything my father had left behind, in his rage.

The bags of money. Our home.

I slipped in the mud as I circled the house, head down in the rain, but the front door was locked—he must've secured the doors behind him, after he snuck inside.

But there was another way.

I darted to the back, to the crawl space door, and dislodged it from its position, where I'd tried my best to secure it earlier. I pushed the kayak aside and crawled across the blue tarp, until I could stand upright underneath the house.

It was pitch-black and claustrophobic, and the rain echoing off the gutters only made everything feel smaller, darker. With the light of my phone, I moved through the crawl space, making my way to the ladder in the back corner and the secret hatch that led into Caden's closet.

I climbed now, pushing the hatch open overhead, pulling myself into the enclosed space above. The closet door creaked as I exited into the bedroom, and then I slowly moved down the hall.

I listened to the house. Listened for him. But the rain was too loud.

A flash of lightning lit up the back windows, the empty rooms. Thunder resounded from somewhere in the mountains, echoing down into the valley, in a delay.

I took out my phone, to set it to record. I needed proof. It was the only way to stop him.

I made it into the kitchen, to the gun box open on the table. I shone my light onto it now: empty.

A creak of the floorboard behind me. The click of a gun. "Put down the phone."

I did, lowering it slowly onto the table.

I raised my hands, turned around.

"I really don't want to do this, Hazel."

The Holt voice. I had expected it. I had suspected my father, and then Gage. Now I'd been ready for Caden. But I'd had the wrong Holt all along.

My father thought Gage had done something horrible. Gage thought the same about my father. But they had both been wrong.

Roy stood before me in the dark, my mother's gun in his hand. Cold and stoic. No longer the man I knew.

"Then don't," I said, my voice wavering. "What do you want, Roy?"

"I want you to stop, Hazel." I noticed, then, that his arm was trembling—but I didn't know if it was from nerves or the thrum of anticipation. "Do you *know* the things your father has done? How I've protected him?"

"Yes," I said. "I do, Roy. Did he tell you what happened to Audrey?" My phone may have been out of my hands, but it was still set to record on the table—I could get a real confession, inside the walls of this house.

"Oh, he didn't. But Caden did . . . he always had interesting things to say, as a kid," Roy said. "He had those terrible nightmares, would wake up screaming. The things he told me about . . . He really should've seen a specialist, but Perry couldn't have that, now, could he?"

I closed my eyes. How traumatized Caden must've been by the things he'd witnessed that night.

"I know everything, Roy," I said. "All his secrets."

His arm twitched, making me flinch. "Let me ask you this, Hazel. Did you know that when Audrey left Perry that night, she was coming to *me*? Had made a *plan* and everything. But Perry wouldn't let her leave. Apparently, he'd rather she die than be happy."

I stared back at him, his shadow coming into focus in the dark. *Ask your uncle.* Sonny had told me that. She knew Roy, growing up, just as she knew Audrey. Rumors didn't keep here. People knew. They knew what had happened with the Holts.

"Her death was an accident," I said.

"An accident he covered up! Like she was collateral damage he could just throw away."

He moved around me now, so that I had to pivot, just to watch him. He picked up my phone, the display illuminating his face in a ghastly horror, before tucking it into his pocket.

"Sonny tried to warn me—"

He let out a bark of laughter. "A real shame about that one. She *was* my most consistent customer."

I was a step behind, even now. Piecing together what he was confessing. The call to her dealer—the man suddenly standing in my kitchen, with a gun.

"Where did you find all that money, Hazel?" A smile played at the corner of his lips, like this was a game. A game he suddenly thought he could win.

My heart pounded. I was running out of options. Trapped inside, with no way out. I needed to keep him off balance. Find help—

"Were you looking for it?" I asked, suddenly understanding. He was the person who had been keeping an eye on my father's email. Checking his accounts. Searching for where he'd hidden it all away.

"You always were the smart one," he said, smiling for real then. "Not as smart as me, though." I could see him clearly then, the puppet master behind the scenes. Manipulating us, playing my brothers and me against one another. An evil lurking in this family. In this town.

"You blackmailed him," I said. My father must've been desperate to keep the money out of his brother's hands again. Roy could take it from Gage, maybe even Caden, with the things he knew—but not me. I was the one who could keep it safe. Dad had even made him the executor, so he would know: *Leave my children alone. There's nothing here for you.*

"Blackmail?" Roy said incredulously. "No, no. We helped each other out, despite everything. I got into some trouble, after Audrey—Perry thought he was going to send me to *jail*, Hazel." He laughed, a single horrible wheeze. "Jail or rehab, he said. Thought he could strong-arm me, over some pills . . . Can you believe it? He didn't know what Caden had told *me*." His smile stretched, in the dark. "His tone definitely changed after that."

I backed away, closer to the door, trying to remember if it was locked. How quickly could I get outside? "I cleaned up my act real fast then," he said. "But those pills do come in handy, when you control them. . . ."

Roy reached around me, unlocking the door himself. As if this had been his plan all along.

He slid open the back door, gun still pointed right at me. "I have to hand it to him, though. Perry helped me get back on my feet. Helped me clean up. Start a new practice. We always helped each other. We're family."

How long had he kept my father under his thumb, owning him, once he knew about Audrey? The favors and the money and whatever else he must've demanded. My father replaced the money stolen from his accounts, because what was the alternative?

"My father never knew about you and Audrey, did he," I said. I couldn't imagine he would've helped him, if he did, no matter what else Roy threatened.

"Your father was blinded by *himself*, Hazel. All the time. He never even saw me. That's something he never understood. It's easier to stay in control when you keep yourself under the radar. That was *not* one of *his* strengths." And then he tapped the gun against the open door. "This was your mother's weapon, is that right?"

I didn't answer. I'd told him as much earlier. And, I realized with horror: I'd given him a plan.

"Your father always said you had to be careful with these, didn't he? That they could be used against you, so easily. That people were more likely to have accidents . . ." He pressed his lips together. "You must be so upset. *So very upset*. Just like Sonny. And your mother." He gestured with the gun. "It's time to move. Out."

"Where are we going?" But I thought I knew. Out to the lake. Where there would be an accident, with my mother's gun. Where the evidence would be washed away, once more. Where I, too, would disappear.

He pushed me forward when I hesitated, and I tripped over a wood slab, catching myself on the rail.

"Down," he said, walking behind me on the deck.

I thought, for a moment, about running. I was faster than him, I knew. How many steps to the lake. To the woods. To Nico's—

But he grabbed my wrist, and I felt the press of the gun in my side.

He was a killer, plain and simple. He had killed, and he would kill again—

"My father knew who you were, Roy. He knew, and he wanted to keep the rest of us safe."

"Well, look how well that worked out," he said, pushing me toward the edge of the water. "He's got a pretty shitty track record of keeping the women in his life safe, if we're keeping score."

"What did you do to my mother?" I asked. I didn't have the phone recording him anymore, but I needed to know. I needed to know the truth.

"Your mother was a firecracker, Hazel. Not unlike you. Could talk her way into anything, including my business. She was always doing more than she should. Tried to figure out why the finances weren't adding up. Thought someone made a *mistake*. I found myself a little underwater for a time. Made a few bad deals. Needed some extra cash. But I was going to find a way to cover the funds."

My mother had noticed the missing money. She hadn't stolen anything. It was Roy, skimming from the accounts, stealing from his clients, to cover himself for a mess of his own making.

"Sonny came to see you," I said, shaking in the rain. "*You* gave her those pills." Her bike, outside the ABC liquor store. Her phone call to the unknown number, after I'd gone to see her. She'd tried to do something. She'd tried to help her daughter.

The gun dropped away from me for a moment, as he waved his arms in exasperation. I needed to keep him talking. Keep him distracted.

"She came to me about my nephews. Thought one of them was dangerous. I have *always* done what I had to do to protect this family."

"She was just trying to help Jamie!" Did she think Roy would be on her side, because of his history with Audrey?

"She's been coming to me for years. I helped her with the pain. You'd be amazed the things I know about the people of this town. They all think they have the power. Sonny barged in demanding something of me, like she could threaten me." He scoffed. "I gave her something, to calm her down, before she started talking *somewhere else.* No one was even surprised to hear she overdosed. I bet even Jamie isn't. Just like no one was surprised by Nico's father. Or, for that matter, your mother."

I was right. Sonny hadn't died in her house. The depths of his depravity hit me full force, and my knees went weak. Death, following death, to keep covering his tracks. He'd gotten away with it once, and it had fueled something else, dark and true, that had lived inside of him.

"Did you kill my father?" I asked, the thought seizing me in another moment of horror.

"Of course not," he hissed. "How could you think that? He was so important to me. Very valuable. Always willing to help, in more ways than one."

I was going to be sick. As if the rest—Sonny, Nicholas Pritchard, my mother—were nothing at all.

He was so much more dangerous than I thought. I needed to push him off guard, off balance.

"My mother was on to you, Roy. She left a note. She said we weren't safe."

That surprised him. I could tell by the pause of silence. He stopped for a moment, but I kept moving, backing slowly toward the lake.

"Your mother was only scared of her past catching up to her. I told her, replace the money, or I would tell Perry she had taken it. I'd tell Perry what she'd done to her last husband—how she left him. She worked for me—it was very easy to track her history. Her ex had some *very* interesting things to say. And she did it—she went to the bank and got the money from their account. She made me whole."

And yet he'd let my father believe a debt was still owed.

"But like you, she was trying to get some evidence. She was going to run. She couldn't be reasoned with. There was nothing to keep her from going to the police somewhere else. I tried to get her to stay, but . . ."

"You killed her," I said. I needed him to say it. Not my father. Not Gage. *Him.*

He shook his head, rain hitting the hood of his coat. "Seems fitting, in some Shakespearean-tragedy way. He killed the love of my life. And I, his."

"Where is she?" I asked.

But before he spoke, I knew. The way he'd insisted on renovating, instead of moving. The projects that he'd tackled, little by little, across his backyard—

She had never made it back to our house that night. It was Roy who had come, to cover his tracks. He was a desperate man, and he was so very dangerous.

"You killed her at your house." My voice dropped, and everything sank. I felt sick, my limbs heavy. The gravity of the truth, pulling hard and fast. "You brought her car back in the night, made it look like she was running. And then dumped it in the lake behind our house." I didn't even recognize my own voice. It was low and furious and laced with something just as dangerous.

"She came to me with demands. It wasn't a good look, Hazel. She thought she was smarter than me. Just like you."

"But you didn't know she'd bought a gun," I said. "And you didn't know she'd left me a note. It still exists, you know. You made a mistake." About me, about my father. About all of us. I took a step forward. "Tell me *where*, Roy."

"You're in no position to be demanding anything here either, Hazel—"

That's when the beam of a flashlight shone through the rain, illuminating us both.

"What's going on here?" Caden stood at the top of the yard, standing over us both. He'd gotten my texts. He'd come. He was in uniform, holding his service weapon.

"Caden?" Roy said, lowering the weapon. "What are you doing here, son?"

Caden cocked his head. "Why do you have a gun, Roy?" His voice was cold.

Caden's flashlight left nothing to the darkness anymore.

"He killed my mother," I shouted. "He was blackmailing Dad, because of what happened to yours. *That's* why he left the house to me. So I could protect us. I found the money, Caden. It was in the walls."

"Caden, really. She's talking her way in circles, just like her mother. Threatened me—"

"Ask him what happened to Sonny!" I said, eyes on the gun in Roy's hand. "Ask him what happened to Nicholas Pritchard!"

"Hazel, I *told* you to stop." Roy raised the gun again, and I put my hands up between us, as if that could stop anything.

But Caden was armed too. "Put down that gun, Roy," he said.

"Why, Caden?" he asked, gun still on me. "What's she to you?"

"Roy," he continued, "*please* put it down."

"She'll ruin our lives, just like her mother did," Roy said. "I've always looked after you. I've protected you. She's got everyone fooled. Even your father was a fool for her."

Caden looked between us. He could let me die—I could see it. How easy it would be, to do nothing. Let Roy shoot me, claim it was an accident. Or self-defense, even. Who would miss me? Nico? Who would question it? Caden could take the money. The house would be his.

It was his moment to decide.

"Run, Hazel," he said. I didn't wait. I ran, straight into the woods, toward the Pritchard property. I needed the cover of darkness. A place I knew so well. I needed to get to a phone. Get help.

A shot rang out in the darkness. Only one. A thump, audible even in the storm. A body falling.

And then silence.

CHAPTER 36

I pressed my back into the nearest tree, breathing heavily.

One shot. One shot meant someone fired, and someone fell. Caden was trained. He had good aim—

A bolt of lightning lit up the night, and shadows crisscrossed the darkness. I couldn't even see Nico's house from here. I was sure he was at the school vigil, where Gage had been heading. I didn't know if he'd replaced the hidden key, or if there was another way in—

"Hazel!" Roy's voice, somewhere inside the trees.

My muscles seized in horror. Caden. He could be injured and bleeding out, in the night. Or worse.

"Hazel, come out! Let's talk this through!"

I had to get back to Caden. The sound of rain covered for me as I darted through the woods, back toward home.

Roy's flashlight scanned the trees looking for me, but I remained hidden, protected by the shadows. He spun around, the light skimming across the expanse of our backyard. And *there*—a dark shape, lying on the ground in the yard.

The light arced away again, and I heard Roy step into the trees, heading uphill. I took my chance and ran straight into the clearing—fully exposed. I fell to my knees beside Caden, running my hands across his body in the dark, looking for signs of injury.

He was breathing rapidly, hands pressed to his side.

"Hold on," I whispered. "Please don't die. Please, Caden."

He sucked in a breath. "I couldn't do it," he said, then grunted in pain. "I didn't think he would do it either. He's family, he—"

"Okay, shh," I said, pushing down on his hands, covering the wound.

"Hazel!" Roy yelled from somewhere in the woods. I peered over my shoulder, saw the beam of light cutting through the shadows—heading this way again.

I pulled Caden's phone from his pocket, crouched low over him as I called 911.

"My brother's been shot," I whispered to the operator on the other end. "Roy Holt did it." I gave the address. "Hurry. He's coming back."

"I'm sorry," I whispered to Caden, leaving the phone beside him, line open. "Help is coming."

And then I pushed off the ground and took off running down the slope of the yard. There was nothing to shelter me from view. If Roy was looking this way, he would probably see me, darting through the night.

A flash of lightning illuminated everything then. Roy, at the edge of the trees, gun hanging by his side. Me, by the water. A curtain of rain between us.

The rain felt heavy in my clothes, my hair—shoes sinking into the muddy shoreline. I slipped them off at the edge—a trail to follow—so they would know: *I was here.*

I understood then that Roy had nothing to lose. Caden was shot. Sonny was dead. Why not me? I knew the truth. *I* was the most dangerous thing to him right now. Of course he'd kill me.

Roy's light shone directly on me then, and I spun, running straight into the water, diving into the surface as a shot rang out in the night.

I emerged again, just as the flashlight scanned the surface, searching for me.

"Listen, Hazel," he yelled. "Don't do anything rash here! We can say it was him, okay? You keep the house. We'll call it even."

I watched as the light moved closer.

He took a step into the water. Another.

I swam for the platform, one hand slapping onto the edge, fingers slipping off the slick surface. Roy waded out into the water. I saw the moment the lake took him—the weightless feeling I knew so well. He dropped to his neck, gun held over his head, the light slipping under the surface.

And then, suddenly, I heard something else. The sound of a siren. Coming for Caden. Coming for Roy. He must've known it too. He could stop right now. He could surrender, confess. But he wouldn't. It wasn't in his nature.

"Hazel, get out of the water!" Roy said as he swam my way. I'd thought the water would protect me. Keep him from seeing me. Keep his shot from reaching me.

But he kept coming, gun in hand.

I knew he wasn't going to stop now. He couldn't. He'd come too far, and he was desperate.

I turned and kept swimming—I was faster than him, I knew.

The sirens grew louder, but he followed, calling after me. I swam toward the end of the inlet. Toward open water.

The water felt so heavy—pouring down from above, and pulling from below. My muscles were burning.

But I'd spent my childhood here. I could outswim anyone. I knew the borders of the lake, the pockets of depth, the places where the current moved, swift and unexpected, under the surface.

I felt the moment I made it to the main channel—the current started to *move*.

I turned to see if he was still coming—and he was right there, passing from the inlet into the main channel. I watched him start to swim against it, in a desperate struggle.

"Hazel," he called, but it came out pained and desperate this time. "Wait." Like he was begging me for something instead.

It was the last thing I heard.

He fought it—fought to get back to the inlet. But it was too late. The night fell eerily silent under the storm.

He didn't know: You had to let it take you. You couldn't be afraid.

In the next bolt of lightning, I saw nothing. Just the rain, spilling onto the surface. And nothing, nothing, from here to the trees.

I tipped my head back, arms out to the side, and I let the current take me too.

At the next curve, where the current ebbed and the water dropped, I pulled myself out. The woods here would cut back to our property, from the other side. I was shaking, and soaked through, and the rain was still falling, so that it was nearly impossible to orient myself.

But in the distance, I could see bright lights moving through the trees.

They were looking for me.

Flashlights were scanning the perimeter of our property—guiding my way home.

I started running through the trees, waving my arms at the closest light. Someone was looking for me at the top of the inlet, where the water reached the main channel.

"Hazel?" a familiar voice called.

Nico was there, moving toward me now—like he knew exactly where to find me. Like he understood exactly what I would do.

I crashed into his chest, sank into his body, my legs nearly giving out.

"Where's Caden?" I began.

"They're working on him," he said, just as another flashlight illuminated us.

Serena came to a halt behind Nico, eyes darting between us. "Where's Roy?" she asked, gun out in her other hand.

"Gone." I gestured to the lake behind me. The churning black hole, pulling everything toward it in the night. And then I raced back through the woods, for home, for Caden, with Nico and Serena following behind.

When I finally stumbled out of the tree line, into our backyard, I saw Gage rushing toward me. But I didn't stop. I kept moving to the front of the house, where the ambulance was still idling in my driveway, back doors open.

Caden's abdomen was packed, the EMT worker pressing down. He was shaking from the shock. "I'm so sorry, Caden. You're going to be okay. You are."

He had to be. For Skyler. For Jamie.

"I told your mother." He winced, his face pale, clothing soaked through from the storm. "I told her the truth about what happened to mine. I thought she left because of it." He turned his head away, eyes glazed. "I thought she left because of me."

"No," I said, climbing into the ambulance beside him. It was the least I could do. "She was coming back for us." I could still see his fear—all the secrets he'd had to keep. "She left a note. She was coming back for all of us. You did the right thing, Caden. We were only kids." I realized we were both shaking now. I grasped his hand in mine, and squeezed. "Thank you for coming back for me tonight."

Caden nodded once, just slightly. As if he were still stuck there—watching as his uncle aimed a gun at him, and fired.

"Caden," I said, trying to pull him back. "He was going to kill me. You saved my life."

He looked me over then, like he was surprised to find me here still.

"You saved mine," he said.

EPILOGUE

A handful of ashes to the air. A handful of ashes to the water.

I stood at the edge of the lake for another memorial. Another goodbye.

A small one, this time. Just family. Just us.

I couldn't think where else to do it. She'd made this place our home. And home seemed like what she would have wanted. She'd been buried for a very long while. It didn't take much time for them to find her. I knew by instinct where to look—the gazebo was the first thing Roy ever built on his property.

She'd been waiting for us long enough. It felt right to bring her home.

———

Afterward, we walked back up the yard, toward the house, Gage on one side of me, Caden on the other, still moving with a slight limp. There was a lot between us we needed to forgive, but that would come.

"Ready?" Nico asked, sitting on the patio with Jamie.

"Ready," I said. I'd be back next weekend, anyway.

Two hours isn't really that far, I'd told him, and he agreed. The lake had given up all its secrets. The past no longer had a hold on either of us.

We were free.

Inside, Skyler was showing Keira and Luke her room—the same one her father had grown up in—after we'd finished the work on it. We had enough money to do it now.

The house would be owned by the three of us in equal shares. But it would be lived in by Caden's family, for the time being.

It felt like the right thing to do.

It felt like the thing my father would've wanted.

The house full of noise, and life, and our family.

A reason, always, to come home.

ACKNOWLEDGMENTS

Thank you to the fantastic group of people who helped support this project from the initial story idea to the finished book:

I'm very grateful for the continued guidance and brilliant insight from my editor, Marysue Rucci, and agent, Jennifer Joel, along every step of the way. Thank you to the entire teams at Marysue Rucci Books and Simon Element, including Richard Rhorer, Clare Maurer, Elizabeth Breeden, Suzanne Donahue, Jessica Preeg, Nicole Bond, Sara Bowne, Emma Taussig, Laura Wise, and the many other people who have had a hand in bringing this book into the world. And to the team at CAA, including Sindhu Vegesena and Josie Freedman. I'm so fortunate to get to work with you all!

Thank you to retired Detective Sergeant Lee Ann Oehler for taking the time to answer my questions and provide extra insight. And to Elle Cosimano and Ashley Elston, for all the brainstorming and support on this (and every) project. I'm so grateful for your friendship!

As always, a huge thank you to my family.

And to all the readers—thank you.